Praise for
RACHELLE MORGAN'S
WILD CAT CAIT

"Only on a place called Wildcat Mountain
can a sexy loner and a woman hiding
from the world fall in love. I adored it!
Don't miss *Wild Cat Cait*."
Pamela Morsi

"Rachelle Morgan skillfully weaves laughter
and heart-wrenching moments to create
a triumphant story of two lonely people
who discover the courage within through
love. *Wild Cat Cait* is a thoroughly
enjoyable and unforgettable read."
Lorraine Heath, RITA Award-winning
author of *Texas Glory*

"An excellent read filled to the brim
with adventure, animals, conflict, humor,
and love . . . Ms. Morgan's *Wild Cat Cait* is an
historical of the first caliber, and her
writing style delivers first rate entertainment."
Rendezvous

"Rachelle Morgan's *Wild Cat Cait* is wild and
tender! A sensational mix of emotions!"
The Literary Times

Other **AVON ROMANCES**

RACHELLE MORGAN

WILD CAT CAIT

AVON BOOKS ◆ NEW YORK

AVON BOOKS, INC.
1350 Avenue of the Americas
New York, New York 10019

Copyright © 1998 by Rachelle Nelson
Inside cover author photograph by Dobbs Photography
Published by arrangement with the author
Visit our website at **http://www.AvonBooks.com**
Library of Congress Catalog Card Number: 98-92457
ISBN: 0-380-80039-X

First Avon Books Printing: September 1998

AVON TRADEMARK REG. U.S. PAT. OFF. AND IN OTHER COUNTRIES, MARCA REGISTRADA, HECHO EN U.S.A.

Printed in the U.S.A.

WCD   10   9   8   7   6   5   4   3   2   1

To Eve Gaddy for every frantic conversation, for every "you can do this," for every "take-your-time" read, I owe you my undying gratitude. Thanks for always being just a phone call away.

To Rosalyn Alsobrook—had you not braved the wilds and manned the camera, the cats wouldn't exist. Thanks for making my research such an adventure.

To Trana Mae Simmons for the best steak dinners in Texas, for listening to hours of babbling, for hanging in there when things were really grim. . . . Thanks for always taking care of me when I forget to.

To Lorraine Heath—you held my hand during the tough times and cheered me on, never wavering in your belief. Thanks for an especially treasured friendship and your constant inspiration.

To Dee Pace—from the day we "met," you have been one of my staunchest supporters and dearest friends. Thanks for helping to make this story better than what it might have been.

To Mike and Mary Irons for providing the research that almost ate me. Without your generosity and experience, this book would not have had as much personality. And to Kitty, Katrina, Nala, and Chuffers . . . all stars in my book.

To Cecilia Oh for your brilliant ideas, your

immunity to foot-in-mouth disease, and your incredible understanding. I hope I'll do you proud. Thanks from the bottom of my heart.

And most especially, to David for being an ordinary man who does extraordinary things . . . thank you, honey, for handling the house, the kids, the mood swings, and the sleepless nights, and for making that last heroic effort to see this book in print. Each day I am reminded of how lucky I am that you are mine.

Always,
S.

No good deed goes unpunished.

WILD CAT
CAIT

Chapter 1

Montana Territory, 1887

Ordinarily, Ethan Sawyer wouldn't have given a second thought to one of Newt Hullet's men riding hell-bent-for-leather through the center of town; the rancher employed one of the rowdiest crews of Ethan's acquaintance. Not a Saturday afternoon passed that the Hullet Bunch, as the Circle H hands were known throughout Roland, didn't stir up a little bit of dust, a little bit of ire, and a whole lot of trouble.

But this wasn't Saturday.

And Jim Tooley wasn't just any of Hullet's men.

The noise outside reached a level bordering on frenzy. Ethan set his swivel cutter down on the heavy pine work table strewn with strips of rawhide and carving tools, stamps and bevels, mallets and punches. He rose from the four-legged stool and headed toward the front of his shop, dodging a doweled rack that held pieces of leather he'd dampened and soaped, then hung out to dry. Beside it a sawhorse boasted the cantle and seat of one half-formed saddle.

Ethan parked himself at the full-sized window overlooking Main Street just as the Circle H foreman dismounted from a stocky piebald near the saloon. From the looks of it, the poor horse had been ridden fairly into the ground. His head bowed; his sides heaved; foam had formed a dripping beard under his muzzle. . . .

What could be so all-fired important that Tooley would risk killing his prized cow pony to reach town?

Frowning, Ethan removed his heavy apron and hung it on a wall peg beside the door before stepping outside. Crisp, cool spring air hit him in the face, a welcome respite from the stuffy odors of soaps and leather and vegetable dyes permeating his workshop.

He paused on the plank walkway and watched through cool, assessing eyes as the crowd multiplied. Just about every settler and shop owner, tradesman and teamster in town that day dropped what he was doing to investigate Tooley's arrival. Ethan couldn't hear the foreman's words, but whatever he had to say was getting folks plenty fired up.

Hooking his thumbs into his front pockets, Ethan strode with deliberate casualness across the rutted road bisecting town. No one paid him any mind as he circled the outer perimeter of the gathering, but he was used to that. In fact, most of these people had made it no secret that they wished he'd disappear altogether.

Sometimes Ethan wondered why he didn't.

But he kept his expression impassive as he made his way around the fringe of the crowd to the front, where Tooley stood on the elevated boardwalk: the natty trousers, flannel shirt, and black vest on his wiry body carried a layer of Montana dirt; his sunken cheeks were red and chapped by dust and sun.

Bits and pieces of conversation filtering in from the crowd explained the foreman's unexpected visit—it seemed there'd been another cougar attack on Hullet's herd.

"I'm tellin' ya, that cat took down a six-hunnerd-pound steer!" Tooley's gravelly voice rose above the din.

Ethan leaned against a support post and scoffed under his breath. He didn't doubt the attack. But a mountain lion taking down a six-hundred-pound steer? More like a two-hundred-pound calf. Everyone knew that Tooley exaggerated, though few ever called him on it.

"That's three head Newt's lost this month," Tooley went on to report, "and he's willin' to pay top dollar to any man who brings that varmint down." He waited until the rumbling spread to the far end of the crowd, then goaded, "Is there a man among ya up to the job?"

"Why doesn't he hunt down the cat himself?" Ethan called out.

Silence fell over the crowd, and several of the more pious folk cut narrow-eyed looks his way. Ethan ignored the silent reprimand for daring to open his mouth in public. Far as he knew, he still had a constitutional right to speak his piece in this country.

Tooley hitched up his baggy britches and rocked back on his heels in a manner that had always grated on Ethan's nerves. "Well, nah, Ethan, I expect if you was a real man, ya'd know that answer t' that."

A few snickers rose from the assembly. Ethan's blood simmered but his gaze never left Tooley's gaunt face.

Just when he figured the foreman wouldn't answer his question, Jim tipped back the brim of his grimy Stetson and drawled, "In case you ain't checked yer calendar, Sawyer, this is brandin' season. A respected businessman like Newt don't just leave his ranch in the midst of his busiest spell to hunt." Thin lips curved in a smile of false cordiality. "But then, I don't expect you'd know much about that, would ya?"

A muscle ticked in Ethan's jaw. It took all his self-control not to knock Tooley down from his self-appointed pedestal. If anyone knew busy seasons and obligations, he did. His fingers carried scars of his trade, crafting and designing Sawyer saddles all winter long to fill his orders before spring. Still, he knew better than to let Tooley, or anyone else, see his aggravation. "Tracking down a mountain lion is a dangerous job, though. What's Hullet willing to offer a man for his life?"

Steely blue eyes fixed on Ethan in silent, mocking challenge. "One—hunnerd—dollars."

A gasp rose at the staggering amount.

In spite of Ethan's resolve to remain unaffected, his brow lifted. A hundred dollars? He whistled under his breath. Impressive. It took most folks six months or more to make that kind of money—if they were lucky.

He had to give Hullet credit: the rancher knew just how to lasso in the volunteers. Nearly everyone in the area was riding on lean times. Montana winters were harsh, but this past one had been especially brutal. In fact, Ethan knew that if his saddles weren't in such high demand by ranchers and military alike, he'd be sitting in the same sorry pasture with the rest of his neighbors.

"So how about it, men?" Tooley addressed the crowd once more. "Who among ya is brave enough to go after that cougar?"

Low murmurs grew in volume, and in seconds the street erupted in chaos. One loud-mouthed rowdy lit off a round of yips and catcalls. Excitement spread like a bad case of smallpox, infecting everyone with feverish hysteria.

Despite the jostling and shoving by men forcing their way out of the center of the crowd, Ethan didn't budge. Instead, he quietly observed his fellow Rolanders making mad dashes toward horses tied to the hitching rails or buckboards parked along the road. The scene reminded him of one played out three years earlier when the thrill of the chase alone had many a young man's blood racing. Now, with the reward Hullet offered tacked on, even those without a shred of experience couldn't resist joining the hunt.

Hell, even his old friends Billy Gray and

Louis Anderson intended on going after the cat.

The men stopped near a couple of brown geldings tied to the split rail fence that extended from the livery, prattling to one another like old biddies at a barn-raising. If either man noticed Ethan standing a few paces away, neither gave any sign.

Ethan glanced down at the scuffed toes of his Brogans. The slight still shouldn't bother him after all this time, yet it did. Once the three of them had been closer than tar on a shake roof. He'd thought nothing would come between them.

He'd thought wrong.

He grimaced and pushed away from the post. The loss of his pals was only one consequence of that long ago day, but what good were regrets? The deed was done, the consequences clear. He'd had no choice but to pick up the pieces left of his life and go on.

Spine straight and shoulders squared, he headed down the road toward his shop. But as he passed his former friends, snatches of their conversation had him slowing his steps and perking his ears.

"Bet it's one of them cats that belongs to the savage in the hills," Louis said, tightening the cinches on his horse.

Billy pushed his wolf-skin cap back, revealing curly blond hair two shades lighter than Ethan's. "Oh, c'mon, Gypsy-man . . ." He squinted over at Louis, whose dark hair, lean features, and restless nature had earned him the nomadic nickname. "How many times do I gotta tell you ain't no woman who would keep wild animals for pets?"

Louis grinned; his deep-set black eyes glittered. "Ain't no woman gonna be livin' alone in the mountains either, yet Wild Cat Cait does it."

Wild Cat Cait? Ethan glanced back, his step faltering.

"I think you need to stop listening to Tooley's campfire tales," Billy scoffed. "The only wildcat in those mountains is the one I'm aimin' to plug with ole Chester here." He patted the silver-plated Winchester rifle before sliding it into its saddle holster.

Strangely enough, Ethan had to agree with Billy. Hell, stories of Wild Cat Cait had been circulating around Roland for years. Some claimed she was a ferocious creature, half catamount, half woman, who wrestled beasts three times her size. Others said she'd been raised in the mountains by wildcats and held mystical powers over them, which accounted for the outlandish name people had given her. And Louis, who at twenty-three was the youngest and most imaginative—not to mention impressionable— of their former trio, held the title for being one of Wild Cat Cait's biggest believers.

To Ethan's way of thinking, the legend of the female mountaineer was just that—a legend. Nothing more than a myth perpetuated by folks to keep children away from the dangers of the Mission Mountains.

In spite of his skepticism, though, tales about her had always intrigued him. Once on a dare, he and Billy had even hiked into the Mission

Range, fired up to prove the stories either true or false. All they'd gotten for their trouble was a seat full of blackberry thorns.

Ethan's smile over their youthful foolishness disappeared as quickly as it had formed. The days of him and Billy Gray raising Cain had long since passed into a season of tarnished memories.

With a curt shake of his head, he started across the street again, away from the men, away from a past that couldn't be changed.

"William Gray, what in heaven's name do you think you're doing?"

The shrill voice stopped Ethan in his tracks. He turned, and bittersweet affection flooded his chest at the sight of the young woman sailing down the center of the road like a runaway prairie schooner. She had the folds of her simple brown skirt fisted in both hands. Flour dusted her plump cheeks and flaxen braid. Gravy drippings stained a wrinkled apron that did nothing to hide the prominent roundness of her belly. Yet his sister Josephine had never looked prettier.

She reached the stout figure of her husband and grabbed his arm just as he prepared to mount. "Have you gone crazy, Billy?"

"Get back, woman, I'm on a man's mission," Billy snapped, shaking free of her hold.

"More like a fool's folly. You are not going after that cougar, Billy, it's too dangerous."

"The hell I'm not. For that bounty, I'd go after a grizzly."

"What of your responsibilities here? We've got a baby on the way and a restaurant to run!"

Casting a swift glance toward Louis, Billy wrapped his fingers around Josie's elbow and ushered her out of earshot. The rest of their exchange fell to harsh whispers, and Ethan couldn't help but grin. He suspected his little sister was ripping Billy a new ear. He'd been on the receiving end of one of her tongue-lashings often enough to recognize the signs.

Then Billy said something that hushed her instantly and made tears well up in her clover green eyes.

Ethan's amusement faded. His fists clenched. He stepped forward, ready to knock the stuffing out of his brother-in-law for upsetting Josie, especially in her condition—until he recalled Josie's response the last time he'd come to her defense.

"Stay out of it, Ethan. What goes on between me and Billy is none of your concern. Anything you do will just make matters worse."

Dragging slow, heavy breaths through his nostrils, Ethan manage to quell his flaring temper. The haze of red receded, the temperature of his blood dropped a few degrees.

Billy strode back to the sorrel and settled into a saddle of Ethan's creation. His eyes fixed on Josie, and for a moment his whiskered features softened. "Don't worry now, little darlin'," came his gruff assurance, "we'll be back in time for supper."

She tipped her chin, nodded once.

To Louis he said, "Let's move out, Gypsyman."

With a whoop and a holler, Louis kicked his heels against his horse's flanks.

Billy tugged on the reins to bring his horse around only to still at the sight of Ethan a short distance away.

Ethan stared back, meeting the simmering hatred rising in Billy's eyes with cool reserve of his own. The mastery over his emotions paid off after a few moments when Billy, tight-lipped with fury, kicked the sorrel into motion, leaving behind nothing but the dust of his hooves.

Other parties followed soon after, until the only folks left in the street were wistful old men, chattering women, boisterous children. . . .

And Josie.

She stood where Billy had left her, her wrist resting on her distended belly. The misery in her eyes as she watched her husband disappear pierced Ethan like a rusty nail. The rift between the couple had never been more apparent.

And it was all his fault.

Sheer power of will kept him from going to her, putting his arm around her and drawing her close like he used to when they were both younger.

Instead, Ethan did the best thing he could for his little sister—he spun on his heel and walked away. Before she spotted him. Before she approached him. Before he caused her more pain.

That thought pounded through Ethan's skull as he plowed his way down the boardwalk. He paid no notice to folks passing by other than to sidle closer to the sturdy lumber buildings lining the main road through town. Only when the prongs of a parasol stabbed into his chest did the blinders fall away; at the same time, his arm knocked against a decidedly feminine figure.

Reflex had him reaching out to steady her before he remembered that folks—womenfolk, in particular—didn't welcome his touch.

None more than the woman in front of him.

Amanda Hullet, Newt Hullet's niece.

She looked fetching, as always. Spun gold hair done up in one of those fancy knots, fat curls dripping over one shoulder. A plum silk gown with the tiny pearl buttons that went all the way up to her chin was as spotless and fashionable as ever.

Ethan retracted his outstretched hand and curled his fingers into his palm. "Amanda." He nodded stiffly.

Perfect pink lips formed into a circle of distaste. "Mr. Sawyer."

His own mouth flattened. His back stiffened. There'd been a time when Amanda had called him names a whole lot less formal than "Mr. Sawyer." She'd whispered endearments like "darling" and "love" against his neck, against his lips, into his ear.

And there'd been a time when she liked hearing him whisper those same endearments back.

Now that same mouth barely spoke to him; when it did, even "Ethan" had become a vulgarity.

"Are you going to stand there all day, or will you let me by?"

He backed up until his spine hit the rough log wall of the general store.

Amanda gathered a handful of skirts then strolled on past him. To his surprise, she turned around after two steps and arched one dark brow. "Have you a mind to go after that cat, too?"

"I'm not a hunter, Amanda," he answered flatly. "You know that."

"Oh, yes. How could I have forgotten?" At that, she snapped the frilly cloth mushroom back into place overhead and spun away with uppity disdain.

Long after her departure, the words hung in the air. Loathsome. Searing.

Ethan pushed away from the wall. He told himself it was better that he'd found out her true feelings before they'd exchanged vows. It still stung, though, to discover that in the end, the woman he'd planned to marry was just as stiff-hearted as the rest of the town.

With a self-deprecating shake of his head, he walked into his shop. What did it matter what these people thought of him?

He took a seat behind his work table and shoved the rolled cuffs of his sleeves past his elbows. But as he began to push a grooving tool along the edge of the leather saddle skirt, in the same manner as his father and his father before him, Ethan couldn't lie to himself. It did matter what his neighbors thought. It mattered a lot. Not about him—he could handle the hostility. But when they took their anger out on an innocent bystander . . . when his unpopular decisions caused problems between a wife and her husband, a woman and her future. . . .

He'd been the one to commit the unpardonable sin, and yet Josie was the one bearing their contempt.

Who among you is brave enough. . . .

His fingers fumbled over the leather. Slowly his gaze raised, centered on the waning activity outside the front window, then veered east toward the range of mountains capped in fire and ice. Afternoon sun cast a layer of gold dust along the rugged aspen-covered slopes and snow still coating the peaks glowed like a halo against a backdrop of azure blue.

How hard could it be to catch a wildcat? You find it, you shoot it. Simple.

As the idea sank its roots, temptation built inside Ethan, so strong he could practically taste it.

He tore his gaze away, focusing his attention back on the scrolling designs. Gawd A'mighty, who was he trying to fool? The closest he'd ever come to going after a wild animal was that bison hunt a few years back with Billy. It had been nothing short of slaughtering for sport. Not an experience he'd like to repeat.

Then again. . . .

He raised his head once more to the beckoning mountains. This was different. This was survival. Protection against an element threatening the lives and livelihoods of innocent people.

Ethan's fingers clamped so tight around the carving tool in his palm that he felt the ribbed grip cut into his callouses. *Who among you is brave enough. . . .*

An image of a feisty young woman with yellow-gold hair appeared before his eyes—standing beside him as they cooled a woman's fevered brow; standing against the town when word escaped about who was staying in the Sawyers' home; standing alone in the street while her husband rode off into the horizon.

Tossing the cutter onto the table, Ethan jumped from the stool and grabbed his sheepskin coat off the freestanding rack in the corner. Maybe he'd fail. More than likely he'd fail. But he had to try.

For Josie's sake, he had to try.

An hour later, Ethan strode grim-faced from the Valley Emporium, loaded down with more supplies than a pack mule. Hershel Sinclaire might not cotton to him much, but he sure pocketed his money fast enough. Ethan had no doubt it was one of the only reasons the good citizens of Roland didn't drive him from town.

Not that he'd ever give them the satisfaction. His family had been one of the first to settle the area—had, in fact, helped to found Roland. He'd be damned if he'd turn tail and run to suit the town's whims.

Besides, he'd discovered long ago that even though most folks wanted him about as much as a toothache, they needed him—or more accurately, they needed his money.

The knowledge rankled, but Ethan continued to do business with Sinclaire and all the other shop owners, finding perverse pleasure in his small power over them.

"Ethan Sawyer!"

The sound of his name brought him to a quick halt. Ethan glanced over his shoulder and spotted Josie hurrying toward him.

Damn her reckless hide!

His mood darkening, he headed in the opposite direction toward the livery before she could waylay him. The street had begun to empty as folks broke away from one another and returned to their normal activities, but he wasn't about to take the chance of someone seeing her with him. Folks gave her enough grief already.

He should have known escaping wouldn't be that easy. Rapid clicks warned him that she followed. He picked up his pace, hugging the shadows cast by the overhang until the boardwalk dropped to the packed dirt road in front of the livery yard.

"You can't avoid me forever!"

Maybe not, but he'd do his damnedest trying.

"Stop this instant or I'll cause a spectacle the likes of which you have never seen."

With a vile curse, Ethan froze at the corner of the split wood corral, his spine stiff, every muscle tightened in dread. He watched her elongated shadow bob along the packed road, heard the rustle of starched hems. A moment later, five feet and a hundred and fifty pounds of maternal outrage barred his way.

He clenched his teeth and hissed, "Go away before someone sees you talking to me."

"You're my brother. Of course I'm going to talk to you."

"Not in public, Josephine. You gave me your word."

With a hand propped on an ample hip, and her head tilting defiantly to the side, Josie dared, "What can they do that they haven't already done?"

"I'm not willing to find out. Just go on about your business. I've got my own to tend to."

"What sort of business does a saddle maker have with gear like that?" She pointed meaningfully at the traps slung over his shoulder by an anchor chain.

Ethan refused to look at her. Instead, he focused on the distant mountains behind her.

Unease coiling down her spine, Josie followed her brother's line of vision. "Oh, Ethan, no!" Her gaze snapped back to his rugged face. "Tell me you're not going after that cougar, too!" She hoped, she *prayed*, he'd deny it, tell her how silly she was being for even thinking he'd go on such a foolhardy quest.

But he didn't answer.

He didn't have to.

Josie's blood turned ice cold in her veins. All too well she recognized the stubborn set of his jaw, the determined glint in his golden eyes. It was the same expression he wore every time he meant to do something he knew she wouldn't agree with.

Her gaze swept over his long, lean body with disapproval. "And here I thought you were the one man in the town who hadn't lost his senses."

"That animal is a danger to the community," he said tonelessly.

"Then let someone else go after it, someone with more experience," Josie cried. "You aren't a hunter, Ethan, and we both know it." She jabbed a finger into a chest built of solid muscle from years of strenuous labor. That Ethan was also twice her size and eight years her senior had no bearing. "In fact, not a one of those men has the foggiest notion how to hunt a cougar, including that foolhardy husband of mine."

He whipped around to face her, his features harsher than she'd ever seen them. "Would you rather I stayed behind and turned a blind eye to a dangerous situation? That's something I'm seasoned at—ask anyone."

"This is not the same thing at all!"

"Isn't it?"

Josie searched his eyes and her stomach sank at the suffering she saw in the pale brown depths. Being treated as a pariah for a simple act of kindness had wounded him deeply. Only a person who knew him as well as she did would see it, for he did an admirable job of hiding his feelings from the world.

Would he ever find peace within himself for the choices he had made?

"Oh, Ethan . . ." She reached toward his face, wanting only to smooth away the lines carved into his narrow brow. He reared back as if her hand were made of fire instead of flesh.

Josie folded her fingers into her hand and glanced away before he could see the tears springing to her eyes. Normally she could bear her brother's touch-me-not behavior. Unfortunately, her emotions had been in a wringer since the onset of her pregnancy, and it was harder to disguise how his reaction stung.

"Josie . . ."

The gruff remorse in his voice had her biting her lower lip to keep it from quivering.

"These people have treated you like dung on their heels for the last three years. They won't eat at your restaurant, they don't invite you to their social gatherings . . . they barely look at you unless they can't help it. Because of me. If I can catch that cat, prove that I do care what happens to the people of this town, then maybe they'll start giving you the respect and courtesy you deserve."

She drew in a shuddering breath through her nostrils and tilted her chin. "You did nothing to be ashamed of nor do you have anything to prove. Neither do I. I stood beside you because I believed in what you did—"

"And look at the price you've had to pay."

Josie balled her hands into fists and cried, "When are you going to accept that it doesn't matter to me what these people think?"

"What about your husband?" Ethan countered with a sardonic lift of one tawny eyebrow. "Doesn't it matter what he thinks?"

She blanched. The troubles between her and Billy were hardly a secret. In fact, if the decision had been left up to her, she'd have quit this town a long time ago. Still, she hadn't expected to have the subject arise so abruptly. "You know he has reasons for feeling as he does," she said, feeling compelled to defend her husband. "He'll come around someday."

"Then until that day, you'd be wise to forget you ever had a brother."

Chapter 2

Standing on the front porch of her cabin, Caitlin Perry lifted her arms in a slow, fluid stretch and absorbed the evening. Although winter was barely over, a faint scent of spring had settled already within the canyon— the tangy bite of evergreen, the purity of sweet mountain grass, the mellow dampness of snow clinging to the ground in patches. An owl *who-whoo*ed high in a nearby tree, insects hummed their nightly lullaby, and in the distance, she could hear the muffled roar of the mighty falls an hour's brisk hike away.

She lowered her arms and released a contented sigh. Moving to the mountains six years ago had been one of the wisest decisions she'd ever made, and she wondered if her grandfather had any idea how grateful she was for the precious gift he'd left her. She wished she could tell him. Unfortunately, communicating with spirits wasn't a habit she practiced, although from the stories told about her, one would never believe it.

She supposed it didn't matter, though. The

important thing was, thanks to John Perry, she'd been given the freedom to spend her days as she saw fit. She could go where she wanted, when she wanted, and be accountable only to herself—a scratching sounded behind her—and to her comrades, of course, she added with a smile.

Cait glanced over her shoulder just as the master of the house stuck his head out the doorway. Brassy gold eyes studied her from a wide, whiskered face.

"It's about time you decided to get up, lazybones." Cait patted her buckskin-clad thigh. "Come on out and join me."

Sawtooth looked undecided. But apparently the glorious tint of the sun sinking behind Wildcat Peak to the west beckoned to him as it had to her. Huge paws padded lightly across the porch as he rounded the willow hoop frame holding the stretched elk hide Cait had spent the afternoon scraping.

A pace away from her legs, the Siberian tiger lowered his upper torso. Inch-long claws hooked into the wooden platform; sleek muscles rippled awake beneath the vibrant orange and black striped coat; huge fangs gleamed like polished ivory when he yawned.

Rising back up, Sawtooth butted his head against Cait's thigh. She reached down to scratch the coarse tuft of fur between his ears. "I suppose you're hungry."

He responded with a rumbling mewl, then sat back on his haunches and licked his powerful jaws.

Cait chuckled. "I figured as much. You're al-

ways hungry. Well, there's the forest." She
swept her hand toward the dark line of trees
surrounding the clearing. "Happy hunting."

Four hundred pounds of solid feline sprang
up. Though he still sat on his hind legs, his
paws landed on Cait's chest and knocked her
back a step. She laughed at the familiar ploy.
"You big, spoiled baby." She rubbed her forehead against the broad bridge of his nose. He
really was just an oversized pussycat—and the
best companion a girl could ask for. "Oh, all
right, I'll do the hunting tonight. Let me feed
Ginger and Faw Paw, then we'll see what we
can scare up for you."

With uncanny understanding, Sawtooth
dropped to all fours and led the way off the
porch toward the back of the cabin.

Cait lifted the bar of the split log gate and
crossed the rear quad to a shed built into the
hill where she stored meat. She stepped inside
the dim doorway, unsheathed her knife, and
cut the rest of the elk she'd taken down yesterday into several large chunks. She tossed
Sawtooth a scrap to tide him over until later,
then cranked a portion through the grinder for
Ginger.

A ten-foot-high pen built of slender saplings
and lashed together with rope took up a good
part of the rear enclosure. The instant Cait
opened the slatted door, Ginger leaped down
from a spruce bough.

"Hello, pretty lady." Cait smiled.

The lioness moved toward her in a graceful
rolling gait. Ginger had been with Cait nearly
as long as Sawtooth, even though she was

twice his age. Whereas the Siberian tiger had
been some Russian aristocrats' not-so-smart
idea of a pet, the lioness had been the victim
of a circus trainer's cruelty. A childlike scribble
of lashmarks scarred her golden rump, one ear
had been lopped off at the tip, and on especially cold days she walked with a hitch in her
step from a hip that had once been broken and
not properly set—if it had been set at all. But
the most unforgivable atrocity was that all her
beautiful teeth had been removed.

She stopped several feet away, sat, and
waited. Cait waved the bowl of ground meat
back and forth, trying to coax her closer.

Ginger would have none of the bribery. Cait
sighed and told herself not to get discouraged.
When she'd first fetched the lioness four and a
half years ago, it had been a battle just to get
into close proximity of her, much less touch
her. At least Ginger no longer attacked the moment Cait opened the gate. Those endless days
and nights of speaking of anything and everything in a soft tone seemed to have paid off in
that regard.

Unfortunately she still refused to eat if Cait
was anywhere near. And setting her free was
impossible. Without teeth, Ginger would never
survive in the wild.

But one day, Cait assured herself as she set
the bowl down and left the pen, Ginger would
reach a point where she'd eat from Cait's hand,
just like Sawtooth. At least, Cait hoped she
would.

Faw Paw came next. His cage, with its thick
pine walls and stone base, had been made nec-

essarily smaller and more tightly lashed than Ginger's. Cait untied the rawhide thong of the door, then lowered to her hands and knees inside the entrance.

Using a slow approach and soothing sounds, she crawled across the dirt floor scattered with conifer needles. Wary green eyes watched her every move from the far corner. Halfway across the cage, the seven-month-old cougar curled back his lips and hissed. Gray fur bristled along his nape, his ears flattened against his head, glazed eyes reflected pain and anxiety.

Cait stopped. "Easy, baby, I just want to check your leg."

Several tense moments passed, amplifying the distant hoot of an owl and the occasional trill of insects.

Only when Faw Paw rested his head on his front paws did Cait move again. Discreetly she pulled an elk hide mask from her waistband. Even though the cougar had settled considerably during the weeks of his captivity, Cait still felt it necessary to protect herself from those wicked fangs. She'd clipped his claws already, so had less worry that they'd do much damage.

At the sight of the muzzle, Faw Paw hissed again, even tried to get to his feet. But the bulky splint on his useless hind leg prevented him from rising, and he fell back down onto his side with a low, agony filled *mreeew*.

Cait's heart contracted in sympathy. She reached his side and stretched her hand toward him. He bowed back and swiped at her.

"It'll just be for a minute, baby. I can't have

you taking another chunk out of me." Already she'd have a permanent scar below her elbow from their first encounter.

Quickly she slipped the muzzle over the sharply angled face. Faw Paw struggled as she expected he would, but to Cait's pleasure and relief, he didn't make any further threatening moves. No laudanum-laced meat would be needed to sedate him this time. They were making definite progress.

She slid around to the injured leg and unwrapped the bandages holding the splint in place. At the sight of the pink gash circling Faw Paw's hind shinbone, Cait once again cursed the game trappers that set iron jaws around the mountainside, hoping to add a new pelt to their collections. She'd learned long ago that most didn't care what got caught in their traps, as long as it brought them a profit. And from her biannual visits to the trading post in Pine Bend, she knew that cougar pelts and teeth were worth a pretty penny.

Cait gently removed the splint and gave the wound a close examination. "Looks good, boy. No sign of infection." In fact, the scabbed flesh looked well on the mend. The snapped bone was a different matter. Cait guessed it would take another few weeks before it knitted together. "I don't know how bad the tendon damage is, or if you'll ever have normal use of this leg again, but I've done all I can do." And once the leg healed sufficiently, Faw Paw would return to the wild.

That thought filled Cait with a mixture of pride and sadness—pride that she'd had a hand in Faw Paw's recovery; sadness that his impending freedom would again leave him open to the cruelties of man.

She finished cleaning the wound with soapy water, applied bruised comfrey leaves, then re-set the splint and wrapped it tight. After slipping the muzzle off the whiskered face, Cait backed out of the cage and tossed Faw Paw his reward of elk meat. A round of growls and hisses vibrated through the cage as he curled a forepaw protectively around the food.

Knowing how fierce he got with his meals, Cait secured the door behind her and left him to eat in peace.

She entered the small cabin of native pine, built by her grandfather back in the thirties, when trapping was still profitable and rendez-vous was the highlight of every mountain man's year. The single room was divided into two sections by a three-paneled screen: the living area, marked by a wall-size stone fireplace that she used for both cooking and warmth, and the sleeping area, which boasted a double-wide bed stuffed with feathers.

Cait dug out her hunting clothes from the chest at the footboard and quickly changed from her loose skirt and blouse into a set of buckskins. Brushing and braiding her hair took much longer. Once she had the wavy mass confined to a single brown plait down her back, she tied a simple rawhide headband across her forehead to keep loose strands from getting in her eyes.

Catching her reflection in the tin bottom of a skillet hanging from the mantel, she couldn't help but wonder if her father was smiling down on her. From what she could remember, he'd been fervently proud of his Blackfoot blood.

She lifted the Remington off the antler rack holding three other rifles of various sizes and calibers. The weapon fit naturally in her hands, the maple stock worn smooth from repeated handling.

A half hour later, with the Remington resting against her shoulder, Cait headed down a well-worn path leading out of the hidden canyon. The fringe of her long-sleeved tunic swished softly with each step, and leggings protected her from bramble from thigh to ankle. The soft soles of her deerhide boots crushed the new shoots of grama and fern struggling through the snow.

Sawtooth strode soundlessly along beside her, stopping now and then to sniff at the moist layer of needles upon the forest floor. Cait had lost count of how many times she and the tiger had hunted in the five years they'd been together, but it never failed to fill her with a sense of purpose. Sawtooth, Ginger, and Faw Paw, along with any other strays she managed to collect, staved off the soul-deep loneliness she had borne upon first coming here, the bewildering sense of rootlessness.

If every now and then she longed for something a little more than her feline friends could provide, well, she had only to remember what it had been like back in what some termed the "civilized world."

A mile outside of the narrow canyon, Sawtooth came to a sudden stop. His body tensed, every instinct inside him went visibly on alert.

Cait froze. "What is it, boy?"

His ears went flat against his skull. Striped fur stood on end along his spine. His tail stretched straight out behind him.

Alarmed by his behavior, she scanned their surroundings. Beyond the dense stands of pine, not a bough stirred, not a shadow moved.

Yet Cait trusted Sawtooth's keen senses. Something had him ready to come out of his skin.

She strained to hear over the pounding of her heart.

The blowing whinny of a horse reached her first, followed by human voices.

Cait dropped to a stealthy crouch. Pressing her finger against her lips, warning Sawtooth to silence, she crept toward the voices. Sawtooth prowled close behind.

They stomach crawled over a granite ridge overlooking a wide and tumbling creek bordered by craggy rocks and sweeping willows on either side. Curling rapids sent white foam crashing against rocks spanning the water's width.

Two men—hunters, judging from the weapons propped against nearby trees—sat around a small campfire near the bank, drinking what smelled like coffee. The first man had curly daffodil-yellow hair and one of those long, drooping mustaches she thought looked ridiculous but seemed so popular among the whites. Nearby, a leaner, dark-haired man with narrow features and a spade beard reclined against a rock. From the lived-in look of the place, they'd been camped here for several days.

The knowledge sent a coil of unease down Cait's spine. It was bad enough that hunters tromped all over her mountain, taking what they wanted, when they wanted. But to find them so close to her cabin. . . . The canyon meadow where her grandfather had chosen to build had been a well-kept secret for many years. If these men stumbled upon it, whether by accident or design, they might tell others. Then what was to stop every cutthroat and sportsman from invading her haven, destroying the peace and freedom she'd been so careful to protect for herself and her unusual animals?

Cait cast a worried glance at Sawtooth. He looked back at her, his mouth set in a grim line, his muscles tense. Once again she could have sworn that he knew exactly what she was thinking.

The harsh tone of male bickering rose up to the ridge.

As one, she and Sawtooth turned their attention to the men and listened. . . .

"I'm telling ya, we ain't going to find it!" Billy cried, clambering to his feet. He tossed the dregs of his coffee into the fire. Logs sizzled; a ball of smoke billowed into his whiskered face. "We've been scouring this mountain for four days and ain't picked up that cat's scent yet."

"Don't bust a seam, Billy." Louis stabbed

one of those nasty cigars he favored into his mouth and lit it with a twig from the fire pit, then pumped out smoke like a steam engine. "We'll catch that cougar before it strikes again."

"That cat could wipe out Hullet's entire herd, for all I care," Billy snarled, waving his hand to clear the air of the stinking fumes. Nothing would make him happier than if Newt Hullet lost that government contract he was so damned proud of. Maybe then all those worthless reservation Indians he fed with his beef would finally die out. Slow starvation was the least the murdering bastards deserved.

As he fixed his gaze on the flickering light of the campfire, a grisly image began to form in the flames. The trout Billy had eaten earlier began to churn in his gut.

He pressed his lips together in a grim line and closed his eyes. Sometimes he could block the memories, but other times they hit him so damned hard that he could feel himself back in Nebraska. Smell the blood and smoke. Taste the fear and loss. Hear the screams and yips, and worse, the silence. . . .

Billy wrenched himself from the past before his emotions got the better of him and frowned at Louis. "The only reason I'm wasting my time up here at all is to collect that bounty."

"That bounty ain't nothing compared to what the pelt'll bring in," Louis said, taking out his cigar long enough to suck down a swig of coffee from a battered tin cup. "After we show Hullet the carcass and collect the reward, we'll take the hide to that trading post in Pine

Bend. They'll give us ten times what Hullet's willing to pay."

Billy lowered himself to the rock and grumbled, "They ain't gonna give us dirt if we can't find the damn thing."

"It's here somewhere," Louis insisted. "I can smell it."

"I don't know how you can smell anything over the stench of that damned stogie."

"Christ on crutch, Gray, who's been pissing in your porridge?"

"What are you talking about?"

"You've been in a sour mood ever since we left Roland, and it's gettin' mighty old."

A deep scowl pulled at Billy's brow as he broke a twig into bits and threw each piece into the blackened pit. Louis was right. He hadn't been the most pleasant company lately. "I just didn't reckon it would take this long, is all. If I don't get back to town soon, Josie'll have my rump through the grinder."

"So go back." Louis shrugged. "We need supplies, anyway."

Smoothing down the mustache bracketing the sides of his mouth, Billy considered doing just that. Normally he wouldn't have taken a job that had him away from Josie for so long, but with business doing poorly, and their first baby due in three months . . . hell, the pressure just kept piling up. If he didn't come up with some money soon, he was gonna wind up losing everything. The business, his wife. . . .

"Naw, I ain't about to give you open season on that cat," he grumbled. "Besides, if I see that good for nothin' brother of hers, I'm liable to snap."

"He's a nervy s.o.b., I'll give him that," Louis chortled. "I'd have staked a week's winnings that he meant to take a swing at you before we left."

"Yeah, well, the day he tries is the day I walk a mud puddle into his ass and stomp it dry."

Only the promise of Josie never forgiving him had kept him from doing it long before now. But maybe it was for the best. He wanted Ethan Sawyer to suffer far more than a good walloping. Once he caught this cat, he'd have enough money to take Josie so far away that the bastard would need a search party to find her.

Billy knew he just had to bide his time.

"Ya know, Billy-boy, I still can't figure out why Josie stood up for him, especially knowing what the redskins did to your family."

Billy stared at the short remainder of the stick. He couldn't admit even to Louis how deeply it still hurt that his wife had taken her brother's side against his. Ironically, the only man who would have understood without thinking him weak was the one who'd driven the knife into his back.

Choosing his words carefully, he told Louis, "She's got it in her head that she owes him her loyalty."

"There ain't no accountin' for taste, I guess." Louis kicked his feet out in front of them, crossed his ankles, and grinned. "After all, she married you."

Billy eagerly grabbed onto the shift in subject. "You're just green because you wanted her, too."

"Maybe once, but that's before I heard about the little feline hidden in these hills." He cupped his hands behind his head and leaned back against his saddle with a sigh. "Yep, I'm savin' myself for Wild Cat Cait."

"Oh, cripes, give it rest, will ya, Louis?"

"You wait and see, Billy-boy, she's here somewhere." His gaze swept the surrounding wilderness. "And I'll wager that when we find her, we'll find our cat, too."

Ducking low to avoid being spotted by the obnoxious smokestack, Cait's jaw tightened with a combination of fury and disgust. She could brush off the arrogant remark about her—it wasn't the first time she'd heard comments of that ilk and it probably wouldn't be the last.

But the conversation about the cougar?

The temptation to set Sawtooth loose on the men nearly choked Cait. Only the knowledge that she'd be inviting more trouble stopped her from having them ripped to shreds. Surely someone would come searching for them if they didn't return to where they'd come from.

Besides, she reminded herself, the last thing she needed was for one of the men to set their sights on her cat. If cougar pelts were worth a fortune, she could only imagine what exorbitant price a Siberian tiger's coat might bring in.

Reason prevailing, Cait motioned to Sawtooth, then backslid off the ridge before their presence was detected. She reached level ground and broke into a sprint. Sawtooth followed close at her heels.

But by the time they arrived back at the cabin, her outrage had soared. She flung open the door, jammed the rifle on its rack, and paced the hearth in agitation. "Can you believe the nerve of those men, Sawtooth? How dare they hunt cougar on our mountain!"

The wide black stripe over his eyes that resembled a brow notched low in the center.

"It's bad enough we've got poachers setting their traps everywhere; now we've got bounty hunters to deal with." She spun on her heel and crossed to the other side of the cabin. "Where's their proof that a cat attacked that rancher's herd?" she cried, flinging her hand in the air. "It's just as possible that a pack of wolves did it. But no, a cow gets killed, and they blame a wildcat. And not just any wildcat, but one of you!"

Cait pushed her hair to the back of her head in frustration. Oh, it wasn't unheard of for a mountain lion to strike a herd of cattle. Especially after as harsh a winter as they'd just experienced.

But to blame one of her cats? The thought had fury rising like bile in her throat. Ginger and Faw Paw weren't even capable of hunting! And Sawtooth . . . he hadn't left her side in over five years. Why would he start now?

She knelt in front of the fireplace and jabbed the poker into the glowing coals. No, by damn, if a cat was responsible, it would have to have been one of the wild cougars that prowled the mountain—

Cait's hand went suddenly still. The image of a tiny cougar cub, found alone in a hollow beneath an overhang of rock, formed in her mind. Cait had called her Halona—"the fortunate one." Even at the tender age of two weeks, she'd been a fierce little feline, all hiss and claw. Nothing seemed to have daunted her—not the disappearance of her mama, not the slow starvation of her twin.

She'd be full grown now, big enough have cubs of her own, bold enough to. . . .

Take down a calf.

"Oh, no. . . ." The blood left Cait's face. Just the thought of what those men would do to Halona if they managed to catch her made Cait's stomach revolt.

"Sawtooth, if they find Halona, you know what'll happen." Cait dropped the poker and lunged to her feet. She had to do something. No, she wasn't one-hundred-percent sure that Halona was their target, but mountain lions were solitary creatures and highly territorial. And there were so few left. . . .

Setting her jaw in determination, Cait swiftly gathered a few necessities and stuffed them into a pack, then headed for a small shed out back where she'd stored all of her grandfather's trapping gear. If those fools thought they could trespass on *this* mountain and make a profit off a wildcat, then they were in for a rude awakening.

Chapter 3

By week's end, Ethan wondered what had ever possessed him to think he could play Daniel of the Wilderness without paying a serious price.

Arms weighted down with saturated gear, he trudged from the water onto the silty bank, each step pumping what felt like half of Mission Creek out of his boots. The broken stirrup of the horseless saddle resting on his right shoulder trailed a gouge in the mucky earth. A pair of traps slung by anchor chains over his shoulder clapped against the bruises already on his hip.

He should have known better than to trust a horse with the prophetic name of Trouble; the roan he'd been riding had lived up to it in spades. Every shift of the wind blowing across the valley, any sudden motion or unfamiliar noise, had sent the animal into a crow-hopping fit.

And as they'd climbed higher into the mountains, Trouble hadn't stopped at throwing him at every opportunity. No, he'd also managed to ruin one of Ethan's finest saddles by scraping it against every tree in its path before hightailing back down the mountain.

If there had been any other mount in the livery, Ethan would have traded Trouble in an instant. Unfortunately, the stock had been cleaned out by the time he'd arrived at the livery, so he hadn't had much choice; it was either borrow Trouble, or make the ten-mile hike on foot, carrying two weeks' worth of supplies on his own back.

He'd chosen Trouble.

And had gotten his money's worth.

Well, good riddance, Ethan thought, reaching a fallen log. After that last flight into the creek, he was better off without the contrary beast.

He dumped his gear to the ground and lowered his battered body with a groan. The birch handle of his black powder pistol dug into his ribs. He removed the gun from his waistband and tipped it up. Water streamed from the barrel.

Scowling, he tossed the useless weapon onto the packs, then let his hand fall limply across his knee. A heavy sigh pushed from his lungs. He rubbed a damp palm across his forehead.

Right now he'd give just about anything for a decent meal, a warm bed, and dry duds.

Ethan glanced around the dense tangle of timber and underbrush populating the snow-encrusted mountainside.

A human voice wouldn't be unwelcome, either.

He hadn't seen a soul in a week. Given his

reception in civilization, it struck him odd how much he missed the company of people—even ones who made him feel about as wanted as a weasel in a henhouse.

But as much as he longed for the comforts he'd left behind, there was no going back. Not without the cat. Josie's reputation, her very future, depended on him doing something that would earn him the town's respect again. Catching that cougar would prove that he did have their best interests at heart—in spite of what most of them believed.

The problem was, he hadn't found so much as a paw print since leaving Hullet's land, where he'd first picked up the cougar's trail. Not that paw prints were easy to spot in the thick foliage, but with all the snow still on the ground, there should have been some sign of the cat by now.

Another weary sigh sent a cloud of vapor into the crisp air as Ethan dragged himself off the log. No job ever got done by a man sitting around feeling sorry for himself. With so little left of the afternoon, he might as well take advantage of the creekside clearing; it seemed as good a place as any to make camp and dry out before he continued his search in the morning.

He spread his blanket and extra clothes over rocks and bushes, then hiked around the area in search of dead fall for a fire that would help dry the items. He found several chunks of pine and tossed them into a pile. Just as he reached for a fourth, he caught an unpleasant whiff of . . . what the hell was it? Rotting timber? No, too rancid. Dead animal?

His brow crimping, he cautiously followed the nose-curling odor. If it was a carcass stinking up the area, he hoped it would be small and easily disposed of. He was too tired to move camp.

The smell grew stronger the closer Ethan came to a high-branched pine tree set back from the creek's edge. Each footstep sent pine cones and other debris skittering out of his path, and Ethan didn't pay much mind when the toe of his boot caught on the viny underbrush, until—

Snap! Whoosh!

"What—?" He glanced down just as the ground swooped up around him, whipped him off his feet, and yanked him into the air.

For a moment he was too stunned to react. Curled into a ball, feet at the top, shoulders at the bottom, knees tight against his chest, Ethan gaped at the ground ten feet below. His traps lay in a bed of dried needles like petrified skeletons. Beside them, his saddle, weapons, packs and bedding. . . . everything he owned except the clothes on his back.

His curses began softly, then gained in strength. When he ran out of all the ones he knew, he created others so colorful that even the pine trees blushed.

Daylight died and the night came alive with hoots and whirs and eerie rustles.

Ethan wasn't sure how long he'd been up here, but it had been beyond long enough. It felt as if every last drop of blood in his body had drained to his head. His scalp tingled, his eyes stung, his lips had gone numb. Not a bone in his body didn't ache.

He'd tried everything he could think of to get out the snare, but nothing had worked. Whoever had made it sure knew his business. Whipcord ropes made of twisted hemp had been woven together into small squares. At the top, the ropes gathered like the drawstring of a lady's purse.

And inside he lay, bound tighter than a caterpillar in a spun-steel cocoon.

He rubbed his hands up and down his arms to try and warm himself, even knowing it wouldn't do any good. Falling temperatures combined with his still wet clothes had started his teeth to chattering some time ago, and as he stared through the branches at the tip of a crescent moon, he wondered if he'd survive the night.

Wouldn't that make everybody in Roland ecstatic?

Of course, the only way they'd learn of his fate was if someone came upon him. Like Billy. Or Louis. Or any one of the men out for the cougar.

The prospect of someone from town finding him in such a humiliating position left a sour taste in his mouth. Yet by the time the darkness gave way to dawn, Ethan decided he'd be happy to see the grim reaper himself if it meant getting out of this tree.

He must have fallen asleep at some point, though, for the snapping of a twig startled him alert.

Ethan twisted as far as his binds would allow. "Hel—" The plea for rescue came out in a raspy whisper. He'd hollered his throat raw already, and he barely had a voice left, but he licked his chalky lips and tried again. "Heeelp."

All sound stopped. Not even a bird chirped.

It occurred to him that anything could be out there. Bears were beginning to come out from hibernation, and of course, mountain cats. . . .

Tension mounted and time stretched into an endless river of anticipation as he waited for his mysterious visitor to make an appearance.

Just when he started to think his mind was playing tricks on him, a shadowy figure separated from the tree.

"Who's there?" he demanded.

"I might ask the same of you," came a stern response. The pitch struck him odd, sounded unnaturally low.

He hesitated to give his name. If whoever was down there recognized it, they might hightail it in the opposite direction purely out of spite. But if he didn't identify himself, they might leave anyway.

Figuring that he didn't have much to lose, he answered warily, "Ethan Sawyer of Roland."

"Well, Ethan Sawyer of Roland . . ." His visitor moved boldly forward into a triangle of twilight. "Looks like you've gotten yourself in a bit of a bind."

Ethan's senses jolted when the buckskin clad figure stepped into full view. He sucked in a swift breath as his gaze locked with eyes so strikingly pale they glowed like moons against her coppery gold skin. Dark brown hair the color of freshly brewed coffee framed her rounded face, and lips that made a man think of nights full of sweet temptation and sinful pleasures curved into a faint smile.

His dumbfounded gaze followed the long-sleeved tunic hugging every curve and hollow from neck to thigh. Fringe trailed down the side seams, and beadwork decorated the yoke and hem. Legs as long as a sixteen-hand filly were wrapped in leggings so snug they might as well have been baked on, and calf-high moccasins adorned her feet.

While the craftsman in him couldn't help but appreciate the fine details of the costume, the man in him responded to what lay beneath. The womanly flare of hips, the nipped in waist, the generous swells of her breasts.

Needs Ethan had long since forgotten himself capable of slammed into him like a cast-iron mallet. It felt as if he'd been living in a dead man's body until this moment. His blood rushed through his veins like a gully-washer, heat spread like wildfire across his skin, and the unmistakable bulge developing at the front of his trousers would have been embarrassing if he'd thought she could see it.

Not since his first trip to Peachy's House of Pleasure when he was fourteen had the sight of a woman caused such a swift and powerful reaction. Even Amanda, whose golden beauty had been turning the head of every male in Roland for the last decade, didn't hold a candle to this sultry vision.

Who *was* she?

His awkward position made it hard to see her features clearly. Those blue eyes clearly marked her of white blood, and yet . . . Ethan took in the rifle gripped in one hand, the hide pack belted around her waist, and a bone-handled knife strapped against her hip. This was no ordinary white woman. She looked far too comfortable with herself, fit in too well with her surroundings, almost as if she'd been born from Mother Nature's womb onto this mountain.

In fact, dressed as she was, she could easily be mistaken for a sav—

The connection pushed to the surface of Ethan's mind. His eyes widened. Gawd A'mighty, it couldn't be . . . "Wild Cat Cait?"

One dark, slender brow arched. "So they call me."

Ethan blinked. His jaw fell. This curvaceous beauty was the legendary heathen of the hills? The mysterious mountaineer who wrestled beasts three times her size? She couldn't be more than five and a half feet tall, and looked hardly strong enough to choke a gnat!

He fell back in shock. Never in his wildest dreams had he imagined he'd meet up with Wild Cat Cait. Hell, to be honest, he hadn't really believed she existed!

Yet here she stood—in the flesh.

"You keep staring at me like that, I'm likely to take offense." Full wine-dark lips curved into a smile of wicked smugness. "And you aren't in much of a position to be offending me."

Ethan blinked and gave himself a mental

shake. She was right, he couldn't afford to rile
his only hope of rescue. "I'm sorry," he said.
"It's just that . . . you're not what I expected."

"I file my fangs down once a month and my
nails grow only during a full moon," she replied wryly.

She *knew* of the tales told about her?

"I have to say, I've found some unexpected
creatures in my snares, but you beat all."

Her snares? he thought, jolted from the stupor she'd cast upon him. What the hell was she
planning on catching in this contraption?

Then again, did it really matter at the moment?

Ethan cleared his throat. "Would you mind
seeing what you can do about getting me
down?"

"Mind telling me how you wound up
there?"

Hot embarrassment climbed up his neck. It
would have been bad enough had any of the
men from Roland come upon him, but being
caught in such a humiliating lurch by a woman
of her reputation made him feel about two
inches tall. "I was out hunting."

"Interesting technique. Let me guess—
you're the bait."

Ethan scowled, the amusement in her tone
adding another bruise to his already battered
ego. "A little help would be much more appreciated than the jokes."

With a casual hip-swaying stroll that had his
mouth going dry and his pulses picking up,
she wandered further into the clearing. He'd
never thought a woman's walk could be se-

ductive. Then again, he was learning a lot of things on this excursion.

A skittering *clank* sounded below as she kicked the trap he'd been toting around half the Rockies. "Quite a set of jaws. What are you after? Bear?"

"Mountain lion," he corrected tightly.

Her head jerked up. "You're one of *them*."

Her silky-smooth voice became brittle and cutting. The mood around him shifted, turning frostier than a winter dawn.

"One of who?" Ethan asked.

"Those hunters after the bounty."

Ah, she must have had a run-in with a party of Roland's finest. He couldn't help but wonder if they'd come away from the encounter unscathed. "Not exactly. Look, just get me down—"

"So you can destroy an animal in danger of being wiped out in this area? You're out of your mind, hunter."

Ethan gawked at her. "That *endangered animal* is killing livestock."

"Oh, goodness gracious, forgive me for not being more sensitive to some fancy cattleman's purse when an entire breed is being slaughtered. I'll wager you hunted buffalo, too."

Slack-jawed, Ethan could hardly believe his ears. She was defending the vicious predators? He snapped his mouth shut and countered, "There are also innocent children on those ranches. If one of your precious mountain lions attacked one of them, would you still be so quick to jump to its defense?"

"Mountain lions rarely attack a human unless they are invading their territory or threatening their offspring. They don't pounce on people just for sport. Jesus, ignorance like yours just turns my stomach."

She twisted on her heel, her hair whirling around her like a sable cloak before it settled against her bottom.

A moment passed before Ethan realized she meant to leave him. His fingers curled around the ropes. He lurched forward, crammed his face against his prison. "Wait, you can't just walk off!"

Without a backward glance, she hollered, "Watch me."

"Wait!" Ethan thrashed inside the net. He swore the ropes clutched him tighter just to make him suffer more. "God damn it, wait— I'm freezing, I'm starving, and I can't feel my feet anymore. If you leave me up here, I'll die."

She kept walking.

Desperation slammed into him, made his heart thump erratically in his chest. He raised his voice. "Look . . . I'll do whatever you want—" He hated the pleading in his tone. He'd never begged for anything in his life, not even the day his father had walked out on him and Josie. But the thought of spending even one more night stuffed like sausage in a casing sent panic rushing through his veins.

She came to a dead stop at the edge of the clearing and snapped her hand against her hip. "Anything?"

"Just name it."

"Go back to where you came from and forget about that cougar."

A dozen images flashed through his mind as he stared at her: Josie's misery. Billy's hatred. A restaurant that had barely known a customer in years.

She would have asked for the impossible.

He released his grip on the ropes. His frantic heartbeat slowed to a resigned rhythm and in a low, firm voice, Ethan replied, "That I can't do."

"Then you can rot up there."

Cait stormed through the forest, so mad she could spit. She'd spent the last four days scouting the territory for telltale signs—repeated patterns of tracks and claw marks on the ground and around trees—in order to best decide where to set snares in places the cougar revisited. She'd laid out five of her grandfather's best nets, using raw meat laced with laudanum as bait, and had taken time away from her own animals each evening and each morning in order to tend the snares.

And for what? To catch a *man*? Worse—an egotistical, demanding, tender-footed hunter!

How *dare* another one of those ignorant, money-grubbing . . . *vultures* swoop down on her mountain and roost where he didn't belong?

Was there no end?

It didn't matter to them that mountain lions had been roaming these lands for thousands of years. That they didn't understand barbed wire or trespassing—all they knew was a natural need to eat.

But of course, if their way of life dared to

threaten a few measly cows, the ranchers' answer was just to destroy the animals. Hell, they'd been doing it for years!

None of them cared that the number of mountain lions in this area was shrinking at an alarming rate. No, they wouldn't be happy until the cats were completely wiped out.

Then again, Cait thought, flinging her hand in the air in frustration, why should she expect any different? Hadn't they done the same thing to the buffalo? To the Indians?

And to think she'd actually believed this hunter harmless when she'd first come upon him. Ha! He was just as dangerous as the first two she'd encountered—maybe even more so. Because he cloaked his actions under a noble guise. Because he'd recognized her.

Because he'd stirred something inside her. Fascination. Amusement.

Compassion.

Her footsteps slowed. She cast a hesitant glance over her shoulder and furrowed her brow. Was he still hollering? His voice had sounded a little . . . chafed.

Cait whipped back around and stormed on. Who cared? He shouldn't be on her mountain, anyway. And this *was* her mountain—she had the deed to prove it. If he died in that tree, it would serve him right.

She didn't make it another hundred yards before her conscience kicked in with a mighty vengeance.

Cait stopped, bowed her head, and took a few deep breaths to try and regain control over her emotions. Yes, the survival of wildcats was a sensitive issue with her, but she'd not get a wink of sleep knowing she'd left a human being to the mercy of the elements.

Not even one of *them*.

With a defeated sigh, she retraced her steps back to the snare. She would have felt better having Sawtooth at her side, but with all these men swarming into the area, it had seemed wiser to leave him at the cabin. Not only would he be some protection for the other animals, but he wouldn't be spotted by those pelt-hungry vipers out to make a fast dollar.

She reached the tree. Sawyer was swinging slowly back and forth in the net, whistling softly, as if enjoying a lazy morning nestled in a hammock instead of crumpled like old newsprint in a sock.

Cait bristled and almost left him again. Only the annoying voice in her head kept her from doing so.

Besides, she decided, she wanted her net back. Preferably without him in it.

Before she changed her mind, she used her hands and thighs to maneuver herself up the coarse-barked trunk to the branch supporting the snare.

The snare shook and wobbled. She could make out the vague shape of him thrashing around. Then all went still, and she heard him sigh her name with relief.

It sounded like a caress.

She ground her teeth against the glow that swept through her and announced, "I came back for my net."

"Gee," he countered sarcastically, "and I

was just starting to get comfortable."

"Get your own net, then, this one's mine."

A single swipe of her Bowie knife severed the rope. The snare fell.

Sawyer landed on his back with a ground-quaking thud while the cords of the net slithered around him like vipers.

An agonized groan rumbled through the air. His arms lowered, his broad hands drifted slowly to his chest.

Cait bit the inside of her cheek to keep from asking if he was all right. Any conversations with this man might lead him to believe she welcomed his intrusion. He was still breathing—that salved her conscience well enough.

Shimmying back down the tree, she moved to stand over him. Little in life surprised Cait anymore, but the sight of the man on the ground sent astonishment speeding to every nerve ending in her body.

Until now, the thickly woven ropes had disguised his features and prevented her from getting a good look at him. But lying in a circle of gauzy sunlight, nothing came between her and a good view of the ruggedly handsome man at her feet. Hair the tawny brown of a lion's coat swept back from a low brow, revealing almond-shaped eyes the color of aged whiskey, the steep blade of a nose, and a mouth no woman in her right mind could resist; a strong jaw boasting several days' growth of golden whiskers gave him a roguish appeal.

He lifted his head and squinted up at her. "Did you have to be so brutal?"

His voice, like worn velvet—smooth, warm, masculine—left her skin tingling.

Cait shook off the sensation and jammed her knife back into the sheath at her waist. "You're lucky I cut you down at all."

"For that," he panted, "I am eternally obliged."

Before she could decipher whether he meant that sincerely or sarcastically, he drew in a deep breath and rolled to his feet. Following the fluid motion of his body, it was all Cait could do not to gasp. He had the solid build of a warrior, with wide, muscled shoulders that even the loose white cotton shirt couldn't hide. Buff-colored trousers bonded to the lean length of him, then disappeared into dusty black boots that reached to his knees.

Though he stood only half a foot taller than she, he seemed so much bigger. Stronger. More powerful.

And Cait began to fear that she'd made a mistake in letting him out of the net.

She swallowed the disturbing thought and tipped her chin. She'd let no man intimidate her, especially not one in her own territory. "Just so you don't get any ideas, I set you loose for one reason and one reason only—to deliver this message to your friends: Get the hell off my mountain and stay away from that cat, or the next time I see any of your trespassing hides, buckshot will be kissing your backsides."

Without giving him a chance to reply—or herself more to regret—she disappeared into the forest.

Ethan glared at the spot where she'd stood. Buckshot kissing his backside, huh? He clenched his jaw. Cold fury and hot humiliation roiled in his blood. Just who in the hell did she think she was to threaten him? Oh, that's right, he scoffed, she was Wild Cat Cait. Hell, her reputation was almost as notorious as his! The difference was, he'd been made into a leper.

She'd been made into a legend.

Well, he didn't give a damn who she was. If she thought she could intimidate him with her skinny rifle and her frosty eyes, she had another thing coming. He'd been dealing with difficult people long enough in Roland; no gun-totin', buckskin-wearing wildlife champion with a tongue as sharp as the knife she carried would scare him off.

Legend or not, he wasn't leaving this mountain without the cat.

Fueled with determination, Ethan turned to collect his gear only to freeze at the shambles left of his camp. His shoulders slumped; he ran his hand through his gritty hair. God, this was all he needed. No horse, a she-devil threatening him with both barrels, his belongings strewn from here to infinity by critters who must have decided that his things were free for the taking. . . .

As Ethan set out to search for whatever items he could recover, he couldn't see how things could get any worse—until he rounded a tree and came face-to-face with Billy Gray.

Chapter 4

"Well, lookee here, Billy. It's our old pal Ethan." A grinning Louis planted the butt of his rifle against the ground and angled it away from his body.

The move appeared innocent enough, yet Ethan's senses went on full alert. His glance slid from one man to the other. While Louis's eyes held a cocky recklessness typical of him, Billy's burned with a fire of loathing that had become as much a part of him in recent years as his mustache and wolf-skin hat.

Both men, Ethan knew, would just as soon cut out his heart as let him pass without incident. The question was, which one would make the first move?

Tension strung around them like barbed wire. No one spoke. The rush of water, the dulcet twitter of songbirds, and even his own heartbeat sounded abnormally loud and out of place in the taut silence.

And though every muscle in his body tightened in readiness, Ethan kept his hands loose at his sides, his expression indifferent . . . and waited.

Billy finally broke the silence, his tone frigid with scorn. "What the hell are you doing here, Sawyer?"

Ethan braced his weight on one leg in a deceptively casual stance. "Same as you, I expect."

"You're hunting that cougar?" Louis snickered.

A muscle twitched at Ethan's eye. He was getting damn sick and tired of everyone ridiculing his decision. Only the knowledge that a calm front had avoided trouble in the past helped him keep a solid grip on his control. "I don't want the community in danger any more than the next person," he said with a shrug.

"You sure as hell didn't feel that way three years ago," Billy sneered.

Three years ago they hadn't been talking about hunting cougar, either. But Ethan wasn't about to let himself get baited into defending his actions during that fateful summer. He'd done what he'd felt he had to do, and if he had regrets, well . . . they were his regrets.

Smoothly he countered, "You fellas just here to admire the scenery, or you got business with me?"

"That depends," Louis drawled, eyeing the mound of netting with calculated interest. "You run across any wildcats yet?"

The image of a brown-haired, blue-eyed hellion in buckskins appeared instantly in Ethan's mind. He scanned the treeline. Intuition told him that Cait had left the immediate area, but she could not have gotten far in the short span of time since they'd parted.

A strange compulsion to protect her gripped him with relentless force. As capable as she'd seemed, he doubted that even she'd be any match for Billy or Louis if they caught her unawares. There was a time when he wouldn't have thought either man capable of harming a woman, but given Billy's hatred toward Indians, and Louis's obsession with the myth of Wild Cat Cait, what would stop them from preying on her—especially if they guessed her identity, as he had, or thought she could lead them to the cat?

"There's no cougar here that I've been able to find," he said, hoping to steer Billy and Louis in the opposite direction and buy Cait time to get further away. "In fact, I wouldn't be surprised if it got its fill of Hullet's herd and moved on."

"Then maybe you should do the same," his brother-in-law challenged, "and leave the hunting to real men."

Coolly, Ethan returned, "And maybe you should go back to your wife."

Billy took a menacing step forward, chest thrust out, eyes livid with fury. "Mind your own gawddamn business, Squaw-man."

"Josie *is* my business, Billy-boy."

A fist crashed against Ethan's jaw. His head snapped to the side, pain exploded through the entire right side of his face.

He shook away the stars circling inside his head, then moved his jaw from one side to the other, testing the hinges.

Assured that nothing had been broken, he fixed an unrelenting stare on Billy, who stood a pace away, shaking out his hand.

"Josie ain't nothin' to you anymore, got that?" Billy fumed. "You ain't even fit to say her name, you yella-bellied traitor."

Ethan's restraint snapped. For three years he'd taken verbal shots at his manhood, his honor, his pride. For three years he'd kept his temper in check and pretended that popular contempt didn't bother him.

No more.

He doubled his fist and let it fly. Knucklebones connected with Billy's chin and the shorter man fell from the impact.

Ethan stared at his brother-in-law, sprawled in the dirt. "And you ain't fit to call her wife."

For any other man, the fight would have ended there, but Billy never had been one to give up. He stayed on the ground long enough to spit out a mouthful of blood, then staggered to his feet. "You sonofabitch!"

With a cry of rage, Billy dipped his shoulder and charged, slamming into Ethan's gut with the force of a wild bull. Ethan took the brunt of their fall and hit the ground with a bone-jarring grunt.

They rolled in the dirt for several turns, each wrestling for the upper hand. Dimly Ethan heard Louis urging Billy on but found himself a bit too occupied to pay attention to the words.

Billy finally gained top position. He pressed his thumbs into Ethan's windpipe, laughing maliciously when the veins began to swell in his face.

Though Ethan was the bigger and more powerful of the two, Billy had rage feeding his strength.

But Ethan had something more—a desperate instinct to survive. He clubbed his forehead against Billy's. The instant his grip loosened, he hooked his leg around Billy's knee and flipped him over.

Ethan then rolled to his feet and put a wide distance between himself and Billy. Sweat stung his eyes, blood filled his nose. He wiped his sleeve across his face. A peripheral movement had him spinning a quarter turn on his heel just as Louis leveled his rifle.

"Scuffle's over, Sawyer, be on your way."

Billy pushed clumsily to his hands and knees, shook his head, lumbered to his feet. "Leave off, Gypsy-man," he commanded. "This is between me an' him." Then he reached behind his back and the next thing Ethan knew, a knife had appeared in Billy's hand. "I'm gonna slit you a new gullet, Sawyer."

Ethan crouched low and circled, keeping his eyes on the blade, cursing the fact that his own knife lay somewhere under the pile of netting behind him.

How in the hell had it ever come to this? Once they'd been closer than brothers. They'd skipped school to fish at the local swimming hole. Raced horses at every Founder's Day festival since '72. Courted the ladies, drank themselves into oblivion, and come to each other's rescue more times than he could count. . . .

"C'mon, Squaw-man," Billy taunted, wiggling his fingers in invitation. "There ain't no skirts to hide behind now."

His throat tight with the deluge of memories, Ethan hoarsely confessed, "Damn it, Billy, I don't want to fight you."

"You should have thought of that before you brought that pox-ridden savage into town."

Ethan continued watching the knife being jabbed repeatedly into the space between them. "She was sick, Billy. I couldn't leave her to die. You of all people should know that."

"All I know is that saving a redskin's worthless hide was more important to you than protecting your family and friends."

Ethan didn't bother refuting the charge. What was the use? Billy wasn't the only one who thought he'd endangered everyone around him the day he'd found the Flathead woman and brought her home. "Fighting won't change what happened. What's done is done."

"No, but it'll give me the satisfaction of wiping your sorry ass all over this mountain."

The scorching glint in Billy's eyes told Ethan that anything he said would only feed the anger. He could talk himself blue in the face and there would be no more reasoning with Billy now than before.

No, the only way to get through this deadlock with any semblance of pride was to call Billy's bluff.

Reverting to the days when all that mattered were winning hands and fast horses and loose women, Ethan manufactured a slow, cocky smile designed to make Billy wonder what he had hidden up his sleeve. "Kill me then, Billy-boy, if it'll make you feel better"—he paused for effect—"and if you think you can."

He bent at the waist and mentally prepared himself for the onslaught of hatred that had been festering inside Billy since he was ten years old and saw his family massacred.

For long moments they stared at each other. Circling, searching, waiting for a weakness . . .

Then, to Ethan's surprise, Louis stepped in and grabbed Billy's arm. "C'mon, Bill, he ain't worth it."

"Stay out of this, Louis."

"You ain't thinkin' clear, pal." Lowering his voice, he added, "What do you think Josie'll do if she finds out you killed her brother?"

Something flickered in Billy's eyes. A glimmer of doubt, a hint of reluctance. . . .

Then a vile oath littered the air. Billy shook free of Louis's grip, straightened, and jabbed his knife back into the sheath. The anger blazed hotter than before, making his voice quiver as he said, "Just stay the hell out of my way, Squaw-man. If I see you again, I'll be dragging your carcass back to Roland along with that cougar's."

At that he motioned to Louis, who flipped his rifle against his shoulder.

Ethan kept his attention fixed on the men as they walked toward their horses. Once they were out of sight, his shoulders slumped. He bowed his head and slowly released a pent-up breath.

Damn, he was tired of this. Tired of the

games and of pretending he was invincible and of being hated by everyone he met.

He walked stiffly to the creek and lowered to his knees. Every muscle in his body screamed at the abuse he'd put it through over the last week. Between being thrown by Trouble, spending the night in the net, and the fight with Billy, he felt like he'd been chewed up and spit out.

A groan escaped him as he caught sight of his reflection in the rippling surface. Hell, he didn't look much better than he felt. Blood streamed down the steep bridge of his nose from a gash in his forehead. More blood dribbled from the corner of his mouth, and one eye was already beginning to swell shut. He hadn't had a shiner in ages, but by tonight he'd have a whopper of one for sure.

And for what? To prove his manhood?

He could hear Josie now—"A man doesn't fight with his fists, a man fights with his convictions."

Ethan sighed. Maybe she was right.

Though he couldn't dredge up any remorse over slugging it out with Billy, there had been no satisfaction in it, either. Losing control hadn't served any purpose; it sure as hell wasn't going to change anything. Not Billy's hatred, not Josie's misery, not his own status in the community he'd helped found.

He closed his eyes and splashed his face, wincing when the water flushed out his wounds. Hellfire, he didn't even know what his convictions were anymore. They used to be so clear. Now. . . .

He shook his head.

Part of him wished Billy had done him in; dying couldn't be any worse punishment than what he'd already endured.

Yet another part of him embraced the fact that he'd been given another day. For the first time since this whole farce had begun, he saw a glimmer of light at the end of the dark and dank tunnel he'd been living in.

All he had to do was track down a cattle-killing beast.

Ha! Now, that was almost funny. As if competing with half the male population of Roland didn't cause him enough problems, he also had to contend with an untamed little she-cat that would rather see him strung up by his toenails than find that mountain lion.

Gawd A'mighty, she'd been a fetching piece. Just the sight of her had been like hitting a hot stamp to cold leather. The image burned into his mind of her standing there in those curve-molding buckskins, armed with nothing more than a shotgun and wild fury, made his blood sizzle and his palms sweat all over again. He imagined winding that fall of sable hair around his wrist. Peeling away the tunic. Pulling her close and tasting—

A sudden shove from behind sent Ethan diving face-first into the creek. An instant later he came out of the frigid water sputtering and flung himself around.

On the bank stood Trouble.

Ethan sprang to his feet, swiped his sleeve across his face. "You! You low-down, good for nothing, pitiful waste of hide and hoof!" he cursed the roan. "Do you know how much trouble you've caused me?"

Even as he said the words, Ethan realized how ridiculous they sounded. Of course, the horse knew. Trouble was, after all, his name.

"If I had any sense, I'd shoot you right now," Ethan thundered, stomping out of the creek. Unfortunately, as much as Trouble aggravated him, he needed the critter too much to make good on the threat. The mountain range was vast, his gear weighed almost as much as he did . . . unless he wanted to finish the hunt carrying all his supplies on his back— or unless God took quick pity on him and produced another pack animal out of thin air—he was stuck with the difficult beast.

He made it to the bank, dropped to the ground and yanked off his waterlogged boots. Damn it all. If this kept up, he was going to wind up trekking around the mountain in his socks!

It was his own fault, he admitted. If he hadn't been preoccupied, he'd probably have heard the horse come up behind him. But nooo, he'd let himself get so distracted with thoughts of a bright-eyed hellion that he hadn't noticed anything around him.

Ethan propped his elbow on one upraised knee and let his forehead fall into his palm. What the hell was the matter with him? She was Indian, for God's sake! That fact had registered shortly after he'd hit the ground. Even if he hadn't heard the stories, even if she had been wearing different clothes, the faint coppery tone of her skin, the high forehead, and the prominent cheekbones gave away her heritage; he'd lived in the area long enough to recognize the characteristics of a native.

That sure as hell hadn't stopped him from reacting to her, though, he thought with a grimace. Yes, it had been a while since he'd lost himself in the softness of a woman, but that was no excuse. If he ever acted on the fantasies he'd had about Wild Cat Cait . . . he shuddered just thinking about the trouble that would bring him.

Ethan pulled on his boots, determined to push thoughts of her out of his head and concentrate on finding the cougar.

And yet, as he circled the area in search of his scattered belongings, she lurked in the back of his mind like a shadow. Haunting him. Taunting him. Tempting him until all he could see was the sky in her eyes and the sunshine in her smile.

Who was she really? Where had she come from?

Turning to Trouble in frustration, he cried, "Just what the hell had she been doing wandering around the mountain on her lonesome, anyway? Doesn't she have any common sense?"

The horse nickered.

"And where are her menfolk? They ought to be shot for not keeping a tighter reign on her," Ethan ranted, ripping one of his shirts free of the thorny underbrush.

She'd just been lucky that she'd stumbled onto him and not Billy or Louis. If word ever got out that Wild Cat Cait wasn't just a tall tale, but a flesh-and-blood woman who could tempt a rock, he'd bet his last shipment that she'd be hunted more fiercely than any four-legged animal.

He paused and gripped the shirt to his chest. Concern. Yeah, that's what it was he felt for her. As capable as she'd seemed, a shotgun and those flashing blue eyes wouldn't be any match for a man set on claiming her. If—and it was highly unlikely—he did happen to meet up with her again, she had a right to know that she could be in danger. What she did with the knowledge would then be up to her.

Ethan settled the matter in his mind at the same time he located his bedroll, with two holes now showing daylight through the wool, under a pile of bramble. He grimaced and wadded the blanket into a ball.

Luckily the varmints had managed only to chew through one side of his saddlebags, leaving his extra clothes intact, but the other side that had contained a good portion of his foodstuffs and cooking gear had been cleaned out. He found his tin plate wedged between two rocks, his cup caught in a pile of rocks near the creek bank, his coffeepot in the water, lodged against a fallen tree. Where they'd taken his eating utensils off to was anyone's guess.

He packed up the rest of his gear on Trouble's back and swung into the saddle. "Now, you'd best behave yourself. I've got a cat to find, and I'm in no mood for your tricks."

With that stern warning, Ethan guided Trouble along the edge of the creek. Several miles upstream, they veered off into the woods and scouted the area in an ever-widening circle until it got too dark to see.

Hunger gnawed in his belly and weariness became an ache in his soul as Ethan pitched camp at the bend of the brook. He brushed down and then hobbled Trouble, devoured a soggy piece of jerky and barely managed to undo his bedroll before he fell on it, asleep.

He awoke late the next morning. Even the knowledge that the sun was already an hour high in the sky couldn't hurry him. Too little rest, too little food, and too much abuse had taken its toll on a body more accustomed to the comforts and conveniences of town life. He sluggishly rolled off the pungent layer of pine needles that had served as his mattress.

He'd never known a body could ache this bad.

After a quick cup of coffee, he saddled Trouble and packed his gear securely. He refused to think about yesterday; today was all that mattered. And today he was going to find that damn cat if it was the last thing he did.

The temperatures had dropped again, making it colder than a corpse's skin. Trouble's hooves crunched through the thin crust of frost that had formed during the night.

Even so, it was almost a pleasant ride.

The wind soughed through the trees. The brook gurgled softly nearby. Squirrels chattered from one of the trees.

Ethan absorbed the scenery even as he studied the ground for signs of the cougar—paw prints, scratch marks . . . the cougar itself. The eroded slopes above the creek provided haven to a horde of small critters—rabbits, fox, even a mink or two. An eagle soared above, claiming the vast blue sky as its own, and in the background, higher slopes of the Mission Range touched heaven.

What would it be like, Ethan wondered, to have the run of something this vast, this peaceful? That had its appeal. He hadn't known peace in so long. . . .

He should have known it wouldn't last.

Trouble started up his usual mischief. Sidestepping, balking, tossing his head—and for no apparent reason other than to torment him, Ethan thought, grinding his teeth. He gripped the saddle horn and reins and tried to soothe the animal. "Come on, Trouble. Easy, boy."

With Ethan's attention focused on calming his fractious mount, the distant rumble that swept through the forest didn't register in his mind until it was too late. Trouble reared back with a shrill whinny.

"Oh, shit, not again!" Ethan lurched forward and grabbed the roan's dark mane seconds before hooves hit the ground with a teeth-jarring impact. Trouble then began to fishtail, bucking and kicking, seeming determined to rid himself of the load on his back so he could gain speed. Ethan clamped his knees around the horse's girth, just as determined to keep his seat.

Then a shriek rent the air, followed by a thunderous roar.

And Trouble was off like a bullet.

Ethan could only hold on for dear life as the gelding stretched out into a full hair-raising, spine-tingling gallop. The scenery passed by in a blur. The scent of evergreen and fear rushed through Ethan's nostrils and into his lungs. Branches tore at his face, and something—a stick, maybe?—tore through his trousers and scored his thigh. A burning sensation cut clear to the bone. Sweat, cold and salty, stung his eyes. His hands ached from clenching the reins, his seat felt like a tenderized slab of meat.

At the crest of a bluff, the ride ended as fast as it had begun.

Trouble went bowstring tight, locked his forelegs, skidded across the earth like an ice skater's blade.

Ethan went soaring over the roan's head.

He *oof*ed as his shoulder took the brunt of his fall. A sixth sense warned him of the wicked hooves descending. Ethan curled into a ball and tossed himself out of the way and found himself rolling down, down, down. . . . Rocks, bramble, pine needles, and dirt ground into his skin, scalp, and clothes.

He came to a sharp stop against something hard and immobile.

Breathing heavily, every muscle weeping in agony, Ethan opened his eyes. Sunlight beamed through a weblike tangle of branches stretching across a pale blue sky. When the dancing speckles cleared from his vision, he lifted his head. The movement caused a shard of pain to shoot across his neck and down his arm.

He fell back and waited for the throbbing to pass. Then he rolled awkwardly to his feet. A bolt of lightning-hot agony shot down his leg, buckling his knees. He grabbed his thigh, sticky with blood and dirt and God knew what else. He ripped a strip of flannel off the tail of his shirt with his teeth and bound the wound. If nothing else it would stop the bleeding until he could wash it out.

Brushing soil from his clothes, Ethan scanned the area but saw little more than the erect assembly of tree trunks surrounding him like prison bars, and the clinging green foliage beneath.

There was no sign of Trouble.

Muttering curses filthy enough to make a two-bit whore blush, he limped down the slope in search of the aggravating animal and tried to ignore the throbbing in his leg and shoulder. He'd just as soon shoot Trouble as see him again, but he needed his supplies. Everything he'd brought with him was tied to the horse.

He'd just reached a break in the timber several hundred feet away when a flash of vibrant color caught his eye.

Eyes narrowing, then widening on the source, he watched in horror as a black and orange creature the likes of which he'd never seen reared back, then pounced on a slim brown figure kneeling beside the ribbon of a stream.

The air resounded with a high-pitched squeal that sounded almost. . . .

Female.

Ethan's heart stuttered. *Cait!*

Allowing himself no thought beyond reaching her, he charged the rest of the way down the slope.

*　　*　　*

Cait's laughter dwindled to breathless giggles as she pushed Sawtooth's head away from her hip. "Okay, that's enough wrestling, you big oaf. We've dawdled enough for the day."

With one last ruffle to the tiger's fur, she rolled to her feet and grabbed up the buckets she'd been filling before Sawtooth had decided he needed attention.

Instead of falling into step beside her as she headed for the cabin, he nipped at her sleeve and retreated, nipped and retreated, obviously not satisfied with their brief tussle.

She gave him a scowl of mock irritation. "I said quit, Sawtooth, we have work to do."

Of course, he had the annoying ability of ignoring her when it suited him. He paced a tight figure-eight pattern around Cait, tangled himself in her legs, and upset her balance. She let loose a squeal and landed on her rear end. The buckets went flying, water soaking both her and the thirsty ground.

Cait picked herself up off the dirt and glowered at the tiger. "*Now* look what you did!" She seized the buckets. "Damn it, Sawtooth, I've got enough work to do without you heaping more on me." She had cages to finish cleaning, clothes to wash, hides to tan. . . . Shoot, she thought, retracing her steps back to the shallow stream that wound through the canyon, she'd fallen so far behind on her chores that she'd need a week to catch up.

The disruption of their routine was for a good cause, though, Cait reminded herself as she dipped the buckets into the water. She wasn't about to let a bunch of no-account hunters get away with killing one of her cats. Even though it had been nearly three years since Halona had been returned to the wild, Cait still considered the cougar her responsibility.

Yes, it was time-consuming and tedious work, setting the snares each evening and checking them before dawn, but it was well worth the effort if it saved Halona.

Unfortunately, Halona wasn't being very co-operative. Cait couldn't be sure if the cat detected her smell or the faint bitterness of the sedative she'd sprinkled over the raw meat she left in each net, but so far she hadn't eaten any of the bait. As frustrating as it was not to have caught her yet, Cait understood the need for patience and persistence.

The only thing Sawtooth understood was that he wasn't getting as much attention as usual.

As if he'd read her thoughts, he sidled up to her, stuck his face in hers, and emitted a close-mouthed growl that sounded more like a plea.

Cait sat back on her heels, looked at him, and sighed. "Look, I know you think I've been neglecting you lately, but how would you feel if it was you out there and a band of hunters wanted to strip you of your coat?"

He whined and covered his eyes with his paw.

"Exactly. So I don't want to hear any complaining, is that clear?"

She didn't wait for an answer. Full buckets in hand, she forged on toward the cabin, her thoughts still heavy with the task of catching an animal that didn't want to be caught. Cait supposed she should be thankful for one thing—she hadn't found any more surprises in her traps. It was too much to hope, though, that Ethan Sawyer had heeded her warning. He didn't strike her as man who gave up easily, in spite of his questionable hunting skills.

Well, with any luck, he'd dropped into a hot spring and boiled himself skinless, or something equally as satisfying.

The grin that formed on her face at the thought got knocked off by a hard nudge from behind. Then Cait felt herself wrenched back a step. She glanced over her shoulder at the four hundred pounds of sheer orneriness latched onto the back of her tunic by his teeth.

She narrowed her eyes and scowled. Sawtooth loosed his toothy grip, sat back on his haunches, then peered up at her with the innocence of a cub waiting for a treat.

Ohhh . . . how could anyone stay annoyed with a face like that? Even knowing that she was being worked like a piece of doeskin, Cait knelt, set the buckets down, and scratched him between the ears. "You big baby," she grumbled. "You're going to keep pestering me until I give in, are you?"

Sawtooth rubbed his fuzzy face against her neck and chuffed in reply.

"These last four days have been tough on you, haven't they?"

He licked her cheek.

She hugged him tightly and whispered, "I'm sorry, Sawtooth." The big cat wasn't made for confinement. Nobody understood how he felt better than she did. After all, she'd spent nearly twelve of her own twenty-four years cooped up behind stone walls.

Cait closed her eyes against the bitter memories threatening to surface.

This was different, she assured herself. She'd *had* to leave Sawtooth behind these last few days for his own safety as well as that of the other cats, not as some sort of punishment or idealistic "betterment for his own good." She just couldn't risk taking him outside the canyon, not while men were crawling all over the mountain.

"It won't be for much longer, Sawtooth, I promise. Once Halona is safe and the hunters can't find her, they'll eventually give up and go home. Then things will return to normal around here." Releasing her hold on him, she pushed to her feet and smiled. "Tell you what, let me clean the cages, then we'll take a walk around the canyon. Maybe even go for a swim?"

Sawtooth leaped into the air in frisky joy at the mention of his favorite pastime.

Cait laughed at his antics but remained firm. "*After* I clean the cages."

The rest of the short journey to the cabin passed without incident. Cait hauled the buckets into the quad and set them outside Faw Paw's cage while Sawtooth wandered off, no doubt to prowl the perimeter of his "territory."

Looking forward to casting her worries aside for a short while and simply enjoying the warm breath of spring, Cait quickly doused the cages, then layered the floors with fresh pine straw. After checking Faw Paw's leg, which

improved more with each day, she left Ginger
free to roam the quad, secured the gate, and
went in search of Sawtooth. But he wasn't
waiting on the porch. Nor did she spot him
roaming the clearing in front of the cabin.

"Sawtooth?" Cait cupped her hands around
her mouth and repeated the call. *"Saaw-
tooooth."*

Hearing only the echo of her voice, she
propped her hands on her hips. "Now, damn
it, where could he be?"

Chapter 5

It was the biggest, meanest, most forbidding-looking creature ever put on this earth.

And it straddled over him like a variegated archway.

Ethan lay still as a stone, unable to do anything more than stare into the glittering gold eyes boring into him. The striped beast had come out of nowhere, leaping through the air, tackling him to the ground, driving the breath from his lungs.

Instinct told him that one wrong move, and his carcass would be strewn from here to perdition and back. Of course, with his shoulders pinned to the ground by a massive set of paws and his torso trapped by the animal's hind-legged spread, he didn't have much choice but to stay put.

Still, it was torture, lying under the critter, feeling its hot, humid breath press against his face. And the stench of it was nearly unbearable—a mixture of wet dog and winded horse, and something more ... an exotic muskiness that curled his nose.

His only consolation was that Cait was nowhere to be seen, so he hoped he'd saved her from being mauled.

Unfortunately, there was no one around but him to care.

After sifting through his options, Ethan decided that his only hope of survival rested in taking the beast by surprise. He wished he had his rifle. His pistol, even. But the rifle had been carried away with Trouble, the pistol had gone flying when the beast tackled him, and he didn't see any possible way to reach the knife in his boot with an animal the size of a small horse on top of him.

Ethan slid his gaze from one side to the other, searching the ground for something that he could use to protect himself. He spotted a rotting limb an arm's length away. The branch hardly made an ideal club; it would undoubtedly crumble the minute he touched it. But a slim chance was better than no chance at all.

With survival his sole thought, he began to move his hand slowly across dirt and forest debris.

A low, beastly rumble of warning came from above, halting the movement and turning Ethan's blood to ice. The creature's fur stood on end from the tips of its flattened ears to the end of its stiffly extended tail. And when its mouth opened, revealing white fangs as long as Ethan's thumb, his heart nearly quit beating.

"Oh, shit...." he whispered, hating the

tremor that rocked through him, yet unable to stop it. He was a dead man.

Wasn't this just his luck? That instead of being hailed as a hero, his last memory would be of cowering beneath the jaws of the very opportunity that could've restored his rank in Roland?

Ethan let his eyes drift shut and felt a peculiar sense of peace and acceptance begin to dull the edge of fear.

And then, as an uninvited vision of Cait appeared in his head. . . .

"There you are, pal. What did you—"

A jolt of alarm shot straight through Ethan at the sound of the voice. Cait? His eyes snapped open.

"Well, well, well, if it isn't the mighty hunter. Good job, Sawtooth, you saved me a couple of bullets."

Gawd A'mighty, what did she think she was doing? A cry of *"Run!"* built in his throat, only to get stuck there with the sudden realization that for someone he'd just seen being attacked by the beast, she sounded far too casual in its company.

Her words sank in, then, and giddy relief warred with heightened dread. Ethan licked his lips and croaked, "This—*thing*—belongs to you?"

"Actually, we belong to each other."

Hellfire, the legends were true—she *did* wrestle beasts three times her size!

"What are you doing here, Sawyer? I distinctly remember telling you that you aren't welcome on this mountain."

Peacefulness and acceptance, relief and dread abruptly disappeared and angry irritation filled him to the marrow. "Having a tea party. What the hell does it *look* like I'm doing?" His started to jerk his head toward Cait.

A ghastly hiss changed his mind.

"I wouldn't make any sudden moves if I were you," she said unnecessarily. "Sawtooth might get the idea you're trying to escape. He'd have to give chase." She tut-tutted. "Messy business, that."

Ethan could imagine. Vividly. He swallowed the hard knot that shot into his throat and licked his lips. "What is it?"

"A Siberian tiger, one of the largest cats in the world."

He managed a weak smile. "Nice kitty."

The "kitty" licked his jaws.

Ethan's stomach plummeted to his spine. "He looks . . . hungry."

"He hasn't eaten yet. But this must be your lucky day—he prefers blonds."

"I am blond," Ethan replied, though it was probably hard to tell with all the grime and debris in his hair.

Then the cat lowered his head and began sniffing Ethan's neck, making strange blowing noises from his nostrils. Hot, heavy breaths stirred the sweat trickling down his temple and neck. "Uh, what's he doing now?"

He could have sworn he heard a chuckle.

"He likes to play with his food before he takes that first savory bite."

As if to support the claim, a tongue of coarse velvet swabbed his cheek.

The blood drained from Ethan's face and pooled somewhere against his spine. "God have mercy . . . call him off."

This time her laughter was unmistakable. It came in a rush, like wind-tossed chimes, but with a hint of blood-chilling glee before it dwindled away on the breeze.

Panic throbbed anew in Ethan's veins. Could Cait be so cruel as to let this animal tear him to shreds and not do a thing to stop it? Cold sweat popped out on his brow, his skin turned clammy. "Call him off!"

She crouched beside him and leaned so close to his face that the stench of the tiger faded. He could smell the fresh sunshine scent of her skin, feel the minty dew of her breath whisper across his cheek. "You didn't say the magic word."

Ethan closed his eyes. The word, rusty and alien, squeezed past his tight throat. "Please . . . call off your guard."

Silence wound around them so tight that he could practically hear her mind ticking its decision.

After an eternity's hesitation, she backed away and Ethan heard a sharp command, "Sawtooth, off!"

The tiger's long body swayed to and fro in a regal triumph as he swaggered off Ethan's chest. Ethan couldn't hold back the whoosh of relief. His nerves went weak; every muscle felt like it was melting. He'd never admit to anyone how terrified he'd been.

With a safe distance between him and the beast, he rolled to his side and pushed himself carefully to his feet. He brushed off the seat of his pants, then looked at the unusual pair in front of him.

The tiger was leisurely licking a paw the size of a pie tin. Cait stood beside him, wearing a worn pair of moccasin boots and a snug set of buckskins much like the ones he'd first seen on her, only dyed a creamy butternut color. And she was grinning from here to Sunday: it reached all the way to her eyes, making them sparkle like sapphires on a sunbeam.

Ethan's heart bucked in his chest, and once again a sizzle of awareness seared through him.

Nothing could have pissed him off more. "Are you crazy?" he exploded. "What the hell do you mean, letting a beast like that roam free?"

"Don't tell me the great and mighty hunter is afraid of a little ole cat." Her eyes widened, she batted a set of spiky black lashes.

Ethan's mouth fell open. "He was going to eat me!"

Her eyes dimmed to the color of deep waters and her smile went brittle. "You'd do well to remember that the next time you think about trespassing on private property."

"Trespassing . . . ?" He gnashed his teeth together. "Lady, I was just lookin' for my horse when I saw that animal attacking you."

"Sawtooth?" She set a possessive hand on the tiger's head. "He'd never hurt me."

"How was I supposed to know that? I only know what I saw, what I heard. . . ." He drew in deep breath in an attempt to control his temper. It didn't work. Especially not with Cait standing there looking so calm. So controlled.

So—unharmed.

Ethan flung his hand in the air, and with a frustrated snarl, told Cait, "Never mind. I don't know why I even bothered thinking you needed me to come to your rescue."

"I don't know why, either," she replied. "This mountain has been my home for a long time now, and I've survived just fine without help from you or anyone else." She paused, tilted her head, and scanned the length of him with a critical eye. "In fact, from what I've seen, the only one who seems to need constant rescuing around here . . ."—her smile returned, toying at the corner of her mouth until Cait could hardly contain it—". . . is you."

To her perverse enjoyment, a variety of emotions choked him into speechlessness—fury, shame, humiliation; the colors flashing across his face revealed them in striking clarity. Visitors were few and far between, here in the canyon, and Cait found herself getting quite a tickle out of making him suffer.

But fully aware that she could lose the upper hand as fast as she'd gained it, she forced any trace of humor she felt in taunting him out of her system and said, "Now, consider this your final warning, hunter—" She swung the shotgun up and aimed it at his midsection. "Get off my mountain or I'll plug you with so many bullets you couldn't hold paste." She jerked her head toward the tiger. "That is, if there's anything left when Sawtooth gets through with you."

She almost expected Sawyer to argue with her, but to his credit, he must have decided that it would be in his best interest just to do as she'd said, for after casting a wary glance at Sawtooth, then at her, he muttered a curse and limped across the clearing.

She waited until he'd climbed out of the canyon and disappeared over the rim before lowering the shotgun. "Well, we chased him off this time," she told Sawtooth, "but something tells me that this isn't the last we've seen of Ethan Sawyer."

Strangely, that intuitive suspicion didn't worry her as much as it probably should have, considering that he now knew about the hidden canyon. Cait supposed it was because the man had a knack for annoying her more than alarming her. Anybody who tripped into nets and tangled with tigers couldn't be the brightest taper in the candlebra.

That didn't make him any less fascinating, though. In fact, it made him even more so. She suspected that there was more to Ethan Sawyer of Roland than he let on.

Feeling the pull of Sawtooth's stare, she darted a glance down at the tiger only to find him wearing an accusing expression. Cait's grin wilted to a frown. "What?"

He emitted a half-whine, half-gowl and cocked his head.

"You're judging me? Hell, *you* licked him! How could you do that? You might as well have invited him to stay for supper!"

Sawtooth turned his attention back to the forest that had swallowed the hunter's broad-shouldered form. Cait followed suit, her brows narrowing into a troubled V. "Yeah, he seems different to me, too." And that's what bothered her. From the very beginning she'd sensed that he wasn't like the other hunters. It was more the way he carried himself than anything he'd actually said or done.

And he was awful handsome.

Even in those wet and filthy clothes, his hair rumpled and his face scratched, she couldn't forget that he cleaned up rather nicely.

Nor could she forget that he'd tried to "save her skin"—even at the risk of losing his own. Never mind that he'd botched the job. She couldn't remember the last time someone had cared enough about her well-being to make such a sacrifice.

Why? she wondered with a puzzled frown. Why would he do such a crazy, reckless thing?

Was he a glutton for punishment? Did he get some boost to his vanity playing the hero? Or could it be something more elemental? Like maybe he'd felt as strong an attraction to her as she'd felt to him?

Oh, this was ridiculous! Cait thought, spinning on her heel and marching back toward the cabin. Why was she making excuses for a man she had about as much use for as a festering boil? Had she lost all her senses?

Even if he hadn't admitted to being one of the hunters, she knew better than to let down her guard when it came to strangers. No matter how harmless Ethan Sawyer seemed, or that he was a handsome son of a gun, or that he intrigued her like no other—she'd learned long ago not to trust someone on physical appearance alone. Some of the most innocent-looking people were the ones who posed the greatest threats.

For all she knew, he could have been following her, and searching for a horse had been a handy explanation when he'd been caught. Or maybe he'd already discovered the canyon and had been spying on her, waiting for the moment when she was alone, when he could catch her unawares. . . .

Cait came to a sudden halt, swung around and searched the ridge. Why, knowing all the logical reasons it was best to have him gone, did she find herself fighting the illogical temptation to call him back?

By the time Ethan climbed out of the canyon, his lungs were pumping like bellows, his thigh hurt like he'd been slashed with a hot poker, and his temper had spiked to nearly uncontrollable heights. For the second time in two days, he struggled with the urge to hit something.

Instead, he scuffled to a low boulder and sat. The pain in his leg prompted him to peel back a torn angle of his trousers, and Ethan hissed as the material ripped away from the skin, revealing a two-inch gash scraped across the muscle. It probably needed a couple of stitches, but he had neither the materials nor the experience to do the job.

And for damn sure he wasn't about to go groveling to that vixen down the hill for help.

A fresh wave of hot humiliation swept

through him as their encounter replayed itself in his mind, and he wondered how in the hell that woman always managed to twist his good intentions into some pathetic gesture gone awry. All he'd done was try and save her life; he'd narrowly escaped with his own.

Would he never learn?

It wouldn't surprise him if she thought him the most bumbling, incompetent fool on the face of the earth. And who could blame her? She'd found him stuck in a damned tree, then trapped under an oversized hairball.

Ethan shook his head and felt his rage slip several degrees. Gawd A'mighty, that had been one amazing animal. All fang and fur and claws sharp enough to split wood. He had no doubt if Cait hadn't shown up when she had, her furry friend would have made jerky strips out of him.

He knew more than a few folks who wouldn't shed tears over that. He could see the epitaph on his tombstone now:

HERE LIES ETHAN SAWYER—
TURN-TAIL, TRAITOR, AND TIGER BAIT
ROT IN HELL

Ha! Some hero.

Two weeks. He'd been up here for two weeks and had suffered more misfortune in that time than in all his twenty-nine years put together. And for what? To be snared, beaten, tossed down a cliff, almost eaten by a fur-ball. . . .

In one split second, Ethan's mind spun back

to a remark Louis had made the day they'd left Roland. *Bet it's one of them cats that belongs to the savage in the hills. . . .*

His heart thudded with the possibility. He twisted at the waist and peered down into the canyon. Why hadn't he thought of it before? After all, a cougar couldn't bring down a full-grown steer. Could it?

What if neither Billy nor Louis nor any of the other men in the Mission Range couldn't find the cougar because it wasn't a *cougar* attacking Hullet's herd? What if they'd all been chasing after the wrong predator? What if the true killer was an oversized, snaggle-toothed bag of stripes and bones?

It would sure explain why Cait was damned and determined to chase him off the mountain. . . .

As fast as they'd soared, Ethan's spirits plunged, and his shoulders slumped. No, though it was certainly possible that Cait's tiger was their target, it wasn't probable. Ethan had gotten a chillingly close-up gander at that animal's paws. Even a man of his limited experience would have recognized that the tracks on Hullet's land were half the size and depth. As unlikely as it was for a cougar to have killed that steer, the tracks clearly belonged to one.

Ethan drew his hand down his face, then pushed himself off the rock. Yeah, he wanted to catch the cat killing Hullet's cattle. But he wasn't about to hold the first one he saw responsible just to claim the glory of the hunt. Especially when the odds were against it having been the one to commit the crime. That

was the easy way out, the coward's way. He'd
been the cause of an innocent's needless suffering once; he couldn't bear the burden a second time.

But then, neither had he come all the way up
here to let himself be threatened off the hunt.
Finding that cougar meant as much to him as
it did to Cait or any of the men after it—if not
more. Because he had so much more at stake
than livestock, and so much more to gain than
a bulging pocketbook. He had Josie's future.

Cait couldn't say what made her decide to
follow Ethan. She wanted to believe it was a
simple matter of keeping tabs on a potential
threat. Except that didn't explain why she
hadn't felt the same compulsion to spy on the
other two men.

After securing Sawtooth back at the cabin
with orders to watch over Ginger and Faw
Paw, and a promise to take him for that swim
when she returned, Cait climbed out of the canyon shortly after Ethan had disappeared over
the ridge.

She quickly spotted a set of bootprints and
recognized Sawyer's mark instantly. The prints
belonged to a man of substantial height, at least
six feet tall, weighing close to two hundred
pounds, and wearing wooden soles. Store-
bought soles, at that. That he made no effort to
hide them made her shake her head in dismay.
The greenhorn left a trail so simple a child
could find it. But then, she doubted he expected anyone to be on his tail. Another critical
mistake. Ten years ago, he wouldn't have sur-

vived two days in this area. He'd have been tracked down and slain before he knew what hit him.

The prints led around the base of a rocky slope, crossed a narrow hazel-colored meadow spattered with snow mounds, then entered the thick forest once again.

A flash of moving white amid the needled greenery drew Cait deeper into the forest. Branches snapped in the distance like brittle bones, birds fluttered away, squawking at the intrusion, and once more, Cait shook her head at Sawyer's disregard. Following in his noisy wake, she maintained a safe distance, her feet falling soundlessly on the thick evergreen floor.

The sun rode high in the sky. Other than stopping a few times to quench his thirst at tiny springs or ribbony brooks, Sawyer didn't falter. But neither did he seem to know where he was going. Instead, he hit dead ends, narrowly missed plunging down into ravines, and got himself tangled in thickets so many times that Cait began to wonder if he was lost.

She could have told him that they were only a few miles north of the valley, and not far from the spot by the creek where she'd first seen him, but knew it was much wiser if Sawyer stayed unaware of her presence.

Soon she couldn't hear his footsteps anymore, for the mild roar of the little falls blocked out all sound.

Taking cover behind a clump of tall grasses bordering the creek, Cait dropped to her knees and parted the reeds, and caught Sawyer looking at the twelve-foot tumble of water off a ledge.

His expression, one of pure wonder and utter gratitude, had a strange effect on her. She felt her heart soften, and her emotions seemed suddenly ... fragile. Seeing the falls through his eyes reminded her of the first time she had happened upon this place. How enchanted she'd been by the steady pounding of water against water, the smell of lush foliage and clean earth, the sound of freedom whispering in the wind.

And she remembered with heart-wrenching clarity how the first taste of nature's sweet ale had revived her spirits and given her hope that maybe, just maybe, she'd fulfill the promises she'd made to herself.

She'd forgotten that first time. But now, as she watched the hunter gaze at the waterfall with the same yearning she'd once felt and the experience rushed back on a current of memories, she couldn't help but wonder if he'd ever felt trapped and alone and desperately afraid he would fail.

Cait ducked on reflex as he suddenly turned his head from side to side as if searching for company. Apparently not having noticed her, he turned back to the waterfall, and then. . . .

Oh, God have mercy, he began to strip.

Chapter 6

One by one, articles of clothing dropped to the earth. Coat, boots, socks, shirt. . . . Trousers.

Cait's breath caught.

In utter stupefaction, she gawked at the nude form standing on the bank. From head to heel the man was a fluid blend of golden skin and solid muscle. Wide shoulders tapered to a straight waist. Narrow hips extended to corded thighs dusted with tawny gold hair. And oh, heaven help her . . . he had the nicest seat. Taut, firm, perfectly proportioned with the rest of his long, lean body.

She swallowed the lump lodged in her throat, her heart skipped several beats. Without a doubt he was the most magnificently built man she'd ever seen. Not that she'd seen a lot of naked backsides to compare, of course, but . . . she couldn't imagine anyone as fit. As powerful. As utterly beautiful as the one filling her vision right now.

He stepped onto a ledge of rocks where the

water showered down into a shallow end of the creek. His movements were sleek and graceful and oh, so incredibly masculine.

The instant the falls deluged him, he arched his neck backward and let the water pound down upon his face. His eyes were shut, his mouth open. Broad hands scraped his hair back from his temples and ears.

She couldn't help but wonder if the pressure of the falls hurt the scrapes and bruises on his face, but his expression was one of such bliss that she doubted anything could cause him pain at this moment.

If only she could remain as numb. Aches developed in places she'd not thought possible. Her throat, her chest, low in her belly. Pinpricks of awareness spread along her arms and back. For heaven's sake, even her toes were curling!

And when he reached up to wash his shoulder, the muscles of his arms whipcord tight, she thought for sure she was going to faint. Her gaze followed the water trickling down the indentation of his spine, over the firm curve of his rear, along the length of his legs, and God, she envied its journey.

Heat sparked low in her belly and uncoiled outward, spread downward, consuming her with a stream of sensations the likes of which she'd never felt before.

For a fleeting moment she felt herself thrown back in time to a stark stone classroom filled with somber dark-haired, dark-eyed students. An equally somber man in unrelenting black save for the white collar around his throat paced the front of the windowless room, hands behind his back, head bowed, his monotone voice lulling the children to sleep.

It had been ages since Cait had allowed herself thoughts of Father Joseph. But watching the golden hunter indulge in nature's shower, she began to understand the priest's ardent lectures on carnal temptation and sins of the flesh. How giving in to either would condemn one's soul to purgatory.

She even began to understand why some people might not care, because right now, Cait couldn't bring herself to leave this spot if the flames of hell itself were licking at her heels.

Maybe it was reckless rebellion to experience the forbidden, or maybe it was simply a woman's curious wonder that kept her staked to the spot. She didn't know. Nor did she care. She only knew that she'd never felt such a powerful need to touch—and be touched by—someone in her life. To explore his every plane and knoll, to have him explore hers.

Cait's breathing became more labored, and swallowing heavily, she placed her hands on her breasts, awed and vaguely disturbed by their response to him: the stiff peaks, the swollen eagerness. Her nipples felt unusually sensitive, chafing against the fabric of her tunic, aching for relief that she sensed only he could give her.

Had he ever touched a woman? Surely he had. Surely his hands knew how to ease the longings she felt. Inside. Outside.

Intense and burning.

She rose slowly, drawn to him in a way she couldn't explain. Her weakened knees barely supported her. Her hands felt sweaty and clammy at the same time.

But the moment he started to turn on the ledge, a spear of alarm cut through Cait's dazed mind. Without pausing to examine her sudden attack of cowardice, she turned and bolted away from the waterfall before she got a full-front view.

Swift, heart-pounding strides carried her around the base of the mountain and through the forest, to the canyon's narrow entrance, then across the meadow to the cabin.

Sawtooth was pacing the front porch. Cait spared him a brief pat on her way to the rain barrel. Closing her eyes, she cupped her hands into the water and splashed her face. When that didn't cool her fevered cheeks, she plunged her head into the barrel.

Cait stayed under until her lungs burned, then whipped her head back, her braid spraying water every which way. Gasping, she braced her hands on either side of the barrel rim.

At length, her breathing regulated, her heartbeat steadied, the flush left her skin.

What had come over her?

Of all the men in the world, how could she have reacted so strongly to that one?

Worse, how could she have run from him? Never in her life had she run from anyone, and it shamed her to her soul that the sight of a bare Ethan Sawyer had sent her dashing through the woods like a spooked doe.

Her eyelids drifted open and she stared into the depths of the rain barrel. From the water's dark surface, a rounded face pinched with confusion and anxiety stared back at her through eyes of stormy blue.

Cait sighed heavily at her reflection. All right, so it hadn't been so much the sight of Ethan Sawyer that had sent her running as the alarming feelings he'd awakened inside her. Pine Bend brimmed with men of all walks of life; handsome, strapping men of all races, creeds, and color, and not a single one of them had made her pulses leap or her skin tingle.

How could one heartless hunter affect her when none of them ever had?

It just didn't make any sense! She flung herself back against the cabin wall and pushed her hand across the top of her head. He'd declared himself her enemy, said loud and clear that he was hunting a mountain lion that some believed she owned. He had even discovered her canyon, the only place she'd ever considered a sanctuary. Was he aware that few were privy to that secret? If so, would he use it to his advantage?

Damn, the combination of all she'd learned of Ethan Sawyer made him little more than an animal himself. Cunning. Unpredictable.

Dangerous.

She had to get him off her mountain. And if he wouldn't heed her warnings—Cait's mouth pursed in determination—she'd just have to persuade him another way.

Ethan emerged from the falls feeling more refreshed than he had since he'd begun this cursed quest. It seemed that Lady Fate had finally decided to smile on him; he'd have been downright stupid not to take advantage of her generosity. Though the water had been this side of frigid, it had soothed both his aching muscles and his wounded pride, and managed to revive his strength so he could continue searching for that blasted runaway horse.

But to Ethan's further surprise, when he reached the bank of the creek, he found Trouble pawing a mound of snow, digging for whatever grass might be growing beneath. Ethan's relief at seeing the roan outweighed his aggravation.

After throwing on his clothes, he approached Trouble. "Either you've got the nose of a bloodhound, or Fate is being especially kind to me," he told the animal. He wasn't about to question Trouble's appearance, not when hours of tramping through the wilderness for the blasted beast had been saved. He'd learned the hard way that when he went looking for Trouble, he usually found it.

Taking a quick inventory of his supplies to make sure everything was still there, Ethan felt his fingers graze a familiar object in his saddle pocket. His tool case. He pulled the hard leather pouch out from beneath the flap and examined his initials stamped into the front. Inside, a host of sewn loops held various tools of his trade: a miniature mallet, assorted metal stamp heads of different decoration, two files, a stippling, and a tap beveler.

The kit had been a present from Josie, to carry with him on every journey so he could keep his hands busy and his craft honed.

He hoped she was faring well. With him and Billy both gone, she'd been all but left to fend for herself. He wouldn't worry so much if she wasn't so far along in her pregnancy, but few if any of the townspeople gave two hoots about her well-being, and he feared that if the baby decided to come early, no one would be there for her.

Ethan crammed the case back into the saddlebag with a muttered curse and swung himself into the saddle.

He needed to find that cat and get home.

It was around here somewhere, he thought, scanning the border of trees. Sometimes, he got the sense of being watched. Of being ... stalked, even. But he couldn't say for certain whether the cougar was spying on him from some hidden perch, or if it was just a result of being alone in the wilderness.

Well, not alone exactly, he thought with a wry grimace.

He was out here with a living legend.

And hell, she hated him, too.

It didn't matter, Ethan told himself as he navigated Trouble through the forest. Soon this would all be over with, and she would be nothing more than a story to tell his grandkids—if he ever had any.

The morning wore on, and as the sun rose to high noon, the chill lifted, making the day rather pleasant. Trouble's hooves punched a lulling beat into the earth. Ethan easily saw why Cait was so protective of this mountain. There was a tranquility about it, untouched by human industry, and such a purity that he could taste the cleanliness of the air.

Beginning to recognize landmarks where he'd laid one of his traps, Ethan hobbled Trouble a safe distance away, unsheathed his rifle and covered the remaining yards on foot.

The sight of an object sticking out at an angle from the trap had him reining in his pace.

"Why, that sneaking little she-cat," Ethan whispered, lowering the Spencer. As he wandered toward the black and orange striped pole jammed between the jaws, he wasn't sure if he wanted to throttle her or laugh.

He examined a single feather lashed to the hilt of the lance. It had Cait's name all over it.

In spite of himself, Ethan had to admire her gall. That woman didn't back down from anything. In fact—he twanged the lance—she had a hell of a way of getting her point across.

He scanned the area, half expecting to see her pop out from behind one of the trees.

She didn't. But then, she didn't need to. Her message was clear. She meant to get rid of him, even if it meant sabotaging his hunt.

Well, two could play at that game, Ethan decided. He was fed up to the hilt with every effort being thwarted. Cait could threaten him, she could insult him, she could destroy his gear—no matter what she did, he'd eat leather before he let the bloodthirsty mountaineer drive him away.

Yep, if the wildcat wanted to tangle, then she'd met her match. Strangely, the thought of pitting his wits against hers had his adrenaline pumping harder than it had in a long, long time.

*   *   *

Over the next few days, Ethan discovered a certain pattern to the way Cait set her snares. Since he had only two traps, he was pretty much forced to lay them at random and move them around often to create an element of surprise, whereas Cait's snares remained in the same spots. He'd counted four so far. Only God knew how many he hadn't yet found, but he figured if he scouted around watering holes and cave-riddled bluffs long enough, he'd come upon a few more.

Since neither of them had caught the cat yet, he couldn't say whose way was more effective. But her way was definitely more predictable—probably the only thing about her that was predictable—and it played to his advantage.

He tossed away the branch he'd used to erase his tracks and smiled. Satisfied with the day's work, Ethan brushed his hands together, mounted Trouble, and headed back to his camp by the waterfall for a well-deserved rest.

"It was here," Louis remarked.

Billy glared at his partner. "I know it was here, damn it, I saw the signs as well as you."

Rising from a squat, Billy's foul curse sent a squirrel dashing up the trunk of a tree. He didn't give a damn. In fact, as mad as he was right now, the fluffy-tailed rodent had been smart to get out of his way.

He couldn't believe he'd spent the last two hours following tracks through every draw and wallow in a two-mile radius only to have them vanish as soon as they'd crossed the creek.

This wasn't the first time, either, come to think of it. The other day he thought he'd seen part of a print down by Golddigger Pass, but it hadn't been clear enough for him to be sure of which animal had made it.

The tracks he and Louis had found today, though, had definitely belonged to a catamount—until they'd up and disappeared, that is.

Billy circled the area, searching the ground for some clue they might have missed during the first search, while Louis strode back and forth along the banks.

He noticed something odd about a bush to his right. Studying it, Billy strode toward it and yanked out a branch that had been jabbed into the others in an attempt to make it look natural. It probably would have, too, except that a film of damp dirt clung to the leaves of this branch, while the rest of its brothers were simply dusty. "That gawddamn sneaky bastard," he snarled. "I should have gutted him when I had the chance."

"Did you find somethin'?"

Billy wielded the branch toward Louis. "This is where the tracks went!"

"Well, I'll be damned," Louis said, coming up beside him. "Looks like someone don't want us catching the cat."

"And I know of only one person underhanded enough to go around erasing the tracks."

"You think Sawyer did this?"

"Who else? He's the only one we've seen up

here, and I wouldn't put it past him to try and swindle us out of that bounty."

"Well, it could have been W—"

Cutting Louis off, Billy whipped the branch to the ground and cried, "If you mention that woman's name, I'll bust you one. I'm sick to death of you going on about Wild Cat Cait."

"But they say she's got a way with the weather. What if she sent the wind down to blow away the tracks? It has been gusty lately."

"They also say she's magic, and we both know there's no such thing as magic."

Louis's shoulders came back, and when he pushed out his chest, he looked like an underfed bulldog. "Maybe she is. Maybe she's cast a spell on the mountain and that's why we can't find the cougar."

"It was Sawyer, I'm telling you!" Billy glared at the faint brush strokes in the dirt. "He's gonna pay for this."

"Jeez, Bill . . . you ain't thinkin' on killing him or anything, are you?"

The thought had crossed his mind more than once in the last few years, but had never been more tempting than now. Billy had to remind himself that death was too good for the likes of his squaw-lovin' brother-in-law, that there were more lasting ways to make him regret the day he'd betrayed them.

"Do you ever wonder where it went wrong, Billy-boy?" Louis asked, as he pulled a cigar from the box he kept in his coat pocket.

Billy's shoulders tensed, and his hand gripped ole Chester so tightly he practically dented the stock. There was no use pretending that he didn't know what Louis was talking about. "Not as much as you, it appears."

"Can't help thinking about the old days," he said, scraping a Lucifer against his sole and lighting the fag. "Things were fun then." He gave a short chuckle. "Remember that time you and me and Ethan shaved Mrs. Livingston's goat then let it loose in her house?"

Billy's throat went tight. "Yeah, I remember," he said, his voice deep and scratchy. "Took her two days to realize it weren't Mr. Livingston eating the *Roland News*."

It had been one of the many pranks they'd pulled as boys. Lots of times they'd dragged Josie along, because she was daring and because she was willing and because she was often more devious than they.

As the film of memories cleared from Billy's vision, and he once again saw the brush strokes on the ground, he wished he could look upon the erased tracks as one of Ethan's antics. Except he knew there was nothing funny intended, and too much muddy water had passed under the bridge, and Billy just couldn't forget, or forgive, Sawyer for turning on him. And if it was the last thing he did, he'd see the turncoat pay.

The bait was gone.

Her brow pleating, Cait glanced up into the lofty branches of the spruce tree, then scanned the area. The prints that had originally persuaded her to set the snare beside the shallow brook were still visible in the dirt, along with a few fresh marks. She couldn't say for certain whether they belonged to Halona or not, but given a cougar's solitary nature, the odds were in her favor.

How had she gotten the meat without springing the snare, though? And how had she escaped the laudanum's lulling effects?

Cait unfolded herself from a crouch and wandered cautiously in an ever-widening circle about the area, searching for a distinctive tan lump that would tell her the drug had worked its power.

A buzz of flies called her to a clump of blade-like jonquil leaves. She knelt to inspect the patch of earth. No claw marks to indicate burial of droppings. In fact, the dirt looked suspiciously packed, as if by something hard and flat—

Like a boot heel.

"Why that dirty, no-good . . . bait stealer!" Her mouth pursed in annoyance. Even a simpleton would have noticed that the print belonged to Ethan Sawyer. The depth and width matched those of a man of his size and weight. Not to mention the fact that any seasoned woodsman would know better than to leave behind such visible evidence.

But what was she going to do now? She'd used almost all the laundanum. Though the nets and bait would still work well enough to catch the cat, she knew better than to approach an untamed mountain lion not under sedation. She rubbed the underside of her forearm where a reminder of Faw Paw's attack remained.

Damn Sawyer's stubborn hide! Why couldn't

he just go back to where he had come from? Why did he feel it so blasted necessary to disrupt her peaceful life?

A sudden prickling at Cait's nape had her stilling. The scent of worn leather and warm male drifted on the breeze behind her.

She turned to find the object of her thoughts leaning against the peeling trunk of a pine tree, his arms folded against his chest, one ankle crossed over the other. His steady, mocking gaze and the ghost of a grin struck a raw nerve.

Cait rose slowly and brought her shoulders back in silent challenge. After her folly at the waterfall, she'd told herself that if she ever saw him again, she'd remain cool. Calm. Detached. She was good at that. Twelve years of living under strict direction in the mission school had taught her well.

And yet, as he stood so casually beneath the thrusting branches of a pine, shadows flirting with the rugged planes and angles of a face and form she couldn't seem to forget, the last thing she felt was cool or calm or detached.

Especially when his gaze traveled down, then back up, the length of her with excruciating slowness. His eyes darkened and became hooded. As if he were planning to devour her whole.

A fever rose in her blood and flowed through her veins. Her pulses sped up to a frenzied pace. A sizzling current connected her to him so she couldn't tear her eyes away, no matter how badly she wanted to.

Cait folded her fingers into her palm and

pinched her lips together. Damn her body for betraying her like this!

And damn him for making it happen.

"You know," he said with a hint of scorn, "for someone who claims to know so much about survival, you take some really stupid chances."

She angled her head and lifted one brow. "Is that so?"

He uncrossed his arms, let his hands fall limp, yet ready, at his sides. The reckless gleam in his eyes sent a sliver of alarm down Cait's spine.

"This is the third time I've found you wandering around this mountain alone."

Defiantly she raised her chin. "It's my mountain. I'll go wherever I damn well please."

"Not without protection, you don't."

"Don't ever assume that I don't have protection."

"Oh?" Brows raising, his gaze circled the forest around them. "Then where is that man-eating menace of yours when you need him?"

"Looking for a man to eat—seen any?"

His eyes darkened with irritation. "You can't smart-talk your way out if this one, wildcat." The timbre of his voice dropped to a growl. "Don't you realize how vulnerable you are out here alone? This mountain is crawling with men who'd sell their souls to get their hands on you and wouldn't think twice about using whatever means necessary. It wouldn't matter to them that you're a—" He broke off in mid-sentence.

Her breaths coming fast and heavy through

her nostrils, Cait narrowed her eyes at him. "It wouldn't matter that I'm a what?"

A mask seemed to drop over his face. "A legend," he said calmly.

Her lips pinched together. She doubted that had been what he'd nearly said, for he'd looked appalled. But she didn't demand the truth, wasn't sure she even wanted it.

"Damn it, Cait, I know you're aware of the stories about you. You've become something of a mystery to people. Most folks seem satisfied just talking about you, but there are others who'd do whatever it took to *have* you."

"Should I be flattered?"

"You should be careful!"

Cait reared back, stricken by the intensity of his voice.

"What if it hadn't been me who came upon you?"

She recovered her lapse of control and grabbed onto a weapon that had served her well in the past—sarcasm. "But I knew it was you. I could smell you a mile off." She didn't dare tell him that the musky odor reminded her of the forest at sunset, warm and smooth and compelling.

After a moment his features relaxed. Suspicion and wariness had Cait's eyes narrowing. He stepped forward with a lazy grace that drew her eyes to his torso. She swallowed and wished that she wasn't so aware of the body beneath the loose linen shirt and buff-colored trousers. The way it had rippled with strength, gleamed in the sunlight, glistened under the water. . . .

"Are you so sure I'm such a safe bet, Cait?"

The underlying edge of his tone, the savage glint in his eyes, had her pulses quickening and her breasts tightening even as prickles of apprehension raced down her arms and spine.

"What makes you think I'm no less a danger than any other hunter prowling this mountain?"

He drew closer, a slim three paces away. Cait fisted her hands and gritted her teeth, resisting the urge to take a step backward. Instead, with a flick of her head, she sent her braid soaring over her shoulder and taunted, "My, my, aren't we full of ourselves today." She framed her jaw with her thumb and index finger. "Let's see, what kind of animal do you compare yourself with? The buzzard? The weasel? No, wait—" She jabbed her index finger in the air. "The raccoon! Irritating little thieves that scurry around in the dark, stealing whatever strikes their fancy."

One step away, he looked down at her and quirked a brow. "Leave my traps alone, I'll leave your bait alone."

"I've got a better idea—" Cait snapped back, hating the sudden quickening of her pulses, knowing he was the cause. "Why don't you just leave, period."

"I told you, I'm not leaving without the cougar." His eyes remained steady on her; his voice dropped to an intimate level that had her senses spinning. "I'm a patient man when I need to be, Cait. No matter what you do to interfere with this hunt, I will win this little contest you seem determined to play. You can bet on that."

Disturbed by the way he so easily threw her off balance, Cait's lip curled in disdain, partly at his arrogance, but more at her own weakness where he was concerned. She swept him with a scathing look. "You just don't get it, do you, Sawyer? You don't find a wildcat, a wildcat finds you."

"Not if I find it first."

Then he winked at her.

As he whistled off into the forest, a growl of outrage burst from Cait's throat. Of all the stubborn, pigheaded attitudes!

Who'd he think he was? Acting so damn smug. Insulting her skills. Her capabilities. And *then*, to make the arrogant assumption that he could best something as swift, as cunning, as a wildcat in its own territory? Ha! A greenhorn like him probably didn't know the difference between a mountain puma and a barnyard tabbyc—

Cait's mental tirade came to a screeching halt. Ethan Sawyer thought he could outwit a wildcat, did he? A grin of pure wickedness spread over her face. The time had come to teach the overbearing ass a lesson he wouldn't soon forget.

Chapter 7

"So you think you can find a wildcat before it finds you, huh? Who's being stupid now?"

Ethan's eyes snapped open; his system was jarred awake by a keen edge of alarm down his spine, a sharp taste of danger in his mouth—

A cold blade of steel at his throat.

Lying on his side with his assailant behind him, he fixed his gaze on a dappled patch of dawn and forced himself to stay calm, not make any sudden moves.

By degrees he became aware of light, even breaths shifting the hair by his ear, the brush of a velvety sleeve against his chin, the scent of wildflowers and wilderness in his nostrils.

His forehead creased. Only one person he knew of carried such a distinctive natural fragrance. "Cait?"

"That's right, mighty hunter," she whispered against his ear. "You're quicker than I gave you credit for being."

"Gawd A'mighty, what are—"

The blade pressed tighter against his windpipe and shut him up.

Relief that he'd been surprised by Cait and not Billy or Louis or any one of his numerous enemies quickly disappeared. Cait was as dangerous as any of them, if not more so. She had a way of catching him in the most vulnerable of positions . . . assaulting not only his pride, but his senses as well.

Even now, with injury a mere wrist-flick away, Ethan couldn't control the sudden flare of desire.

"You see how easy it was for me to sneak up on you?" she practically purred. "To catch you unawares? That's what a wildcat does, Sawyer. It stalks you, studies you, and when you least expect it—*wham!* It goes for the jugular." He felt her smile. "Its quarry doesn't have a chance."

The truth of her softly spoken words hit him like a mallet to metal. Trepidation rang through his vitals. Cold sweat popped out on his brow. His throat went dry as rawhide.

His only saving thought was that if she wanted him dead, he'd already be dead—several times over. She'd had plenty of chances, that was for certain. But for some reason, she seemed to enjoy taunting him. Toying with him.

Like a cat with a mouse it planned to have for supper.

Well, he had news for this devious little claw-in-his-side, Ethan thought with a stubborn set of his jaw. He was nobody's willing meal.

He relaxed his tense muscles; as he'd hoped, the pressure of the blade against his throat lessened.

It was all the advantage he needed.

Grabbing her wrist in one hand to keep her from slicing his throat, Ethan brought his free arm up in a swift arc, hooked it around her neck, and flipped her over faster than she could gasp. One quick roll and he had her pinned beneath him, her wrists trapped to the ground above her head by his grip.

She blinked in surprise.

He grinned in triumph. "*Now* who's caught who unawares?"

Her eyes flashed like bolts of blue lightning. She gritted her teeth and began to struggle. "Get off me."

"So you can decapitate me? I don't think so."

"Damn you, Sawyer, get off me right now, or—"

"Or *what*, Cait?" he taunted, giving her a taste of what she'd been giving him. "It doesn't seem like you're in much of a position to be making threats."

She kneed him between the thighs.

His agonized cry ricocheted through the mountains as he rolled off her and doubled over on the ground, holding himself. White-hot pain shot clear through his groin to his stomach. His eyes watered. Blinking furiously, grinding his teeth, he waited for the pain to subside.

When it finally dulled to tolerable, he opened his eyes and immediately noticed that the spot where Cait had been was now empty.

Ethan rolled onto his side, his gaze frantically searching for her.

A flash of brown streaking through the forest captured his notice.

"You vicious little wildcat," Ethan hissed. Clenching his teeth, he staggered to his feet and stumbled toward Trouble, hobbled a short distance away behind a clump of young pine.

A swift flick of the button loosed the cowhide cuffs around the roan's front shanks. Ethan clambered onto Trouble's bare back and heeled him in the flanks. Trouble jumped, and as he gave chase, Ethan had no other thought than to catch the vicious little hellion.

Her figure came into view and grew more distinct as the distance between them closed.

The sound of galloping hooves brought her attention swinging over her shoulder. Ethan noted the widening of her eyes with a surge of triumph.

Her legs pumped harder. He urged Trouble faster, wanting to head her off before she reached the fissure in the rock ahead.

Though she moved through the forest with the fleet-footedness of a deer, even she was no match for Trouble's speed. Distance between hunter and hunted quickly closed.

Pulling up beside her, Ethan dived off Trouble's back. At the last moment he twisted in midair just as his arm hooked around Cait's waist, and they both landed on the ground with a thud, Ethan taking the brunt of the fall.

The wind knocked out of them, both lay on a bed of moss and fern and sweet grass, gasping for breath, Ethan's arm slung around her hip, her back from heel to shoulder pressed against his front.

Feeling Cait begin to stir, Ethan brought one leg around, trapping her legs, and slid over her, pinning her beneath his weight, before she could escape again.

A vicious threat rushed into his mind as he once again clamped his hands around her wrists.

But the instant his gaze clashed with Cait's, the words lodged in his throat. She lay tense and silent, staring up at him with incredibly blue eyes, until Ethan couldn't remember his own name, much less what he'd been about to say or what he meant to do to her when he caught her.

There wasn't an inch of her that he didn't become aware of. The frailness of her bones under his hands. The firm muscle of her legs under his. The smooth line of her ribs, no corset, under his midsection.

To make matters worse, each heaving breath she took pushed her breasts against his chest in a teasing rhythm that sent his blood rushing through his veins and his heart bucking against his rib cage. And shockingly enough, the blow she'd delivered to his groin didn't stop him from hardening against her belly.

Ethan tried his damnedest to master his body's reaction to her but realized he'd have more luck weaving a rope of sand than stopping the desire coursing through him. This woman had the ability to drive a man well past his endurance.

And yet somehow Ethan recognized that the

sensations building inside him went beyond
carnal desire, beyond physical attraction.

As he stared at her, mystifying threads
swirled through him, spun around them, connecting him to her in a baffling way that sent
ripples of shock to his very core.

He let go of her wrist and brought a shaking
hand to her face. He couldn't believe how
clumsy and inept he felt. But she looked so
damn pretty, her hair fanning out beneath her,
those big blue eyes staring boldly up at him.

And she smelled so damn good, of crushed
sweet grass and forgotten dreams. In the scent
of her he could almost recapture a sense of belonging.

With one fingertip he traced the contour of
her jawline from temple to chin. Her skin, with
its faint mahogany tones, felt softer than the
finest chamois. Ethan closed his eyes briefly
and marveled at the texture. How long had it
been since he'd touched a woman who didn't
shrink back in disgust? Didn't cringe in fear of
being poisoned?

When he opened his eyes, he discovered that
the wary defiance in her azure eyes had
changed to astonishment. Her slender brows
pulled together, her ripe lips parted as if she
felt the same confusion he did. "Ethan?" she
whispered, his name sounding like a song
coming from her.

He shook his head. He didn't have the answers any more than she did. But drawn by
her innocence, lured by her passion, his mouth
inched forward, hesitating again and again, until they were breath to breath.

Heartbeat to heartbeat.

Her sooty lashes fell; she swallowed thickly.

Unable to hold himself back any longer, Ethan brushed his lips across hers and nearly cried out at the sheer pleasure such simple contact brought him. It skidded down his arms and spine, made him feel weak and powerful at the same time.

Wanting more, needing more, he kissed her again, sealing his mouth to hers. Cait's arms crept around him. She angled her face to better receive his kiss, and this time he couldn't contain a blissful moan. Lips had never tasted as sweet. As warm. As welcoming.

His hold tightened around her. He wanted to crush her to him, pull her inside his skin, keep her softness with him—anything to keep alive this feeling he'd once taken for granted, had once thought would be his for the taking when he married Amanda. But even Amanda hadn't filled him with such a sense of wonder.

He teased the seam of Cait's mouth with his tongue, and when she opened for him, he slid inside. Ethan took his time, lazily exploring the moist honey within, coaxing her tongue around his, drawing her lips into his mouth.

Kissing her was so incredibly sweet, and yet the more confident she became, the bolder she got, and the more greedy he became. He stroked one hand down the column of her neck, over the swell of her breast, until he cupped the heavy weight in his palm. Cait whimpered into his mouth, pushed herself closer against him, seeking, seducing, making him want every dream he'd had of her to come true right here, right now, in the sweet grass and sunlight.

His leg slid up her thigh, causing an intimate scrape of canvas on buckskin that made him groan in blissful agony. Cait's fingers raked down his shoulders, then up again. Through his hair, then back to his shoulders. He felt her hunger climb with his. His arousal grew harder and more urgent against the soft flesh of her belly. And when she arched against him, he thought for sure he would explode.

Reaching the brink of his endurance, Ethan broke the connection of their lips before he lost control and suffered the ultimate embarrassment.

His forehead falling against hers, he lay there for long, taut moments; their hearts hammered in unison, their heavy breaths mingled, their bodies fit together as if they'd been tailor made for the other.

"Gawd A'mighty," Ethan panted. Never. Never had a woman brought him to such a fevered height. Even now, he smoldered like a bed of banked coals, and he fear that if Cait so much as shifted beneath him, he'd go up in flames again.

How could he be so affected by a woman who, not long ago, had tried to kill him? Why did this particular one twist his senses until he couldn't think straight? Just who was Cait that she could hold this incredible power over him?

Thoroughly baffled, he raised up and studied her, the drowsy, passion-glazed eyes, kiss-swollen lips, flushed skin. He brushed aside a wisp of silky hair. "Who are you really?"

A slow, sultry smile pulled at the corners of her mouth. "Haven't you heard?" she asked in a throaty whisper. "I'm the Heathen of the Hills."

The words, meant in jest at the stories Cait had heard told about her, seemed to hit the man holding her like a bucket of ice water. His face blanched instantly, and she swore she felt every nerve in his body go numb.

A second later, he flung himself off her, onto his back beside her.

It happened so fast that Cait didn't know how to react. Neither her mind, dazed by surprise, nor her body, still humming with the sensations he'd awakened, could seem to grasp his sudden withdrawal.

One moment he was kissing her senseless, wildly stirring up needs she'd never known she could feel, the next moment, a simple remark had him flying off her faster than quills off a porcupine.

Cait knew then, suddenly, why he had been so quick to throw himself away from her. The wild need drained from her in a rush. Her blood turned frigidly cold in her veins. A knot of disappointment that bordered on betrayal formed in her stomach. It made no sense. She'd pinched off that nerve a thousand seasons ago.

And in one foolish moment she'd let it open again.

Tears burned at the back of her eyes, but she refused to let them surface. She never cried, never let anyone get past her carefully guarded emotions to cause her pain.

She'd be damned if some barbaric ass from

the valley would make her bawl like a jilted bride.

She sidled a glance at him lying next to her, close enough to touch, close enough for her to feel the heat of him reach out to her like a sunbeam. His arm rested over his eyebrows and he stared at the sky, his chest rising and falling in a deep, hypnotic rhythm.

"What's the matter, hunter, never kissed a *legend* before?" She'd meant it as a sarcastic jab; it came out in a raspy whisper.

"Gawd, no."

"You could try sounding a little less disgusted. It isn't contagious, you know."

With a startled glance in her direction, he said, "I'm not disgusted, I'm . . ." He hesitated. "Cait, I'm sorry. I don't know what came over me."

"Yeah, I figured you were." She tamped down the bitterness uncoiling inside and sat up abruptly, wincing at the stiffness in her neck. "Jesus, you could've broken my neck," she grumbled, rubbing her sore nape.

He rolled his head to the side and gaped at her. "You would've sliced mine! Not to mention trying to ruin me for life."

Cait latched onto her anger, finding it a less dangerous emotion to deal with than the turmoil he'd roused inside her. "I warned you to stay away from here—twice, in fact. But did you take my warnings seriously? No, instead you insult my ability and my experience and then you pounce on me like a bear on fresh meat."

He laughed, a harsh, hollow sound. "So you go for first blood?"

"If that's what it takes. Did you expect anything different?"

"No. Yes." He rocked to his feet, swiped a broad hand down his face, and shook his head. Shaggy mellow brown hair brushed his shoulders. "Hell, with you I never know what to expect."

"Good. You never will, either." She got to her feet, picked up her knife, and wiped the blade clean across her tunic before slipping it back into its sheath. "Everywhere you go, you're going to wonder, 'Will this be the day I take my last breath?' Because I'll be watching you, and if you get anywhere near that cougar, your scalp'll be hanging from my war lance."

She turned, meaning to leave him choking in the dust from her heels, but his voice brought her to a standstill.

"Do you hate me so much, Cait?" he asked softly.

Caught unprepared, she twisted around and met his questioning gaze. Remnants of dried needles and soil on his rumpled clothes and in his mussed hair triggered a memory of lying beneath him, his mouth plundering hers, his hands taking liberties with her body that she'd not let any man take before.

She should hate him. She wanted to hate him. But heaven help her, she couldn't.

Because from a distance she had admired Ethan Sawyer. Wondered about him. Dreamed of him. Up close, though . . . oh, up close he'd exceeded all her fantasies.

She felt as if she'd been waiting forever for Ethan's kiss, but when it happened, it had only made her restless and aching for more. Even now, watching him watching her with those intense green-gold eyes of his, she longed for him to take her in his arms and do it again.

How could she hate someone who made her feel so damned alive?

Averting her eyes lest he see the turmoil in them, she stated, "I hate what you stand for. That cougar never did anything to you and yet you are bound and set on seeing her punished."

"Why are you so determined to save that cat?" he cried.

Because I know what it feels like to be part of a dying breed! "Why are you so determined to kill it?"

After a silent moment, he shook his head. "You are never going to see my side of this issue, are you?"

"And you are never going to admit that your side may not be the right one. There are other ways to exist with what one fears without destroying it, you know."

"Name one."

"Live with it. Respect it. Learn from it."

"That animal didn't bother learning to live or respect or learn from the cows it killed."

"It's following its instincts," she countered in frustration. "Had those cows not been put there by some self-serving cattleman, the cougar would have been perfectly content with the elk or deer or rabbit that come naturally to this area.

"But no, man had to move into its territory and either scare off or kill most of the wild game it had survived on. What choice do the animals have?"

"What of people, Cait? Don't they have a right to live where they can prosper?"

"Not at the expense of those who were here long before. Wild creatures deserve no less than the people you're so bent on defending."

"So you'd place more value on an animal than on human life. Hellfire, Cait, who turned you so against your own kind?"

"The kind that turns against its own kind," she hissed. She regretted the words the instant they left her mouth, for they came from a place so deep inside her that most often she could forget it existed. And now she'd all but blurted out one of her darkest recollections to this . . . tenderfoot trapper, a man who of all people did not need to be made privy to her weaknesses.

But if he had any inkling what she'd done, he didn't show it. Instead, he sighed and pushed his hand through his hair, then let it fall to his side. "What do you suggest, Cait, that we allow that beast to continue slaughtering calves and threatening human lives?"

"Of course not," she snapped back. "But I don't see any reason why this cougar has to be killed. The same purpose can be served by catching her and taking her to a less populated area. It would be for her own protection as well as that of the people in the area."

"That's not solving the problem, it's moving it to someone else's shoulders," he returned with barely concealed disdain. "What about the next one, wildcat? And the one after that? You can't save them all."

"Maybe not, hunter, but I'll damn sure try."

The encounter with Cait replayed itself over and over in Ethan's mind for the next two days as he and Trouble scouted the area for the cougar's tracks.

Move it, she'd said. He could hear the townspeople now, they'd really agree to that. Hell, a crate was moved. A rock was moved. You didn't move a vicious killer.

He just didn't understand that confounding woman's reasoning.

So what had he done? He'd kissed her. Ethan shook his head. Gawd A'mighty, he still couldn't believe he'd done that. He sure hadn't meant to. Hell, his life and his reputation were in enough of a jumble without throwing an attraction for Wild Cat Cait into the stew pot.

She was Indian. A legend. A champion for the very animal he'd vowed to destroy.

Yet it didn't change the fact that he'd wanted her like he'd never wanted a woman in his life. Lying atop her, feeling the brand of her curves and inhaling the sweet smell of her skin, he'd felt his normally staunch reason blow away like seeds in the wind until he could focus on nothing but her as woman. Beautiful. Untamed. Deadly.

The sight of prints in the dirt provided him with a much welcome distraction. He dismounted Trouble, then looped the reins loosely around a branch. If the cougar was nearby and came close to Trouble, the horse only had to give a good pull to escape.

As an afterthought, Ethan decided to stash his saddlebags and bedroll under a bush—just in case. Then, grabbing his Spencer from the scabbard and dumping a handful of cartridges in his coat pocket, he followed the tracks.

They meandered along the ridge for a while before forking left, down a rugged incline into a box canyon closed on three sides by steep pine-populated slopes, leaving open only the farthest side, where the creek cut through; on the opposite bank of the creek stretched a wide, grassy meadow.

A sense of unease twisted in his gut, but he knew he'd come too far to turn back now.

He picked his way carefully down the slope, mindful of the last canyon he'd landed in. The difference between then and now was that he'd prepared himself for anything.

Or thought he had.

Until he reached the bottom of the canyon and found himself staring at an animal that made Savagepaw or whatever that tiger's name was look like a child's toy in comparison.

Grizzly.

Chapter 8

Ethan poised in the meadow, not daring to move. He knew even less about bears than he did about tigers and cougars, but one thing was crystal clear—this was no trained pet that could be ordered off him by a curvaceous mountain woman.

It was almost a thousand pounds of muscled fury that could kill him in one swipe.

And there was nowhere to run.

The thing hadn't noticed him yet, though, either because it was too engrossed in whatever snack it was eating beneath the trees at the edge of the forest, or because Ethan was too far away for it to see him, since a good stretch of open meadow divided them. Either way, its lack of interest played in his favor.

Wracking his brain, he tried to decide what course to take. He remembered Billy once saying that bears couldn't see well, but that their sense of hearing and smell were remarkably keen. With that in mind, he narrowed his choices down to three: stand here like a halfwit until the bear did notice him and turned him

into its main course; shoot, and hope to God
he killed it in one shot, because he wouldn't
get a second one; or try and make a clean and
quiet escape.

Even though he was surrounded by canyon
walls eighty feet high, the third choice still
sounded the most achievable. He figured that
as long as he didn't make any sudden moves
that might attract its attention and the wind
didn't shift, he might come away from the encounter with his skin intact.

He took one cautious step back, planning on
reaching the wall behind him, then scaling as
fast as his hands and legs would take him.
From there, Trouble would be his wings to
safety.

When the bear continued to feed on its meal,
Ethan took another step, then another, and yet
another. And just as he thought his plan might
actually work, a pinecone crunched under his
boot.

Ethan froze. The bear lifted his head. Sunlight bounced off the shaggy fur, turning it to
a shimmering coat of gold and brass.

He lifted his pointed nose into the air and
his head rolled to the right, to the left.

And then he reared up.

As if hearing the chill that rattled down
Ethan's spine, the bear swung its head in his
direction. A nasal bellow erupted from him
loudly enough to make the Rocky Mountains
tremble.

Fear left a metallic taste in Ethan's mouth,
and as he whispered an urgent prayer, he
hoped God was listening.

Apparently not.

Even before the bear charged, Ethan had begun to make a run for it, keeping close to the base of the hills surrounding him. He knew there was no way he'd make it up the slope now. Nor could he break for the forest, since the bear was between it and him. No, the creek was his only chance of escape—even if it meant throwing himself over the falls.

His legs pumped furiously. His lungs began to burn. He could feel the ground quake beneath his feet and knew that the bear was closing in on him.

From some well deep inside, he found a surge of speed. Soon he could hardly breathe for the intense pressure in his lungs. The sound of the falls grew louder. Out of the corner of his eye, he caught sight of the bear cutting a diagonal course, as if to head him off, and he knew an instant flash of utter panic.

He wasn't going to make it.

Was this it, then? The final draw in a hand that had dealt him three years of punishment for one act of kindness?

He hoped it wouldn't hurt. He hoped he'd earned enough mercy that when the bear caught him, it would be a quick and painless blow.

He was so damned tired of hurting.

A curdling roar yanked Ethan's attention behind him. He glanced over his shoulder in time to see the bear stumble; it fell, then tumbled head over rump into a still heap.

Ethan didn't think; he just swerved sharply to the left and dropped to his knees. He'd never be able to outrun the beast and he knew it. No, his only chance lay in taking a stand.

He planted the Spencer butt down on the grass. The cartridges spilled from his pocket to the ground.

The bear gained its footing again. Body swaying, feet staggering.

Ethan fumbled to open the chamber of the rifle. Fear made his hands clumsy.

The bear shook his head, made a lumbering charge.

Death closed in with choking swiftness. Fifty yards, thirty yards, twenty yards ... Ethan started shoving shells down the barrel. Fifteen yards, ten. . . .

Again the bear crashed to the ground like a drunken giant. Ethan didn't know what the hell to make of the animal's behavior, but neither did he question it, for it gave him time to finish loading the Spencer, stand, and take aim just as the beast rose again.

He got off one shot, then a second and a third. He kept firing until the rifle gave the ominous click of an empty chamber.

Less than fifteen feet away, the bear collapsed.

And then, silence. And smoke. And the overwhelming sting of gunpowder filling Ethan's nostrils. His knees buckled. He sank to the ground, every muscle, nerve and bone turning to liquid.

The succession of shots rang in Cait's ears long after the echo faded. Dropping from a branch where she'd been repairing a loosened snare, she raced through the forest in the direction of the reports. Oh, God! Her heart thundered with a mixture of fear and dread and disbelief. He'd killed her. Ethan had finally killed Halona.

How could she have fooled herself into thinking he was different from the others? He'd told her time and again that he meant to see the cougar destroyed no matter what. . . .

Cait's legs pumped harder across the ground. Her feet stamped through large patches of snow that refused to melt and churned up sharp twigs, shredded pinecones, and needles. Branches tore at her hair, wind slapped her face.

Splashing through a branch of the creek, then racing along the bank, she finally reached a meadow backed by a wall of rocks. She spotted Ethan kneeling on the ground beside one of her snares, a rifle gripped in his hand.

She burst forward. Noticing her, he started to rise. "Cait?"

"You bastard!" She rammed the heels of her hands into him with all her might, but succeeded only in knocking him back a step.

Her fury escalated. "Are you pleased with yourself?" She slapped at his arms, pounded his chest, called him every filthy name she'd ever heard.

He dodged each blow with the agility of a warrior, and Cait became dimly aware that she was fast losing any semblance of control over rational action, yet found herself unable see past the haze of rage clouding her senses.

Finally his hands gripped her arms and he

gave her a sharp shake. "What's the matter with you?"

"You won!" she screamed into his face. "You got what you came here for . . . are you happy now?" Ignoring his look of confusion, she struggled against his hold and wildly scanned the scraggly grasses and shredded ropes. "Where is she?"

"Who?"

"Halona! The cougar, you self-serving cut-throat!"

"What are you talking about? I haven't seen the cougar—"

"I heard the shots," Cait hissed. How *dared* he act like he didn't know what she meant!

"I wasn't shooting at the cougar, I brought down a bear."

Cait abruptly stilled. "A what?"

"A bear. He charged at me, and I shot him."

Her jaw fell. Her brows shot up. "*You* brought down a bear?"

His brows narrowed and his shoulders rolled back in a proud stance. "Yes, a bear."

"I'm supposed to believe that you—"

He grabbed her shoulders and steered her in a circle. "A bear," he asserted, and pointed to a massive hump of brassy yellow fur not far from where they stood. "A really big bear."

The blood drained from her face. Her mouth parted in surprise. "My God, you shot a *grizzly*?"

"That's what I've been telling you."

"I know, but—" She just couldn't seem to stop repeating herself. It was so hard to absorb, it seemed so unreal! She started a cautious approach toward the bear.

"Are you sure it's dead?" There was nothing more formidable than a wounded grizzly. She'd seen the consequences of an attack once during a visit to Iron Eye Mary's trading post.

"I'm sure," Ethan said, falling into step beside her as she cautiously circled the prone beast.

She barely heard him, barely noticed his presence beside her. In her mind's eye she saw again the torn and bloody remains of the attacked man, but his features had been transformed somehow, became so strikingly similar to Ethan's that nausea rolled in Cait's stomach.

She swung around to face him, and for the first time noticed his wind-tossed hair and rumpled shirt with one tail hanging out and a tear at his shoulder. She also detected a disturbing calmness lurking in his eyes, bloody scrapes on his hands, and fresh scuff marks on his boots. He appeared healthy and unharmed otherwise.

A powerful wash of relief made Cait's knees weak. "I'll be damned, hunter, you killed a grizzly bear."

He looked startled for a moment. "Yeah—" He wiped a hand down his face and let out a shuddering breath. Then, beaming from ear to ear, he said, "Yeah, I did, didn't I?"

The broad grin of his seemed so boyish that she couldn't help but be charmed by it.

Unsettled by the reaction, when only moments before she'd been ready to rip out his heart with her bare hands, she focused her attention on his prize. "What are you going to do with it?"

"Well, there's too much there for one man. So I thought . . . well, I thought you might be able to use some of the meat. And the coat, of course, since I have no need for it."

"You want to split your kill with me?"

"Seeing as how you're partly responsible, it seems only fair."

"Me? What did I do?"

"It was eating some of your bait when I happened by." He gestured toward the forest line where Cait remembered setting one of her snares. "Whatever you've been putting in the meat had him stumbling all over the place. It was mostly dumb luck on my part. If he hadn't been drugged, I'd be supper for the buzzards right now."

Still reeling over the fact that this tenderfooted hunter had killed a grizzly, Cait shook her head. First, he gave her a share of the credit for the kill, now he was offering her part of the meat? She'd never heard the like!

Her eyes suddenly narrowed. "What's the catch?"

With a terse laugh and a flip of his hands, he exclaimed, "Why do you think there is always an ulterior motive? I don't believe in waste—or are you too proud to accept a gift freely given?"

"Nothing is freely given, Sawyer."

His gilded lashes fell, shuttering his eyes. After a moment's pause, he met her gaze and sighed. "All right—there is one, small catch."

* * *

Ethan nearly lost his stomach at the first slice into the carnivore.

He closed his eyes and willed the nausea down. When he opened them again, he found Cait looking at him, her eyes twinkling.

"What's the matter, never dressed your own kill before?"

He swallowed and glanced at the beast, then at the bloody knife in Cait's hand. "I'm more accustomed to handling the skins, not the innards."

"Strange method for a hunter."

"I'm not much of a hunter, I make saddles back in Roland."

She gaped at him, baffled. "But what do you do for food?"

He thought fleetingly of Josie and shrugged. "What most bachelors do, I guess. There's a restaurant in town that I favor. Now and then I'll catch a fish or rabbit. Before that, on the rare occasions when I did hit a deer, I could usually bribe Billy to do the messy work."

Her hand stilled, her voice sounded tight. "The hunter friend of yours?"

"Used to be."

"Used to?"

"We had a . . . difference of opinion."

The locking of his jaw must have warned her that Billy and their friendship—or lack of it—was not a subject to pursue, for she turned back to her task and said, "We'll need a litter to carry back the meat. Maybe you'd rather find a few sturdy pines to cut down."

"I'd rather do what you're doing." He gestured toward the bear.

Once more, her gaze sought his, and there was no mistaking the surprise in her sapphire depths. Surprise and something else. Could it be . . . approval?

"Are you sure?"

The question held a mixture of concern, doubt, and challenge. The last chipped at his pride.

He couldn't explain this sudden need to prove he could gut the bear as well as her. Except, the idea that he might earn this woman's respect, even if grudging, compelled him to nod. "I think I can handle it."

She held out her knife. With a wry tilt of his mouth, Ethan unsheathed his own, a blade of forged steel and stag antler.

Side by side, they worked together, Cait's gentle voice washing over him as she gave him direction on where to cut, what to remove, which areas to avoid to prevent from spoiling the meat.

He found his confidence building with each move, and the nausea he'd first felt gave way to something more unexpected—a powerful sense of pride. He'd brought down a damned grizzly bear. He was actually field dressing the animal. His father would be astounded if he could see him now.

In more ways than one.

He cast a sly glance at the woman beside him. Her face was flushed, wisps of hair had escaped the tight braid down her back, a strip of blood smeared her cheek. And yet he'd never seen anyone quite so breathtaking. She had a natural beauty, and like the wilderness, seemed kissed by the elements. Hair the rich, dark brown of aged bark. Eyes like a morning sky. Skin as soft and smooth as buffed oak. As if she'd been born of the majestic Rocky Mountain Range itself, and raised as its child.

Maybe there was some truth to the legend, after all.

Venturing into territory he'd refused to tread earlier, Ethan asked, "Did your people teach you to do this?"

"My people?"

"Of your tribe. Did they teach you how to carve like this?"

"I taught myself."

He didn't doubt it. She was one of the most independent women he'd ever met. And he wondered if it was one of the traits she'd been born with or one life had shaped into her. "Even split between the two of us, there is an awful lot of meat here. What will you do with it?"

She shrugged. "Dry some, smoke some, salt some—and eat some, of course. But a bear's weight is made up mostly of fat, so the meat is best used in stews or ground up."

"I suppose you taught yourself how to do all that, too."

"There was no one else to do it."

He watched her rise and walk to the creek, where she washed her hands and face. His gaze followed the proud line of her back, the flare of her hips.

An instant tightening in his groin had him glancing away with a curse.

He unfolded his body and knelt at the rocky

bank, keeping a good six feet or so between himself and Cait. She cleaned her knife with sand in silence, and he did the same.

In spite of the distance, he remained all too aware of her. He stole another glance at her. No trace remained of the wild female that had attacked him a short time ago. She'd reminded him a little of Josie, the way she'd ferociously come to the defense of the cougar she'd thought he'd shot.

He couldn't help but wonder what would it be like to have someone care for him that passionately. Amanda never had; she'd have married him for security, and he'd asked only for a son in return. Even Josie, for all her loyalty, focused on pleasing her husband first, as it should be.

But Cait . . . she projected as much of her energy into a simple kiss as she did protecting a wild beast.

He knew he shouldn't let himself think about the day she'd snuck into his camp. It was always there, though, playing in the back of his mind like a song he couldn't forget. The feel of her arms around his neck, the taste of her lips pressed against his, the sultry vision of her dark brown hair fanned around her head, and her pale blue eyes drowsy with desire.

But there was more to her than a physical allure; there was an essence he found himself constantly fighting to resist, a spirit that beckoned to him like a whispering wind.

He envied her. Her freedom. Her tenacity. Even her courage. She had more of it than he did, that was certain, shunning society and all its restrictions.

But then, he had to remind himself, she didn't have the responsibilities he had. She wasn't accountable to anyone or anything. He had Josie and his shop, contracts that needed fulfilling.

Still, he couldn't help but wonder what it would be like to live life on one's own terms, as she did. To trade the bustle of civilization for the comforting peace he'd discovered here in the mountains.

"Cait?" His brows knitted together. "Do you ever get lonesome up here, all by yourself?" The minute the words were out, he cursed himself. No telling what she might think he meant—of course, if she thought he wanted her, she'd be right.

"I'm not by myself. I have Sawtooth—"

"I mean, for people. Do you ever just wish for someone to be with? To hold a conversation with?" To hold you at night when the world gets too dark?

He didn't say that, of course . . . but he wanted, needed, to know what compelled a woman of such seemingly fragile stature to exist out here alone, to take on all the risks of wilderness living. It surprised him how much he wanted to know about this woman, beyond the myths that had been created about her.

She sighed and looked across the water at a wall of rocks that rose several feet up from the water's edge. There was a vulnerability in her expression that he hadn't seen before.

"Before I came here, I lived in a place with

more people than some meet in a lifetime. I learned to read, to write, to sew and cook and garden—all the things a decent woman needs to know to survive in this modern world."

She fell silent, but not before he detected a faint trace of scorn in her words. "Why did you leave?" he asked, unable to stop himself from questioning her any more than he could stop the sun from rising.

"Because if I hadn't, I would have died."

The statement shocked him. Rocked him. "I don't understand—were you sick?"

She shrugged. "I suppose you could say that. But it was more a sickness of the soul."

Something in her quietly spoken words touched the deepest corner of Ethan's heart. And when she lifted her face to his and he looked into the guileless blue of her eyes, the sorrow there, the bleakness, called out to him like a grieving child.

She seemed almost . . . lost. Scared. And so damn alone. The same way he'd been feeling for the last three years, though he could never admit it to anyone. A need to protect her rose inside him so swiftly and strongly it nearly suffocated him.

Disturbed by the power of his own emotions, Ethan forced down the lump in his throat and glanced at his hands, then grimaced. "Gawd, what a mess."

"I know," she said, sounding almost relieved. "I'm tempted to bathe under the waterfall like you did."

Ethan laughed. "Yeah, me, t—" His chin

jerked up. "How do you know I bathed under the waterfall?"

She went still as a stump. Ethan thought he even saw color fade from her cheeks. But she didn't answer. Instead, she got to her feet. In a brisk no-nonsense tone, she said, "It'll be dark soon. We need to get this meat packed up, or we'll be fighting the wolves for it."

In silence, Ethan wiped his blade on his shirt and returned it to his boot, but it nagged the hell out of him how she knew about him and the waterfall. The only way she could know was if she'd seen—his head snapped around with sudden dawning. She'd watched him? She must have. There was no other way she could know.

But when?

Ethan brushed his hair back across his scalp. She'd watched him, and he'd never noticed. The thought left him feeling vaguely uneasy, but more, it gave him a strange pleasure.

Images punched into his mind, then, of the two of them under the falls. Their bodies wet and slick, pressed together under the showering water. Skin against skin. Mouths fused. Hands exploring.

Cait pointed out two sturdy but slender pines and instructed him to remove the branches after chopping down the trees.

Ethan gulped and looked at her. She was acting as if nothing had happened, as if the incident were of no importance to her and could be easily forgotten. Feeling his face flush, he mentally doused the pictures of them together and gratefully took the hatchet she handed him from her belt loop.

He brought back the saplings a short time later and watched as she fashioned a triangular carrier, using the same type of rope as her snares. Together they spread out the bearskin, and laid half the meat within, then bound it securely to the poles.

"I'll be right back," he said. "I hobbled my horse up at the top of the canyon. If he's still there, you can use him to haul this back for you."

At Cait's nod, Ethan crossed the meadow and scaled the wall to the upper ridge.

The minute he disappeared from sight, Cait let out a gusty breath, overwhelmingly relieved that he was gone—even if for a few minutes so she could gather her wits.

How could she have made that stupid slip about the waterfall? It had been her secret, the one she took out at night to explore and savor.

Glancing around, she was struck for a fleeting moment by how easy it would be to make her escape.

No, she'd run from him once. She'd not do it a second time. Besides, she'd have to leave the meat behind, and she needed it too desperately to do that.

Better to continue acting as if she'd never seen him under the falls, she decided. And if he didn't buy that, then behave as if the incident had meant nothing to her.

By the time he found his way back to the box canyon, a saddled roan in tow, Cait had recovered her usual aplomb. Man and beast navigated the wall, then kept to the edge of the forest, moving with a grace that sent tingles racing up and down Cait's arm.

Until the horse caught the bear's scent.

Rearing onto its hind legs, it loosed a shrill whinny and ripped free of Ethan's grip. The horse swerved past Cait and galloped on through the creek, headed for the open meadow on the opposite bank.

The look of absolute shock on Ethan's face caused a bubble of laughter to well up inside Cait. And then another, and another, until her whole body shook and her stomach muscles hurt.

"Damn it, damn it, damn it!" she heard him cursing, as he flung the saddlebags he'd had over his shoulder to the ground. His rifle and what looked like a bedroll suffered the same abuse.

Cait cupped her hands around her mouth and called, "Problem?"

"I hate that critter!" he yelled back. Storming to her side, he jabbed his finger in the direction the horse had gone, and said, "*That* was Trouble."

Cait giggled. The only thing left of the horse was the echo of hooves pounding down the mountainside. "Will he come back?"

"I don't know and I don't care anymore. He's caused me more aggravation than he's worth."

"Some animals just aren't made for the mountains."

"Yeah, but now we'll have to drag this load

ourselves," he said, taking one handle as Cait grabbed the other.

Her amusement over the horse fled. She looked at Ethan in surprise and with a sliver of apprehension. *"We?"*

"It's too heavy to carry on your own."

Maybe. But accepting the meat he offered was one thing, letting him help her take it to her cabin quite another. "Thanks, but I'll manage."

"You don't trust me?"

"Trust you?" she scoffed. Hell, she couldn't trust anyone. People used trust to get what they wanted, then they ground you under their heels and left you to wallow in their dust. The government had done it to her father's people for years; the priests at the mission school had done it to her for half her life—if she couldn't trust a man of the cloth, how could she trust a man of the world like Ethan?

His eyes softened, and he brushed her cheek with his thumb. "If I'd wanted to hurt you, Cait, I could have done so long before now."

She almost laughed at the absurdity of the claim. Who had been besting whom this last week?

"And if it's that flea-bitten thunder box you're worried about," he went on, "you can put your mind at ease. He's not what I'm after."

She knew that. And that was the problem.

Yes, taking him up on his offer would save her the dozen or more trips she'd have to make to haul the meat herself, raising the chances of her being spotted by the other hunters. At the same time, bringing this man to her home would be just like giving him her approval to hunt at will. And he'd know something about her that only one other living person knew: he'd know precisely where she and her animals lived. She felt confident that she could protect herself. But what about her cats? Up until now, they'd been only extensions of the fables. If Ethan saw that they did, in truth, exist, what was to stop him from blaming one of them for the attacks on the cattle? Or leading other people to her home?

As if he had the power to read her thoughts, he tipped her chin and said, "I give you my word, Cait. Whatever secret you're hiding will go with me to my grave."

She weighed the sincerity in his eyes with her own conflicting feelings. Had she, and was she still, misjudging him? Being too harsh on him as a result of her own experiences? From the beginning she'd sensed he was different from the others. More honest and more honorable. More compassionate.

What if she did bring him home? Let him see Ginger and Faw Paw the way she saw them, see their beauty, see the damage being done to these majestic animals ... what if she could somehow appeal to the "humane" side that she glimpsed so frequently? Would he give up the hunt, maybe even convince others to do the same?

Cait swallowed heavily even as a weight in her heart lifted. Yes, she'd be taking a huge risk, but nothing else was working. Besides, he'd already met Sawtooth. And if he really wanted to, he could probably find her canyon again, and her cabin. By showing him willingly, did she really have more to lose than she had to gain?

With a singular somber nod, she gave her consent.

And prayed she'd made the right decision.

Chapter 9

After hanging his share of the meat in a tree, out of the reach of four-legged thieves, Ethan picked up one side of the litter while Cait picked up the other.

The journey through the forest went slowly, but Ethan didn't mind. He and Cait stopped often to rest and shake out their arms, which grew numb from a combination of the load they hauled and the vibration of the travois scraping along the ground. They even talked a little, mostly about the weather. Nothing personal. Nothing invasive.

Yet he got the most pleasure from simply walking alongside her. In spite of his longer legs, they seemed to fall into a natural, almost companionable pace. And every now and then their legs would brush, or their elbows would bump, and sparks of awareness would shoot through his system.

He kept the pleasure to himself, though, worried that if Cait knew how she affected him she wouldn't feel as comfortable in his company. He didn't know why it was important to him that she not hate him, because nothing could ever come of getting involved with her. He only knew that right here and right now, he liked being with her, and if he could help her with this one small thing, taking the meat to her home, then maybe it could make up for what she saw as his greatest fault—his hunting the cougar.

So he kept his silence, and she hers, while all around them the sounds of the wilderness abounded. Unseasonably warm weather had brought out all manner of wildlife, from the tiny muskrat to the imposing moose, their chitters and bellows filling the crisp air.

After a while, Cait licked her lips and he heard a catch in her breath just before she spoke.

"Look, about the way I acted back there . . . the way I jumped on you. I don't normally lose control like that. It's just that I thought . . . when I saw—"

"You don't have to explain," Ethan interrupted softly.

"But maybe if I do, you'll understand. I've told you that the number of mountain lions in this area is shrinking at an alarming rate. What I didn't tell you is that . . . well, I believe the cougar all of you want to kill is one I helped several years ago, when she was a cub."

"You can't be sure of that."

"Not completely, no—but my gut tells me they're one and the same." She readjusted her grip on the litter handle but kept her sight on the horizon. "So I suppose that makes me a little more protective of her than I would normally be of another puma. When I thought you had killed her, I just . . . well, I guess I went a little wild."

Ethan stayed silent for a long while. He didn't know what to say to her. He empathized with her cause and her reasons behind it. He even found it admirable that she gave so much of herself to it. But at the same time, the cougar was nothing more to him than a means to an end, a danger that must be dealt with.

He couldn't tell that to Cait, though. She knew how he felt, and she disagreed with it. Why ruin the evening by voicing his views again, when nothing he could say would change her mind, anyway?

Instead he listened to the sound of the litter poles scoring the earth, enjoyed the feel of the wind ruffling his hair, savored the company of the woman beside him.

"What did you put in the meat that the bear ate?" he finally asked.

"Laudanum."

"Isn't that dangerous?"

"I tested it first before I decided to use it. It leaves you a little muddleheaded when you wake up, but otherwise there are no lasting side effects—unless one takes too much of a shine to it. Then it's like liquor—one drop and you just can't stop."

"Maybe that's why the bear couldn't seem to get enough."

She laughed shortly, and he found the sound just as addictive as any drug or liquor.

"I feel like such a fool," she said. "It never

occurred to me that another animal might eat the bait."

"Sometimes we do things for what we believe are all the right reasons without thinking through the consequences."

"True. Even so, it's the only way I could think of to capture Halona without causing her harm."

They reached the canyon then, and the descent prevented further conversation, much to Ethan's relief. Continued talk about the cougar left him with an uneasy feeling, partly because his main motive for hunting it wasn't exactly selfless, and partly because it reminded him of the unbridgeable gulf between himself and Cait.

It took his and Cait's combined weight and strength to keep the litter from toppling over. Slipping, skidding, gritting their teeth, and grunting, they had made it halfway down the incline when Cait's heel slid on a patch of snow and she landed on her bottom with a shriek.

"Cait?" Ethan shot around the litter toward her only to skid on the same patch and slide into the spot beside her. Pine needles and dirty clumps of snow sprayed out in front of him; a wrenching spear of pain shot up his spine. "Oh, shit."

She started laughing so hard he wondered that she didn't pop something. "You just can't help yourself, can you, Ethan? You always gotta be a hero."

He couldn't reply immediately for the sharp pressure throbbing in his back. "Yeah, something like that."

Gritting his teeth, he rolled to his feet, reached for her hand, and hauled her up alongside him. The warmth of her palm in his stayed with him long after she'd let go to smooth down her hair.

"How do you do this all the time?" Ethan asked, taking hold of his side of the litter.

"A lot of trips back and forth," she said, brushing off her leggings. The motion brought his attention to the fine fit of fabric stretched across her backside. "Sometimes I get Sawtooth to help me, but he tends to eat more than he carries."

That remark had him scanning the area. "He isn't out here somewhere waiting to pounce on me, is he?"

Cait laughed. "No, I keep him in the quad when I'm away. I don't want him wandering around without me."

They finally reached the bottom, and misty echoes of Cait's laughter rang in his mind as they crossed the meadow. A butter white moon illuminated the area and gave the tall, sweet grasses an enchanted rippling appearance.

He found himself wanting to take Cait's hand again and stroll off into the horizon, where nothing existed but the two of them. Dangerous thoughts, he knew, yet he couldn't seem to stop them from seeping into his mind and soul.

He glanced at her only to discover her already looking at him. The instant their eyes met, her gaze darted away, and damned if her cheeks didn't turn red.

Charmed, he wondered what had been going through her mind to make her blush. Was it possible that she too had been caught under the spell of the moon, the serenade of the wind through the reeds, the enchantment of a mild spring evening?

"There it is . . . home sweet home."

Ethan tore his gaze from Cait's moon-kissed face and looked through the trees. A small log house sat back in a clearing surrounded by tall evergreens. Four poles rose from a step-high plank porch and held up a shingled overhang. A rain barrel sat at one corner, a six-foot lance and a tree stump table at the other. Above the stump, curtains fluttered through an open window, the only touch of frivolity Ethan could see in an otherwise rusticly masculine setting.

Awed, Ethan asked, "Did you build this?"

"No, my grandfather did." At the surprised lift of his brows, she gave him a wry grin. "Why, what did you expect to find me living in? A tepee?"

Ethan found his face growing warm. "Well, actually . . . yes, I guess I did."

She chuckled. "Sorry to shatter your illusions, hunter, but this Injun happens to like the comforts of the white man."

To Ethan's relief, she sounded more amused by his assumption than offended. "But your clothes. . . ."

"I'm making a statement of rebellion."

"Against what?"

"Pick a topic." She grinned. It came quick, natural. And sent a shaft of sunlight straight to his soul. How long had it been since someone had smiled at him? Even Josie, for all her loyalty, seemed to have forgotten how.

"Actually, I wear these for practical reasons. I don't have to buy the material, they're warm in the winter and cool in the summer, they repel water, I don't have to worry about my petticoats or hems catching on fire . . . need any more reasons?"

"So are you a white woman living like an Indian, or an Indian woman living like a white?"

"Both. Neither. Why does is have to be either?"

He started to reply, but she cut him off with a sigh. "Look, Sawyer, my blood runs as red as yours, so do me a favor—don't make this a matter of heritage."

How could he not, when the red blood that ran in her veins came from a warring people? When the enmity between the Indians and his own people still ran swift and deep? When his life had been ruined by a single call of judgment involving one?

The subject died as they entered the rear quad. No sooner did Ethan shut the gate behind him than a ball of orange and black came flying out of the blue.

Once more Ethan found himself flat on his back with Cait's tiger on top of him. "Hellfire, I knew my luck wouldn't last!"

Cait grabbed the scruff of the tiger's neck and pulled. "Sawtooth, get off of him."

"That animal is going to be the death of me yet."

"He's very protective of me."

"I can see that."

"I'll tell you a secret, though."

"What's that?"

"I think he likes you."

Rising to sit, Ethan rubbed the ache in his back. "I'd hate to see him hate me."

"You wouldn't. You'd be dead." She flashed him a teasing grin and swirled away.

While Ethan struggled to recover from the power of her smile, she tossed the tiger a hunk of bear meat off the litter. With a roar and a leap, the cat caught the scrap in his jaws and dragged it to a darkened corner of the quad almost before Ethan could blink. "Gawd A'mighty!"

"I know, isn't he amazing?"

"I've never seen anything move so fast in my life!"

"That's how they attack their prey in the wild."

Blanching, Ethan brought his hand to his neck.

"Just don't go anywhere near him while he's eating. As tame as he is, even I keep my distance until he's through."

He could have told Cait that she didn't have anything to worry about; he'd have cut Hacksaw a wide berth even without the warning. As he stared in fascination, it was hard to believe that the snarling, growling savage was the same gentle creature that licked Cait's face and nuzzled her neck with affection.

"Would you like to meet the rest of the tribe?" Cait asked, drawing his attention away from the tiger.

"The rest?"

"Yeah," she chuckled. "Come on, let's get

this meat put up, then I'll introduce you to the others. That first building is a cold shed. It's where I store the game."

As they dragged the litter across the moon-bright quad, they passed by a cage built around the trunk of an evergreen. The walls reached about ten feet up into the branches.

He wondered what she had in there, but figured his curiosity would be satisfied soon enough.

Working together, it didn't take them long to hang the meat on hooks or wrap it in skins that Cait kept in the shed for that purpose. Then she led the way to the structure that had caught his interest. She untied a thong on the door without a hint of hesitation, then entered the cage.

Cautiously Ethan stepped inside behind her. It was roomier than he'd expected. A ridge of rock lined the back wall next to the tree trunk, and a layer of pine straw had been laid on the dirt floor.

Startled by a swift movement to his right, Ethan swung around. The stunning sight of a light brown animal making its way toward them had him falling on his rump and scooting backward. "Oh, Jesus! What is that?" It looked a little like the tiger, only smaller and without the colorful stripes.

"This is Ginger. She's a lioness." Cait smiled at the animal and cooed, "Hello, my lady. You have a visitor."

With a slow yet fearless stroll, Cait approached the lioness and crouched low to pet her head. The animal was the size of a small horse, with a shiny light brown coat almost the same shade as Ethan's hair. At first she shied away from Cait's touch, but after a few minutes of listening to Cait's soft coaxing, Ginger rubbed her head against Cait's palm.

"Gawd A'mighty," Ethan breathed in awe. "I've never seen the like!"

"Don't know why you would unless you've been to Africa. Lions are native there."

He didn't want to admit that he didn't know where Africa was, so instead he asked, "Is that where you got her?"

Again laughter trickled into the air like rain on a tin roof. "No, it's too far away, across the big ocean. Actually, I found her in Billings a few years back. One of those traveling circuses had been setting up for the weekend. I'd never seen one before, so I went wandering around the rail cars. I remember seeing some of the most amazing animals! Elephants, monkeys, even a leopard!"

The excitement in her voice and eyes captivated him, despite the presence of the deadly looking creature drawing near.

"Anyway, there was one flat car with several cages on it filled with cats. That's where I found Ginger."

Cait's voice dropped. She lifted her hand to the lioness, inviting her closer. "She'd been lying in the cage. The straw around her was soiled and foul. Her eyes were glazed over. And a man was screaming at her and poking her with a long stick to get up. He kept calling her lazy, kept hitting her with that stick. She wasn't lazy, Ethan, she was sick."

"What did you do?"

"I took her. The man wasn't happy, of course, and hollered for a few of his friends, but I told him if he came anywhere near this animal again I'd blow his goddamn head off."

Ethan grinned at the image of her holding a group of men at bay with only a shotgun and ferocious outrage. Of course, he thought wryly, it wasn't like *he'd* ever been on the receiving end of Cait's temper. . . .

"It was appalling how they treated her. I just couldn't let them—" Shaking her head, Cait abruptly unfolded herself. "Wait here a minute while I get her something to eat."

Before Ethan could protest, Cait left.

He pressed as far back against the cage wall as humanly possible. The lioness paced the ground in front of him, keeping him in her sights. Back and forth, back and forth, she went, making him dizzy.

She didn't look sick anymore. In fact, she looked incredibly healthy.

And very hungry.

"So . . . Ginger, is it?" He chuckled uneasily. "I'm Ethan." Of course, he'd probably be *dinner* in another second if the way she was looking at him was any indication. He licked his dry lips and tried to discourage her. "I really wouldn't make a good meal. Tough meat, you know."

Footsteps outside provided a welcome distraction. Cait stepped inside the cage, an earthenware bowl in her hand. "Suppertime, Ginger."

The cat stopped and studied Cait with glowing yellow eyes.

"That meat won't hurt them, will it?"

"I doubt the bear ingested enough of the drug. Would you like to try and feed her?"

"I don't think so." Ethan shook his head adamantly.

"She won't bite, if that's what you're worried about—she doesn't have any teeth."

"Now she tells me," Ethan muttered. "What happened to them?"

"Her former keepers ripped them all out after she bit one of them for whipping her."

Just the thought of having his teeth torn out of his jaw made him cringe. He looked at the lioness, now accepting Cait's tender strokes upon her head. It might have been the knowledge that she couldn't bite him, or maybe a need to show Cait that if she wasn't afraid of the critter, then neither was he, but Ethan mustered his courage and took the bowl. "Well, why not? You only live once, right?" Crouched beside her, the bowl stretched out in front of him, Ethan snagged the lioness's interest.

She dipped her head, her eyes always steady on him. She took a step forward. Then a second, and a third.

Ethan kept still. Cait didn't twitch a muscle, either. The lioness kept coming. She sniffed at the bowl. Ethan held his breath. Any moment he expected her either to bolt away or to pounce on him; she might not have teeth, but claws could do just as much damage, if not more.

She did neither.

She licked his hand.

Cait gasped.

He felt her surprised gaze shoot to his face, but he kept his eyes locked with Ginger's. Somehow, as he gazed into the gleaming tan eyes, he keenly understood her caution, her longing to trust, her fear of man. Almost as if he'd experienced her life—a crazy, illogical feeling, yet there it was all the same.

When she angled her head to eat out of the bowl, a triumphant smile broke out across Ethan's face.

"I can't believe it!" Cait exclaimed in a whisper. "I've been trying to get her to eat from my hand for years, and it takes you only a few moments."

"I guess I've got a magic touch with wildcats."

To his astonishment, she blushed for the second time that evening.

"Yes, well," Cait cleared her throat and rose to her feet.

Reluctantly, Ethan set down the bowl, ran his hand down Ginger's neck, then followed Cait outside.

They skipped the next cage after Cait told him it was empty and moved on to the third, a log box on a stone slab that looked oddly forbidding. The warm sense of achievement he'd felt drained out of him when a series of blood-chilling hisses and snarls met them through the narrow slats of the cage.

He gave a nervous laugh. "I'm afraid to see what you've got in there."

"You should be," Cait retorted. "Faw Paw

won't be as easily charmed as Ginger—he's as wild as they come."

"What is a Faw Paw?"

"A cougar." Ignoring the surprised lift of his brows, she put a match to the lantern she'd brought with her from the shed and held it high. "He's just a cub, though, so I'm hoping he'll settle down a bit."

Ethan pressed his eye against a narrow space and peeked inside. He barely made out a gray ball curled up in the corner. It looked as if he had bandages around his hind leg. "What happened to him?"

"He was caught in one of your fancy traps." She handed him the lantern. "Stay here and don't make a sound."

Ethan grabbed Cait as she lifted the latch, preventing her from entering the cage. "You can't go in there—are you crazy?"

She looked at his hand on her arm, then at him. "Yes, I can. He needs help, and I'm the only one around here willing to give it to him."

The last thing Ethan wanted to do was let her go inside that cage. But he'd been around Cait enough to know that she did as she pleased. Other than physically restraining her, he didn't see how he could stop her.

With his heart pounding at the speed of a comet, he watched through the slats as she crawled across the floor toward the gray animal curled up in the corner. The cougar watched her, too. Each time it hissed, Ethan's blood stopped flowing and his stomach dropped. He had to remind himself that Cait had been doing this for a long time, that she knew what she was about, that these animals were familiar with her.

But he nonetheless gripped the wooden bars tightly, prepared to charge inside the cage if that cougar decided he didn't want to be bothered.

An eternity seemed to pass while Cait examined the cougar's leg, then tossed it its meal.

She stepped out of the cage with a "Phew!" Ethan fell back against the outer wall and wiped a trembling hand down his face.

Cait laughed. "What's the matter, hunter, too close for comfort?"

"I don't know how the hell you do that. Aren't you afraid of being attacked?"

"Of course. But you watch their eyes." She pointed to her own. "They'll always tell you just before they strike, then you turn and run like hell and hope they don't catch you."

With a casualness he couldn't understand, she strode across the quad and took a seat on a bench built against the back of the cabin. Since she hadn't yet asked him to leave, Ethan joined her, sinking onto the seat beside her. Gawd A'mighty, the woman exhausted him. "Anybody ever tell you that you've got strange taste in friends?"

"They are unusual, aren't they?"

That was an understatement, Ethan thought, watching Sharpjaw tear apart his meal with his teeth. "Why isn't he caged like the others?"

"A couple of reasons. He's capable of surviving in the wild; Ginger and Faw Paw aren't—at least, not yet. And two, I promised

Sawtooth when I brought him home that I'd never cage him up."

"Did you find him at the circus, too?"

"No, he came to me through a friend in Pine Bend who owns a trading post. Sawtooth had belonged to a man who seemed to think it would be impressive to own an exotic animal, except Sawtooth was really wild. The man's idea of taming a tiger was keeping him locked up." Her voice dropped, her eyes went stormy. "You can't change a creature's instinctive behavior just by locking it up. It takes love, compassion, understanding, and patience. Even then, you don't want them to change completely, because it's that spirit and uniqueness that attracted you in the first place."

There it was again, Ethan realized, studying Cait's profile—that hint of something deeper than the words she spoke, a glimpse into her soul that made him want to pull her close and yet keep her at arm's length.

He agreed with her about the spirit and uniqueness being an attraction. Each moment he spent with her drew him further under a mysterious spell he couldn't explain and was afraid to examine.

Glancing away, he let his gaze land on the cougar's pen. "Are you planning on taming that cub?"

"Some wild creatures can't be tamed; it would kill their spirit."

Like Cait?

"Faw Paw is one of those creatures. He would fight for his freedom or die trying, rather than submit to captivity."

"What will you do with him, then?"

"Set him free. Not here, of course, and not now. When it's safe, I'll take him to a place I know of where he won't be a threat to people—or their precious cows. If I let him loose now, he'll only be killed by one of you."

The statement snapped him out of the enchantment of the evening. Ethan slowly got to his feet and wiped his palms down his pant legs. "I think that's my cue to leave. . . ."

Cait didn't argue, for which Ethan was thankful. If she so much as looked like she would object, he had a feeling that no power on earth would move him from this place.

It was getting late, though, and he had a long walk back to camp, thanks to Trouble's desertion. Besides, if he stayed any longer, they'd just wind up arguing again. And the day had just been too nice to end in an argument.

Cait pushed herself off the bench, and together they headed for the quad gate in silence.

"Oh, wait—I almost forgot!" She dashed toward the cold shed where they'd parked the litter.

She returned a minute later with a bundle wrapped in a scrap of bearskin. She stroked the long, coarse hair, took a deep breath, then handed the bundle to Ethan.

He took the offering, frowning in puzzlement. "What's this?"

With a proud tilt of her chin, and a glimmer of respect in her eyes that both surprised and humbled him, she answered, "The heart of the bear. May its spirit and yours become one."

Chapter 10

At the first sound of thunder, Cait set aside the shears and scraped elk hide she'd been cutting for a summer tunic, rose from the ladder-back rocking chair, and wandered to the window. Wildcat Peak was nearly obliterated by low, heavy clouds whipping themselves into a charcoal froth.

She opened the front door just as a gusty wind shrieked through the canyon, strong enough to peel the bark off the trees. The tops bowed over, then flung back, as if waving to an angry heaven.

Pulling her shawl more snugly around her, Cait stared at the sky with a worried frown. Distant crackles of thunder and faint flashes of lightning behind the clouded peak warned her that one hell of a storm was approaching.

She hoped Ethan had enough sense to take shelter.

No, that really wasn't fair, Cait decided. He wasn't a stupid man, just inexperienced. And dangerously ignorant about the perils of the mountains. Worse, if he'd stayed by the waterfall, hoping to find decent shelter, he was in for a surprise. There weren't any caves on that side of the mountain to hole up in, just jutting shelves of rock that would offer little protection against the elements. He could get struck by lightning, or hit by falling rock. Or, if he made it through the storm, a night spent in the cold and rain would leave him susceptible to lung sickness. . . .

"Oh, damn it," Cait cursed. She shut the door and leaned back against it. She'd told herself she wouldn't do this. Wouldn't think about him, wouldn't worry about him. . . .

She began to pace the room. So he'd shared a bear with her. So his concern for her safety had touched a tender chord within her. So he made her feel alive in a way that she couldn't remember feeling in all her twenty-four years.

It didn't change the fact that the two of them were on opposite sides of an issue.

And yet, she sighed, no amount of self-control or lengthy lectures to herself seemed to rid her mind of Ethan Sawyer.

For the last three days, his image had been her constant companion. Awake. Asleep. When she played with the animals or when she did her chores. It didn't matter. She saw him in striking clarity—the tawny hair, the golden skin, the lionlike amber eyes. An autumn warrior she was finding hard to hate, and even harder to resist.

Licking her lips, she swore she could still taste the flavor of a kiss nearly a week old.

Even his scent seemed to have woven itself into her clothing. No matter how hard she scrubbed, she could smell him. Evergreen needles and spring water. Wood shavings and saddle soap. Ordinary smells that on him didn't seem ordinary at all. For there was something more, a subtle essence she hadn't recognized, couldn't define. She only knew that it was both mystifying and alarming, and so, so inviting.

And always, always, the sight of his hands, the sound of his voice as he had said, "I'd rather do what you're doing," haunted her. She'd sensed a thirst for knowledge so like her own that it was scary. A proud eagerness to learn a way of life foreign to him, a willingness to try something new.

A lifetime of instruction and criticism and punishment came back to her in a single wave of stomach-turning bitterness. She couldn't recall a single time when someone had allowed her the chance to teach. Always to learn. To sit. To watch. To mimic. Pass all the tests. Obey all the rules.

Rules, God, so many of them.

And the consequences if they weren't followed to the letter. Raps on the knuckles with a willow switch. Extra chores that kept a child up until the wee hours of the morning. Time in the closet. Sometimes alone, sometimes not. . . .

And that was when you'd hear the whimpering. The kind that made your chest hurt and your soul weep.

Cait shuddered. Though she'd been spared time in the closet, she often thought she'd rather take a hundred days in there over the alternative. At least then, the ones you loved didn't suffer. They didn't get their rations suspended. They didn't get whippings. You didn't hear in mind-numbing detail how they'd tried to see you and had been dragged away by their hair and locked up for days and days and days. . . .

But you were promised a better life if you complied. If you followed the rules and obeyed the instructors and kept your life divided into two parts: who you'd been, and that whom you must be.

Well, the day she'd broken free of the school, she'd seen the better life they offered. The filth and the humiliation and the degradation.

And that day she'd sworn never to live under another's thumb again based on promises.

She hadn't, either. Not once since leaving the mission school had she surrendered to another's will. But Ethan made her realize that in an effort to shield herself from the bad, she'd also cut herself off from the good.

"Don't you ever get lonely up here by yourself?"

Oh, God, he had no idea.

She leaned her temple against the window and watched the treetops bow over. Sometimes she longed so desperately for another human voice that she thought she might go mad. Only the cats had saved her, had filled her life with meaning. She'd thought it would be enough. And it had been.

Until Ethan.

Cait closed her eyes. What was she going to do about him? Bringing him to the cabin, letting him meet the tribe, seemed to have accom-

plished little. Though he'd shown a genuine
interest in her feline friends, he still feared
them. And fear was a powerful obstacle.

She knew. It had kept her a prisoner for
twelve years.

And damned if it wasn't keeping her a prisoner now.

Cait straightened, stunned and ashamed by
the realization. Why was she letting herself be
ruled by a fear she'd sworn to overcome?
Damn it, she was Wild Cat Cait! A woman
who, according to the tales she'd overheard,
could rip a man's throat open with her fingernails. A woman who ate raw meat. A woman
who could sneak up on prey without making
a sound.

And that barely scratched the surface of the
outrageous yarns told about her.

They'd all be very disappointed if they
learned she was just a woman who wanted
peace.

She stiffened suddenly, struck by a lightning
bolt of an idea. *Peace*. Could that be the answer
to talking Ethan out of the hunt? A truce with
him? They'd gotten along fairly well the other
day, hadn't they? She hadn't fought him . . .
well, not after she'd realized he'd shot the bear
and not Halona, anyway . . . and he hadn't
fought her. Neither of them had tried to kill the
other.

Yes, a truce—at least for this one night—
might be just the solution she'd been looking
for.

Bolstered by the idea, Cait made a beeline for
the trunk to trade the woolen skirt and shirt

she wore for thicker clothes. Inviting him in out of the storm had nothing to do with her feeling a little lonesome tonight, she told herself. Or being a mite worried about him. Or needing to prove nothing more than she wasn't afraid of him. It was a way to save the cat. And if he asked, she'd tell him that she was simply repaying his kindness for filling her larder with meat, a necessity she'd found dangerous to do herself with so many men about.

What could it hurt?

Her decision made, Cait finished dressing, stepped over Sawtooth, and grabbed her coat.

Sawtooth lifted his head abruptly and started to roll to his feet.

Cait stayed him with an upraised hand. "No, Sawtooth, you stay here and hold down the cabin. I'll be back in about an hour."

So much for Lady Fate smiling down on him, Ethan thought, huddled under a tattered blanket beneath a scanty ledge of rock. She was probably laughing her fool head off.

Not only had his horse abandoned him, but he'd done so just before the worst storm in memory. Freezing rain and hail pelted Ethan's legs and arms like bits of lead. The falls crashed down with trembling force and the creek had become a churning mass of foam and spray, hungrily devouring branches that the shrieking wind tossed into the current.

The violence of the weather starkly reminded him of Mother Nature's wicked temper. He wondered if that was a womanly trait. When Josie got riled, she threw things. He and

Billy both used to run for cover—usually down to the nearest fishing hole.

Amanda stomped her foot and cried.

And Cait. . . . He leaned his head back against the stone wall and sighed. Ah, Cait. She had the most savage temper of all. Hell, she used weapons. Some had fangs, some had razor-honed blades, but the most dangerous one was that sharp tongue of hers. With a few well-chosen words she could cut a man to the quick.

Or lift him to the highest of heights.

His hand slid out to fondled the wet scrap of fur beside him. Just when he thought he had her all figured out, she went and did something completely unexpected.

He had no idea what he was supposed to have done with the bear heart, but it had seemed mighty important to her that she give it to him. And since the last thing he wanted was to shatter the fragile truce they seemed to have formed, he'd taken it. And he'd buried it. He doubted that that was what she'd intended. But he figured as long as she didn't know what had become of it, her feelings wouldn't get hurt.

He wasn't sure when it had become vital not to hurt Cait's feelings. Maybe when he'd seen that moment of sorrow on her face. Or maybe when he'd seen her blush—he couldn't be sure. But under all that spit and fire, somewhere beneath all the sarcasm, he'd glimpsed a woman who had suffered pain. And he didn't want to be the one to cause her more of it.

But he would, he admitted with a heavy

heart, and he knew it. The day he actually did bring down the cougar she was so determined to defend, he would hurt her badly.

And he just didn't see any way to avoid it.

"*Ee-thaan?*"

Startled by the sound of his name above the roar of the falls, the drum of the rain, and the howl of the wind, he jerked forward and peered around the rocks. "Cait?"

Her face appeared above the rock he sat on. Her hair was plastered against her head, rain ran in rivulets down her face and clothes.

He blinked, unable to believe his eyes. "Gawd A'mighty! What are you doing out in this weather?"

"Figured you might need rescuing," she quipped with a blinding smile that had his heart somersaulting.

"You came out in this"—he gestured around him—"to look for me? Have you lost your *mind?*" In spite of his blustering over her reckless behavior, he couldn't help but feel touched that she'd not only been worried about him, but had gone to the trouble of seeking him out.

"I know a place nearby that takes in strays. It isn't much, but there are four sturdy walls, hot food, and warm blankets."

"What's the catch?"

She laughed. "*Now* who's being suspicious?"

He chuckled. "You were the one who said nothing comes without a price."

"I owe you for the bear."

He arched one brow.

"You don't believe me?"

"I would if you told me the truth."

"Oh, all right." She sighed, and then peered up at him through damp, spiky lashes. "I figure if I'm nice and offer you a place to stay for tonight, you'll be nice and call off the hunt."

"So you're trying to bribe me."

"Yep. Is it working?"

"That depends.

"On what?"

"On how long you want me to call off the hunt."

The mirth in her eyes dimmed. "Let's just take this one night at a time."

He shouldn't. Damn it, he knew he shouldn't. Cait had a way of getting under his skin. Making him think about things he didn't want to think about, long for things he had no right to long for.

Yet how could he resist the offer of decent shelter and a warm fire? Besides, he couldn't very well do any tracking in this weather, so he wasn't losing anything.

"It's a deal," he said, grabbed his gear and rifle before she changed her mind. Or he changed his.

It was only reasonable that Cait take the lead, since the night was so black you could feel it and she knew the way better than he did.

They sprinted across the wind-tossed turf for what seemed like miles. The rain hit in one icy sheet, frozen pellets that nicked his skin clear through his clothes.

In the forest, the thick spread of overhead branches shielded them some from the downpour and lightning, but it all returned in full force when they finally descended the canyon.

They slipped and slid down the soggy slope. Cait lost her footing and took a face-first spill. Ethan was beside her in a flash, grabbing her arm and helping her to her feet. He couldn't help but laugh. She was so covered in mud that all he could see were the whites of her eyes. With her hand tightly clasped in his, they continued across the canyon.

They reached the porch, both soaked to the bone and shivering so badly their teeth chattered.

"Go on inside and get out of those wet clothes," she yelled above the wind. "I'll be there in a minute."

"Where are you going?" he shouted back, as she reached for the quad gate.

"To check on the cats."

"I'll help you."

She hesitated, looked at the sky.

"It'll go faster with the two of us," he urged her.

A clap of thunder decided for her. "All right."

Inside the quad, the clatter of rain against the cabin roof sounded like applause and cut visibility to almost naught. Intermittent flashes from the sky provided their only light.

"Shoot, the tarp came loose."

"What do you want me to do?"

"Grab the lower corners of the canvas and make sure they're lashed tightly to the stakes in the ground. Faw Paw's pen needs to be kept as dry as possible or he could slip and reinjure his leg."

Ethan did as she'd directed while she hurried to Ginger's cage. Catching the tarp was like trying to catch a maverick pony. Each time he grasped it, it ripped through his fists and whipped away, only to twist around and snap at him.

After several aggravating minutes and a dozen vivid curses, Ethan jumped, grabbed the tarp, and wrestled it to the ground. With a good portion of it clamped between his thighs, he knelt in the mud and wound the rope around the stake.

"That's it, hunter, show it who's boss!"

Ethan glanced up and saw Cait standing a short distance away, her arms crossed over her chest, the wind tearing at her hair and clothes. He swore he saw her eyes dancing.

He clamored to his feet and headed toward her. He pointed a muddy hand toward the tarp. "The damn thing *bit* me!"

"And you thought my cats were vicious . . . ?" Her laugh stayed with them all the way to the front door of the cabin. Ethan shrugged out of his muddy coat while she opened the door and propped her rifle against the doorjamb. "There's a blanket on the bed that you can wrap around you while I fetch some tow—"

A low-pitched growl cut off the sentence. Ethan's head snapped up just as a load of stripes went airborne.

"Sawtooth, no!" Cait cried.

Too late.

Paws outstretched, fangs bared, the tiger leaped past her.

Ethan's eyes widened. "Oh, no, not agai—"

Sawtooth landed against his chest. His weight drove Ethan backward, out the door, across the porch; the railing splintered as he went crashing over the platform and landed in the mud with an *"Oof!"*

"Sawtooth, damn it!" He heard Cait yell. A second later she wrapped her arms around the Tiger's neck. *"Off!"*

The tiger resisted her orders. Instead, he laid his full crushing weight on Ethan and rubbed his face into the crook of his neck. Hot, sweaty breaths blew against his cold skin, and wiry whiskers poked the underside of his jaw. After several unsuccessful tugs and pushes, Cait finally managed to heave the tiger from Ethan's chest. The next thing he knew, she had dropped to his side. "Are you all right?"

Gasping, sputtering, trying to get his wind back, he let several moments pass before he answered, "I really wish he wouldn't like me so much."

A noise that sounded suspiciously like laughter drew his attention to Cait. Her hand covered her mouth, her shoulders shook. Finally she lost the battle and her laughter spilled forth. "You look like a drowned pup."

"Look who's talking." And he found himself laughing along with her. Without thinking, he reached up and wiped a smear of mud off her cheek. Silence fell. The current that sizzled between them appeared to shock her as much as it did him. They stared at each other in bewilderment for a moment, rain pouring down their faces, lightning streaking above them, wind tossing their hair. Ethan knew he'd never forget the breathtaking sight as long as he lived.

Recovering first, Cait abruptly shook her head and climbed to her feet. "We'd better get inside before we drown."

"Or lightning fries us to a crisp," he added, his voice raw in spite of the light remark. He rolled to his knees. The fiery pressure in his back nearly sent him sprawling face first in the mud. Ethan bit back a curse, straightened, and stiffly mounted the porch steps after Cait. Sawtooth waited near the door, looking properly chastised.

Inside the cabin, Cait lit an oil lamp on a table near the door. "As I was saying, wrap yourself the blanket and hang your clothes over the chair to dry." To Sawtooth, she ordered, "And you, you big bully, go to your room."

The tiger cocked his head and whined, but Cait was firm. She pointed to a wide bed built into the far corner of the room, covered with a patchwork blanket. "Go."

His head hanging, he trudged through the doorway like a doomed convict and crawled under the bed.

"That's his room?" Ethan chuckled. He'd left his filthy coat on the porch but brought his gear inside and set it by the door.

Cait strolled over to light another lamp sitting on an old flour keg beside the bed. "As you can see, there aren't many to choose from."

True. In fact, the whole cabin would probably fit inside his shop in town. But then, he supposed Cait didn't need much space for herself.

While she opened a steel-banded trunk at the end of the bed, Ethan wandered further into the cabin. The mixture of modern and natural furnishings inside her home amazed him. A porcelain bowl sat beside stone tools on a waist-high shelf stocked with cans and pouches. An imported clock with brass works hung alongside hand-fashioned willow hoops on log walls chinked with a mud mixture. Copper kettles dangled from hooks on a pine beam mantel, and above the fireplace an assortment of shiny rifles rested on a broad set of antlers.

Polished wooden frames displayed atop the mantel caught his eye. He pulled one down for a closer study of the black and white sketch. A man in his fifties sat in a chair, wearing a coonskin cap and buckskins and holding a rifle; a fair-haired girl of about ten stood beside him with her hand on his shoulder.

Ethan's gaze slid to the next sketch. It portrayed a version of the same girl in her early twenties, standing beside a seated man obviously of Indian descent. He wore intricately designed regalia, a feather wound into his long black hair.

"My grandfather sketched those."

Ethan started to replace the picture; Cait stepped up beside him and took it from his hand. "He did this one looking in a mirror."

"He's very talented."

"Was. He died when I was a little girl. Jean-François LaRoque was his name, but folks took to calling him John Perry because his accent made Paris sound like Perry and I guess the name stuck. The little girl is my mother—her name was Jeanette."

"Was?

"She's dead, too," Cait answered quietly. "They all are." She brought down the second frame and handed it to him.

"This is my mother when she was my age. My grandfather used to take her with him when he traded furs at the rendezvous point on the Canadian border. That's where she met my father." She pointed to the man in the drawing. "He was very handsome, don't you think? Half Scottish, half Blackfoot. And proud. A noble warrior in youth, or so I was told before—"

"Before?"

"Before everything changed."

A guarded look came over her eyes, and once again Ethan wondered what secrets she hid. Yet he didn't press. He had secrets of his own he wanted to keep.

"You had best get out of those wet clothes before you catch a chill," she said brusquely, replacing the frames. "Here,"—she pushed towels and a soft brown garment into his arms—"I even found a shirt for you to put on instead of the blanket."

Ethan lifted the velvety brown fabric for inspection. Fringe decorated the seams from sleeve to hem. Animal teeth had been sewn into a brightly colored yoke. "Yours?" He lifted one brow.

"No, my grandfather's. You can keep it if you want. It's much more suited to the mountains than that flimsy cotton thing you wear."

"I can't take this, Cait. It belonged to your grandfather."

"He doesn't need it anymore. Besides, I think you earned the right to wear real mountain clothes after killing that bear." She started walking away. "When you're finished changing, if you'll stoke the fire, I'll make us a pot of coffee." Over her shoulder, she asked, "You do like coffee, don't you?"

"As often and as black as I can get it."

"Good. We have something in common, then."

With a twinge of regret, Ethan realized that it was probably the only thing they had in common. He turned back and looked at the pictures. At John and Jeanette, and at Cait's father. Cait seemed to have inherited bits and pieces from each of them. Her grandfather's round face, her mother's straight nose and full mouth, her father's broad forehead and high cheekbones. A striking combination; no doubt they would be proud if they could see their creation now. Cait really was a beautiful woman.

"What did they name you?"

"Pardon?"

It took him a moment to realize he'd voiced his question aloud. "Your parents. What did they name you? I can't imagine you were born Wild Cat Cait."

"Depends on who you're asking."

In spite of the lightness of her tone, Ethan sensed an underlying edge that was both puzzling and intriguing. "I'm asking you," he said softly, meeting her gaze across the cabin.

Several moments passed. The thunder rolled above, the wind shrieked down the chimney, stirring the coals into a frenzy of red and orange and blue flames.

Cait clutched a bundle of clothes close to her chest with one hand and held the trunk lid open with the other.

Finally she licked her lips and said, "Well, I was given a Blackfoot name, but I can't remember it. Caitlin Jeanette Perry is the name I was born with, though, after my father's mother and my mother. What about you?"

"Just plain old Ethan Sawyer, no middle name."

With a short laugh, Cait let the trunk lid drop shut. "There's nothing plain or old about you, Ethan Sawyer." The remark appeared to startle her as much as it did him.

As if suddenly embarrassed by what she'd said, she turned her back and started to pull up her tunic.

Ethan's mouth went dry at the inch of bare skin she revealed before stopping abruptly and glancing over her shoulder. "You plan on watching?"

A guilty flush crept into his cheeks as he quickly averted his eyes and faced the fireplace. If she hadn't said anything, that was undoubtedly exactly what he would have done.

In an effort to keep his mind off the fact that she was taking off her clothes, he concentrated on unfastening the buttons of his shirt.

But he could hear Cait behind him, hear the peel of buckskin, the clink of beads, the slap of wet clothes hitting the floor. His hands froze on the third button. His breathing grew unsteady. He started to turn his head, then jerked back with a silent curse. He doubted Cait would appreciate him abusing her hospitality by spying on her like some pubescent youth.

Determinedly he fixed his gaze straight ahead.

He nearly choked at the sight of Cait's silhouette reflected on the wall. His heart stopped, then started up again at a full-speed gallop.

"Oh, Gawd A'mighty," he whispered in reverence. She had the most perfect shape. Her breasts were round and full, the nipples erect, her stomach flat, her buttocks gently curved.

The cabin became suddenly hot and steamy and smothering. His lungs swelled, along with another part of his anatomy. Speechlessly Ethan watched as she reached back and slid one arm into a shirtsleeve, then the other, in a provocatively graceful movement.

The pressure in his loins increased to a painful level.

Muttering another epithet, Ethan forced his gaze off the enticing curves of her body and finished unbuttoning his shirt. He shrugged free of the wet material, wrapped a towel around his neck, then dropped to a crouch in front of the fireplace. Jabbing at the embers with a poker, he wished to hell that he was back in Roland, out by the waterfall, stuck in a net . . . anywhere but here.

He should have known that staying with Cait wasn't a good idea. Or maybe he had known it and hadn't cared. But after that little display, he wondered how he would survive the torture of sleeping in the same room with her all night.

"I'm finished."

Relief coursed through him when he discovered that Cait's shadow now moved around the cabin. "Me, too." Hellfire, he sounded like a bullfrog.

"No, you're not, you still have your trousers on."

Damn right he did. He wasn't about to take his pants off in his condition. "I figured I'd get a fire going first," he said evasively.

She knelt and took the poker from his hand. "You change. I'll start the fire."

Too late, he thought. She'd started a fire in him almost from the day they'd met.

Even now, she looked soft and clean and so damned appealing that it was all he could do not to drag her down on the floor and have his way with her. She wore a simple sleeveless cotton camisole and tanned doeskin trousers that fit her like a glove. Her hair, loose and flowing around her shoulders, begged for his touch. The wan light from the coals gave her face an ethereal glow.

Ethan shot to his feet. Instantly a sharp pinch ripped down the center of his back, and with a vicious curse he grabbed at the muscle running parallel to his spine.

"Is your back still bothering you?"

He drew in a deep, steady breath and forced a smile. "It's nothing, just a little crick. . . ." Call it pride, call it stubbornness, but he didn't want her getting the idea that he couldn't han-

dle hauling a load of bear meat or a pouncing
tiger. Hell, she did things like that all the time
and he didn't hear her complaining of sore
muscles.

The next thing he knew, Cait was on her feet
and steering him in a circle. "Lie down on the
floor."

"What?"

"Lie down—I'll rub your back."

"Uh, thanks, but I don't think that's such a
good idea—" Especially with Cait's stimulating performance still fresh in his mind. If she
touched him now he'd probably bust a seam.

"Don't be silly. You got hurt helping me. It's
the least I can do."

She pulled on his shoulders before he could
object further, and caught unprepared, Ethan
dropped to his knees with a hiss. A firm push
sent him flat against the floor.

"Besides," she went on, settling herself on
the rise of his rump, "I remember pulling my
back when I put Ginger's cage together. Just
twisted wrong, I guess, but it hurt like hell. I
was down for a week before I could stand up
straight."

She sounded completely unaware of his agony. She whisked the towel off him. Cold air
brushed his skin.

Ethan dragged air into his lungs, trying to
get a grip on the biting soreness. Just when he
thought he had it under control, Cait grabbed
two fistfuls of flesh and muscle—hard.

Ethan nearly came out of his skin. "Ow,
damn, woman!" he cried out in surprise, "that
hurts!"

"Sorry. I didn't expect your muscles to be so tight. Most men get flabby over the winter, but you, you feel strong as a moose."

"Saddles," he croaked, gingerly lowering back down to the floor.

"Saddles?"

"They weigh a lot. Some up to a hundred pounds. Guess lugging them around has some rewards."

Shutting his eyes and gritting his teeth, Ethan braced himself for more torture. To his relief, her hands were gentler as they kneaded the tender area beneath his shoulder blades. Still, each grasp seemed to push the pain into every other nerve in his body. He supposed it was a good thing, though. At least it distracted him from the fact that he had a beautiful woman perched on his backside.

She soon fell into a soothing rhythm. The pain gradually ebbed, and Ethan found himself beginning to relax. A sense of peacefulness seeped through his bloodstream.

He listened to the wind and the rain and the thunder, and Cait's even breathing as she worked the knots out of his tense muscles. Every now and then a snuffle would remind him that Saberjaw was still under the bed.

It was hard to believe that just a short time ago he'd been sitting smack in the midst of the storm raging outside, cold and wet and miserable. Inside the cabin, he felt far removed from the rest of the world, as if only two people existed—him . . . Cait. The crackle of the fire. The smell of roasting pine and warm lamp oil and a faint scent of wet sweet grass.

He couldn't say exactly when the pain ebbed and the pleasure began, it happened so gradually. A subtle lift of pressure from her fingers. Nails dragging with curious gentleness across his shoulders, up his nape, behind his ears.

Ethan's eyes opened wide. He lay with his cheek pressed against the cool, damp floor. A languid warmth spread through him that had nothing to do with the fire a foot away and everything to do with the woman sitting on top of him. Rubbing his shoulders.

Gripping his sides with her thighs.

Making him hard all over again.

He wished he could blame his growing arousal on abstinence, but he knew better. No other woman had the power that Cait did to arouse him with just a look, just a touch.

He tried to just enjoy the attention she paid him, tried to remember why he'd vowed to keep his distance from her, why he couldn't let the sensations she created inside him rule his actions.

But as the lazy exploration of her fingernails along his skin continued, the only thing he could think of was how she'd tasted that day he'd kissed her—like sunsets and summer mist and hope newly born. And how she'd felt beneath him, as if her body had been created solely to fit his. And how she'd looked at him then, and again outside, with undisguised wonder and curiosity and desire.

She leaned forward. Her womanhood rocked against his spine. Full breasts brushed against his scorching skin. "How does that feel?" she asked.

Oh, Gawd A'mighty. . . . "Better," he croaked. But inside he swore that every drop of blood in his body had centered in his loins.

He balled his hands tightly to keep from touching her, closed his eyes to keep from seeing her. It only made matters worse. Clearer somehow. Keener, as his other senses awakened. The smell of her, a seductive storm of rain, wind, fire, and woman. The sound of his heart hammering. The erotic brush of doeskin against his bare sides, the crush of her soft bottom against his.

She made a sound—a sigh, a purr—hell, he couldn't tell. But the last thread of his resistance snapped.

"That's enough," he said gruffly. Rising swiftly to his knees, he felt Cait slide off him. Knowing only that he had to get away from her before he threw her to the ground and took her like a cowpoke off a three-month cattle drive, he shot to his feet. He passed a shaking hand through his hair, released a ragged breath, then grabbed his shirt. Shoving his arms through the sleeves, he didn't give a damn that it was still wet. He couldn't stay here. Storm or not, Cait wasn't safe with him anymore. He needed to get as far away from her as fast as possible before he lost what little control he had left.

Then he made the mistake of looking at her. She stood in front of the fireplace; flames chased across her face. Her cheeks were flushed, her eyes glazed with a desire that rivaled his own.

It didn't make him feel any better to see that she'd been affected, too.

It made him hotter.

"If you don't quit looking at me like that, wildcat, we're both gonna find ourselves in a heap of trouble."

She stared at him for what seemed an eternity. Then, damned if she didn't flick her hair over her shoulder and prop her hand on her hip. "Is that a threat, hunter? Or a promise?"

The saucy invitation had need slamming into Ethan like a thunderclap.

In three swift strides he crossed the cabin and captured Cait in his arms. His mouth swooped down on hers, hard, hungry. She matched his kiss with one so wild and lusty and desperate that the world shattered into a thousand fragments of feeling.

He thrust his tongue into her mouth, seeking more, delving deeper, then withdrawing only to do the same thing over again until his limbs trembled with a bone-melting weakness.

Lightning forked outside the window; sleet and hail came down upon the roof like a thousands bullets. Ethan barely noticed. He knew there were reasons why he shouldn't be giving in to the lust raging inside him, but at this moment he could think of nothing except the feel of Cait in his arms and the sweltering taste of her mouth on his.

Cupping the back of her head in one hand, the soft curve of her bottom in the other, he pulled her so tight against him that it was impossible to tell where he ended and she began. The rigid flesh of his arousal rubbed against her pelvis, her breasts crushed against his ribs. And when Cait arched into him, he thought he'd explode.

He didn't realize he'd started walking backward until the backs of his knees bumped the bed frame. They fell onto the mattress; the bed ropes strained and creaked beneath their combined weight.

Somehow the sound reached deep into his consciousness.

With a strength he didn't know he had, Ethan tore his mouth away and panted, "Wait, Cait, this is insane."

She caught his neck in the crook of her arm and dragged his mouth back down to hers. "No waiting."

He clamped his hands around her arms, forcing her away. "Damn it, listen to me, wildcat."

The urgency in his voice, the earnestness in his eyes, gave Cait pause. His cheeks were taut, his lips drawn tightly, and she wondered how he could have such a firm grip on control when flames were licking through her bloodstream like a forest fire gone wild.

"I want you," he told her in a voice rough and raw. "Have since the first day I saw you. And right this minute I need you so badly that I can hardly stand it. But if you don't want me here, on you, inside you, say it now."

At the words, something gave way inside her. A band loosened around her heart. She had never been needed by anyone but her cats before. Hearing that this gentle hunter, this tender warrior, needed her nearly brought tears to her eyes.

She lifted her fingertips to his whiskered jaw. "I want you here," she kissed his lips. "On me." She kissed the bristly underside of his chin. "Inside me." She kissed his neck. "No waiting," she repeated. She felt as if she'd been waiting her whole life for this moment and she'd be damned if she'd let him deny her now.

She watched the struggle on his face. Hunger warred with honor.

Then, hunger winning, his mouth returned to hers and he kissed her with a fervor that matched her own.

They rolled onto their sides, mouths greedy, hands anxious, limbs tangled.

She cast a startled glance at his face. The firelight behind them cast him in an aura of sparkling gold. His hair was a wild, tawny mane of silk upon her pillow. Rich brown lashes shuttered his eyes. A sheen of sweat glistened on his brow.

Her gaze traveled down the harsh line of his jaw, along the cords of his neck to the gap in fabric covering his chest.

The wet shirt clung so tightly against his skin that it formed around the muscles of his chest, outlining the squared pectorals. She could see the golden hue of his flesh and the dusky circles of his erect nipples beneath the damp material.

She brought her gaze back up to his and found him watching her closely. In his slumberous eyes she saw flecks of green come alive in an amber sunrise, like the forest at dawn.

"I saw you once, beneath the waterfall," she told him in a husky voice she hardly recognized as her own. Keeping her gaze fixed to his, Cait peeled back the edges of his shirt. "I wanted to touch you then, I want to touch you now."

"Oh, God."

The plea—or curse—she didn't know which, barely left his mouth when she spread her hands against the breadth of him. His pupils expanded; he drew in a hiss, then released a groan. A burst of power filled her at the knowledge that she could create sensations in him that he created in her.

With a smile of wicked delight, Cait leaned forward and drew the dusky nipple into her mouth. She felt a shudder rock through his body. His heartbeat clamored against her palm.

His hands shaped themselves against her hips, then slid up beneath the hem of her camisole, blazing a path up her rib cage. The filmy material bunched. The touch of his fingertips against the outer swells sent tingles speeding down her arms and legs.

He bared her breasts, muttered a prayer. . . .

Without warning, she felt herself spinning through the air. Then the thick mattress sank beneath her back and Ethan loomed above her.

The instant his mouth closed over her nipple, a bolt of pleasure ripped through Cait. Crying out, she gripped handfuls of his damp, silky hair in her fists and arched. He pampered one breast, then the other, squeezing them gently together, shaping them, molding them with his hands and his mouth until she thought she'd melt.

She didn't remember him ridding himself of his trousers, barely recalled him shimmying hers down her hips.

He wedged his hand between them. His fingertips caressed the indention of her thigh, toyed with the curls, urged her to open for him. Moist and warm, Cait parted her legs. He touched her then. Cait bucked. The cabin spun.

"Please, Ethan—" she whimpered against his mouth.

She didn't know what she was begging for as she clawed at his back and pulled at his hair. She only knew that she needed him to feed this hunger he'd created inside her, this living beast he'd let loose.

He didn't ask if she'd done this before, and she didn't want to waste words telling him she hadn't. She simply let nature and instinct take over. And when he began to ease himself inside, Cait lifted her hips to receive him.

She felt no fear, no shame, nothing but an aching void and an almost unbearable sense of anticipation. She writhed against him, beyond longing, beyond restless.

He lost all pretense of restraint. With a savage growl, he plunged himself inside her. Cait clutched him tightly. The pressure inside her climbed and her nerves hummed and the sweet length of him filled her, stretched, brought her ever closer to the edge of some unknown vortex.

She chanted his name, afraid and exhilarated at once. He drove harder, faster, into her. And the spasms began. Riding on the sensations taking her higher, Cait dug her nails into his back, clamped her teeth into the salty sweat of his shoulder. And as her heart took wing and her spirit soared, she cried out in sheer bliss. Ethan reared up, and with one last thrust, an animalistic roar reverberated through the cabin at the same time she felt a powerful surge of warmth inside her.

Breathless, blinded, Cait sank back against the pillow and waited for her soul to reconnect to her body.

Trembling, flushed, Ethan lowered onto the bed beside her, his leg draped across hers, one arm flung over her belly. She stared unseeingly at the ceiling while her heartbeat slowed and her breaths became less labored.

As the mist of her mind cleared, Cait became aware of the pop of logs, the steady drum of rain, a sleepy whine from beneath the bed. Ethan's leg was warm and deliciously heavy on hers.

"Cait?"

Lethargically she turned her head to the side and found him staring at her. "What?"

She watched him lick his lips and was surprised at the stirring the sight caused in her belly.

"You haven't . . . this was your first time, wasn't it?"

"Does it matter?"

He rolled onto his back and brought his arm up across his eyes. "Did I hurt you?"

She smiled. "No. Did I hurt you?"

This time he smiled. It made his face look

younger somehow, almost carefree. "I think you left scars on my back."

Feeling reckless and incredibly invincible, she rolled onto his chest and quipped, "I'm the Wild Cat, remember? The Mountain Savage, the Heathen of the Hills."

His arm shifted higher up his brow; his lashes lifted and he met her gaze. "You say that like it means nothing to you."

"Oh, it means something, just not what you might think."

"And what do I think?"

"That it should matter, what people say about me." Cait laid her cheek against his chest, felt the steady throb of his heartbeat against her skin. "It doesn't, though—not any-more."

And as his arm came down around her back and he dragged her close against him, the last thing Cait remembered thinking before she fell asleep was that for the first time in forever, she didn't feel so damn lonely.

Long after Cait fell asleep, Ethan lay wide awake beside her, watching the steady rise and fall of her chest beneath the blanket bound around them.

He tenderly brushed a strand of her long, glossy hair behind her ear.

He eased himself onto the side of the bed and sat there, his hands limp between his knees, his head bowed. What had he done? What had she done to him?

The last thing he'd meant to do when he'd accepted Cait's offer was bed her.

It shouldn't have meant anything.

But it had. Gawd A'mighty, it had.

Slipping quietly off the bed so he wouldn't wake her, he donned his trousers and boots, then reached for his shirt. His hand paused in midair. Beside it, over the back of the chair, lay the rich brown buckskin shirt Cait had given him.

Draping it over his arm, Ethan touched the fancy stitching around the collar, brushed the fine hide. She'd said he'd earned the right to wear a mountain man's clothes.

Bullshit. A mountain man was strong. Wise. Courageous. He was none of those things. If he'd been strong, he'd have resisted her. If he'd been wise, he'd never have accepted her offer to stay in the first place. If he'd been courageous, he wouldn't have felt such bone-chilling fear after being intimate with her.

Ethan pinched his nose and sighed. Why hadn't he just walked out? Of all the women to have bedded, Cait was the most forbidden. So she'd been wild and willing and writhing in his arms, reacting like no other woman had before her. So he'd desired her with every fiber of his being. So she'd made him feel more wanted than he'd ever felt in his life.

That didn't excuse the fact that he'd done what he had done. She'd been untouched. He'd taken that from her, and he had nothing to give her in return.

Nothing, that is, but misery.

He carefully hung the shirt over the back of the chair, picked up his saddlebags, and walked out the door.

Chapter 11

The slide of a rough tongue across the back of Cait's hand roused her from sleep the next morning, a sleep wrought with fantasies beyond any she'd experienced before. Until last night, she'd had nothing to base her dreams on, but after the delight she'd found with Ethan. . . .

With a slow smile and a languid stretch, she rolled onto her side, seeking the embrace of the man who'd kept her warm and snug throughout the night—only to find herself alone in bed, the sheets beside her cold.

Her smile faded. A gnawing uneasiness settled in the pit of her stomach. Cait sat up suddenly, clutching the blanket to her breasts. Even as her gaze darted around the cabin, she knew what she'd find—or wouldn't find. The gear he'd set by the door was gone, the shirt she'd given him remained folded across the chair where she'd put it the night before. There was no sign of his presence, no indication that he'd even been here at all. In fact, if not for the mild tenderness between her thighs, she might have believed the whole night had been an illusion.

Cait swung her legs off the bed. Her eyes burned and her throat clogged with unshed tears. In spite of herself, a sense of abandonment welled up inside her, twisting into an almost unbearable ache. She didn't know what she'd expected from Ethan after the pleasures they'd shared last night, but his leaving before the crack of dawn hadn't occurred to her.

Had she done something to frighten him off? Replaying the events in her mind, she couldn't think of anything she might have done—

It hit her then. As surely as if he'd told her himself, Cait knew why he'd left: he'd gone after the cougar.

"Damn him!" She pounded her fist against her thigh.

And damn herself. For thinking for one minute that he'd come to consider her more important than his almighty hunt. For throwing herself at him, urging him to take her, knowing ... oh, God—she covered her face with her hands—knowing that once the storm had passed, all deals were off.

Cait scraped her tangled hair back from her temples and blinked back the infuriating moisture in her eyes. Well, if that's the way he wanted it, then that's the way he'd get it.

She flipped back the blanket, and ignoring the chill in the room and in her heart, she grabbed her hunting clothes out of the trunk. After dressing, she marched to the fireplace and lifted the hinged lid of a polished wooden box. Within she found a tiny brown bottle. Beside it lay an assortment of darts that could be shot from a blow pipe or rifle, if properly loaded.

She'd not wanted to resort to such drastic measures; the consequences of the tranquilizer were unpredictable and potentially harmful, according to her grandfather's journal, but if this was what she had to do to save Halona and get Ethan Sawyer off her mountain and out of her head, then it was a chance she'd have to take.

The only decision left to make was whom she should use the darts on. The hunter? Or the hunted?

"Billy-boy, I think we've finally been dealt a winning hand," Louis exclaimed, hunkered down beside a set of prints in the moist dirt.

Billy bent low and examined the tracks. "Well, I'll be damned," he breathed. Four indentions, fresh as spit. Hell, the mud hadn't even dried yet. He scanned the surrounding area. The tracks continued along the bank of the creek. "C'mon, Gypsy-man. Let's get that cat before something else goes wrong so we can get home."

This gawddamn hunt should have been over a long time ago. It probably would have been if Sawyer had kept his yella-bellied self out of this one like he'd done three years before. Instead, he'd stuck his grimy hand into every camp from here to the lake and back—stealing traps, erasing traps, throwing weapons into the creek. . . . Christ, it had gotten so bad that he and Louis couldn't even sleep without their

weapons in the bedroll with them for fear that
Sawyer would sneak up on them and steal
them out from under their noses.

Louis still claimed that the savage was responsible for sabotaging their belongings. Billy
knew better. Wild Cat Cait was nothing but a
campfire yarn. Sawyer, though . . . hell, he'd
probably planned to destroy their chances of
capturing the cougar from the beginning.

Billy wished for the umpteenth time that
he'd done the world a favor and blown out
Sawyer's lamp a long time ago. Only the fear
of Josie leaving him after finding out—

Billy came to a quick stop and cocked his
head. "Did ya hear that?"

"What?"

"Listen!"

It came again, the hollow tumble of gravel.
Billy backtracked its path up the side of a
mountain, a smile of malicious delight spread
across his face. "Well, well, take a look up
there."

Louis followed the direction in which he
pointed. "What's he doing up there?"

"Same thing we're doin'." He glanced
swiftly at Louis. "Put that stinkin' thing out
before he smells it."

Louis ground out the cigar under his heel
while Billy propped Ole Chester on top of a
rock.

"Oh, this is just too good to pass up," he
cackled softly, and aimed.

"Wait a minute—"

A sudden jerk on his arm brought the rifle
down.

"What the hell are you doin', Billy?"

He yanked loose from Louis's grip and hissed, "I ain't gonna kill him, just scare the tar out of him."

"You'll scare the damn cat away!"

"If I don't do something, Sawyer's gonna get it first."

"What if you hit him?"

"I won't." But as Billy raised the rifle once more, the thought stole into his mind that if he did happen to hit Sawyer . . . well, hunting accidents happened all the time.

Cait knelt beside the junction of three sets of human prints and one belonging to an adult cat. She easily recognized the mark of Ethan's store-bought boots. Unfortunately, though she could track with a fair amount of skill, she couldn't read the stories the prints told well enough to decide whether the meeting of men had been planned or coincidental.

But a terrible sense of foreboding had her heart tripping and her mind screaming, "Caution!"

Had this been Ethan's intention all along? To wear down her defenses and lead his hunter friends to her canyon?

Sprinting soundlessly, Cait reached the base of the mountain. The impressions split, two sets going up the mountain, two sets veering to the east.

Torn between which pattern to follow—man and cat or man and man—Cait relied on her senses to guide her. She closed her eyes, lifted her nose, perked her ears.

The distant muffle of the falls. The squawk of hawks.

A breeze kicked up, carrying the scent of rain-washed air, damp moss, and . . . she stilled. Frowned. Her nose crinkled. Smoke? Eyes snapping open, Cait scoured the area. Smoke, yes, but tainted with a foul element that reminded her of burning stinkweed.

She'd smelled the odor one time before, but couldn't place where—until her roving gaze lit on a fair head topping a shaggy coat. Recognition hit Cait like a slap. Just then, a second, darker-headed man appeared beside the blond. It was the same fellow who'd boasted of one day finding her—and her cats.

Both crouched behind a rounded rock, clearly lying in wait, hardly distinguishable among the drab terrain. The blond man's rifle trained on something high up the mountainside.

She followed the direction of the rifle. Shadows played a game of tag across the face of the mountainside with rocks in shades of brown and gray. Scraggly grasses and a splash of wildflowers lent a bit of color to the otherwise stark appearance. Darker blotches marked concave indentions in the slope, and a musty odor clung to the surface.

But almost a hundred feet up, Cait glimpsed a painfully familiar figure wearing a worn sheepskin coat and buff-colored trousers navigating a ridge above.

"No," she whispered, shaking her head in denial.

*   *   *

He'd spotted the tracks at the base of a ridge where mammoth-sized rocks made natural stepping stones to heaven.

His heart a battering ram against his chest, Ethan fitted his hand around another rock and pulled himself up to the next level, climbing higher. The wind flared up, perfuming the air with musty earth, tangy pine, and a nip of anticipation.

He'd told himself not to get too hopeful when he'd first seen them; he'd found tracks before that had led either to nowhere or to places he'd rather not have ventured. But spotting another smeared print, and another, he couldn't quell the surge of energy pumping through his blood. After nearly three weeks of searching and tracking and pursuing, it seemed he might finally end this interminable hunt.

And after what had happened between him and Cait, getting the hell off this mountain was the smartest thing he could do.

As he hoisted himself onto a narrow ledge, he tried not to think about what her reaction might have been when she woke up to find him gone. He couldn't see any other way to leave without hurting her, though. Telling her the truth was out of the question. A man didn't tell the woman he'd just bedded that it had been the biggest mistake of his life—especially a woman like Cait, who'd likely chop him up and feed him to her cats.

And he couldn't blame her in the least.

Ethan hardened himself against the seed of shame trying to embed itself under his skin, focused on the prints, forged his way up the steep and jagged incline. No, he didn't want to hurt Cait. But there was so much more at stake than a mountain woman's sensibilities. His sister's future, maybe even her unborn baby's, hung by a thread in the community. His first responsibility must be to her and to making sure that she was safe and secure and happy. Unless he could raise his worth in the eyes of the people, she would continue to suffer for his fall from grace.

The rocks gave way to a narrow ledge about thirty feet from the base. Ethan hoisted himself onto the shelf and paused to catch his breath and scan his surroundings. A prickling sensation crawled along the back of his neck. He glanced up, to his right. And there, on an upper ridge less than fifty feet away, a mountain lion prowled along the narrow ledge.

He lifted his rifle, and as he sighted down the barrel, a picture of his neighbors' faces when they saw him hauling back the killer's carcass appeared in his mind. Amazement first, probably. Then skepticism—how many had voiced their doubts of his skills? Too many to count. But once the astonishment wore off, he hoped they'd finally reexamine their opinions of him. Maybe a few of them would even admit that he wasn't the cowardly traitor they accused him of being.

The sudden crack of a gunshot ripped through the air.

With a jerk of surprise, Ethan dived onto the shelf, flinging his arm up instinctively to shield his head. Rock sprayed around his feet. A beastly scream ripped through the air, followed by an eruption of gunfire.

He whipped around and . . . oh, Jesus. Halfway between him and the base of the mountain, hidden behind a tree on a ridge, stood Cait, her back pressed against the trunk, pumping the rifle in her hands.

Shock clutched his vitals; disbelief stunned his brain. Cait was trying to shoot him?

No sooner did the question pierce his mind than she swung out from behind the tree, but instead of aiming at Ethan, she fired toward the west.

Ethan swung his attention that way and caught sight of Billy and Louis looking as startled as he felt. A split second later, both men turned their aim on the tree Cait hid behind. Bullets plugged the trunk, ripping and scattering the bark while Cait hunched to avoid the flying debris.

In the pause it took them to reload, Cait once again blasted at them.

Ethan shouldered his Spencer. Without understanding why, he shot at Billy and prayed his poor marksmanship would stand him in good stead; he didn't want to have to tell his sister he'd killed her husband. He just wanted to give Cait some cover time to make her getaway.

Suddenly faced with gunfire coming from two different directions, though, Billy jabbed Louis in the arm. Apparently deciding not to chance their own deaths, they skedaddled, hell at their heels.

Smoke and the acrid odor of gunpowder and hot metal rose into the air.

In the thick of it, Ethan saw Cait step out from behind the tree onto the open ridge. Patches of mud and bark stuck to her buckskins, the rifle hung limply from her fingers, twigs and dirt stuck to her hair.

He forgot the cat, forgot Billy and Louis. Cait became the center of his focus, of his relief.

Of his anger.

His blood boiled at the thought of the risk she'd taken. "Are you crazy?" Ethan yelled. The harsh and bitter words packed an additional wallop with the echo resounding through the mountains. "What the hell are you doing out here, getting yourself involved in a bullet fight like some gunslinger in a saloon brawl?"

"I—" She touched the back of her head, a stunned look on her face. "Ethan? I've been hit . . ."

The words hardly registered before Cait began to weave in place. Ethan's heart dropped into his stomach. He vaulted off the ledge, and had just started toward her when he caught a flash of pale gold out of the corner of his left eye.

In horror he saw the mountain lion leap through the air, over the jagged boulders, down the mountainside, onto Cait.

And then she dropped out of sight.

"Cait!"

He scrambled along the rocks and skidded

down the slope, sending a spray of gravel down the ledge. *"Caaait!"*

He reached the ridge she'd been standing on and peered down. His heart stopped.

Chapter 12

The scent of blood was a powerful lure. It brought out the beast in man and animal alike.

Lying on the ledge with the cougar upon her, Cait expected at any moment to feel death take her by the throat. It amazed her that she felt no fear. In the golden eyes of the feline she saw her own reflection. Expectantly pale. Strangely peaceful.

She'd never purposely courted her own death—not consciously, anyway. In fact, all her life she'd rebelled against it, fought against defeat in any form. Self-preservation of body and mind had become a way of life. Sometimes hissing and clawing, other times with a fragile mien of acceptance.

Presently, though, as the very creature she'd sought so desperately to protect stared at her with feral measure, Cait felt nothing but numbness down to the marrow of her bones.

She was conscious of the fact that razor-tipped claws bit into the meat of her shoulders, heard succinctly the monotone growls emanating from low in the animal's throat, became keenly aware of the musky, primitive odor of the cat.

The smell mingled with the metallic scent of her own blood, pooling from her head, seeping into the rocks beneath her. She knew she'd been wounded, understood that she'd been hit by a small spear of fire.

And yet . . . it all seemed so . . . distant. As if the world had narrowed itself down to this moment between herself and Halona.

Cait wanted to speak, to remind the cougar of who she was, to assure her that she meant her no harm. But her tongue had swelled and her throat seemed to have closed off. She could only look into the feline's glowing yellow eyes and wait.

Gradually the mood shifted, became gauzy, like a veil of cloth flapping gently in the breeze. Cait struggled for consciousness as she felt herself plunge into another realm, where a clash of steel rang in her ears and mournful wails blended with cries of rage.

Her breath came in shallow gasps, and the horror of the scene gripped her relentlessly. Red. Black. Blue. Colors swirling, dividing, merging.

Her heartbeat escalated as she felt a sense of being chased. Hunted. She saw herself hiding behind a wall of logs. Heard twin roars of thunder. Black and orange. Tawny gold. Her friends, she dimly realized. Sawtooth and Ginger . . . no Faw Paw in the picture. Puzzling.

A predatory calm, then. A sense of being herded into a pit of blackness, like a box with the walls slowly closing in on her. Suffocating until she thought her lungs would burst.

The vision shifted, became a man of gold. Skin. Hair. A woodsman bearing the scent of saddle soap, so strong she felt it being absorbed into her skin.

And the cougar, Halona . . . surrounded by a sea of green, legs stretching in a bid for freedom. Freedom . . . and peace.

The distortion cleared and Cait found herself once again staring onto Halona's yellow eyes. She didn't understand what had happened. Maybe she'd died for a minute. Maybe she'd experienced one of the sought after visions she'd been told her people coveted. She didn't know.

But she did know, without a shred of doubt, that this cat must remain free. Unharmed. And that Ethan was the key.

A bright glitter of silvery light gripped the edge of her vision. Halona's head whipped to the right, her face twisted into a savage snarl.

In almost surreal motion, Cait turned her head in the same direction, and for the first instant since she'd fallen, she knew raw fear.

On the ledge stood Ethan, her tender lover, her fair warrior, her relentless hunter, the steel barrel of his rifle aimed at Halona.

The lack of sound was deafening. The echo of the shots had long since faded, leaving behind an eerie calm.

Below, on a shelf of rock no more than two feet wide and six feet long, lay Cait. He could barely see her, save for her feet and the tangled mat of her hair.

The mountain lion covered the rest of her.

Ethan blinked. Sweat stung his eyes. He kept the rifle aimed at the cat. His finger curled over the trigger, applied pressure just shy of actually firing. He could hardly distinguish between the brown of Cait's buckskins and the tan of the cat. "Move, you bitch. Give me a clear shot."

As if sensing his desperate fury, the cougar hissed. Penetrating golden eyes stared at him, challenged him.

Every muscle in his body went taut with apprehension. Tension stretched between them like fresh kill. *Shoot, Sawyer!* his instincts screamed. *Take out the beast—it'll all be over. Cait'll be safe, the cat'll be dead. You'll have gotten what you came for.*

He knew he wouldn't get a better chance.

But if he hit, and the bullet went through the cat to Cait . . . or if he missed the cat altogether, and hit Cait. . . .

Damn all the times he'd turn down the chances to hunt or develop sharpshooting skills!

He blinked again. His muscles trembled from holding his position. His finger twitched against the trigger.

Then Cait looked at him, her blue, blue eyes reaching across the distance between them, piercing clear into the core of his soul, imploring.

And one word formed on her lips, silent and

strained, yet it seemed to resound through him like shout.

Please.

"Damn it!" He lowered the gun. His shoulders sagged. "God damn it!"

As if waiting for just that moment, the cat bared her teeth, and with a screamlike "*Reeowwr*," leaped away.

Ethan wasted not a second. He scrambled down the slope and dropped to Cait's side. She lay on her back, her arms raised on either side of her head, her eyes nearly closed. The only thing that had saved her from tumbling further onto the rocks below was the sturdy trunk of a bare-needled pine.

With trembling fingers, Ethan touched Cait's cheek, brought her face around to his view. Her lashes fluttered upward. Pain clouded the blue of her eyes. "Hurts, Ethan."

His glance lit on the dark pool spreading over the gray rock. "I've got to get you to a doctor." His voice quivered with fear and panic.

She licked her chalky lips. "No doctor."

"You need help, Cait, and I don't know what to do."

"If you . . . want to help . . . stop the bleeding."

"I can't see the wound."

"It burns . . . behind my left ear."

He brushed aside her hair and sucked in a breath, hit by the smell of singed hair and burned flesh resulting from the two-inch groove carved into her scalp.

"Pressure," she said, her voice weakening. "Needs pressure."

Spurred to action, Ethan stripped off his shirt and tore several strips off the tail, then wadded the remains. His hands shook as he pressed it against her head. There was so much blood . . . so much damn blood. He glanced at her face, so white. Her eyes, moist and dark with pain, began to drift shut. "Don't go to sleep on me, Cait." He didn't know why it was so important that he keep her awake. "Talk to me."

She blinked. Heavy-lidded, she stared blankly over his shoulder and licked her lips. "About what?"

About what? He didn't know. They didn't understand each other, couldn't begin to agree on anything—most especially that damn cougar! She wanted to save a cat that he wanted dead. She lived life on her terms, while his every action reflected on another. "Tell me what the hell you're doing up here!"

"Looking . . . for Halona." A wan grin. "Found her."

"Is that why you shot at me?"

"I didn't—the pale-haired man. He was . . . aiming at you. Rescued your sorry ass . . . again, hunter."

Ethan's jaw almost hit the dirt. Billy? Billy had shot at him? Did he hate him enough to try and kill him?

He couldn't grasp the fact, but the proof was right here, in blood. In Cait's blood.

"I've got to get you off this ledge," Ethan said, pushing Billy out of his mind for now.

"Cabin," she whispered. "Want to . . . go home."

He knew he needed to get her off this ledge, out of the dirt. But the cabin? Hellfire, it was almost as far away as Roland, and twice as desolate. What was more, Billy and Louis were still somewhere around here. They'd just as soon shoot her as see her, and carry the tale back to every ear in Roland.

Yet how could he deny her? She'd taken a bullet meant for him.

There was no decision to make. If Cait wanted to go home, then he'd take her home.

With one arm under her neck and the other behind her knees, Ethan lifted her into his arms. He couldn't help but cradle her a little closer, his chin against her temple, as he began the trek back to her cabin. She felt so frail. His untamed mountaineer, his fierce wildcat.

After what seemed an eternity, he reached the clearing. Cait's tiger was sprawled on the porch. He lifted his head off his paws. Spotting Ethan, he came to his feet in a single fluid movement.

Though he couldn't help but remember past encounters with Cait's pet, Ethan's stride never faltered as the animal loped toward him. "Get the hell out of my way, you flea-bitten menace, or I'll turn you into a rug." He was in no mood to battle the oversized furball. Cait needed help, and he'd be damned if he would let the striped beast stop him from getting her into the cabin.

The tiger seemed to understand that something was wrong. He crept forward and sniffed

Cait's hand, hanging limply, then backed off with a deep whine.

Inside the cabin, Ethan gently laid Cait on her bed—the same bed where just a few short hours ago he'd found pleasure beyond belief. The images came back to him in one fell swoop. Tangled bodies and slick skin and passion more powerful than he'd thought possible.

Jerking himself from the memory, he searched Cait's trunk, bringing out shears, soap, and cotton cloth. He filled the pitcher with rain from the rain barrel, and by a stroke of luck, a half-empty jug of liquor that smelled so lethal it almost took the skin off his nose.

Cait remained unconscious, and so still that if not for the regular rise and fall of her breasts, he'd have thought her dead.

After piling the items on the keg, he cut the silky sable strands away from the gouge and gently bathed the area with soapy water. She moaned at his touch, and Ethan reveled in the sound, for it let him know she was still coherent enough to feel pain. Over and over again he soaked the cloth and washed the blood, until the water in the basin turned a dull red.

Once he got the wound clean, he realized that in spite of the frightful amount of blood, she hadn't suffered a life-threatening injury. But it struck him—hard—that she'd escaped death literally by inches.

He'd just finished wrapping a long strip of linen around her head when Cait's sooty lashes fluttered open.

"Ethan?"

Tenderness spread through his chest at the

sound of his name on her lips. He brushed her hair off her brow with his palm. "I'm here."

"My cats . . . they'll need to eat. . . ."

Ethan glanced down at Sawblade. The tiger lifted his head, looked at Ethan, and blinked. Then he rested his head back down on his paws. In spite of himself, Ethan couldn't help but admire the animal's loyalty to his mistress. Sharptooth might be an aggravation he could do without, but to the animal's credit, he hadn't budged once from the spot on the floor beside Cait's bed.

Shifting his attention back to Cait, he promised, "Don't worry, I'll take care of them."

Assured, she drifted off into sleep once more.

He tied the linen into a knot, then went to clean up the mess accumulating on the keg. His hand hovered over the shank of hair he'd cut from around Cait's wound. Unable to bear the thought of throwing away her hair, he gathered up the small mass as if it were made of spun glass. He rinsed out the blood, then tied it with a rawhide strip. If he never had anything else of Cait's, he'd have this one keepsake of their time together.

After dumping the soiled water and putting away all the items, Ethan pulled up a chair to her bedside and sat watching her, his hands clasped between the spread of his knees. Though a frown marred her otherwise flawless brow, she seemed to be resting peacefully.

He absently dragged the soft lock between his fingers, as images of her in different stages flashed through his mind. Fearless Cait. Vul-

nerable Cait. Passionate Cait. Reckless Cait. So
many people wrapped up in such a little body.

A lump rose in his throat. He couldn't identify the emotion. Deeper than sorrow, more intense than fear, what he felt for her was unlike
anything he'd ever felt for anyone before. The
only thing he could say with absolute certainty
was that he never felt more alive than in the
weeks since he'd been caught in her snare, and
the thought of losing her left a gaping hole in
his chest.

Ethan gripped the lock tight in his fist. A
shudder shook him at the image of the cougar
atop her. She might have taken the bullet because of him, but that cat was just as responsible, for if it hadn't been attacking the cattle,
none of this would have happened in the first
place.

Well, there'd be no more mercy on his part.
Once he was assured of Cait's recovery, he'd
track down that killer and see it destroyed once
and for all.

"Damn it, damn it, damn it!" Billy whipped
Ole Chester to the ground while his curse grew
in volume and color. "It ain't good for nothin'
but the melting pot anymore."

"Which is where this hunt has gone, thanks
to you."

Billy swung around to glare at Louis, who
knelt by the creek, splashing water on his arm
where a stray bullet had creased the flesh. "I
can't help it my rifle jammed."

"That ain't what I'm talking about and you

know it. Christ, Billy, what were thinking back there?"

He jabbed a warning finger toward his partner. "Leave off, Gypsy-man."

Louis sprang to his feet and fisted his hands. Pink water streamed down his wounded arm. "The hell I will. We're supposed to be after the cat, not Sawyer!"

"If I hadn't shot at him, he would've gotten that cat," Billy yelled back.

"He couldn't hit a target pasted to the mouth of the barrel." Louis angrily twisted his kerchief around his arm, all the while marching toward the horses.

"Where are *you* going?" Billy had just about enough of everyone turning on him.

"I ain't gonna be no part of killin' a man!" Louis hissed.

"I wasn't tryin' to kill him—"

"Bullshit! I saw where you were aimin'. If he hadn't ducked, you would've plowed lead smack between his eyes!"

The truth of Louis's words crashed into Billy like a falling boulder, exploding through his mind, stealing his breath. Suddenly it seemed like too much effort to keep standing.

"Billy, I don't know what's been going on in your head lately, but you're startin' to scare me."

Hell, he was startin' to scare himself.

He dropped to a crouch beside the creek and plunged his hands into the water. They were shaking so bad he spilled more than he cupped.

Always before he'd kept a tight grip on his

rage toward Ethan. But today . . . the realization that he could have easily picked the man off with one shot rattle the blazes out of him. As many times as he'd imagined killing his brother-in-law, he'd never really thought himself capable of doing it.

And he'd never thought he really wanted Ethan dead.

Billy pressed water on his hot face, trying to calm the tremors. He blotted his skin with his sleeve. "You think he knows it was us?" Gawd, if Sawyer had seen them . . . and if he told Josie. . . .

Louis plowed his hands through his short hair and started to pace in front of the horses. "I don't know. Once the shootin' started everything else happened so fast. And that second gun—I bet it was Wild Cat Cait!"

Billy arced his head impatiently. "Gawd damn it, Louis, I ain't in any mood to hear that crap now."

"It was her, I'm tellin' ya. Tooley said she had hair long enough to lasso the moon, and from the length of the braid I saw—"

"You can't see something that ain't real!"

"Then who was shooting at us? Those bullets were real!"

Billy couldn't argue that. Christ, the blasts still rang in his ears. One had popped Louis in the arm. And when his gun jammed, leaving them sittin' there like ducks. . . .

A bullet could've hit him just as easily. He'd never see Josie again. Never hold his baby. . . .

"Look, Bill," Louis sighed. "Maybe we oughta just call this hunt quits."

Billy's head snapped up. "I ain't quittin'."

"We'll find the money for your kitchen some other way."

"I ain't quittin'. We're this close to gettin' that cat. All we gotta do is go back and pick up the trail—"

"And then what? We're almost out of ammo, and if Sawyer's got Cait on his side, we might as well throw in our cards. For all we know, the two of them could be huntin' us now."

"Well, then, you'd have found your legend," Billy said through clenched teeth.

"Not this way—"

"I want that cat, Gypsy-man. If we quit now, Sawyer wins."

"*What* does he win?" Louis asked, exasperated.

Billy's chin dropped to his chest. The back of his eyes burned as he swallowed the thick lump in his throat. "Josie."

"If we go back up there now, we ain't comin' back down. Do you know what Cait does to her enemies? She tears off their scalps with her fingernails, then leaves the rest of them for her cats. What will Josie do then? What's she gonna win if an Injun leaves her a widow?" Louis jammed a cigar between his teeth.

Billy blinked back the sudden flare of memories that Louis's remark conjured. Still, they pushed at this mind. Ramming, ramming, ramming. His vision started to fade. A blackness crept in. He clamped his head in his hands as if to shield it from the encroaching madness.

Josie.

He called up an image of his wife's face. He

needed to see her. She'd always been the one sane link in a world teetering on insanity. She appeared in his mind. Instant calm. Soothing, making the noise and the blood fade far away until they were once again just distant images he could safely lock out of his mind.

Gradually his surroundings began to shift into focus. The rush of the creek. The smell of Louis's cigar. The whinny of a horse nearby.

"All right, we'll go back to Roland and restock." They could always come back. He *would* come back. But right now, he had to get out of here, before he slipped over the edge of no return.

Chapter 13

Scorching pinpricks of pain at the side of her head hit Cait first thing when she awoke. She brought her hand up to the spot behind her ear with a moan. Her palm encountered a wad of cloth held in place by a fabric band circling her brow and knotted at her nape.

God, she felt like she'd been creased by a brimstone.

Or a bullet.

The events leading up to the moment fell into place. The hunters, the cougar, Ethan's face just before he'd lifted her against him.

The rest fell into a black void.

Cautiously rolling her head to the side, Cait gave her surroundings a sweeping glance. Two lamps burned low, filling the room with the odor of oil and burning wick, and shed a mellow glow upon the sparse but sturdy wooden furniture. A tree stump table, two ladder-back chairs, a cabinet holding a mismatched washbasin and pitcher set. Cait recognized the speckled tin dishes on the shelves along the walls, the weapons racked above the fireplace, a dream catcher above her bed, given to her by her friend Iron Mary at the trading post.

Obviously Ethan had brought her back to the cabin. And night had fallen.

But how many? How long had she been asleep?

And most important, where *was* everybody? She sure as hell hadn't expected Ethan to stick around, but Sawtooth would never stray far, especially with her hurt.

A sense of foreboding made her skin prickle and her heart race. Cait told herself not to panic. The cat was around here somewhere.

But the longer she lay there waiting for someone to show up, and the louder the quiet came, save for the popping of pine logs in the fireplace, the less assured she felt.

What if Ethan had decided to take advantage of her unconsciousness to slay her cats? To take their lifeless bodies back to Roland and collect the bounty?

She brought her legs over the side of the bed and sat up. The cabin spun. Nausea rolled in her stomach. Her limbs trembled uncontrollably. Cursing her weakened state, Cait braced her hands on the mattress, closed her eyes, and paused until the effects subsided.

Then, drawing in a deep, bracing breath, she pushed off the bed and shuffled to the door. It had been left open, and a gentle breeze ruffled the limp hair around her face. The flutelike notes of insects crescendoed, then waned in a repeated and deceptively peaceful rhythm.

Her legs shook as she stepped onto the

porch, down the step, onto even ground. She had to stop twice to gather her strength, but finally made it to the quad gate.

The latch lifted silently beneath her touch. The gate swung open.

A rumble of soft, masculine laughter brought her to a surprised halt. In a circle of lantern light near Ginger's cage, Cait made out Ethan's familiar form crouching in front of Sawtooth and Ginger. Cait closed the gate behind her and leaned against it, unable to stop the knee-buckling relief flooding through her.

As she watched Ethan hand-feed Ginger bits of meat, the lingering dregs of panic dissipated. Beside Ginger sat Sawtooth, licking his chops, patiently waiting for his treat.

It was a sweet and unexpected sight, yet all Cait could focus on was the fact that Ethan had stayed. He hadn't harmed her cats. And the longer she observed him, the sillier she felt for thinking him capable of doing either when he'd clearly shown her—on several occasions—that he wasn't a mercenary killer, but a protector. Even Sawtooth and Ginger, with their uncanny feline intuition, seemed confident that he wasn't a threat to them.

As if to prove that point further, Sawtooth planted a paw on Ethan's shoulder.

"Looks like you've made a friend for life," she remarked softly.

Ethan jumped with a curse. Ginger dashed into the darkness, tail tucked between her legs. Sawtooth jerked his head up in startlement, then loped to her side and licked her hand. Cait stroked his ear but kept her eyes on Ethan.

"What are you doing out here, wildcat?" he demanded gruffly, even as swift, long-legged strides carried him toward her. Reaching her side, he wrapped a supporting arm around her waist.

Cait fought the urge to sink against him. She'd let him get close enough once to hurt her; she couldn't afford to repeat the mistake.

And yet the woodsy scent of him was so overwhelmingly comforting, the strength of his arms so beckoning. She lost the battle and leaned against his chest. "I needed to check on the cats."

"They're fine," he said, his arm tightening around her, his cheek resting against the top of her head. "Me and Bandsaw already fed them and cleaned the cages."

"Sawtooth—and I can see that." Glancing up, she added, "Frankly, I'm surprised to see you."

"I couldn't leave until I knew you'd be okay."

In spite of herself, the confession touched Cait. She took note of the tiny lines extending from the corners of eyes that looked as weary as his posture. His clothes, she noted, were also rumpled and streaked with dirt. She suspected he hadn't changed since the bullet had downed her, what . . . one, two days ago? "How long have I been sleeping?" she finally managed to ask.

"All day." He brushed her hair off her brow in a gesture of concern that had her heart stammering. "How are you feeling?"

"Never better," she fibbed.

"You're a lousy liar, Caitlin Perry."

Though his smile softened the words, she detected dark shadows behind the bright amber of his eyes. She stared at him in speechless confusion. Had he really been worried about her? Given all the strife between them, she would have thought he'd be glad she was in no condition to cause him grief—for now, anyway.

"Now, tell me the truth, how are you feeling?"

Lowering her lashes in chagrin, she admitted, "A little light-headed, I suppose." Cait had the sneaking suspicion that her injury wasn't the cause so much as Ethan's nearness.

His lips clamped together with displeasure. "I knew it was too soon for you to be out of bed."

Cait gasped and her arm shot around his neck as he swept her into his arms. The grim set of his jaw persuaded her not to argue.

Even if she could.

As he carried her out of the quad, Cait became acutely aware of the muscles flexing beneath her hand, the friction of his chest against the side of her breast. And her mind clogged with images she'd tried so desperately to forget, of him walking beneath the waterfall, and later of him laying atop her, her hands spanning the breadth of his chest.

Sensations she'd determinedly banked flared to life once more, bringing a rise of heat to Cait's cheeks. She told herself it was because she was helpless and vulnerable in a way she had never been before, and in no condition to brace herself against Ethan's touch.

He angled them through the cabin's doorway. Sawtooth followed, taking up position a few feet behind Ethan as he peeled back the blanket and set her on the bed. Reluctantly, she unwound her arms from his neck, but to her relief, Ethan didn't move away. Instead, he fussed and fidgeted with the bedding, tucking her feet beneath the blanket, folding it under her hands, plumping her pillow.

Had it really been just yesterday that he'd walked out on her? Stolen away at daybreak without any explanation?

A sudden stinging at the back of her eyes shamed Cait. "Why are you doing this?" she whispered in confusion.

His hands stilled. "What?"

"Taking care of me."

"I don't see anyone else around to do it."

There never had been, she thought. "That's because I don't *need* anyone around."

He fixed a steady gaze on her. "Right now you need me. And I'm not leaving until I know you'll be okay, so you might as well get used to it. Now, are you hungry?" he asked, pulling away. "I made a venison stew earlier. It'll just take few minutes to warm."

Cait hesitated a moment, then nodded. Food did actually sound appealing. She didn't realize she was even hungry until he mentioned it.

He wandered to the fireplace and crouched before the hearth. She stared at the curve of his back as he added logs to the ashy mound beneath a cast-iron kettle. His shirt pulled taut across his broad shoulders, his trousers hugged his thighs.

In spite of everything that kept going wrong between them, it felt so right having him here.

She just didn't understand it, this hold he had on her, this irrational attraction she had for him. But she owed him her life—and Halona's. She swallowed, then whispered, "Thank you."

He twisted at the waist to face her. "For what?"

"For not pulling the trigger."

His jaw tightened, and he turned back to the fire. "I don't want to get into this with you again, Cait."

"But don't you see? You aren't like them. You didn't kill Halona. You had the chance and you didn't shoot."

"I told you, I'm not a skilled marksman. I didn't want to miss and hit you."

"I don't think it's that simple—"

He sprang to his feet and flung the poker to the hearth, where it hit the stones with a clatter. "It *is* that simple, God damn it!" He scraped his hair back with his fingers. "As soon as I know you're going to be okay, I'm going back out there to track that cougar."

"For what purpose?"

"That cat could have killed you."

"She didn't, though!"

"But she could have. I am not willing to take the chance of something like that happening again—not to you, not to anyone else. It has got to be destroyed, Cait, why can't you accept that?"

Pinching her lips together, quelling the tears that burned behind her lids, Cait rolled onto her back and stared at the rough-hewn logs that made up the frame of the roof. He would never understand what had passed between her and Halona, never understand her connection to the cat; never understand why it was so important that the animal remain free and untouched.

If she told Ethan how afraid she was of being imprisoned again, he'd probably think she'd gone mad. After all, how did making sure a wild mountain lion remained free ensure her own independence?

She didn't know how to explain it, nor was she sure she wanted to try, especially to Ethan. He had a complex fascination and disdain for all that she was, and all that she believed, and it both saddened and infuriated her that he couldn't . . . or wouldn't . . . look below the surface of any issue.

But neither could she let the matter drop. "So everything that poses a danger must be destroyed?" she asked, wanting to understand his logic, needing to find that one chink in his resolve that she could use to change his mind.

He sighed. "What other choice *is* there? And don't tell me to move it—I refuse to shift the problem onto someone else."

"Then accept it. Learn from it. Appreciate the beauty and uniqueness while respecting the fact it can also cause you great pain if you aren't careful."

Several moments passed before he asked, "Are we still talking about that cougar?"

His question compelled her to look at him.

His brows drew low in puzzlement, and she saw her own turmoil reflected in his eyes. "I don't know—*are* we?"

The sound of even breathing coming from the bed nearby should have consoled Ethan.

It tortured him instead.

After tossing and turning for more than half the night, he finally flipped the blanket away from him, rolled off the pallet he'd made in front of the fireplace, and shoved his feet into his boots. There was no way he could get any sleep in this room, not with Cait so close. He could hardly see her, but he didn't need to. Her features were ingrained in his memory, the sound of her voice an echo in his soul. And the walls seemed made of her very scent—wild winds and sweet grass and an arousing fragrance that belonged to her alone.

A combination of all three attacked his senses until he knew if he didn't get away from her now, he'd crawl right into the bed with her, and the hell with the injury.

He slipped out the door on silent feet, not wanting to disturb her, yet needing to escape the heat of the cabin. But it followed him outside, into the predawn air. Even the blast of wind that ripped through his clothes didn't cool him.

He braced his hands on an intact part of the railing and bowed his head, cursing this unquenchable lust he'd developed for her. One time should've gotten her out of his system. It didn't. If anything, he wanted her more.

Was this to be his punishment, then? A lifetime sentence of wanting a woman he could never have?

He'd accepted that the first time had been a mistake, one he'd vowed not to repeat. A second time would be courting disaster. Even if there wasn't so much standing between them, Cait wouldn't want him anyway, especially not after their latest quarrel. She hadn't said more than two words to him since the argument.

Hellfire, he should've just kept his mouth shut about the cougar. Anytime they so much as treaded near the subject, they clashed; she defended the animal, and for the life of him he couldn't understand why.

But railing at her because he'd let it get away did no good. Nor did it ease the guilt he felt for not protecting her from Billy's bullet—a bullet that never would have been shot had it not been for him, caused by a hatred because of something he had done . . . involving an Indian woman he had found.

Funny how life came full circle. He might have laughed at the irony if it wasn't so damned pitiful.

Sighing heavily, Ethan lifted his face to the wind and stared at the dark outline of the mountain looming before him. Whereas most of the snow had melted on the ground, a cap of white still clung to the peak.

Ah, Gawd. What was he going to do?

His head told him to leave. Get out before somehow, someone learned what he had done, and that he was here. He'd gotten her back to the cabin, she was a bit sluggish, but surely she'd be fine. . . .

His conscience, though, told him to stay. She could fall or faint. And how was she supposed to eat, in her weak condition? She could hardly stand on her own feet without weaving, much less provide for herself.

With another heavy sigh, he knew that debating the issue was a waste of time. There just wasn't anything to debate. He could no more leave Cait here alone and injured than he could have left that Flathead woman on the side of the road, raging with fever. No matter what he risked, he just couldn't bring himself to abandon a woman in need.

Recalling the way Cait had practically inhaled the stew last evening, he decided that healthy meals would give her a good start down the road to recovery. He stepped off the porch and entered the quad, then headed for the cold shed. The faster she got well, the sooner he could leave, and the better off they'd both be.

In the meantime, he'd just have to call a truce with Cait, that's all. If she brought up the cougar, he'd steer them onto another subject.

Same thing with discussions about her heritage—another touchy topic best avoided.

As for the attraction he felt for her? Hellfire, that was the most complicated thing of all, but he decided the only way to contain himself was to keep his distance from her.

No matter *how* tempting she was.

Chapter 14

Ethan reentered the cabin with a slab of meat from the cold shed only to find his newfound resolve tested to the limits.

Wearing a cotton nightgown, Cait stood beside the bed with her back turned to him. A beam of sunshine pouring through the open door touched on her like a halo, and the provocative view of her figure beneath the flimsy fabric had his mouth going dry and his palms growing damp. Flaring hips, shapely legs, dainty feet peeking out from under the plain hem.

What he couldn't see clearly his memory provided in tormenting detail. Not just by sight, but by feel and smell and taste. Supple silk beneath his hands, the scent of sweet grass and velvet in his nose, the flavor of warm honey and hot desire in his mouth.

Ethan's lids slammed shut. Hellfire. So much for his determination not to let Cait tempt him.

The instant and powerful reaction to the sight of her had him wavering between sweeping her into his arms and reliving that night, and walking right back out the door and diving into the nearest snowbank.

He did neither. Instead, he mustered all his composure and strode to the table where two speckled tin cups waited for the coffee he smelled perking over the fire. "You're running low on meat."

"I know, I need to go hunting."

Startled that she'd even consider an outing so soon after her injury, Ethan swung around and caught her shuffling on wobbly legs toward the clothes trunk. "You aren't going anywhere. I'll go out tomorrow morning and see what I can scare up."

"In lion prides, the female provides the meat," she said without looking at him.

"We aren't lions."

"Then your ass is going to starve," she retorted.

He arched a brow at the caustic jab at his hunting skills. "Need I remind you who killed a grizzly bear?"

She peered at him over her shoulder, one brow arched. "I seem to recall something about dumb luck?"

Ethan took peculiar comfort that Cait's keen-edged wit hadn't suffered from her ordeal, but it didn't change the fact that she could hardly walk without toppling over, much less do something as strenuous as stalk game. He plopped the meat down on the table and stated, "I will do the hunting."

"Fine," she gave in with a gusty breath.

He didn't have much time to take pleasure in his victory. "*Now* what do you think you're doing?'' he demanded, as she pulled out a clean tunic and leggings.

"My cats need tending."

No sooner did she lay the clothing on the bed than Ethan marched across the room, swiped them into his arms, and packed them back into the trunk. "I'll see that done, too. You aren't going anywhere except back in that bed. Hell, Cait, you took a bullet that might have killed you if you weren't—"

"A legend?" she sneered. "I still have eight lives left, you know."

"If you weren't as strong and fit as you are. But what you need is a lot of rest and nourishment."

"If I rest anymore, I'll petrify," Cait snapped. "Besides, what do you know about taking care of these animals?"

"Not a thing, but you'll tell me what to do—" He paused suddenly and wagged a finger at her. "Don't look at me like that. Roll your eyes all you want but you are not getting out of that bed until you get some color back in your cheeks."

"But I'm bored silly! I'm not used to sitting around doing nothing."

He studied her for several long moments. In truth he couldn't blame her for being irritable. For a woman used to doing for herself, the inactivity had to chafe. He knew how crazy it drove him to be idle.

"Tell you what," he relented with a sigh, "I'll put a chair outside for you to sit in so you can watch me take care of the cats. But you have to promise that you'll tell me when you get tired."

"I am not an—" she stopped the biting words in mid-sentence. Her features froze. Then those sooty lashes of hers fell over her eyes as she made her way to the side of the bed and sank onto the mattress. "Maybe you're right . . . I *am* still feeling a little weak."

Ethan's eyes narrowed. Something had flickered in her eyes just before her lashes dropped, shuttering her thoughts. He folded his arms over his chest and regarded her suspiciously.

She glanced at him with almost believable innocence. "What? You win . . . isn't that what you wanted?"

"I'm just trying to figure out why you've given in so easily."

She grimaced but otherwise ignored the comment. "Go outside so I can get dressed."

A short time later, Cait sat on a blanket in the center of the quad, teasing Sawtooth with a stuffed sock while Ethan boldly strode toward Ginger's pen.

He really could be an arrogant ass sometimes, she decided, watching him. Imagine, threatening to tie her to a tree if she dared move from this spot! Hell, she'd been taking care of herself long before he'd come along, and would continue to long after he left—as he surely would.

But hopefully, not for a few more days.

She told herself that her reasons for playing helpless were purely for Halona's sake. As high-handed as Ethan got now and then, he could also be so damned gentle. She'd seen firsthand his patience with the cats, the way he communicated with them, put them at ease with a soothing touch and a calming voice.

That kindness didn't stop at the cats, though; he treated her the same way. In fact, the memory of his remark "I couldn't leave until I knew you were okay" had been what had hatched the plan being carried out now.

Yes, it was sneaky; yes, it was dishonest. Yet Cait had no doubt that as long as Ethan thought she needed him, he'd stay with her. Though she hadn't yet regained her full strength, neither was she as feeble as she wanted him to believe. But if deceiving him could buy her more time to appeal to his compassion, then she'd do it. At the very least, it would mean one less hunter searching for Halona. Anything that might mean one more day of freedom for the mountain lion—even swallowing her hard-won independence—was well worth the sacrifice.

Cait pulled her shawl tighter around her shoulders and watched Ethan kneel before the open door of Ginger's cage to coax her out into the quad.

It didn't surprise her when Sawtooth abandoned the stuffed sock he'd been playing with, loped toward Ethan, and butted his head against his broad shoulder. One thing she'd learned in their years together was that Sawtooth hated not being the center of attention.

"Go away, you overgrown tomcat," Ethan told him, batting him away.

Oh, the man was really naive if he thought

Sawtooth would obey, Cait thought, shaking her head in amusement. Well, he'd figure out his mistake soon enough.

He did, too, the minute Sawtooth clamped his teeth onto Ethan's sleeve and tugged. Ethan glared at him. Cait giggled.

"Let go."

Sawtooth growled and flung his head back and forth, the fabric still secure between his teeth.

Ethan looked to Cait for help.

She grinned and shrugged. "You're on your own. And good luck. When Sawtooth wants to play, he doesn't ask if you want to play, too."

A peal of laughter escaped Cait when Ethan bared his teeth at the tiger and growled. For just a moment, Sawtooth was stunned enough to release his grip. It didn't last. Sawtooth dashed a few yards away and lowered the front of his body. Hind end in the air, head ducked, his tail swishing back and forth, he prepared for attack.

"Oh, no." Cait gave a humor-laced gasp when Ethan also dropped to a crouch. The fool! Didn't he realize he'd just accepted Sawtooth's challenge? She cupped her hands on either side of her mouth and hollered, "Ethan, brace yourself, he's going to pounce!"

The warning was barely issued when, with a bone-quaking roar, Sawtooth took off toward Ethan. Typically, Ethan put up an arm to shield himself as the cat's weight drove him into the ground.

Soon the two were rolling around in the dirt, wrestling like old pals, to Cait's utter delight.

She had no fear that Sawtooth would hurt Ethan; the tiger's ears remained high and round, his tail loose and fluid, the hair on his back relaxed. If Ethan were in any danger, the signs would have been completely the opposite. No, Sawtooth, still a cub at heart, had simply found himself a playmate—and Ethan, whether he knew it or not, had gained himself a loyal friend.

Cait hoped that the time he spent here taking care of the animals in her stead would go a long way toward convincing him that they had just as much to offer as humans, and deserved the chance to prove it.

She couldn't say how long the two wrassled, but she found herself both enamored by the power of the two males in her midst, and at the same time, tickled blue at their antics.

By the time they broke away from each other, Cait's stomach hurt and her head throbbed from laughing so hard. With a mellow roar that clearly said, "I've had enough," Sawtooth strolled proudly up to her and rubbed himself against her thigh. Cait rubbed and patted his dusty coat. "Did you have fun, pal? Ethan's more your size than I am, huh?"

Ruffling the dirt out of his hair, Ethan approached them. "You were a lot of help."

"You were doing just fine on your own," she chuckled, lifting her gaze to his. The same thrill that glowed in her tiger's eyes, lingered in Ethan's, and Cait realized that contrary to his grumbling, he'd enjoyed the rough-romping as much as Sawtooth. "Just one thing—when he makes to jump up on you, shift one of your feet back and brace yourself for his weight. It lets him know that you're the one in charge."

"I'll keep that in mind," he replied with a lopsided smile.

His gruff affection for Sawtooth had already begun to wear down Cait's defenses, but the combination of that charming grin and his tousled appearance had a devastating effect on her senses. Warmth spread through her belly, her heart tripped over beats, her fingers tingled.

Her contentment dimmed. Yesterday she hadn't been able to guard her emotions, much to her dismay. A combination of a weak constitution and Ethan's unexpected, even unwelcome, presence in her life had left her floundering.

But today. . . .

If she wasn't careful, Cait feared she'd wind up falling for him all over again.

A movement at the edge of her vision pulled her attention behind Ethan. Ginger stood in front of her cage, her tail flipping from side to side, while Sawtooth circled her in a ritual she recognized instantly.

"Oh, no."

"What?"

"Put Ginger back in her pen," Cait urged him.

"I thought you wanted her wandering around the quad."

"I did, but that was before—Sawtooth is . . . and she's—" Cait felt her cheeks burn. Breeding had never bothered her before, but then, that was before she'd discovered all the . . . details. Before she'd learned that so many sensations came alive.

Cait shook her head and chided herself for her sudden timidity. Taking a deep breath, she told Ethan matter-of-factly, "He's caught her scent and I don't want him mating with her."

"Ahhh. . . ." Without another word, he gently herded Ginger back into her pen. Sawtooth tried to follow but Ethan's quick reflexes shut him out of the cage before he could slip inside. Even then, Sawtooth paced around the cage, whining and roaring his frustration.

Ethan knelt beside him, said something that Cait couldn't hear, then left him with what looked like a consoling pat to the withers.

Rising, Cait met Ethan halfway across the quad. "She'll need to be kept away from him for the next week or so," Cait said, as they strolled toward Faw Paw's cage. "She can exercise in the quad, but he must be kept in the house, and when he's in the quad, she needs to stay in her cage."

"What would happen if they did . . . ah, breed together."

"I suppose they'd have ligers," Cait quipped.

"Or tigions." He grinned. His eyes crinkled at the corners.

"Joking aside, I don't think it would hurt her. But after the abuse she suffered, especially to her hip, it isn't a chance I'm willing to take. If she couldn't deliver, it could kill her or the unborn cubs—or both."

They reached Faw Paw's cage. Cait peered through the slats and spotted the cougar limping toward a pile of straw in the far corner. A telltale trail of white dragged behind his hind leg. "Damn, he's chewed off his bandages again."

Though she'd intended only to supervise while Ethan fed the cougar, the absence of Faw Paw's splint forced a slight change in plans.

Gesturing to the blanket where she'd left her knapsack, Cait bade Ethan, "Fetch that pack for me, will you?"

A few seconds later she flipped back the flap of the pack he brought her and fished for the muzzle and a pair of gloves. "Take off your coat and put the gloves on, then rub the scent of them onto your shirt. He's used to me, he isn't used to you; the gloves will help." One thing Cait never forgot was that as tame as the animals appeared, they'd all been born wild. Every dealing with them required certain precautions, with Faw Paw more so than the others.

When Ethan didn't reply, Cait stole a glance at him. There was a hardening to his features that gave her an uneasy feeling. "Ethan?"

He shook his head and handed back the gloves. "I can't go in there."

"You won't be alone, I'll be with you. Just stay inside the doorway and don't do anything to alarm him."

"It's not that, it's—" He impaled her with a frigid gaze. "How the hell can you even *consider* helping him, after what happened to you?"

For a moment Cait was too stunned to speak. Not just by the coldness in his eyes, but by the venom of his words. "Are you suggesting I turn my back on him?"

The tightening of his jaw gave her his answer.

"Ethan, if he doesn't have that splint around his leg, he'll reinjure it, and all the work I've done to heal him up till now will have been for nothing. But I can't go in there by myself. If he gets rambunctious, I won't have the strength to control him." The admission cost Cait dearly. She'd spent the last six years proving to herself how capable she could be, and for the second time in as many days, she found herself relying on someone else. And not just any someone, but a man who'd declared himself her foe. A man she trusted with her secrets.

At his continued silence, Cait touched his cheek, brought his gaze around to hers. Searching his eyes, she noticed shadows lurking in the amber-hued depths and suspected that his reluctance stemmed from a deeper, more personal source than yesterday's brush with Halona. "Ethan, don't make him pay for something he didn't do. He's suffered enough already—all these animals have."

She could almost hear time ticking by in the silence that followed. Indecision played on the harsh lines of his face.

She'd just about given up on him agreeing when he pressed his lips together in a firm line and nodded shortly.

The emotion that gripped her heart and spread through her chest was so powerful that tears sprang to her eyes. Whether he had changed his views for the sake of the cougar, or whether he'd done so for her, touched Cait beyond words. Blinking away the mist blurring her vision, she rose up on her tiptoes and pressed a soft, grateful kiss to his mouth, then smiled brilliantly at him and whispered, "You know, hunter, I think there's hope for you yet."

She left him standing there, looking stunned and mystified, and entered the cage.

A hiss from within slapped Cait with a moment's doubt. She paused in the doorway. After all that persuading, had she made the wrong choice? Ethan knew so little about the animals, and Faw Paw could be highly unpredictable.

"Gawd A'mighty, how do I let you talk me into these things . . . ?" Ethan muttered, stepping into the pen behind her.

The sound of his voice jarred her from her thoughts. She shook her head. No, she couldn't second-guess herself. He had a special gift with the cats that she'd not seen in any human before; if not for that, she wouldn't even have considered letting him go inside the cage. Besides, she didn't expect him to tend Faw Paw, just keep an eye on him for her own safety.

After tucking the muzzle into her pocket, she cautiously lowered to her hands and knees and waited for Faw Paw to adjust to their presence. "Hello, baby."

Gray ears lay flat against his skull, warning rumbles filled the cage, his lean body curled back; though he did keep his weight off of the wounded leg.

Cait felt a motion beside her then Ethan's shoulder brushed hers as he also lowered to his hands and knees. She glanced at his face in surprise, but he was looking at Faw Paw. Studying him intensely.

When she turned her attention back to the cougar, amazement jolted through her system.

Faw Paw was making his way toward them—ears up, head low, tail against the floor for balance. He stopped less than a foot away, dropped his head a notch lower, and sniffed at Ethan's hands. He hissed. Neither she nor Ethan moved. In the quiet, she could hear nothing but her own heart drumming within her breast.

Then she detected another sound, a textured baritone rumble, and it took her a moment to realize that it came from the cougar.

Cait's jaw dropped. "Gawd A'mighty, Ethan," she breathed, borrowing one of his favorite phrases, "do you hear that?"

"He's purring."

"I can't believe it! How do you—?"

"Shhh."

He continued staring at the cougar, and a strange aura filled the cage. To Cait's utter astonishment, Faw Paw backed up awkwardly, then sprawled on the floor.

"Let's get this over with," Ethan said.

Cait didn't waste any time. Faw Paw kept Ethan in his sights while she checked his leg. The bone felt sturdy, but the tissue and muscle around the area still hadn't completely healed. She reapplied the splint and bound it tight, then motioned to Ethan.

He stepped out of the cage and had his back pressed against the wall when she met him outside. His eyes were closed, sweat beaded his upper lip.

Cait circled him, staring at him as if she'd never seen him before. In a way, she hadn't—not the way she'd seen him in the past few minutes. "That is the most amazing thing I've ever seen. How did you do that? Do you have any idea how long it took me to get him comfortable enough to let me get into that cage, much less touch him without sedating him first?" She yanked up her sleeve and showed him the scar below her elbow. "See this? That's what I got the first time I got close to him—he nearly ripped my arm off. But you! Two visits and you've practically got him eating out of your palm!"

"It must have been the gloves."

"No." Cait shook her head. "It's you. There is something about you that these cats connect with. First Sawtooth, then Ginger, now Faw Paw. . . ."

"Cait, don't get yourself worked up. Your head—"

He reached for her; Cait dodged his touch. "To hell with my head!" She propped one hand on her hip, flattened the other on against her forehead and began to pace.

"Are you mad?"

"I'm . . . I'm . . . stunned! You don't even like cats—you hate them, in fact!"

"I don't hate them—"

"And yet, one look into your eyes, and they're . . . they're bewitched!" Cait froze, struck by the realization that the same thing happened to her every time she looked into his eyes. The admission shook her to the core. What was this power he held over them?

Feeling suddenly weak, and more frightened than she'd ever felt in her life, Cait whispered, "Ethan, I don't think I'm feeling very well."

He was there in an instant, his arms tight around her, sweeping her off her feet. "Damn it, I knew you'd overdo it."

"I just don't understand," she cried softly.

As if sensing the onslaught of confusion roiling inside her, Ethan brought her close to his chest; she burrowed into his warmth. "Me either, wildcat," he murmured against her brow. "Come on, let's get you inside and I'll fix you a cup of coffee."

She choked on a laugh. "Make that a shot of whiskey, and you've got a deal."

Chapter 15

Cait didn't stop at one shot of the rotgut left in the jug, she had several throughout the rest of the day. While she remained in the cabin, sewing pieces of elk hide together for her new tunic, Ethan seemed driven to find things to keep him occupied outside. Repairing the broken porch railing, chinking a bare seam in the logs, hauling away a few branches that had blown into the quad during the storm. . . .

He kept close enough to the cabin that Cait only had to call if she needed him, yet far enough away that he didn't disturb her from the rest she was supposed to be getting.

Part of her longed to be outside, working right alongside him, if only for the company; keeping up the pretense of poor health was harder than she'd expected.

And yet another part of her welcomed the time alone to make sense of the frightening new emotions churning inside her—emotions that had begun outside Faw Paw's cage. She wished she could blame that on drink, too. Unfortunately, she'd been stone cold sober.

Whatever had happened both inside and outside the cougar's cage had been nothing short of staggering. Ethan couldn't seem to explain the mystery any more than she, yet she sensed it had some connection to her dream or vision or whatever it was she'd experienced on the ledge.

By the time darkness finally forced Ethan inside, cabin fever had set in with a vengeance. Sheer boredom had Cait nearly climbing the walls. If it wasn't so important that he believed she needed him, she'd have been in her hunting clothes and dashing outdoors before he could say "buckshot."

They shared a silent meal of leftover venison stew, then retired to chairs in front of the fire. Ethan dug for something in his saddlebags, while Cait picked up the tunic she'd been stitching and Sawtooth prowled around their chairs.

The intimacy of the setting didn't escape Cait. From the moment Ethan had walked into the room, smelling of wood chips and pine needles, she'd felt as if a piece of herself had come home. As if having him here, with her, was the most natural thing in the world.

Cait swallowed the knot in her throat, pressed her lips together, and set about attaching the second sleeve. She had to stop thinking of him in that light. He'd be gone soon, and life would return to normal—or at least, as normal as it'd been since the hunt had begun. She had to accept that and prepare for another round of "catch-the-cat-before-they-do."

The continuous movement of Sawtooth's

restless pacing distracted Cait from her sewing. She suspected that he pined for Ginger, and though she sympathized with his frustration, he needed to get used to the fact that he couldn't have her. Just as she had to accept the fact that she couldn't have Ethan.

Not that she wanted him, of course.

Finally Cait couldn't stand it anymore. "Sawtooth, go lie down," she scolded. "You're making me dizzy."

Ethan's attention snapped up from his packs. "You're dizzy again?"

"No, I told Sawtooth that he's making me dizzy. All I see is stripes going back and forth, back and forth. It's enough to drive a woman mad." She stabbed the needle into the hide and Ethan chuckled.

"What are you laughing at?" she asked with a frown.

"You. Him. The pair of you are funny."

"Oh, yeah? Share the humor—I could use a good laugh." She'd welcome anything that would divert her thoughts from him.

"The way you treat him, the way he responds to you." He shrugged and laid a peculiar looking case on the tree stump table between them. "It's almost as if you're his mother."

"You just figured that out? Gee, and I thought the resemblance between us a dead giveaway."

He chuckled again, and opened the case, revealing an assortment of slender silver tools that piqued Cait's interest.

"Do you think he misses being around his own kind?"

Cait glanced at Sawtooth, then at Ethan, and wondered if simple curiosity had prompted the question or if it was leading somewhere. From the blank expression he wore, she couldn't tell.

She took a sip from the watered-down glass of rotgut in front of her, savored the biting warmth going down her throat. "Truthfully, I don't think he understands that there are more like him out in the world. This canyon has been his home for most of his life, and Ginger and I have been the only family he's ever known."

"Haven't you ever thought about having your own children?"

She shrugged, and tugged the thread up from another stitch, determined to keep herself focused on the task rather than on the man beside her. "Sure, I've thought about it. But it's hard enough living up here alone with my cats, much less adding the responsibility of a baby."

"But if you married. . . ."

Cait snorted indelicately. "What man is willing to give up the comforts of civilization and live here with the crazy cat woman of the hills and her ferocious friends?"

He didn't seem to have a reply to that. A niggling sense of disappointment pricked at Cait. What had she expected—that he'd put aside his quest and settle here on the mountain with her? Maybe even give her a couple babies to raise?

She jabbed the needle into the hide and chided herself for the foolish notion. Ethan Sawyer had come to this mountain for one reason and one reason only—and it sure as hell wasn't her. She mustn't forget that. The most she could hope for was that his interaction with the animals during her "recuperation" could convince him to give up the hunt.

A rhythmic *wphoo* drew her gaze to him. He had a scrap of hide laid across the stump, and several of the shiny tools in his hand. She noticed that he kept his nails clipped and clean. He deftly flipped one slender metal instrument with arcs on each end between two of his fingers. Holding the hide flat, he pressed one end against the hide and pushed against the grain.

He blew on the groove, which explained the *wphoo* noise she'd heard, then he caressed the line with his fingertip, as if apologizing for leaving his mark.

She watched him quietly for a long time, mesmerized by the way the yellow firelight softened his features and turned his hair and whiskers to shimmering gold, marveling at the agility, the patience of his hands. That same agility and patience had brought her body to life, and yet she hadn't expected him capable of bringing alive a simple piece of hide, too.

Cait took another sip of her drink. Finally, curiosity got the best of her. "What are you carving?"

"My trademark. I tool it into every saddle I make, but I haven't done it in a while so I'm feeling a little rusty."

He paused to glance at her. "I found this scrap of hide, I hope you don't mind that I'm using it."

"Not at all, it's just a leftover piece. Is that an oak tree?"

He nodded.

"You have an amazing talent."

His face turned a charming shade of red.

"I supposed it represents durability."

"I never thought of it that way, but yeah—I suppose it does. I just always thought it represented the Sawyer name."

A lone oak tree. His environment had undoubtedly shaped him just as hers had shaped her.

"What about you?" he asked. "Do you have a trademark?"

Cait shrugged. "Why should I? I'm not a craftsman."

"I just figured that you would have some sort of totem. I've been told that some natives paint a significant moment from their lives on their homes or shields, usually an act of bravery or wisdom. . . ."

Cait's eyes slowly widened. "That's it!" she whispered.

"That's what?"

"I figured it out!" Her blood hummed with excitement.

"What?"

"Your gift with the cats. I figured it out. You have the spirit of the bear living inside you."

His shoulder stiffened almost imperceptively, his mouth turned down in a frown. "How much of that shit did you drink?"

"I'm not drunk, I'm making perfect sense."

"Not to me you're not."

"Mary, my friend in Pine Bend, told me that

some tribes believe that each person has his or her own animal spirit that lives inside him. It's one of the reasons visions are sought—so the person can be told what his animal spirit is. I didn't really give her stories much credit, until—" she broke off suddenly, reluctant to share her experience with Halona just yet, especially when she didn't quite understand it herself.

"What does that have to do with me? I'm not Indian, Cait."

"So? When the human spirit takes on traits of the animal spirit, I doubt it can tell the difference. When you killed that bear, its essence must have become one with yours. It's what gives you courage and wisdom and strength. The cats respect that and bow to it."

Though Ethan's eyes went dark and intense and he seemed especially intent on his task, Cait couldn't stop the flow of excitement in her veins. Everything fit now; everything made sense. His gift with the cats, his hold over her. . . . Somehow, knowing that he'd experienced a wonder like those of her native people made Cait much less afraid of what the future had in store. Somehow, everything would work out between her and Ethan. She just knew it would.

Josie stood inside the kitchen door, peering through the crack at the three men sitting at one of the dining room tables. She would've taken umbrage at the way Tooley had his feet propped up on the table if the conversation taking place between him and Louis and her husband weren't more important than scuff marks on the linen.

"... And plopped us smack dab in the middle of a gunfight!" Louis regaled to Tooley.

Hot color rose in Billy's cheeks. "How was *I* supposed to know he'd have someone covering him?"

"Oh, and not just any someone," Louis added, "but the Heathen of the Hills!"

"Hooked himself up with another squaw?" Tooley spat a wad of tabacco into the basin on the floor. "Don't surprise me none."

The chair Billy sat in reeled back with a viscious scrape along the wooden flooring. Without a word, he grabbed his coat off the back of the chair and stormed out the front door.

"What's with him?" Tooley jabbed his finger toward the door just as it slammed home.

"He don't like me tellin' about the Wild Cat. You want more coffee? From the smell of it, Josie brewed another pot."

Josie let go of the door and scurried toward the middle of the kitchen. She had a rolling pin gliding over a flat of biscuit dough when Louis walked in.

"Hey, Josie."

"Louis. Billy said he was heading back into the mountains this morning. I thought you'd be joining him."

"Naw, I think I'll wait till this hunt is over and done with before I make any more trips into the hills. It's been just a bit too hairy lately—even for me."

Setting the rolling pin aside, she studied the dark-haired man who'd been a part of their

lives for almost as long as she could remember.
"What happened up there between you and
Billy?" In all the years she'd known Louis, he'd
never lied to her. She hoped he wouldn't start
now.

He paused midway between her and the
cast-iron stove in the corner. "Nothin' to concern yourself over."

"Don't try and protect me. I've had as much
of being protected as I can take."

"We had a bit of a row, is all."

"About what?"

"Your brother."

Josie felt the color seep from her cheeks.
"The gunfight—was it between Ethan and
Billy?"

"You heard us talkin'?"

She nodded somberly. Unfortunately, she'd
caught only the tail end of their discussion, just
enough to hint at deep undercurrents.

Louis shifted from one foot to the other in
obvious discomfort. Finally he gave her a
sketchy account of what had happened on the
hill, though Josie suspected he left out a passel
of details on purpose and embellished others
for the sake of the story.

"Why would he shoot at Ethan?" she asked
softly.

"You know Billy's always had a short fuse,
but lately . . . well, he's been like tinder just
waiting for the flint."

"I know. I thought he was getting better, es-
pecially when we found out about the baby.
Now, though, all he thinks about is that cat.
He'll do *anything* to get it."

"He just wants to do right by you, Josie. A man's got his pride. His has been taking a real beating ever since this place went to ruin."

"And he blames Ethan for it."

"That—and other things. You gotta admit he has good reason."

It wouldn't do any good to justify her brother's actions, so Josie didn't even try. As much as she loved him, as wrong as she thought the treatment he'd been receiving, her husband was the one who needed her concern, now more than ever.

She had a bad feeling about him. Since his return early yesterday, there'd been a wild desperation in his eyes that she couldn't recall ever seeing before. And she feared if he went up into the mountains now, one of the men she loved wouldn't be coming back. Ever.

"Louis, don't let him go up there alone—go after him. Please. And if you see Ethan . . . God, just make sure he's warned."

"I have a few box snares around the canyon that you can check for hares," Cait told Ethan the next morning. "And there's a small glade halfway down the mountain where deer and elk tend to gather. I put a map in the knapsack so you can find it easily."

Ethan popped the newly loaded rifle shut. "What do you have to do around here that will keep you out of trouble while I'm gone?"

"Well, I've been meaning to scrape my bearskin. I suppose now's as good a time as any."

Ethan took the full and sweaty water skin she held out to him and looped the strap across his chest. He avoided looking at her.

"I must say, the shirt looks fine on you."

He paused to brush his hand against the buckskin shirt that had belonged to her grandfather. He told himself he'd worn it only because every other stitch of clothing he owned needed washing. "Feels good."

"It lacks just one thing." She whisked her hand out from behind her back and produced a string of black-tipped grizzly claws.

"What's this for?" Ethan asked, as she slipped the necklace over his head.

"Nothing special—just thought you'd like a reminder of what you are capable of."

Humbled by her confidence in him, Ethan's gaze caught and lingered on her eyes. He couldn't miss the sparkle; it had been there since she'd awakened, adding even more of a vibrancy to the crystal blue irises. And the stunning effect on his senses was as strong as if not stronger than it had been the first time he'd seen Cait. Roughly he asked, "Are you sure you'll be all right while I'm gone?"

"I'm sure."

"And do you promise you won't leave the cabin?"

She raised her hand palm out and grinned. "My word as a legend. Now go, will you? Hungry wildcats are not a pretty sight."

Even with her promise, Ethan found himself strangely reluctant to leave her. It didn't have as much to do with a lack of trust as with worry about her health—and to be honest, a fear that if he left, he might not be welcomed back.

But in the wilderness, if a man didn't hunt, he didn't eat. And neither did those who depended on him.

He slung a knapsack containing ammunition and jerky over his shoulder, then gripped his rifle tight and set out across the clearing with a wave to Cait and Sawtooth, who stood on the porch, watching him.

The sight stayed with him as he trod along a barely discernible path, and it spread a bittersweet ache through his chest. It occurred to him that maybe a bit of distance from Cait wasn't such a bad idea after all. He needed some time to sort out the jumble of conflicting thoughts in his head.

Though she never brought up the incident with Faw Paw, the question hung between them: What did he plan on doing about the wild cougar now? He'd been wrestling with that very problem the past two days. He'd had the perfect opportunity to kill it already and yet he'd let it pass him by.

Cait swore it was because he had some spirit living inside him. A bunch of hogwash, in his opinion. Yet he couldn't deny that something extraordinary had happened inside Faw Paw's cage. When he'd looked into that cat's eyes, he felt as if he could see inside its soul. Its pain and confusion. Its desperation for freedom. . . .

Now that he thought on it, similar occurrences had happened with Ginger—and even Snaggletooth. As crazy as it sounded, having an animal spirit inside him, he couldn't come up with any other explanation why none of her cats had torn him to pieces.

But what difference did it make?

Ethan sighed. It was past time he got back to Roland; he'd been up here much longer than he'd ever counted on.

The funny thing was, whenever he was with Cait, he almost forgot why it was so important that he go back. Funny—and troubling, because the urgency to get her settled and return home had dimmed. He'd enjoyed these days on Cait's mountain and would never forget the time he spent with her. Not only did he actually feel useful, but she taught him things he hadn't realized he'd wanted to learn.

Even now, as his feet sank onto the thick meadow grasses and the smell of evergreen surrounded him, he felt a sense of oneness with nature that he'd not expected, a lifting of the spirit. It was just so peaceful here. Nobody condemned him, nobody threw past actions back in his face.

But they would. If anyone ever learned he'd not only been staying with the legendary Heathen of the Hills, but had bedded her—and in all honesty, wanted to again—he'd be run out of town on a rail. All it would take was one glimpse of him with Cait by any of the hunters. In fact, he couldn't be sure that Billy or Louis hadn't seen her during their gun battle on the ridge. And if they did . . . hell, Cait could kiss her haven farewell.

How was it that he eventually failed every woman he got close to? Josie, Cait . . . even Amanda. He hadn't realized it before, but

when he'd betrayed the town by helping the
enemy, he'd also betrayed her and all she'd expected of him. It hadn't been much—just a few
material comforts and a name. The first he
could still provide for any woman, but the second . . . well, his name—and all it touched—
wasn't worth a hill of beans.

Unless he brought in the cougar.

When had things become so damned complicated?

A few hours later Ethan returned to the cabin
with a brace of dressed hares that had made
their way into Cait's traps. The offerings
weren't much, but he couldn't help but feel
pleased with himself. For a man who'd spent
most of his life cloistered behind the four walls
of a trade shop, he was catching on to wilderness living pretty damn fast.

Not that it would do him any favors in Roland, but at least Cait would be proud of him
. . . he hoped.

The sound of her voice had Ethan pausing
outside the door with his hand on the latch.

"You little thief! You ate Ethan's steak,
didn't you? Don't try and deny it, there's only
two of us in this cabin, and *I* sure didn't take
it."

He smiled. She was talking to Fur-For-Brains
again. He noticed that she did that a lot, treated
the animal as if he could understand every
word she said. In fact, as he'd told her last
night, the cats seemed more like children to
her. She provided for them, nurtured them,
healed their hurts, and gave them more love

than he thought a person capable of giving.

His smile faded. More than he'd ever known, that was certain. It had been ages since he'd thought of his own mother. Almost as if the day she'd left them, a door had closed. He'd been what . . . nine?

"What's he supposed to eat now?" he heard her ask. "No, he doesn't like turnips. When he made that stew the other night, they were the only things he didn't eat."

She'd noticed?

"Well, we'll just have to wait until he gets back and see what he brings," she sighed.

She didn't add "*if* he brings something," but Ethan suspected she thought it.

"Yeah, he *has* been gone an awfully long time. You don't think he got lost, do you?"

Was it his imagination, or did she sound worried about him? The thought took him by surprise, made something twist in his chest. He rested his forehead against the door and touched the necklace. Josie had been the only one ever to worry over him, and though he'd appreciated it, it wasn't the same as having a woman like Cait be concerned about him.

"Strange how quiet this place is when he's gone," she continued, her tone softer, so he had to strain to hear. "I never noticed it before. I'll tell you something—and don't ever let on that you know this—it isn't easy letting someone else take care of me."

Ethan almost choked. That was a secret?

"But I kind of like having Ethan around. He's a little bossy, but he comes in handy. And I have to admit, it's nice having someone to talk to. Oh, don't get all bowed up on me, you know what I mean. Someone who answers me back when I talk to him. Not only that, but he listens. Do you have any idea how long it's been since anyone listened to me?" A pause. . . . "Sawtooth?"

Ethan would have liked to have listened longer, except a scratching from the other side of the door spurred noisy activity inside. He hastened to the end of the porch, then turned just as Cait opened the door.

"There you are . . . !"

As always, the sight of her jolted him. She wore the new tunic she'd made for herself, and it seemed to fit her better than the others, if that were possible. Cropped sleeves left her arms bare, and the hem came to a v, calling attention to the naked flesh of her thighs, tanned shins, and bare feet.

Acting as if he'd just arrived, he propped his rifle against the wall and showed her the rabbits.

"Well, I'll be damned, hunter, you brought supper."

The praise in her voice caused a warm surge of pride to stream through Ethan. "I dressed them, too."

"And a fine job you did," she said, taking the game from his hand. "Come across any trouble?"

It took him a second to realize she didn't mean that bedeviled horse. "No, no trouble." He touched the bandage around her head. "How's your head?"

"It stings a little."

"Any dizziness?"

"I've been too busy sitting to know."

He couldn't stop looking at her. In spite of the bandage, she looked pink and healthy and so damned appealing she took his breath away.

"What?"

"You've got the most beautiful eyes I've ever seen." He hadn't meant to say that out loud, yet Cait's dazed expression made him glad he had. It wasn't often he struck the woman speechless.

Her bewildered gaze followed him as he crossed the porch. "Have you been eating wild mushrooms?"

"I didn't see any mushrooms, so I don't guess I could have eaten them." He stopped before a large upright board with a familiar shaggy yellow coat pegged to it. "Is this the bearskin?"

"Yes. I've been scraping it until my hands are raw."

Ethan examined her handiwork. Nearly half of the stretched skin had been scraped smooth. The rest bore a thick, greasy layer of some substance. "What's all over it?"

"You don't want to know," she chuckled.

"Sure I do." But when she told him, Ethan wished he hadn't asked.

"Would you like to learn how to scrape it?"

Memories of other times when he'd taken up Cait's challenges and earned her approval flashed through his mind. Hell, he'd probably never do anything with the knowledge he'd gained from her, yet something inside him couldn't seem to get enough of her praise.

Knowing he wouldn't have many more opportunities to learn her way of life, he ignored his roiling stomach and nodded.

Cait beamed at him, and he swore that for smiles like that, he'd skin the moon.

She swept past him, leaving the scent of wildflowers and tanned hide trailing in her wake. "It's messy work and not the most pleasant smelling, so I do this outside," she said, settling herself on the wide stump.

As he watched her bottom wriggle on the worn seat, Ethan's mouth went dry. The last thing on his mind was learning to scrape a bearskin. The slit up the side of her tunic gave him an enticing view of bare thigh. Warning bells clamored inside his head. Why had he agreed? He knew damn good and well that he'd only torture himself if he sat anywhere near her.

His legs nonetheless carried him to the stump, and before he realized it, he had taken a seat behind Cait. Her back fit snugly against his front; the heat of her body seeped through his clothes. . . .

"This will make a fine winter robe when it's done." She picked up a funny-looking knife from among several rudimentary tools and blades cluttering a second stump and swiped the narrow blade several times along a whetstone with practiced ease. "After it's fleshed and scraped, I'll grease and tan it, then stretch and dry it."

Cait continued talking, seeming unaware of the havoc her nearness played with his system. Her hair tickled his jaw. He inhaled the sweet fragrance of the long, wavy mass hiding her neck. His fingers itched to moved it aside so he could feast his eyes on the slender column. It had been nearly dark the first time they'd been together. He ached to see what his hands had touched, what his lips had kissed. . . .

"A sharp edged blade is important," Cait said. He tried to pay attention to her instructions, but all he could think about was the soft, smooth skin of her nape. How it looked, how it felt, how it tasted. . . .

He nearly flew off the stump when Cait grasped his hand, brought his arm under hers, and folded his fingers around the hilt of the curved tool. The outer swell of her breast against his bicep had him going hard in an instant. Surely she noticed. . . .

"You want to keep the blade at an angle like so, so that you don't tear the skin."

No, he wanted to reach beneath her arms and touch her breasts. Feel the supple weight of them in his hands. Bare them to the sunlight and admire the perfect roundness of them. . . .

The knife fell from his nerveless fingers and clattered to the porch.

Cait went utterly still. Silence fell. Ethan couldn't hear a thing save for the roaring in his ears. It took all the strength he could muster not to crush her against him and act on the thoughts torturing him.

Then Cait turned her head to look over her shoulder. He found himself staring into heaven itself.

"Have you been listening to anything I've said?"

He shook his head dumbly.

Her lashes fell, she stared at his lips. "Is there something else you'd rather be doing?"

Oh, Gawd A'mighty. . . . Ethan nodded.

"Does it have anything to do with my bearskin?"

"Oh, yeah." Her bare skin, her smooth hands, her hot mouth. . . .

Ethan shuddered. Hellfire, he had to get away from her. But as he watched her eyes darken with longing and her lashes grow heavy, he couldn't find the strength to move, much less breath. Did she have any idea how damned difficult she made it to keep his hands off her?

As if knowing she had the power to bring him to his knees, she found his hands and guided them to her breasts; they swelled and tightened under his hands.

And to wind the web of seduction even tighter, she whispered, "Be with me again, Ethan."

Chapter 16

She stared into his smoldering eyes for long minutes, hardly able to believe her own boldness. With the last time they'd been together having ended in such misery, she supposed she should be more cautious where Ethan was concerned.

Things were different now, though. Last night had opened her eyes to the fact that Ethan was a part of her destiny—whether or not either of them had expected it.

She didn't know what she felt for him beyond gratitude and a powerful physical attraction, but she felt something, a stirring in her heart and in her soul. Every time she looked at him, every time she touched him, her world became a little brighter.

His gaze dropped and fixed on her mouth. Cait licked her lips.

"Gawd A'mighty, Cait," he moaned. He closed his eyes, released a shaky breath, then looked at her again. The golden depths were at once troubled and glazed. "Do you have any idea what you are doing to me?"

She nodded slowly. She had a definite idea of what she did to him. She saw it in his darkening eyes, felt it against her bottom where his hardness pressed against her softness. And it gave her a sense of reckless control that she had the power to bring him to this state. "I want you, you want me. Why should either of us suffer?"

With another groan, he dropped his hands from her breasts. She immediately missed the warmth but took heart in the fact that he hadn't budged from where he sat behind her.

"It's just not a good idea," he said.

"Why not?"

He tenderly tucked a strand of her hair behind her ear. "Because you deserve better. Because I can't make you any promises. Because I have nothing to give you."

Didn't he realize that she needed nothing but him? "I don't want promises. They only get broken, anyway." She brushed a curl of his silky blond hair off his brow, traced the side of his face, let her fingertips trail down his neck, around his collar. "Be with me. Make my heart sing like the river and my soul sigh like the wind."

Just for today, she wanted him to forget everything but her, and for a moment she feared he'd refuse her. She didn't think she could bear that, knowing the pleasures he held in store.

"What about your head?"

"It's fine, Ethan. Now, stop making excuses and kiss me." *Please*.

As if hearing her silent plea, he touched her cheek tenderly. She touched his. Through lowered lashes she watched his head drift forward. The scent of him filled her nostrils, blocking out everything but the elemental essence of him. Man. Wind. Heat.

Anticipation made her blood hum and her nerves tingle with remembered awareness.

Finally his mouth covered hers in a tender and searching kiss. Sweet warmth suffused Cait from head to toe, centering low in her belly.

He tasted her lips with his soft tongue. She opened for him, and as he swept inside, teased a response from her, the kiss became a journey of discovery. A familiar ache built, and she leaned into his chest while he brought one arm around her waist to draw her closer.

The kiss changed, grew more urgent, more demanding. Cait practically tasted the steam. The tip of her finger slid to where their mouths joined and traced his lower lip. Ethan turned his head to the side, breaking the kiss to draw her finger into his mouth. Her head fell back, she groaned at the flaming sensation.

He kissed her palm, ran his tongue down each line. Lifting her arm, he blazed a path down the sensitive underside toward her elbow. He paused at the puckered flesh where Faw Paw had bitten her so many weeks ago. As if to heal the old wound, he covered the weblike mark with tender kisses that almost brought tears to her eyes.

He moved her hair to the side, wound the length around his fist, and moved his attention to her neck, sucking gently, taking tiny nips with his teeth that had fire kindling low in her belly and dampness spreading between her thighs.

Taking in shallow gasps, she curled her arm around his neck and arched into the solid wall of his chest. Muscle flexed beneath her back. The seductive pressure of his mouth on her skin, the grazing of his hair against her collarbone sent shivers coursing down her arm. The fact that she couldn't see him made the sensations even more acute.

She felt his hands mold themselves around her hips, up her back, then come around her rib cage to cup her breasts. They swelled so fully they hurt. Biting back a whimper, Cait clutched the hair at his nape and thrust herself further into his broad palms, aching to feel his skin on hers. He rolled the stiff peaks of her nipples between his fingers.

The velvet of her tunic became both stimulating and abrasive. Humid air caressed the moist flesh of her neck in a tantalizing rhythm that had her nerves aquiver. His thighs tightened around her hips, his hands stroked down her stomach to the bare skin of her thighs. Her legs parted of their own will. Rough palms glided beneath her tunic hem. Her breathing grew even more ragged as his fingers neared her damp core only to skim away.

Again and again he repeated the torture. Was he trying to drive her mad?

Cait squirmed against him. The length of him pulsed against her bottom.

Her body cried out for an end to the sweet

torment, yet her heart longed to savor each level he brought her to.

Surely there was a name for how he made her body respond. The crude words she'd overheard in Pine Bend in recent years seemed too vile, the loathsome phrases use by the missionaries too shameful.

No, neither came close to describing the euphoria of being in Ethan's arms, feeling his hands explore her body, his heart pound against her back like thunder. How could something that made her feel so beautiful and so treasured be wicked?

Then his fingers found her, slid inside. "Oh, God—Ethan!" She bucked against his hand. Blinding pleasure exploded through her mind and body when the movement brought him deeper. She felt his breath pick up speed against her neck. He brought one hand to her breast again while the finger of the other slid in and out of her in a reckless tempo that had her body writhing and her senses reeling.

Cait bit her lower lip, ground herself urgently against his hand. Tension, raw and primitive, coiled inside her until she couldn't bear it anymore. She twisted in his arms, brought her leg over his thigh, rubbed herself against the coarse fabric covering muscles of oak.

"I need you," she gasped. Her fingers fumbled with the fastenings of his trousers. A harsh yank sent the buttons pinging onto the porch boards.

He shook his head but made no move to stop her as she freed the rigid flesh. "Not here."

"Yes, here. Where I can feel the sun on my back and the wind in my hair and the smell of pine surrounding me." Pushing him so his back pressed against the wall, she straddled his lap. "And I want to see your face when I put you inside me."

"Bossy little feline, aren't you?"

"Only when it comes to something I want. And I want you more than anything I've ever wanted in my life."

She brought her lips down on his, hard and hungry and urgent, catching his harsh gasp in her mouth. He tugged at her tunic, lifted it above her hips until it bunched around her waist. Rough hands stroked their way up her back, leaving a flurry of sparks in their wake.

Cait impatiently whisked the tunic over her head, then yanked the buckskin shirt up his torso and over his head. The wall of golden flesh and muscle revealed to her had Cait's tongue going dry.

He sucked in a breath as she flattened her palms on his chest. Cait pinched the hard nubs the way he'd pinched hers, and he threw back his head with a primal cry even as he reached for her breasts to shape them with his hands.

Raising slightly, she felt the head of him prod her opening. The nest of golden hair between his legs scraped delightfully against her inner thighs. He felt thick and hot going inside her, and so damned perfect that her mind spun. . . .

She rode him hard. Pressure climbed. Fever spiked. His grip tightened and a haze of euphoria formed over her eyes.

Surrounded by evergreen and sunshine and wilderness, Cait reached her peak. She cried his name and arched at the same time Ethan stiffened beneath her. And when he spent his seed inside her, her name tore from his mouth and echoed through the mountains long after she had collapsed against his chest.

Much later, Cait awoke to find herself in her own bed. For a moment, languid disorientation prevented her from remembering how she'd gotten there, but when she did remember, a flush bloomed in her cheeks.

She sat up with her back against the head-board, the sheet clutched to her breasts, and immediately searched for Ethan.

Finding him, her breath caught.

He stood barefooted in the open doorway, hands braced against the frame on either side of him, his weight shifted to one leg while the other knee was crooked at a relaxed angle.

For just a moment she allowed herself to revel in the sight of him.

He had such a beautiful body. His back was long, lean, graceful. His trousers rode low enough to give a teasing glimpse of his buttocks, as if he'd put them on but left the ties unfastened. She knew every inch of that powerful body, had become quite tutored in the pleasures it could bring to her—and she could bring to it.

She wondered how she could continue wanting him so fiercely after the incredible afternoon they'd already spent together. Once on the porch, once on the floor in the cabin, then finally again on the bed. . . .

But she couldn't seem to get enough of him.

Even now, his presence drew her out of bed. Unable to deny herself the pleasure of touching him again, Cait threw on a cotton wrapper and crossed the room. He turned at the light caress of her fingers upon his arm and gave her a small half-smile. Cait inclined her head, wondering why he looked so tired, why his eyes looked so troubled, but before she could ask, he hooked his arm around her neck and drew her close to his chest.

She slipped her arms around his waist, her hands into the waistband and filled her palms with his irresistible backside.

He kissed her hair, her temple, her forehead above the bandage. Yet she sensed a stiff reserve about him, almost as if a granite wall had fallen between them. Cait pulled back and searched his eyes.

He avoided looking at her.

And then she knew.

Just as she knew that after today, she could no longer hold him here under the pretense of being ill. "You're leaving again, aren't you?"

He continued to evade her gaze. "I don't want to."

"But you are."

"Yes." He swallowed roughly and dropped his gaze to the floor. "It would be better if I didn't see you again."

The anguish in his throaty voice, the utter loneliness in his rugged features stunned Cait. "Better for who?"

"For both of us." He extracted himself from her arms and walked to the bed. "I have responsibilities back in Roland, responsibilities I can't just walk away from."

She watched him pull on his shirt and tried to make sense of what he was doing. Had the bond they'd formed over the last few days been her imagination?

No. Cait shook her head in denial. He felt something for her. He must. Or else he would have left her to die on the ledge. Or brought her to the cabin, then made his escape. Instead, he'd cared for her, provided for her, shared with her hours of laughter and an afternoon of sensual bliss.

Yet now he held back his emotions. Why? What was it that remained such a barrier between them?

The blood drained from her face, leaving a numbness behind. What had always been between them? "You're still going after Halona."

He froze in the middle of the cabin. Cait didn't realize how badly she'd wanted him to deny it until he met her statement with a guilty silence.

"I can't believe it!" she gasped. "After all you've learned, after all I've told you, after what happened at Faw Paw's cage, you still mean to kill her."

He sat on the bed, his shirt open, one boot dangling from his hand. "Cait, I told you I couldn't make you any promises. If I could give up the hunt, I would. But I've got more than myself to consider."

"Is it money?" She hastened across the room

and pried off the face of a fireplace stone. She reached inside, grabbed a pouch jingling with coins, and hurried back. "Take it." She shoved the pouch against his stomach.

"Don't do this, wildcat."

"Take it! I doubt it's as much as what that rancher is offering, but it's all I've got."

"It isn't the money. It's never been about that."

"Then what? What *will* it take?" she cried. "What do I have to do to get you to call off this hunt?"

His forehead crumpled, his eyes reflected almost believable hurt and confusion. "Is that what all this"—he gestured toward the clothes strewn on the floor, the rumpled bedding—"was about?"

"You know damn good and well that this"—she swept her hand in front of her—"had nothing to do with Halona or the hunt. It was about you and me."

"That's just it, Cait, there can't *be* a you and me." He shoved his foot into the boot. "There are people who wouldn't understand what I feel for you."

"And what is that?"

"I don't know, damn it! I don't know!" He raked his hands through his hair. "But I do know it can only lead to hurt—you said it yourself."

When? When had she said that their relationship would lead to hurt? The only thing she ever remembered saying was that he must respect the fact that things that posed a danger could cause pain. . . .

It dawned on her then. The hunt barely scratched the surface of what divided them.

"This isn't really about the cat, is it, Ethan?" she whispered, unable to hide the hurt in her voice. "It's about me." God, how could she have been so foolish? "You just can't stand the fact that you've bedded a breed—and liked it."

She'd seen the signs and had ignored them—no, hadn't ignored them. Wanted to change his mind about her as much as she'd wanted to change his mind about the cougar.

It seemed she'd failed on both counts.

He said nothing in reply, but simply rose from the bed and started toward the open door.

She choked on a humorless laugh. "You know, I kept telling myself that you were different, but you're just like every other narrow-minded, self-righteous, judgmental ass I came up here to get away from. Because I don't fit into your idea of 'acceptable,' I'm not good enough."

He paused, turned to look at her. "I've never thought you weren't good enough."

"Yes, you have! Since the day we met, you've divided us into Indian and white. The only thing Indian about me is the blood that runs through my veins. In fact, if someone hadn't told you, you probably wouldn't know about my Blackfoot blood because in every other way I'm the same as you."

"You don't have any idea what it's like living on the outside—"

"I don't? Just what the hell do you think I've had to do my whole life? My father was half-Blackfoot, half-white, my mother full-blooded white. How much tolerance do you think I've found in a world that judges people by the color of their skin or the culture they practice?"

"I never said it was fair! Damn it, Cait, if I thought there was a prayer in hell for us, I'd do whatever it took to be with you. But I can't stay on this mountain and you can't go back to Roland with me. So where does that leave us?"

She looked at him, her vision blurry, her mouth tight, her soul numb. Where did that leave them? Oh, God. She'd never known there was more to life than survival until this man had become a part of it, showed her that laughter and passion and human companionship went a long way to filling the empty void she'd carried for so long. And now. . . .

Cait spun on her heel, giving him her back, and folded her arms tightly around her middle, as if it could somehow ease the nothingness inside her. How was it possible to feel her heart pumping within her body, yet feel so barren at the same time? "Maybe it's best you do go, Ethan. Go back to your hunt and your damned responsibilities. And do us both a favor, don't come back."

Ethan stared at her stiff spine for many long moments. The transformation from spirited wildcat to tough-as-nails mountain woman created a sense of loss that twisted at his heart.

He wished he could take back the words, wished more that there was some way to bridge this yawning chasm between them. Not just the cat, but Cait herself. . . .

If Josie wouldn't be the one to suffer for his actions, he figured he'd say the hell with what people thought and find some way to make it work with Cait.

But he couldn't take her back to Roland. And he couldn't abandon Josie. Nor could he continue taking chances by visiting Cait. Hellfire, if Billy ever got it in his head to follow him, not only would he place Cait and her animals in danger, but Billy would connect him to Cait.

And the way things stood now, if anyone ever learned that he'd become involved with not just an Indian woman, but the legendary Heathen of the Hills, they'd accuse him of being no better than his father. And Josie would defend him as she'd always done, and she'd pay for it.

He couldn't sacrifice his sister's future for his own happiness.

"I'm sorry, Cait."

With nothing else left to say, he dropped his gaze, picked up his saddlebags, and walked out the door.

As he crossed the clearing leading out of the canyon, it took him a moment to realize that the mist coloring his vision didn't come from the fog settling in the canyon. It came from his own heartache.

He had to leave, he told himself. He had to get out of here, away from this cabin, away from this mountain, away from a life that beckoned to him more every day. Because if he didn't . . . Ethan paused and looked back at the cabin swathed in the rosy glow of sunset . . . if he didn't, he'd wind up falling in love with a wildcat.

Chapter 17

The street was almost eerily empty when Ethan arrived in Roland. At half past ten on a Friday night, there should have been some sign of life—horses tied to the hitching rails, lovebirds out for an evening carriage ride, at the very least a few stragglers lounging on the boardwalk.

Instead, vacant buildings stared out at him with squared black eyes, flies swarmed over dried piles of dung; even the saloon, usually bursting at the seams with ranch hands in town for their weekend binges, looked lost and neglected.

It was probably for the best that no one saw him back in town—even if only for a quick visit. Without the cougar, they'd consider him a failure, and he was in no mood tonight for the scornful comments sure to be directed at him. Since leaving Cait, he'd wavered between wanting to say the hell with it all and go back to her, and wanting to strangle something because he couldn't.

He'd pity the poor idiot who got in his way

tonight; he'd probably lay them flat.

Approaching Josie's restaurant, his brows dipped at the sight of two boards nailed in crisscross fashion across the doors. CLOSED had been crudely painted on one board. His steps slowed. He neared the window and peered inside. As usual, the dining room was neat and tidy, each table wearing a pressed paisley cloth with a bowl of dried apple peels as a centerpiece. And as usual, it was as empty as a ghost town.

A dim light flickering against the wall drew him to the side door that led to the kitchen. He spotted Josie inside the whitewashed room, laying a stack of plates inside a crate on the pastry table. She paused and rested one hand against the small of her back, the other at her forehead, and stretched. He hadn't thought it possible for her stomach to get bigger, but he swore she'd doubled in girth during the time he'd been away.

When he tried the door and found it locked, he rapped his knuckles against the window. The sound startled Josie. Her hand flew to her throat and she whipped around. Her eyes widened with astonishment, and then joy.

A second later, she flung open the door and threw herself into his arms. "Thank God, thank God. . . ."

For just a moment, Ethan held her close and inhaled the milky-sweet scent that reminded him of mother and sister and friend all rolled into one.

"Where have you been?" Josie cried, smacking him lightly on the shoulder. "Everyone else returned ages ago!"

Ethan drew back in surprise. "The cougar's been found, then?"

"Not yet. Word has it that the cat is still terrorizing Hullet's cattle. He hired a few men to ride his property line and he's hopping mad about the money it's costing him."

Conscious that anyone passing by could see them together, he nudged Josie into the kitchen, then shut the door behind him. "What about Billy? Did he make it back?"

She cast her eyes downward before turning away from him. "He did. He left again."

"How long ago?"

"A few days or so."

Ethan flipped one of the ladder-back chairs around and straddled it. "How did he seem to you?"

"He wasn't in a very good mood, if that's what you're asking, but that's not unusual. Why?"

For a brief moment, Ethan considered telling her about the shooting. But as swiftly as the thought entered his head, he decided against it. Why hurt her more? Josie had suffered enough because of their battle; he couldn't have her dividing her loyalties again. No, the quarrel he had with Billy would stay between the two of them. "Just wondering where everyone is. Town looks deserted."

"The Hullet Bunch just got back from taking a herd of cows over to the reservation. They're celebrating with some big shindig over at the ranch. Are you hungry? I made an apple pie this afternoon."

"I'm not about to turn down a slice."

She dug a fork out of the crate and handed it to Ethan. He didn't bother with a plate, though, just ate straight out of the tin.

"Oh, it's so good to see you," Josie exclaimed, sliding into the chair next to him. "I've been so worried. Especially when that horse came back wearing one of your saddles. I thought—well, I didn't know what to think."

So Trouble had found his way home. "As you can see, I'm hale and healthy," he assured her, then gestured toward the dining room with the fork. "What's with the boards on the front door?"

Josie dropped her gaze. Ethan watched his sister push herself out of her seat and pick up a plate. She wrapped it carefully in a sheet of the *Roland News*, then set it carefully in the crate with the others.

"Josie?"

She took a deep breath. "You might as well know...." She lifted her gaze to him and blurted, "I've closed the restaurant."

The chewing motion of Ethan's mouth slowed, his eyes stayed on Josie. She dropped her gaze, tucked a wisp of blond hair behind her ear, and started wrapping another porcelain plate. When no explanation came, he demanded, "What do you mean, you've closed the restaurant?"

She shrugged one shoulder. "Just what I said. There isn't any point in cooking for customers who don't show up."

"Business can't be that bad."

She gave a watery laugh. "No, it's worse." Tears shimmered in her eyes. "It's a complete failure, Ethan. The few folks who came around did so only because Billy lured them here. Ever since he left for that hunt, though . . . well, everyone seems to hanker after Stella Taylor's cooking more than mine."

Ethan tried to digest the information, but it stuck in his craw like a prickly burr. "How long are you planning on keeping it closed?"

"Permanently. Billy might decide to reopen it, but I won't be around to see it." After a moment's pause, she said, "I'm leaving."

"You're leaving Billy?"

"Maybe, maybe not. He's welcome to come with me, if he's willing to try and make this marriage work. If not, then he can stay here and run the restaurant himself. I just don't care anymore."

"You can't fool me, you love him and you love this town—"

"Yes, I do. Or at least, I did. After what everyone did to you . . . well, the only reason I've stayed this long is because of Billy. And . . . because I suppose I'd hoped folks would open their eyes." She turned back to her task, wrapping the dishes in brisk, determined movements. "I've reached my limit, though. My business is a failure, my marriage is a joke, and most of the people around here wouldn't know compassion if it reached up and bit them." She shook her head sadly and placed a protective hand on her bulging belly. "I can't live like this anymore and I refuse to bring my baby up in an environment that breeds such hatred."

Watching his little sister closely, Ethan noticed for the first time a bone-deep weariness beneath the youthful features. Her normally rosy complexion had faded to a dull pink; her pretty green eyes had lost their luster; faint lines creased her forehead.

Damn, she looked tired. Part of it might have been due to her pregnancy, but it seemed more likely that the strain had finally taken its toll.

Ethan shoved the pie out of the way, crossed his arms on the table, and bowed his head. He'd brought her to this point, and the guilt of that wrapped around his chest like a vine of thorns. Hoarsely, he asked, "Where would you go?"

"I don't know yet. Another town, I suppose. Or maybe—"

"What?"

"Well, I've been thinking about going to see Father."

His head snapped up at that. "You can't be serious!"

"Why not? Think about it, Ethan. He was devastated when Mother left. When he met Isolee, do you remember him ever being happier?"

"But he sacrificed us for that happiness, Josephine. He packed up and walked out and left us to deal with this mess on our own."

"That's not true and you know it. He gave us the choice to go with him or to stay. We chose to stay."

"I had my shop and you had a husband and

a restaurant. Were we supposed to give that up?''

''We might as well have, for all the good that's come out of staying.''

''It isn't over yet, though, Josie. We both still have what we had before, even if it has been a little rocky. But if you go to the Flathead Reservation, you might find Pop, but you'll lose Billy. You know damn good and well that he won't come after you. He'll die before he sets foot on Indian land.''

The tears that sprang to her eyes made Ethan feel like he'd taken a mule's kick to the gut. Hellfire, he didn't mean to hurt her, he just couldn't believe the foolishness coming out of her mouth! Closing the restaurant, leaving town on her own, possibly going to see their father . . . that would surely be the end of her marriage.

In spite of Billy's hatred—a hatred that represented the whole town's feelings—Ethan didn't want Josie giving up on Billy, on the future they'd planned here in Roland. Hell, she'd never be happy without Billy Gray; she'd loved him since she was six years old.

And underneath all the pain, Ethan knew that Billy loved her, too. Had since the day he'd set eyes on her sitting on a wagon bed bound for Montana all those years ago.

Ethan stared out the small window overlooking a clothesline with sheets flapping in the breeze. How could he sit by and watch the two people he cared about most split up because of him? And what about Josie's baby? How could he make his unborn niece or nephew suffer from something he'd caused?

He heard the rustle of Josie's skirts, then felt the light touch of her hand on his shoulder.

"Don't take it so hard, big brother," she told him sadly. "This has been a long time coming, I'm sure you know that. Maybe if I leave, you'll finally be free to find your own happiness."

His gaze shot to hers.

"Do you think I don't know what you're doing—and why?"

His jaw tightened. "I don't know what you're talking about."

"Damn you, Ethan Sawyer!" She slammed her hand on the table so hard the dishes jumped. "Stop treating me like a child! I'm a grown woman, and I don't need you protecting me anymore." She rounded the table and sat heavily in the chair next to him. Grabbing his hands, probing his eyes with her own gaze, she said, "I appreciate everything you've done for me and I thank God for you every day. I don't know how I would have gotten through Mother's leaving, or survived the move from St. Louis, or even managed the restaurant as long as I have without you holding my hand. But it's time to let go, Ethan. I've got to stand on my own, if only to prove to myself that I can do it. Do you understand?"

No, he didn't. The only thing he understood was that his actions had done nothing but ruin his sister's life.

And there was only one thing that could salvage it.

"Josie, don't give up yet. Give me two weeks."

"What's the point? Two weeks, two months . . . it won't change anything."

"Maybe, maybe not. If it does, you'll have back everything you lost. If it doesn't, then I'll take you anywhere you want to go."

"What are you planning?"

He shook his head. She'd given him enough grief about the hunt to last him a lifetime; he didn't need any more. "Two weeks," he repeated. "That's all I'm asking, Josie. Will you give me that?"

Her features brightened, then dimmed in a war of hope and skepticism.

Without waiting for her to think up more arguments, Ethan dug into his pocket and pulled out a wad of money. "Here, this will get you by until then."

"I can't take your money, Ethan, you know Billy'll be fit to be tied if he finds out."

"If Billy was here, I wouldn't be giving it to you. Now, take the money, damn it—it'll buy you what you need."

Thankfully she swallowed just enough pride to take the money, and it eased his mind, knowing that she'd not need for any of the basics in the time he'd be gone.

He paused at the back door. "Two weeks, Josie."

With a new mount, a skewbald cow pony the liveryman had acquired during Ethan's absence, Ethan headed back into the mountains before dawn the next morning with renewed purpose.

Since the prints he'd found the day Cait had

been shot had actually led him to his first glimpse of the mountain lion, it stood to reason he should begin his exploration there.

Unlike Trouble, the horse he now rode was a tranquil beast—maybe too tranquil. He didn't startle at every rustle in the brush, but neither did he seem inclined to move faster than a plod.

As a result, he didn't make it into the mountains until well past noon. After a brief rest, Ethan urged his mount across the creek. He scoured the area where he'd left his traps on the off-chance they had worked. It didn't surpise him to find them gone; Cait had probably destroyed them. He'd probably have done the same thing.

Determinedly he pushed her out of his mind, knowing that if he let himself think of her, his resolve would weaken.

But two hours later, when they reached the base of the mountain where she'd been shot, memories assailed him, of the cougar, of Cait, of the bliss he'd found with her during the most unforgettable days of his life. . . .

She'd been so angry at him. He'd wanted to explain to her that he didn't feel the way everyone else did. In truth, her ways fascinated him. And when he looked into the flawless blue of her eyes, he didn't see the color of her skin or the blood in her veins . . . all he saw was Cait.

All he felt was . . . needed.

But what good would explanations have done? Even if she could forgive him for what he *hadn't* said, one fact remained the same. The loose cougar needed to be caught; his visit to

Roland had been a stark reminder of that. And if he didn't do the job, someone else would. No matter Cait's attachment to it, it wasn't one of her pets. It was a wild and dangerous predator still threatening livestock and people. Hell, he'd seen what it was capable of. Just because Cait had escaped a brutal fate didn't mean someone else would.

He tied the skewbald's reins to a tree branch, then began his climb up the side of the mountain.

It all boiled down to what was best for his sister. He'd meant what he'd said—if their situation didn't change by the end of the month, he'd take her wherever she wanted to go. She was the only family he had left, and she'd stuck by him through thick and thin at her own expense. He owed her the same loyalty.

Halfway up the slope, a flaking smear caught Ethan's eye. He paused to scrape a bit of it off the rock with his fingernail and lift it up to the sunlight. Having seen enough of it in the last couple of weeks, he recognized the rusty smear instantly. Dried blood.

A thorough scan of the area showed nothing more than a hawk circling above, nor did his other senses pick up on anything out of the ordinary.

Had the blood come from the cougar? Fresh kill, maybe? Another animal entirely? It could have come from any number of things, but given the location, he suspected it was somehow related to the cougar.

He continued his climb, making his way across the face of the mountain as well as up it. The terrain became more rugged, the air more crisp. He found several caves, some big enough to hold a bear, others so small he could barely put his head in the mouth.

He also spotted several more trails of blood.

Near a bent aspen growing out of the rock, Ethan's ears perked at an oddly familiar sound, a string of callow growls.

He checked his rifle, then cautiously traced the sound to a shallow cave. The noise stopped, leaving behind a spooky quiet. Ethan kept his back pressed to the wall outside the cave and mentally counted to three, then flung himself in front of the opening, rifle ready.

Four spots of blue light glowed at him from the dim interior.

Ethan dug a tinderbox out of the knapsack slung over his shoulder. A moment later, he had a small flame going at the end of a twisted rag. "Well, I'll be damned," he breathed, lifting the light high.

A pair of fuzzy gray cubs, one atop the other, looked startled out of their skins at the sight of him.

Ethan stretched his hand inside the den. The top cub hissed and spit and scrambled back as fast as its little legs could take him, but couldn't escape Ethan's reach. He grabbed the cowering cub by the scruff and brought it into the sunlight. Its eyes were a deep blue, turning brown. It wasn't sleek and tan, like the wild cougar; rather it had a staticky gray coat with black spots, and darker gray fur around its face where whiskers grew like pipe wires. "If you aren't the cutest little crit—ow! *Shit!*" Ethan dropped the cub and popped the heel of his hand into his mouth, tasting blood from the scratches.

He glared at the set of hissing furballs in the cave. So much for his "gift" with the cats. The things were as vicious as their mother!

His eyes widened with sudden acumen.

Finding these cubs could just be the break he'd been looking for. Traps hadn't worked; neither had snares. But the cubs . . . the mother would have to return to this spot to feed them.

And when she did, he'd be waiting.

Chapter 18

E than located a spot just below the cave that kept him downwind so the mother wouldn't catch his scent, yet where he had a good view, and he set up a cold camp. No fire to alert either the cougar or any hunters of his presence, nothing more than his coat to keep him warm, and jerky and beans out of the can to stave off his hunger.

But as night fell, doubts arose. He heard the cubs up there, crying out their needs. Cait had been right all along, he realized. The mountain lion hadn't been attacking the herds for her own benefit . . . she'd had a very good reason for killing those cows.

Two good reasons, in fact.

He stared at the glitter of stars in the deep black sky, his promise to Josie weighing as heavily on his heart as it did on his shoulders. How could he slay the cat for wanting to feed her young? How could anyone? Since when did providing for a family have to mean a death sentence?

At the same time, how was he supposed to

pretend that his own family didn't matter to him?

Yes, by killing the cat, he'd gain the respect he'd lost and with luck they'd forgive Josie for defending him, but then Cait would never forgive him. Yet if he bowed out of the hunt, he might have a chance with Cait, but the town would never forgive him.

No matter what he did, he'd lose.

Unless. . . .

Ethan's breath snagged in his lungs, his eyes widened with a sudden thought. Maybe there was a way he could keep the promises he'd made to both Cait and Josie. Hullet had never said how he wanted the cat brought in. The rancher just wanted proof that the animal was no longer a threat to his livelihood. Wouldn't he be just as satisfied with having the cougar captured and brought to him alive? What he did with it then would be his business and on his conscience. At least Ethan wouldn't have the cougar's blood on his hands.

The change to his original plan sustained him through the night, all the next day, then through another night as he waited for the mother to make her appearance.

By the second morning, he admitted to himself that she wasn't coming back. Possibly she knew he waited for her, but he suspected the blood he'd found on the rocks had more to do with her absence. Either she'd been wounded somehow, possibly in a fight with another animal, and had gone off to die, or Billy had reached the same conclusion he had, returned to her last known whereabouts, and shot her.

If it was the first, then all might yet not be lost—Ethan just had to find the carcass, take it back to Roland, and show everyone that the threat was gone.

If the second, then he'd agonized over his choices for nothing. The hunt was over and he'd lost.

As Ethan gathered his knapsack and rifle, he knew that the only way he'd have any answers was if he looked.

But what of the cubs? he wondered, his gaze drawn up the mountain. He couldn't just leave them there. They'd never survive without a mother, and it didn't seem right to make them suffer for their mother's crimes. . . .

Cait. She'd take care of them.

The tiger was lying on the front porch, sunning himself in the early morning rays. The instant he caught sight of Ethan striding across the clearing, he rolled to his feet and loped across the grass.

Setting his bundle down a short distance from the porch step, Ethan braced himself for the animal's weight as Cait had taught him. Prepared, he managed to keep his footing when four hundred pounds of stripes raised up against his chest and planted two paws on his shoulders.

"Hey, Sawtooth, how've you been?" Ethan grinned. He scratched the tiger between the ears. Chuffing affectionately, Sawtooth rubbed his head against Ethan's ribs.

Funny how he'd missed the exasperating critter.

A sixth sense had him glancing up just as Cait opened the front door. Ethan's smile faded. He hadn't expected the sight of her to jolt him to the bone, but it did. She wore a wrinkled nightdress that fluttered around her figure like a soft sigh on a wind. She'd taken off the bandage, and her hair waved around her face in a mass of tangled temptation.

Had it been only three days since he'd last seen her? It felt like forever.

Sawtooth trotted to Cait's side. She frowned at the tiger. "Traitor," he heard her mutter.

Ethan folded his fingers into his hands and looked away, staggered by the intense need to crush her to him and kiss her until they were both senseless. Until the world, and all its unfairness, disappeared. Until nothing mattered but the pleasure of being with each other.

He hated her for that. For the way she made him forget everything that was important. For making him forget that there were things in his life he couldn't dismiss.

"Get dressed," he ordered hoarsely.

He saw immediately that it was the wrong tone to use with Cait. The wrong tone, the wrong words.

Lips tightly pursed, she started to slam the door in his face. "Get lost."

"Wait . . . Cait. . . ." He slapped his hand against the door.

She looked first at his hand, then at his face, her eyes hard and flinty. "If you don't get your hand off my door and your ass off my property right now, you're gonna find your scalp hanging from my war lance."

He deserved the hostility, he knew, but he couldn't make himself leave. "I brought something for you."

"You don't have anything I want."

Just then, one of the cubs mewled from under his coat, capturing Cait's attention. Her head swung toward the sound. "What was that?"

He almost grinned. "A surprise."

His coat began to wiggle, a fleecy head peeked out from the tentlike fold. Cait's eyes widened. "A cub?"

"Two of them, actually. Watch its teeth," he warned. "I nearly lost a couple of fingers."

But he didn't think she heard him. She strayed off the porch to where his coat lay. Kneeling, she pulled the cub out from under the sheepskin covering and brought it to her shoulder. To his chagrin, it didn't scratch and hiss at her like it had done to him. Instead, it nuzzled against her neck, beneath the thick fall of her hair.

She smiled at the cub, and a lump the size of Montana formed in Ethan's throat. He'd had one of those smiles before, the day he'd helped her fix Faw Paw's leg. There'd been other smiles, too. Coaxing ones, sultry ones, blissful ones. And they'd belonged to him for such a short amount of time.

"If you aren't the sweetest baby...."

His lips curved at her tone; she cooed like every other woman he'd known who was faced with a baby—or two. All soft and feminine. And damned if his heart didn't give a twist of longing.

The other cub poked its head out as if to investigate, and Cait immediately scooped it up next to its twin. She rubbed her face against one downy coat, then the other, and murmured, "They can't be more than a few months old. . . ." With a sudden gasp, she jerked around to face him. "Where did you get them?"

"In a small cave a few miles from here."

"You have to take them back."

"If I take them back, they'll die. These cubs haven't been fed in a couple of days. . . ." He paused, hating that he had to be the one to deliver the news, knowing how it would crush her. "There was blood near the den, Cait."

Her features froze in shock. "They got Halona?"

"I don't know," he said softly. "But it looks that way. A couple of men were still looking for her. I'll be going back out again to see if I can find them. If I can't, I'll head to Hullet's ranch. They'll have brought her there to collect the reward."

"The bastards." Her eyes blazed, her voice trembled with fury. "The greedy, murdering bastards."

Cait's anger cut through him like a flame through paper. That anger would have been targeted at him had he been the one to kill her cat. And it brought home the fact that if nothing else, he could sleep nights without having the cat's death—and Cait's enmity—on his conscience.

"I hope you don't mind that I brought them here." Ethan crouched down beside her as she set the cubs in the grass to watch them play. Sawtooth also wandered closer to the timid young and sniffed at them. "I didn't want anything happening to them and I knew this was the one place where they'll be safe and well cared for."

Her jaw tightened; she said nothing.

Maybe if he gave her something else to think about besides the mountain lion's fate. . . . "Do you have someplace to keep them?"

Cait looked at him. Shadows of grief lurked behind the anger in her eyes. She got to her feet and collected one of the cubs. "One of the empty cages out back."

To Ethan's amazement, while Cait gathered one of the cubs, Sawtooth took the scruff of the other in his teeth. Ethan gawked at the tiger as he led the way toward the quad gate. "Gawd A'mighty, that animal is half mother!"

"Thanks to this damned hunt, he's probably the only mother they'll have."

He couldn't come up with any reply that might console Cait. So he kept his silence and followed her and Sawtooth to the cage that sat between Ginger and Faw Paw's pens. The quiet within indicated that they slept.

Cait settled the cubs within their temporary new home. Her silence disturbed him. She would hardly even look at him, and the void in his chest grew.

"Well, I suppose I need to be leaving now."

"I won't stop you."

He wished she would. To have Cait care about him again, to have her wrap her arms around him, to have her give him one of those smiles that put the sun to shame . . . he'd just missed her so damned much.

"Cait—" He reached for her; she dodged his touch. Though he couldn't blame her, the action cut to the core. His hand drifted to his side. "You have every right to be upset. She *had* only been trying to feed her young. If I'd known—"

She turned on him in a wild rage. "If you had known, then what? Would you have given up the hunt? Let her have her freedom? That's all she wanted, you know! Just a place where she could be safe, raise a family, live by nature's rules instead of man's."

Gawd, he knew what that felt like. He suspected that so did Cait, from all the things he'd learned about her in their brief time together. He searched for the right words to tell her that he understood. And that maybe he'd been wrong all along, late though the realization had come.

If he explained why, if he told her about his reasons . . . Cait might not condone his actions, but at least she'd understand what had driven him to the hunt in the first place.

A sudden blast cut off the words he'd been about to say. Sawtooth froze in his tracks; Cait and Ethan both whipped toward the canyon entrance.

The echo had barely died when a hair-raising scream tore through the mountains, followed by another screech that made Ethan's nerves jump. "What the . . . ?"

Sawtooth dropped the cub. With a mighty roar, he tore out of the quad.

Cait jumped into action, dashing into the cabin. "Lock the gate, we have to follow him!"

Without question, Ethan hurried out of the quad, slammed the bar into place, then raced across the meadow. The skewbald had been tethered beside the brook, safely away from the cats, who might have spooked him.

The horse shied away. Ethan seized the reins in one hand, grabbed the pommel with the other, and vaulted into the saddle. He brought the horse around to the porch just as Cait burst from the cabin, rifle slung over her shoulder, a possibles bag looped across her front, and what looked like her tunic clutched in one hand. Surprise showed on her face briefly at the sight of the horse.

"Shoes!" he cried, noticing her bare feet.

"No time!" She grasped his outstretched hand and swung up into the saddle behind him. "Go!"

The normally complacent mount put his heart and soul into the run. Long, powerful strides carried them across the meadow in pursuit of Sawtooth.

Ethan glanced over his shoulder at Cait pressed against his back, arms tight around his waist. Her nightgown billowed behind them like an eagle's wings. His body acted as a buffer between her and the vicious wind tearing at his face, making his eyes water.

Hours seemed to pass, yet Ethan knew it couldn't have been more than a few minutes when they reached the edge of the forest. There, the horse's frenetic pace slowed to a cautious lope as he picked his way over the rocky terrain.

"What the hell is going on?" Ethan hollered over his shoulder.

"I-don't-know, I-don't-know! Maybe the cougar—"

"Where's Sawtooth?"

"Damn it, I don't know! Somewhere up ahead. Just follow the noise."

With no other source to guide them, Ethan spurred the horse in the direction of sound: branches cracking, the crunch of brittle needles, the muted thud of paws against the forest bed.

Suddenly the mountains trembled with a roar. A scream followed, like the wail of a woman.

The horse gave a shrill scream and reared onto its back legs, nearly spilling him and Cait to the ground. It took all Ethan's strength to control the frightened animal, then he jammed his heels into the horse's girth; Cait's heart pounded against his shoulder blades as they took off. The horse came to a skidding halt at the lip of a cliff.

Below, in a dell between two slopes, a massive beast of black and orange collided with a smaller, swifter creature of tawny brown.

"Sawtooth!" Cait cried, jumping off the horse's back.

Ethan took in the scene with split-second astuteness. The animals divided. Sized each other up. The tiger leaped; the cougar sprang forward; the two clashed in midair once more, a tangle of claws and teeth. Near the combative animals, he spotted a crooked figure that looked frighteningly like Billy.

He flung the reins around the branch of a fallen tree as Cait all but flew down the bramble-covered decline. Reaching the bottom of the grassy sink, she dropped to her knees and dumped out the contents of her bag.

Cait's mind kicked into exigent mode as she opened the chamber of her rifle. She didn't think, wouldn't let herself think of the risk she was taking. She focused on the knowledge that she had no other choice, and no time to come up with alternatives. Nothing short of death would stop the cats from fighting.

Unless she did something.

She rummaged through bandages, bullets, and other odds and ends in search of the small brown vial that represented the only chance she had of stopping the bloodshed.

Finding the vial, grasping it tightly, Cait ripped the cork free with her teeth. She dipped the dart in the murky fluid, then shoved it into the chamber.

A movement out of the corner of her eye had Cait's attention swinging to her left just as Ethan pulled his rifle from the saddle scabbard.

"No, Ethan!"

"They're killing each other!"

"Don't you think I know that? Shoot into the air—try and distract them!"

He hesitated.

"Damn it, Sawyer, just do as I say."

His rifle began cracking bullets one after another. With his shouts also helping to distract the animals, Cait shot the first dart into the cougar's hip.

Her fingers fumbled with the second dart. Tears blinded her vision. *She had no choice.* Swinging the butt up against her shoulder, she sighted down the barrel, choked on a sob . . . and fired.

Chapter 19

One moment the forest rang with the cries and screams of a wild battle.

The next moment, silence. So quiet that Ethan almost heard the dust settling.

He searched for Cait first. She knelt on one knee, a smoking rifle limp in her hand. Their gazes met, then drifted away to sweep the area. Ethan spotted Sawtooth first, lying unnaturally still. The cougar's limp body lay twenty feet or so away. And then he saw Billy, a twisted, broken heap in torn cotton and homespun.

"Gawd A'mighty. . . ."

Ethan rushed across the clearing. He dropped to his knees beside his sister's husband, his most relentless foe. Yet all Ethan saw as he looked into the blood-smeared face was a man he'd once been proud to call friend.

His breathing was shallow, his eyes were closed. Vicious gouges down his chest shredded shirt and flesh and sinew into little more than a bloody pulp. Ethan's stomach heaved.

He knew he had to do something, but what?

Damn it, he was a saddle maker, not a healing man.

The sound of sobbing pulled his gaze toward an achingly familiar figure. Bowed over Sawtooth's prone form, her cheek pressed against his ribs, Cait ran her hands along the tiger's coat. "Oh, Sawtooth, I'm sorry. I'm so, so sorry. . . ."

"Billy, hang on, okay? We'll get you fixed up." With that assurance, Ethan broke away from Billy and cupped his hands around her shoulders. "Cait?"

"I couldn't let him kill her."

He didn't know if she was talking to him, or to herself, but God, the sound of her weeping tore at his heart.

"He would have dragged her away. It's his instinct."

"You did what you had to do," Ethan consoled her.

"But what if I've killed him?"

"You didn't. See?" He gestured toward the tiger. A slight ripple in the stripes told Ethan that the animal was still alive. "He's breathing."

She looked up at him and her eyes swam with unshed tears. "But what if he doesn't wake up? I've never used the darts before."

Darts? Ah, now he understood why she didn't want him shooting at the cats—his rifle held bullets. Hers must have held some sort of drugged dart, like in the meat. "He'll wake up. You have to believe that."

"Halona?"

"She's wounded, but alive. Cait, Billy's hurt.

He's hurt really bad.'' Though he sympathized with Cait, anxiety over Billy made his voice a bit sharper than he'd intended. Softly, he added, "Please, look at him."

Cait drew back, and with a lingering glance at Sawtooth, released a shuddering breath. She wiped her eyes and donned that no-nonsense attitude Ethan so admired. Underneath, though, he knew her emotions were as fragile as meadow grass after a frost.

Gently he pulled her away from Sawtooth and guided her to where Billy lay, needing her collected and composed.

"Jesus," she breathed, kneeling down beside him to examine Billy's wounds.

"I know. Can you help him?"

"He's in a bad way, Ethan. He needs a doctor."

"There must be something you can do for him."

She started to shake her head.

"Please, Cait—he's my sister's husband. They've got their first baby on the way."

"I'm no doctor."

"But you're his only hope. You've tended your animals . . . you knew what to do when you were shot. . . ."

Her eyes went stormy, and he cursed himself for reminding her of the incident. How could he expect Cait to tend the very man who had almost killed her?

He'd never admired her more than he did when she began ripping the hem off her night-gown.

"I can try and stop the bleeding, but these

wounds are deep, Ethan. No matter what I do, he may not make it. He needs medical attention."

"Just do what you can."

With a singular nod, then a deep breath, Cait peeled away the remains of Billy's checkered shirt. She seemed immune, but the gore of the gashes nearly had Ethan puking. He turned away as she poured water from his water skin over the wounds. The woman, he swore, had a cast-iron stomach.

Feeling useless in the face of her competence, Ethan got to his feet. "I'll make a litter, like we did for the bear meat."

She looked up at him, startled. "You remember?"

"I remember everything you taught me."

Their gazes locked. A thousand unspoken memories passed between them like sands through an hourglass.

Cait turned back to Billy. Ethan shook off the regret beginning to settle in his chest and tramped away to search for the slender pines he needed to strip for litter poles.

As he passed by the cougar, he paused to stare at the beast responsible for mauling Billy. A bloody crease along her neck told him at least one bullet had found its mark. If not for the slight expanding of her ribs, he'd have believed Halona dead. A second opportunity to kill her had gone by the wayside, and he wondered why he never seemed to find the will to carry out the task he'd taken upon himself nearly three weeks ago.

Even now he couldn't seem to dredge up the

desire to see her dead. He kept seeing two fuzzy gray faces found abandoned in a cave. And he remembered the incredible experience with another, older cub, injured because of a poacher's greed.

Who were the real victims here? The animals, who wanted only to survive in their own environment? Or man, who wanted only safety and prosperity?

Ethan just didn't know anymore. But when threatened, one was just as dangerous as the other.

He started forward again only to have it occur to him that the drug Cait had shot into the cougar would wear off. If that happened while they were tending to Billy, who could say how the animal would react?

Setting his jaw, Ethan dug in his pack for the coil of rawhide and bound the cat's front and back legs. He'd not take chances with Cait's life a second time.

Her voice reached him from across the divide. "I think the bleeding has stopped, but he still needs to get to town, and I'm afraid the jostling will get him to bleeding again—what are you doing?"

"Taking precautions. I don't want to risk her attacking again when she wakes up." Under Cait's watchful eye, he ran a short line connecting the front bonds to the rear.

He found the saplings needed to fashion the litter. Lacking a hatchet, he sawed at them with his knife until he could bend them in half and snap them. He used the saddle blanket as the base.

Ethan had just finished tying the blanket to the poles when a groan spurred him to Billy's side. Fragile lids fluttered open. Dark brown eyes slowly focused on him.

"Ethan?" Billy croaked in surprise.

"Yeah, it's me, Bill. Stay still, we're taking you back to Roland."

He moved his head to the side. "Who's she?"

"Cait Perry."

"Cait?" He took in her face, her clothing. Then he scanned the immediate area. His eyes widened at the sight of Sawtooth. Thick blond brows drew together in confusion. He licked his dry lips. "Gypsy-man's legend? She's real?"

A flare of jealousy poked at Ethan at the way Billy connected Cait to Louis. "She's real, and she's fixing you up till we can get you to the doc."

"No." Billy's head wagged to and fro. "Don't want no heathen's hands . . . on me."

Stricken, Ethan glanced at Cait. Her lips pinched together, her eyes turned cool. A sick feeling spread through his stomach. Ethan glared at Billy. "Shut your mouth, Gray, she's trying to help you."

"Don't want her." He shoved weakly at her hands. "Get the hell . . . away from me."

"If you don't let her tend those wounds, you'll die."

"Rather . . . die . . . than have her filthy hands on me."

"Do you really want Josie to be a widow? And what about your baby? Do you want him or her growing up without a father?"

Billy didn't answer. His pain-glazed eyes locked on Ethan for several moments. Then, gritting his teeth, he closed his eyes and let his head drift to the side. It was all the cooperation that they'd get.

The flat line of Cait's mouth told him that Billy's words had upset her, but to her credit, they didn't stop her from tenderly washing away his blood.

Ethan watched her for a while, both astounded at her capacity for compassion and enraged that she'd overheard the insulting remarks. "Cait, what Billy said—"

"Forget it. It's nothing I haven't heard before."

But it still hurt her. He saw it. He remembered it. He hated it. And worse, he'd been just as guilty of rejecting what she gave so freely as Billy, though the gifts were vastly different.

"Indians killed his family," he whispered, staring at her, feeling compelled to explain. "An accident with an ax had confined Billy's dad to bed, so Billy had been out hunting for the day. When he came back, he found his home burned to the ground, his parents and younger brothers murdered. Our wagon train came across the carnage, and my father found Billy sitting under a tree, in shock." Ethan swallowed the lump of emotion in his throat and hoarsely added, "He was only ten at the time."

Her startled gaze slid to Billy's face. She brushed his yellow hair back from his brow and looked at him with new sympathy.

Ethan's throat tightened. The depth of her compassion astounded him. At the same time, shame pricked his soul. The day Cait had asked him to take care of Faw Paw, had he done the same thing—rejected that cougar for something another of its kind had done? He hated learning that he'd been capable of doing the same thing he detested in others. The same thing that Billy, and others like him, did with the natives.

"Billy?"

Ethan jerked around at the unexpected yet distant echo through the mountains.

"Billy!"

Oh, damn! "That's Louis, Billy's partner," he told Cait. He cast urgent eyes upon her. "It's best if he doesn't see you. Use my horse and the litter to take Sawtooth back to the cabin."

"But how will you get Billy back to town?"

"I'm sure Louis has a horse, he always does. I'll take Billy up in the saddle with me. You need to get out of here."

"I'm not afraid of—"

"I know you aren't, but Sawtooth, Ginger, Faw Paw, the cubs . . . they need you. They depend on you to keep them safe. If Louis sees you, he'll tell everyone he knows, and there won't be any stopping the curious. You'll be hounded for the rest of your life, and every one of your cats will be in constant danger of discovery."

He watched the play of emotion on her face as she absorbed the truth of his words. Finally she nodded.

And Louis called again, closer this time.

"We have to hurry, Cait, he's coming up the hill."

Scrambling to their feet, they both approached Sawtooth. Cait grabbed hold of the tiger's feet. Ethan supported his shoulders. "On the count of three—" Backs straining, faces flushing, they lifted Sawtooth onto the litter meant for Billy. "Let's try and drag him into the woods for now."

Dragging four hundred pounds of dead weight across the forest floor sounded easier than it turned out to be. By the time they got Sawtooth safely concealed, both Ethan and Cait panted with breathless exertion. "Can you handle it from here?" he asked her.

"I'll figure out something. What about Halona?"

"Leave her to me."

"But—"

"Billy? Where the hell are you?"

"There's no time to argue, damn it! I'm not going to hurt her, Cait, you have to trust me on that."

Ethan hastened out of the forest, away from Cait and Sawtooth, just as Louis, mounted on a sorrel horse, topped the rise overlooking the recent battlefield.

"Louis!" Ethan waved both arms over his head to grab the dark-haired man's attention. "Down here!"

"Sawyer?" Louis urged the horse down the hill and dismounted. "What happened here? Oh, shit—Billy."

"The mountain lion attacked him. We've got to get him to the doc, but my horse went lame." The lie came easily to his lips in spite of years of striving for honesty.

"Is he gonna live?"

"I sure as hell hope so."

After a brief discussion on the best way to transport Billy, Ethan mounted the sorrel. Louis helped him get their fallen comrade sideways across the saddle in front of him.

Then he turned and draped the mountain lion over his shoulders like a yoke.

"What are you doing, Louis?"

"Bringing the cat—don't you want to take it to Hullet?"

Ethan stole a glance at where Cait hid. He couldn't see her for the cover of the foliage, but he swore she held her breath.

He hadn't thought beyond getting Billy medical attention and making sure Cait stayed out of Louis's sights. Now that the cougar had been discovered by another, he found himself floundering over what to do. He'd promised Cait he wouldn't hurt the cat.

And yet, he sure as hell couldn't leave it here. Cait would either set the animal free and the whole vicious circle would begin again, or she'd try and move the creature. At the moment, she had her hands full with Sawtooth—she'd not be able to handle him and a wild cougar, too. Look what it had done to Billy.

That last thought swayed him as no other. "Yeah, I'm taking it to Hullet."

The air went suddenly frigid.

He felt Cait's shock like a physical blow. Reason told him that he had nothing to feel guilty about, but that didn't stop his heart from twisting inside his chest at the pain he knew he'd caused Cait.

And he couldn't bring himself to leave without at least trying to explain to her why he had to take the cat. "Go on ahead, Louis, I'll catch up."

Louis gave him a perplexed look but didn't pry. The instant he disappeared over the crest of the hill, Ethan spurred the horse around toward the trees concealing Cait.

She stood at Sawtooth's side, fists clenched at her hips, blue eyes shooting daggers at him. "You damned filthy liar! I can't believe you let that cutthroat take her! After all you have seen, after all you have learned, and knowing she was only trying to protect her cubs, how can you do this to her?"

The attack had him going instantly on the defensive. "What do you expect me to do, Cait? Men have been after this animal for weeks. And because of her, my sister's husband is lying at death's door. If I try and stop Louis from taking her, don't you think that will look a little suspicious?"

"If you wouldn't have spent so much time interfering, I would have had her out of here and this never would have happened."

"I told you I wouldn't hurt her, Cait, and I'm not. I'm just taking her to Hullet."

"You may not be the one pulling the trigger, Ethan Sawyer, but sure as shots fly, you're the one killing her."

They'd reached an impasse. The compromise he'd come up with had been no compromise at all. Cait wanted it her way or no way, and he

. . . he wanted not to have had to make this choice at all.

Unfortunately, there wasn't even time to soothe her wrath. The weight in his arms reminded him of the risk he took dallying. "I have to get Billy home."

"I will never forgive you for this," she hissed.

Softly, regretfully, he said, "I know."

Chapter 20

While Louis carried the cougar on his shoulders down the mountain, Ethan made the journey beside him on horseback, trying not to jostle Billy any more than humanly possible.

He concentrated on the path ahead rather than on the last words exchanged with Cait. Yet all the focus in the world couldn't erase the horror-stricken face branded into his memory.

Shops had already begun to close when he finally reached the outskirts of Roland. A couple of old timers sat on the front stoop of their hewn log house. They marked Ethan's passage with quiet speculation for several minutes before curiosity overcame them. "Whatcha got there, Squaw-man?" Wally Bullock called out.

One of Cait's smart-assed quips popped into his mind, but he bit his tongue. "Louis, fetch the doc. Josie, too. She'll want to know what's happened."

"What should I do with this?" He lifted the slim, bound legs of the cougar from against his collarbone.

"See if somebody's got a shed to keep it in for now. You might want to send someone after Hullet, too. That cat will be waking up soon."

Louis froze. His face went stark white. "You mean it ain't dead?"

Ethan might have laughed at his stunned expression if he hadn't spotted the stout form of Doc Harris barreling out of the barbershop. Apparently one of the old-timers had notified him before Louis had gotten the chance.

"Somebody doesn't think I work hard enough," Harris muttered. He wiped remnants of lather from his face and helped Ethan ease Billy down the horse's girth while Ethan dismounted.

Just as they reached the doc's combined house and office, Josie came bustling down the boardwalk.

"Louis said you needed to see—" Her hands flew to her mouth. "Billy! Oh my God, what happened to him?"

"Mountain lion," Ethan clipped out, as he carried Billy into the doc's front parlor.

"Take him into the examination room." Harris pointed to an open door at the end of a spartan hallway.

After laying Billy on a waist-high table covered with a white sheet, Ethan stepped back to make room for Josie.

She bent over the pale, still form of her husband, her hand clasping his. "Billy? Darling, can you hear me?"

Billy didn't respond. In fact, he hadn't made a sound since passing out after rejecting Cait's help. Ethan prayed he'd fallen into a deep sleep and not a death sleep, especially after all Cait had done to save him.

Doc Harris, one of the newest and most valued residents of Roland due to his surgical skills, performed a cursory exam. He removed the disclike tool he'd pressed against Billy's heart and looked at Josie with a grim expression. "Mrs. Gray, I won't mince words. Your husband has been gravely injured. He has lost a great deal of blood, and the damage to tissue and nerve is extensive."

Josie's nails bit into the flesh of his forearm. "What are his chances?" Ethan asked.

"It's hard to say at this point, I'm afraid. Both of you need to wait outside. I'll speak with you more when I've finished tending him."

Ethan pulled Josie out of the room and into the parlor. He sat with her all the rest of the day while the doc patched up her husband.

They talked little, almost as if, by keeping their fears to themselves, they wouldn't come to pass.

Actually, Ethan was grateful she didn't press him for details of what had happened in the mountains. He'd start thinking of Cait again, and if that happened, he wouldn't stop thinking of her. About the loathing in her eyes when he'd decided to have the cougar brought to Roland. About the raw derision in her voice when he'd decided to capture the cat.

The time for regrets had passed, though. If she didn't hate him before, she surely did now. He could try reasoning with her until the cows came home and it wouldn't make any difference. Nothing he said would convince her that he had taken into account what was the best for everyone.

So why'd he still feel so damned guilty?

Doc Harris finally met them in the parlor, pulling a scarf off his cropped black hair. His white apron was spattered with blood, his hands pungently clean.

Josie jumped to her feet; Ethan rose more slowly.

"He's still under anesthesia. He has more stitches than a ballgown, but with rest and time, I think he'll pull through—provided no infection sets in."

"Can I see him?"

Doc nodded. After Josie rushed down the hall, Harris started to turn away, only to pause and set his gaze on Ethan. "You did a fine job patching him up, Sawyer."

A lump of guilt lodged into the pit of Ethan's stomach. Hell, he hadn't done anything—Cait was the one who deserved the credit. But the fewer people who knew of her existence, the better. Grudgingly, Ethan nodded at the doc to acknowledge the compliment.

He checked on Josie. She'd settled herself in a chair by Billy's bedside. Grief and worry twisted her face as she brushed a shock of blond hair from Billy's brow.

Knowing that a wedge couldn't pry her from her husband's side, Ethan quietly took a seat in the corner in case Josie needed him for anything.

Unfortunately, the only thing she needed

was for her husband to recover, and that was something only God could give her.

The sense of another presence in the room coaxed Billy to open his eyes. Searching the room, he found Ethan sleeping in the corner chair.

Gawd damn. Almost like old times when they'd gotten so corked they'd passed out wherever their bodies had landed. Except he didn't remember ever feeling stiff as a corpse.

The breeze of a door opening brought the scent of apple peels wafting into the room. Billy turned his head and saw Josie waddling toward him. She looked so tired.

After setting a basin on the table by the window, she wiped her hands on the apron over her bulging belly. As always, a surge of pride washed through him at the knowledge that if he'd done nothing else right in his life, he'd done that. Created a baby inside the sweetest woman ever put on the face of the earth.

They'd been trying for so long.

"Oh, goodness, you're awake!" Over her shoulder, she cried, "Ethan, he's awake!"

While her brother jolted to alertness, Billy felt Josie's cool hand brush the hair off his brow.

"How are you feeling, darling?"

He licked his dry lips. "Like I've been run over by a freight wagon with spiked wheels."

"Dr. Harris says you'll be feeling better soon."

At the moment, soon wasn't "soon" enough.

The whole left side of his body felt like it had been ground up and fried.

"You brought me back?" he asked Ethan.

His brother-in-law nodded. "I wasn't sure you'd make it. Cait did everything she could, but—"

Reminded of the fact that a Gawd-damn redskin had put her hands on him, Billy reared forward.

"Billy!"

He barely heard Josie cry his name. Pain ripped through his chest and down his arm, set his whole body afire. He dropped back against the pillows with an agonized moan, and panted, "Don't ever mention that name to me again."

"Who's Cait?" Josie asked frantically.

"The savage he let poison my arm."

In an instant, Ethan loomed above him, eyes wilder than Billy had ever seen them, his lips drawn back tightly over his teeth. "Don't ever forget that that savage saved your life, you ungrateful son of a bitch."

As Billy glared into the anger-mottled face of his old friend, the memory came crashing down on him. He'd come back from searching for the renegades only to find that Ethan had put one of their filthy breeders in his bed. His bed! The one William Sawyer had given to him. The one he'd shared with Josie, the one they'd loved and laughed and would make a baby in.

And he'd convinced his wife—the woman who made every breath worth taking—to allow it.

Now he was doing the same damn thing. Defending the Gawd-damn murdering heathens. Putting one above friendship and histories. Given time, Ethan would even convince Josie to take his side again, and he'd be stuck on the outside while the rage clawed at him until he feared for his sanity.

"I don't know why I didn't kill you up on that ridge."

Josie gasped.

"That makes two of us. But thanks to Cait, you'll get another chance."

"That's enough, Ethan." Josie grabbed her brother's arms and steered him toward the door. "I think it's best you leave. Billy doesn't need you upsetting him right now."

Just as his wife opened the door and started to push her brother into the hall, Billy cried, "Why, Ethan?" His voice broke. "Why do you always choose them over us?"

For many moments, the only sound was the steady ticking of a clock in the background.

Finally, Ethan turned around and said, "Because, Billy, there is no them or us, there's just right and wrong. Holding a whole people to blame for something a few did is just plain wrong."

Billy watched through a red haze as his brother-in-law stormed out the door, but the memories remained behind, ate at him like the fire ate at his chest.

He closed his eyes. The sights and smells and sounds of that terrible, unforgettable day came back at him with more strength than ever. Pa lying in bed, slack mouthed and blank eyed. The twins, Bobby and Beau, a tangled heap of little arms and legs in the corner. The metallic stink of blood. The bitter rancidity of burnt skin and hair.

The absolute silence.

Billy's eyes burned like acid. He held himself stiff, fighting the onslaught. Somehow the picture blended with that of an older light-haired boy who'd picked him up and carried him away under the watchful eye of a weary-looking man. They took him to a wagon where a pretty, solemn-eyed girl sat clutching a rag-doll to her pinafore. With a "Hip" and "Ha!", the wagon rolled, taking him away from the blood and smoke and death. . . .

A confusion of emotions swirled in his head. Laughter. Recklessness. Joy.

Betrayal.

Rage. Of a power compared to none.

Then the familiar softness of Josie's breast pressed against his cheek as she brought him close. He clutched at her. An unexpected sob jarred his body. Then another.

And for the first time since he'd found his family massacred, the tears came, and Billy poured fifteen years' worth of hate onto his wife's breast.

When Ethan came out of Doc's office, he saw Louis sitting on the boardwalk in front of the saloon, smoking a cigar, surrounded by a rapt audience. "You should have seen him! He hit him over the head with his fist and dropped the cougar in its tracks—there's Ethan now!"

Louis broke away from his fans and jogged to Ethan's side. "Hey, Ethan."

"Hey yourself. What have you been doing, taking lessons from Tooley on story-telling?"

A blush crept up Louis's lean cheeks. "How's Billy?"

For a moment he couldn't answer. Anger continued to simmer in his chest over the quarrel with Billy, and he wondered why he'd ever thought to bring the bastard home.

No, he knew why. Because he couldn't help but remember the man Billy used to be. And deep down inside, he still carried a hope that that man existed somewhere under all the hatred.

"Came through the surgery. Josie's with him."

"Hullet's gone to Helena till next week. Somebody's bringing a cage to hold the cougar till he gets back. Right now we've got it locked up in Mrs. Livingston's goat shed."

Ethan nodded, not knowing what to say.

"I didn't figure you wanted anyone taking credit for your catch, so I told everyone the cat was yours to give to Hullet."

" 'Preciate that."

"Folks are planning a celebration later, though. You going?"

"I'm not feeling up to any celebrating tonight." The only thing he felt up to was a bath and a good shot of whiskey.

Besides, Cait's contempt-filled face was still too fresh in his mind, and the weight on his heart still too heavy to feel any gladness that he'd accomplished what he'd set out to do.

Entering his shop, Ethan shut the door behind him and absorbed the familiar surroundings: the smells of vegetable dyes and saddlesoap and tanned leather; the small stove in the corner that he used for cooking and warmth and heating his tools.

It didn't seem possible that everything could be the same when inside he felt so vastly different. The day he'd decided to go after the cougar felt like a hundred years ago.

He weaved around the worktable, sawhorses and drying racks to the back of the shop and climbed the stairs to the private apartment.

Dumping his packs on the floor, he made it to the bed, lowered onto the mattress, and sighed. He felt like a puppy kicked into the next week, battered and bruised and helpless.

And the only one who had the power to heal him was so far out of his reach, it would take a miracle to find his way back to her.

Several of the most anguish-filled hours Cait could remember passed before Sawtooth finally roused from the drug-induced sleep. His head jerked; a hollow rumble filled the cabin.

She sat beside him on the cabin floor, stroking his coat, murmuring soothing words of comfort and encouragement. His eyes remained glassy, the pupils large. His confusion communicated itself to her. She told him over and over how sorry she was for having sedated him. At the same time, she found comfort in the fact that if he survived the dart's effects, Halona would recover, too.

But for what? So she could feel every ounce

of torture the bloodthirsty scavengers planned
to heap on her?

Fresh fury seized her at the memory of
Ethan's betrayal. Trust him, he'd said. And like
a fool, she had.

Well, she might have been able to forgive
him for rejecting her, but not for taking Halona.
After all he'd learned about the wildcats, and
knowing Halona had only been trying to provide for her young after the terrible winter
they'd endured, he'd sent her to her death anyway.

That she could never forgive.

And if she let them kill Halona after everything, then they would win. They'd continue
invading the mountain, continue killing off the
animal life, continue being a threat to Sawtooth
and Ginger. And Faw Paw—God, when she returned him to the wild. . . .

None of them would be safe unless she
found some way to rescue Halona and set her
free at Logan's Pass.

Yet torn between a need to stay with her cats
and the silent vow that she'd made Halona that
day on the ridge, Cait wrestled with indecision.
She couldn't leave the cats unprotected and un-
attended. The trip would take at least a week.

If only there were someone she could trust
to watch over them—

Mary! Surely her old friend from the trading
post would be willing to stay at the cabin. And
with a horse at her disposal, Cait judged that
a trip to Pine Bend shouldn't take more than a
few hours. . . .

Night fell before she felt confident that Sawtooth wouldn't suffer any lasting effects from the drug. Though still groggy, he appeared to recognize his surroundings. He even managed to make the trip into the quad without crumpling.

Cait piled a mound of pine straw in the far corner where he could continue to recover his bearings.

"I'll be back as soon as I can."

She arrived in Pine Bend just before nightfall. To Cait's relief, Iron Eye Mary readily agreed to stay at the cabin with the cats for as long as necessary.

If the craggy tradeswoman had questions, she didn't ask them, thank God. Cait didn't think she could bear the explanations or the angry despair that would surely come with them.

Trading Ethan's horse for a fresh mount, and borrowing a barred cart from Mary, Cait arrived in Roland just before midnight. The full moon that guided her was both a blessing and a curse. It provided enough light to see by, but also in which to be seen. And she couldn't stop the memory of another time under another moon when hope had been born and dreams seemed within reach.

Light and laughter drew Cait to a gathering at the far end of town. She kept to the shadows cast by buildings lining the main road. The scents of saddlesoap and leather climbing out of the walls of one particular building reached out to assault her senses. She knew instantly that the shop belonged to Ethan.

The wave of longing caught her unprepared.

Cait's eyes squeezed shut; her hands clenched the reins in a white-knuckled grip. She tried to marshal the anger that had protected her emotions and sustained her throughout the many miles she'd traveled. When she needed it most, it failed her.

Just like everything else in her life.

Several deep breaths helped clear her clouded thinking. He'd taken everything she'd offered him and thrown it back in her face, because in the end, the glory of the hunt had been more important.

She secured the horse behind an oak tree in full bloom and crept as close to the gathering as she dared. She recognized the one called Gypsy-man. He slapped his thigh and guffawed. Then, shaking his head, he ambled toward the edge of the gathering, where a smaller group had formed.

And in the thick of it stood Ethan.

Cait's breath caught. Moonlight glistened in his hair, turned it to the color of gold dust. A pressed blue shirt stretched across his back, black trousers embraced his muscular legs. He turned slightly, giving her a glimpse of his profile. He looked haggard and weary and troubled, and though she knew better than to let herself care, her heart went out to him anyway.

Was it his friend who preyed so heavily on his mind? Had Billy even survived the attack? Or might he actually feel remorse for betraying her?

If he did, then what the hell was he doing here?

A motion at the edge of her vision brought

Cait's attention to a beautiful pale-haired woman making her way toward Ethan. Features like a porcelain doll, clothes straight from a fashion plate.

She hooked her arm through Ethan's. A stunning blow slammed into Cait's middle. She hadn't thought Ethan capable of hurting her more than when he'd taken Halona. She'd been wrong. The sight of the woman clinging to his arm—and he doing nothing to avoid it—put such a crushing weight on her chest that she wondered how she continued breathing.

Responsibilities. Yeah, she knew what his responsibilities were now. A lily-pure bonnet-and-petticoat miss.

She cursed herself again for being foolish enough to think she'd mattered to him at all. Hell, he'd probably laughed himself silly at the uncouth mountain girl in animal skins.

Well, soon enough, the last laugh would be on him.

Cait melded back into the treeline and positioned herself.

Ethan couldn't believe he'd let Louis talk him into coming to this ridiculous affair.

No one had expected anyone to bring the cougar back alive. The fact the he—of all people—had done so had met with rowdy approval. Several of the women had hurried to Josie's side with offers to help with the restaurant while Billy recovered. Most everyone else had gathered to gawk at the mountain lion imprisoned in a large wooden box much like the cages Cait had built for her cats.

Standing at the edge of the crowd, he wished this debacle of a celebration would end. They'd been at it all day and well into the night. His shoulder blades hurt from the congratulatory poundings he'd taken. His ears rang with the praises being heaped on him.

He'd gotten everything he'd wanted.

And yet it was a false victory, one that left him empty and aching.

He didn't deserve their adulation. He hadn't earned it. Cait had. And Sawtooth. They'd been the ones to save Billy, not him.

But he couldn't say anything. One word confirming Cait's existence and she'd be in more danger than either of them could handle. The peace she so desperately coveted would be nothing more than a broken dream.

As long as she remained a myth, a mystery, she'd be safe.

Free.

Just the way she wanted.

"You planning on taking the carcass to Pine Bend, Ethan?"

He brought his attention up to Ike Cornell, the saloonkeeper standing next to Louis. "What for?" he asked. He still couldn't get used to the fact that these people were talking to him. Not so long ago, they'd rather have spit on his shadow than address him.

"What for," Louis snickered. "Money—what else?"

"No. I've been neglecting the shop. I need to ride to the fort on business."

"Ethan, I gotta admit, I didn't think you had it in you."

Before he could come up with an appropriate reply, Amanda approached, smelling of expensive perfume and costly silk. She slipped her arm through his and pulled her so close that he felt the stiff stays of her corset along the length of his arm. "I surely hope you won't be runnin' off too soon. You and I have some catching up to do."

The invitation in her eyes made him feel suddenly nauseated. There'd been a time when he would have given anything to rekindle their broken affair, but so much had happened since then.

Cait had happened.

Needing to escape Amanda's cloying presence, Ethan unwrapped her fingers from his arm and excused himself.

The moon beckoned to him. Heeding its call, he wandered a good distance away from the noise, plugged his fingertips into his back pockets and stared into the shadowy face in a star-speckled sky.

Cait, his heart whispered. With a little imagination, he could almost see Cait in the moon, her stubborn chin, her round, awe-filled eyes. A knot of sorrow formed in his gut and spread outward until not an inch inside of him didn't ache. Remembering another time, another moon, he thought that was when he'd really begun to fall in love with her.

For all the good it did him. If she didn't hate him before, she surely did now.

He reached into his pocket and brought out a lock of sable hair tied with rawhide. God, he missed her. He missed everything about her.

The way she tipped her chin and looked down on him through her lashes when she laughed at him. The little sound she made when she was occupied—whether a curse or a mutter or a hum, always some little sound. And the way she looked when she was sleeping. Soft and innocent . . . tame.

She'd been the first splash of color he'd had in his world in years, and the time he'd spent with her had given him a taste of the life he'd always wanted but never known.

How was he supposed to get on with the rest of his life without her?

He'd have to, though. Somehow. He couldn't have her and the cat too. It would always be there between them.

He tried to tell himself that it would all be worth it in the end, that something good would eventually come out of something bad, but as he closed his eyes and clutched her hair to his heart, all he could think about was that there'd never been a time in his life when he'd felt so damned alone.

A burst of laughter distracted him. He tucked the silky keepsake into his pocket and ambled back to the crowd. It had become tight as a fiddle's strings, and as he wandered closer, he understood why.

"It's waking up!"

"Not for long. This time next week, that cat'll be a rug on someone's wall."

The thought of Halona being a trophy on display disturbed Ethan. He shouldered his way through the throng. Folks didn't give him much guff as he moved front and center.

He stared into the cage, watched the cat struggle to her feet. Their gazes met. Gold locked with gold, a conduit of one spirit to the other. Of his despair and her pride. His struggle and her confusion. His guilt and her innocence.

Then her eyes went hard and glassy; she curled back her lips and hissed.

The crowd cheered.

Ethan's soul wept.

He closed his eyes. He couldn't do it. He just couldn't have this cat's blood on his hands, not even for Josie.

He had to let her go.

Chapter 21

Cait didn't get an opportunity to approach the cage unseen until the wee hours of the next night. With the horse hidden nearby, the cart attached and ready, all she needed was to break open the cage, steal Halona, and make their escape.

She crept on her stomach to the door, where a chain and lock were all that stood between her and freeing Halona. As she crouched to examine the lock, the cougar caught her scent and growled a warning.

"It's all right, Halona, I'm here to help you."

The cougar began to pace, low growls spreading from one end of the cage to the other.

Cait withdrew a small pick and began working the lock. A nearby rustle snapped her head to the side. Seconds later, a shadowy figure dashed around the corner of the cage and pressed back against the iron bars.

Cait rolled swiftly to her feet and whipped the pistol out of the back of her belt.

"Cait?"

Her mouth fell open. Ethan? She couldn't see him clearly, for he wore dark clothes and a cloud had passed over the moon, but she'd recognize his voice anywhere.

He recovered from his surprise faster than she did hers, and stepped away from the cage into a wedge of light. A broad-brimmed felt hat covered his head; her grandfather's buckskin shirt stretched across his chest, brown trousers covered his long legs.

"What are you doing here, trying to get yourself killed?"

Cait shook herself from the stupor and cocked the pistol. "One step closer and I plug you."

His hands shot up. "Hold on there, wildcat, sheath your claws. I come in peace."

"And you'll leave in pieces if you try and stop me from taking Halona."

"I don't want to stop you. Hell, I came up here for the same reason as you."

One brow lifted in skepticism. "You expect me to believe that?"

He pulled a hacksaw from behind his back and grinned.

She didn't.

The grin drooping, he spread his hands in front of him. "Cait, I know you have no reason to believe me, but I don't want this animal dead any more than you do."

She scoffed.

"It's true. When Louis showed up on the mountain, it just seemed like the right answer to bring her back. I figured as long as I didn't actually kill her, I'd be able to keep my promise to you and still get the town to forgive me."

Cait's brows dipped at the strange choice in words. Forgive him for what?

"But you were right," he went on. "I should have listened to you a long time ago and helped you set her free, because it doesn't matter who does the killing, I'm the one who would be responsible."

"Gee, what brought about the sudden change of heart, hunter?"

His solemn golden gaze delved deeply into her soul. "You did. The glory just isn't worth your hatred."

In spite of herself, the seeming sincerity of his words softened her anger and burrowed into her heart. "You want to free Halona so I won't hate you?"

"That's a big part of it. But also because ... well, you can call me weak hearted if you want, but I just can't see her pelt stuck on some collector's wall. She deserves better than that."

Cait's mouth fell open. Was this the same Ethan Sawyer who had vowed time and again to destroy the cat, no matter the cost?

Unaware of the impact his words had on her, he went on, "Now, I've been wracking my brain for a way out of this that will cause the least amount of harm to everyone involved, and I think I've come up with a plan."

Cait cautioned herself about believing him so readily. She'd put her trust into him once before.

Yet even if he had an ulterior motive, did it matter, so long as Halona was free? She lowered the pistol to her side and tilted her chin. "I'm listening."

"I hit her in the head with a rock—not hard, just enough to knock her out—and bind her again, then we take her on horseback to your cabin. We can put her in one of your cages— maybe even with the cubs. . . ."

Cait shook her head adamantly. "It won't work. One, a knock on the head won't keep her unconscious that long, and she'll fight to the death as soon as she wakes up; two, no horse will come near her; and three, the hunt will begin all over again. Only this time they'll wind up in my canyon. Halona won't be the only animal at risk, then."

"So what do you suggest?"

"My original plan. She gets set loose at Logan's Pass. It's near the Blackfoot Reservation, but far enough away that she won't be a threat to anyone."

"But how do we get her there?"

"You keep saying 'we.' There is no 'we.' You made that perfectly clear."

"I have to be a part of this, Cait. I gave you my word that I wouldn't hurt her, and I keep my promises. It's because of me that she's here at all."

She studied him in the dim moonlight. That connection she'd felt to him the first time they'd met came back stronger than ever, pulling her to him. Her head called her "Fool!" Her heart urged her to grab onto this last thread of hope and run with it.

Her hand reached up of its own accord and

traced the smooth, shaven cheek. His eyes went soft and dreamy.

Cait tore her gaze away and said tersely, "I have enough of the drug left for one more dart—enough to keep her unconscious so we can safely load her into a box-cart. If I keep her covered with horse urine, and put a blanket over the cage and blinders on the horse, then it won't get spooked."

"It sounds like you came prepared."

"Damn right I did."

"Then let's get to it before someone spots us out here."

Cait withdrew a hollowed-out reed from her pack, prepared the dart, and with a mighty and precise blow, sent the dart flying into Halona's tawny coat. The cougar dropped with a cry of surprise.

"I'm sorry," Cait whispered. But there was no time for more than the quick apology. Cait returned the reed to the pouch while Ethan sawed at the chain. It snapped apart easily under the strength of his grip. Cait opened the door and crept inside to bind Halona's legs and sack her face.

Ethan carried the cougar to the waiting cart. The cubs set up a cacophony of sound at the first sight of their mother after so many days. They scrambled around her, sniffing her fur and burrowing beneath her limp legs in a touching gesture of recognition.

While Ethan went to fetch his horse, Cait doused Halona and the cubs and covered the cage with the foul-smelling blanket. Ethan returned shortly on a familiar-looking mount.

"You brought Trouble?"

"Beggars can't be choosers. Are you ready?"

Cait swung into the saddle, took a deep breath, and nodded.

"Then let's ride, wildcat."

That night they camped on the eastern banks of Flathead Lake. After hobbling the horses, Ethan wandered back to camp. He sighed at the sight of her empty bedroll lying across the fire from his. Though she'd agreed to letting him help with the cougar, she seemed otherwise determined to keep an emotional as well as physical gulf between them. He couldn't blame her, but it stung anyway.

Seeking her familiar curves, he spotted her rising from beside the boxed cart holding the cougar.

"How's she holding up?" Ethan asked, dropping onto his blanket and tugging off his boots.

Cait poured herself a cup of coffee from the tin set in the coals. "She wants out, but otherwise she's faring well. At least she hasn't rejected her cubs—I'd worried about that." As she took a seat on her bedroll, her gaze strayed to the cage. "What do you think they'll do when they find her missing?"

"Probably go hunting for her again, but we'll be long gone."

"And then what?"

"What do you mean?"

"It's going to take us a week or more to get her to Logan's Pass. Surely with you gone and Halona missing, they'll figure out that you set her free."

"Hopefully not. I told Louis and Josie that I'd been neglecting business and needed to go to Fort Benton to gather orders for next winter. As far as everyone is concerned, I haven't been anywhere near Roland since Tuesday morning."

"Josie—is she the washed-out blonde who was hanging on you like wallpaper at the party the other night?"

Ethan stared at Cait, the coffee mug against her mouth. Was it just hopeful thinking on his part, or did she sound snippy? "Josie is my sister. The woman you saw must have been Amanda Hullet."

"The rancher's daughter?"

"Niece. We were engaged once."

"You and the rancher, or you and the niece?"

He gave her a mock scowl and adjusted his saddle to a comfortable angle for his head.

"Who ended it?

"She did."

"And now that you've become a hero, she wants you back."

Ethan shrugged.

"Well, have a good life." Cait grimaced, tossed the remains of her coffee into the fire, then flopped back on her bedroll. "I'm sure the two of you will be very happy."

She was jealous! The realization had Ethan's mind reeling. Unwilling to let this matter drop, he kept his tone level. "Maybe . . . but not with each other."

"Why not? I'll bet she doesn't have a drop of heathen blood in her."

Chagrin stole in his cheeks at the reminder of their most memorable parting. "No, but Amanda is as fickle as they come, and I don't want to marry a woman who'll leave when times are tough. I want my wife to have the courage to stand beside me, to fight with me and for me ... Amanda wasn't that woman. She washed her hands of me when my father married an Indian woman."

"Your mother is Indian?"

"My mother is an *actress*." He couldn't keep the derision from his voice. "My stepmother is Salish—a Flathead."

"Natural enemy of the Blackfoot, did you know that?"

"You don't plan on rampaging the reservation, or anything, do you? We are camping on the agency's border, you know."

Cait chuckled. "Not unless they come after me first."

Ha! He knew who'd win that battle. When Cait came out fighting, there was no stopping her.

Ethan fed a few more logs into the fire. The valleys were still cool, even in the middle of June, but especially at night. And with nothing more than a thin bedroll to keep them covered, they'd need the extra warmth, not to mention protection against any animals that might brave the cougar to venture into camp.

Still, there was no place he'd rather be than out here, smack in the middle of God's country with Cait nearby. He took her sarcastic quips as a good sign. He'd learned that they usually acted as a cover for her vulnerabilities. The idea that she might be feeling vulnerable with him gave him an odd comfort that even if they couldn't be lovers, they might still be able to be friends. It wasn't exactly what he wanted, but he'd rather have her friendship than her hatred. Or worse, nothing at all.

"Ethan?

"What?"

"What's the connection between Halona and Indians?"

Brows raising, he lifted his head and looked at her. She reclined against her saddle, gaze trained on the sky, fingers twirling a slender reed of grass.

How many times had he wanted to—even tried to—explain why it had been so damned important that he achieve his quest?

He set aside the thick stick he'd been using to prod the burning logs, raised his knees, and draped his hands around them. "Three years ago, a smallpox epidemic broke out on the Flathead Reservation, and a band of men escaped. Maybe they'd been trying to outrun the disease, maybe they'd been searching for help—nobody really knows.

"But when word reached Roland that they were on the loose, everyone went up in arms, swearing that diseased renegades were seeking vengeance on the men who'd brought the terrible sickness to their villages. My neighbors formed a hunting party. They were determined to wipe out the Indians before they brought doom to them—either in the form of the disease, or through weapons."

"Did you go?"

Ethan shook his head. "No. I figured that if they came to Roland, I'd defend my town, but otherwise I couldn't see what good would come of destroying those people without just cause."

"Let me guess, they made you a candidate for mayorhood."

"Not exactly. A lot of people were mighty upset by my decision. So I went for a ride to try and put my thoughts in order. And that's when I found her."

"Who?"

"Isolee, my stepmother. Only I didn't know her name at the time. She was lying in the road, maybe trying to leave the reservation, I don't know. But she was sick. I didn't think, I just put her in the back of the wagon and brought her home. It didn't take long before my father was sweet on her." Ethan threw back his head and gave a harsh laugh. "They couldn't even communicate. She didn't know English, he couldn't speak Salish. But my father said, 'Love has a language of its own.'"

"You don't believe that?"

"I didn't at the time. My mother's desertion had almost destroyed him—apparently the thespian's life was much more exciting than that of a saddle maker's wife. But when he met Isolee, he said that something just"—here Ethan snapped his fingers—"clicked."

"What is so terrible about that?"

"I ruined my family, Cait. Not only did I bring an infected woman home, I'd brought an Indian woman into my home. They might have forgiven my choosing not to hunt the rene-

gades. They might even have eventually forgiven that I'd brought the enemy into their
midst. But when my father ran off with her,
they blamed me for turning one of their own
against them—and worse, they've made my
sister's life a living hell."

"Why? What did she do?"

"She agreed with me. In public. And, I might
add, she was very vocal about it."

Several moments passed, and he could almost hear Cait absorbing the facts.

"So you're saying that because you offered
someone basic human kindness, and because
your sister stood up for you, the two of you
were ostracized?"

"People have long memories, Cait, and
many of them, including Billy, had suffered at
the hands of Indians—of all tribes."

"Well, why didn't you just leave? From what
you've said, nobody wants you there anyway.
Why stay where you aren't wanted?"

"Because I helped to found that town, damn
it! Josie is determined to stay with Billy, and
he refuses to leave. And I don't want those
people thinking that their scorn can drive me
from a town that belongs to me as much as it
does them. When the cat started attacking Hullet's cattle, I figured if I brought the cat in,
they'd stop hating me and start treating Josie
better."

"Would you do it again—help that woman,
I mean—if you were given the chance to do it
over?"

Ethan bowed his head and stared at the
flames licking the pine mound. Would he? "I

don't know. If I knew then what would happen
. . . I just don't know."

He felt her studying him, but he couldn't
bring himself to look at her. The admission
shamed him as nothing else had in a long
while. The idea that if he'd been able to predict
what would happen to him and his sister, he
might have abandoned Isolee while she
writhed in pain and fever, left a sick feeling in
the pit of his gut.

"Then answer me this, Ethan—who have
you *really* been trying to redeem all this time?
Your sister? Or yourself?"

He swallowed, then rolled onto his back and
stared at the thousands of stars dotting the sky.
"Both, I guess."

After a long, long silence, Cait asked, "When
you found that woman lying in the road, what
did you see?"

"A very sick woman."

"And when you look at me, what do you
see?"

Feeling her gaze on him, Ethan rolled his
head to the side until the beauty of Cait filled
his vision. He couldn't see anything beyond
the woman . . . he didn't know anything more
than how good she felt in his arms.

His brow furrowed, and he searched for the
words to explain what she had come to mean
to him. "I see . . . I see sunshine in your smile.
Heaven in your eyes. I see the wilderness in
your heart and the freedom in your soul. I see
waterfalls and wildcats, sweet grass and evergreen. I see courage and spirit. I see everything
I ever wanted."

She twisted onto her side and propped her head in her hand. "Know what I see when I look at you?"

He shook his head. Probably a coward. A traitor. A complete failure. Hell, he was all those things and more. "What?"

"I see autumn in your eyes. Life in your hands. I see the kindness in your heart and the strength in your soul. I see oak trees and soft leather, waterfalls and roaring fires. I see courage and honor...." Her voice caught. "I see everything I never knew I wanted."

Their gazes fixed on each other across the fire. The blue of her eyes matched that within the dancing flames, seeming to touch his soul.

Silently she rolled off the blanket and dragged it with her to where he lay.

Ethan regarded her with confusion. "What are you doing, Cait?"

She spread the blanket, then crawled onto it. "I want you to hold me tonight, Ethan."

That was it. Forgiveness given in a simple statement.

And as he held her, a tenderness spread through his chest, along with something infinitely more powerful: a sense of belonging and acceptance that he hadn't felt in years, if ever.

"I'm sorry about Halona," he whispered, tugging Cait a little closer.

"I know."

They journeyed north through pine forests and grassy meadows blanketed in tiny yellow flowers, crossed canyons and forded creeks swollen with a recent rain.

Each day they pushed the horses as far as they could go, rested, then set out again. The more distance they put between themselves and any posse and the faster they did it, the better.

A new and wondrous bond had formed between them. It never ceased to amaze Ethan that what had been unacceptable to a whole society seemed to have earned him the approval of one mountain woman. She laid her bedroll beside his each night, and though his body ached to join with hers again, to seal this level of their relationship somehow, he refrained. Cait didn't deserve to be bedded, then abandoned again by him.

And there was an additional fear—what if he got her with child? What if he had already? He'd marry her, of course, if she'd have him, because he wanted to and because it was the right thing to do and because the thought of Cait having his children practically had him strutting like a twelve-point buck.

But then, who would be the one to suffer?

She would. And their babies would.

Just as Josie had suffered and their father and his Indian bride had suffered. Those few minutes in Billy's room had reminded him of what Cait herself had once said: there just wasn't any tolerance in today's world for a blend of white and red—no matter how diluted the bloodline.

Like the cougar, he knew he'd eventually have to let her go.

* * *

On the evening of the sixth day, Cait reined in her horse at the edge of a cliff. Ethan pulled up beside her, mounted on Trouble, who had lived up to his name the entire journey.

For the moment Cait simply stared in breathless wonder at the panorama below, a valley so rich in greenery that it astounded the senses. It seemed impossible that so many shades of one color existed. The light green of new evergreen, the verdant green of spring grass, the thick green of mountain scrub.

"This is it," she said softly, feeling that old hollow ache build inside her.

"It's beautiful."

"Yes, it is." Deceptively beautiful. "You see that mountain over there?" She pointed to a snow-capped peak in the distance. "The one set apart from the rest?"

He followed the line of her finger and nodded.

"That's Chief Mountain. He's considered powerful medicine. In fact, all these mountains are thought to be home to spirits. It's sacred to the Blackfoot, and they often sought visions here." The memory surprised Cait. She'd thought it forgotten, along with so many other things.

Dismounting, Cait wandered to the cart and peered inside at the cougar, pacing the small confines. The cubs stared at her with those bright blue-brown eyes of theirs and began a chorus of meows that drew a chuckle from Ethan.

"I think they want to be held."

"It's been hard to resist doing just that this

whole time. But if I stick my arm in there, Halona will eat it." And she remembered all too well what that felt like.

"Do you want a moment alone with her?"

She hesitated a second, then nodded.

Ethan gave Cait's shoulder a quick squeeze, then stepped away. "I'll move the horses."

Cait knelt, clasped her hand between her knees, and gazed into Halona's eyes. "Well, this is it, Fortunate One. You'll be happy here, happier than I ever was. No hunters preying on your every move, and lots of handsome males to mate with." A mist covered her eyes, a lump rose in her throat. "I know this is where I'm suppose to bring you, I can feel it. I saw it in my mind that day on the ledge. So when you go out there, if you see any of my family, you tell them that I am well. And that I have missed them." A sob caught in her throat. Cait covered her mouth.

Minutes later, she won the battle for composure. "You take good care of those babies, hear? Don't let anyone get their hands on them."

Knowing that the longer she prolonged the parting, the more difficult it would be, Cait unfolded herself and glanced around for Ethan. He stood quietly a short distance away near the horses, his eyes soft and full of understanding.

She was glad he was here. His presence seemed to give her strength. And God, she needed it, being here again after so many years.

Cait took a deep breath, squared her shoulders, then climbed atop the cage, onto the blanket. She grasped the sliding door with both hands. "Stay back now, hunter!"

With another deep breath, Cait pulled up the door, opening the cage.

Halona stuck her narrow face out and sniffed the air. Cait didn't move a muscle.

The cougar ducked back inside the cage, then emerged a second later with one mewling cub dangling from her mouth; its twin scampered beneath Halona's feet.

And still Cait didn't move. No matter how good their intentions, only a fool came near a mother animal.

Halona picked up her pace at last, trotting along the rim of the cliff, one cub bouncing from her mouth, the other racing and tumbling behind her.

Finally Halona swerved toward lower ground and disappeared.

Ethan approached the cage. Cait accepted his help off the cart, then hastened to the cliff's edge to watch Halona leap down a series of rocks. When she reached a level stretch of ground, she broke into a graceful run and took her cubs to freedom.

Cait didn't realize she'd begun to cry until Ethan ran his thumb along her cheek and caught a tear.

"She's free, Cait," he whispered, wrapping her in his arms. "She's free."

Cait inhaled a shuddering breath. "I know." Her gaze slid to Ethan's face, the tanned planes kissed by sunlight. The last few days with him had been bittersweet torture, riding alongside him under the sun, sleeping against him beneath the moon. She'd thought herself strong and self-sufficient. Freedom had meant everything to her. Yet the closer they had drawn to Logan's Pass, the more she'd found herself clinging to Ethan's strength. Partly because her hours with him were numbered and their future so uncertain; partly because of the storm of doubt brewing inside her over a decision made six long years ago.

She thought of how he'd faced head on and straight-forwardly the worst times in his life, too bull-headed to admit defeat and too loyal to his family to abandon them.

Her eyes turned back to the valley. Maybe she should have done the same. Maybe leaving hadn't been the right thing to do. . . .

The knot of uncertainty in her middle tightened. "Let's get out of here."

"I thought we'd rest up a bit—maybe camp here for the night."

"No, I want to go home."

Ethan gripped her arms, holding her still.

She felt the hysteria build, the desperation to run, as Halona had done. She'd given this place her spirit; what more did it want? "Ethan, I have to get out of here. I've done what I had to do; now I only want to leave."

His brow furrowed. "I don't understand. I thought this is what you wanted."

She brought her arms up, breaking his grip, and marched to where he'd tethered the horses. He caught up to her, but luckily he made no move to stop her.

She'd shatter if he did.

* * *

They rode until it got too dark to see. Cait's behavior confused the hell out of him. She never reacted the way he thought she would, and though it was part of her appeal, it also left him floundering.

After they set up camp and filled their bellies with fresh trout caught from the Flathead River, Ethan wandered to the bank where Cait sat on a rock overlooking the water. A chipped moon cast bright fingers of light on the rippling surface, giving it a soothing, tranquil appearance. Birds had begun to fly back from their winter retreats down south, and a pair of chatty warblers gossiped among the trees.

Ethan swung his leg over the rock and sat behind Cait, wrapped his arms around her. Cait leaned into his chest, and he felt her vulnerability surround him.

"Do you want to tell me what happened back there?"

She didn't reply for a long while, just stared at the moonbeams on the water. Finally her voice came to him, slow and soft and sorrowful. "I used to live down there, in that valley. When I was six, they built a mission school on the reservation. I vaguely remember being excited, because I'd learned as much about my mother's people from her as I had about my father's people from him, and I liked to read."

Ethan rested his chin on her silky head, waiting for her to go on.

"The excitement didn't last. What the missionaries wanted to teach us were things as they saw them—customs, culture, religion. I didn't see much difference between their god and the Great Spirit, but we were banned from practicing our beliefs. After a while, a door closes on the memories. Children—especially the youngest ones—forget where they come from."

"Your parents allowed them to take away your heritage?"

"At first I don't think anyone knew it would be like that, and by the time they found out there was nothing that could be done. If our relatives tried to see us, we were punished. And if we didn't follow the rules, our relatives were punished. No rations, severe beatings . . . things were bad enough for them without making it worse."

Gawd A'mighty, what a terrible burden to put on a child, Ethan thought, closing his eyes. He remembered talk at the forts where he gathered orders for saddles about the treatment of the natives on certain agencies, but he'd had no idea of the extent of their suffering, nor that it had been happening practically in his own back yard. Many of the Indians had already starved, or died from disease or by other means. But to take their children away, too . . . that must be the most horrible death of all.

"I was seventeen when I got the news that my father had died. They had no hold over me anymore, so I left the school. Just . . . walked out. It was the first time I'd seen how the Blackfoot really lived, and it made me sick. They were starving, ill, old, hopeless. . . ."

"What about your mother?"

"I discovered that she had been 'rescued' shortly after the school was built. She was sent back to Billings, where she had friends. So I went to find her, except . . . she'd killed herself ten years earlier."

"Gawd A'mighty. . . ."

"It's all right," Cait whispered, covering his hand with hers. "Truthfully, I didn't grieve so much as I felt regret. We hadn't seen each other in twelve years. And the Blackfoot—well, I'd learned to be white so well that I always thought of them simply as my father's people. I didn't know enough about them to call them my own, and honestly, I didn't want to know. I didn't want to become like those I'd seen. But I couldn't live among the whites, either, because . . . well, you know why. So when I found out that my grandfather left me his winter cabin, I decided to live there."

Ethan plain didn't know what to say to her.

"I'm one of the lucky ones—I had a way out and I took it. To live down there with them . . . it would kill me. On Wildcat Mountain, I go where I want, do what I want, and rely on myself. I feel like I've got some shred of honor. Down there . . . it's just a grave filled with the walking dead."

She turned in his arms and looked at him. Anguish glistened in her eyes. "I can't live like that, Ethan. Does that make me a bad person? Unsympathetic to their plight?"

Ahh, damn. . . . Ethan worked down the lump in his throat and traced her rounded cheek with his forefinger. "I think it makes you more courageous than you'll ever know."

"But I ran—unlike you, who faced a society of prejudice. When you told me what you've been through...." She averted her face. "Maybe I was wrong to leave the reservation. Maybe I should have stayed, been loyal to them instead of striking out on my own."

The doubt and loneliness in her voice and features cut him to the quick. "Cait—" Ethan drew her gaze back to his with a finger to her chin. "Do you remember telling me once that some creatures cannot be caged, that it would kill their spirit? I thought of you instantly. You need the freedom you found in the canyon. The Indian nations just can't provide that for you."

"So what do I do?"

"Learn about your father's people. Respect them and their old ways. They are a part of you. But that doesn't mean you have to give up Caitlin Perry—or Wild Cat Cait." He dipped his head and looked at her though his lashes. "Don't forget, you're a legend—you have a responsibility to the folks who believe in you."

Cait met his attempt at levity with a watery laugh. "Oh, yes, we mustn't forget my mystical powers."

After a moment her smile faded, but at least the haunted look had left her eyes. Cait didn't have a damn thing to feel guilty for, and he hoped she understood that.

The touch of her fingers stroking his bristly cheek took him as much by surprise as the words she mouthed—*Thank you.*

And a week of his resisting the mystical powers she was famed for met its limit. His mouth drifted down to hers. Their lips met in a kiss so tender it nearly buckled his knees. He tasted the salt of her tears, the sorrow in her soul, the freedom in her heart. And he knew that for as long as he lived, she'd always be a part of him—wherever they both might be.

Reluctantly he pulled back, their lips clinging, their breaths mingling, until that very last moment.

Ethan climbed down from the rock and reached for her hand. "Come on, wildcat, let's get some sleep. We've got a long ride ahead of us tomorrow."

"If I go to sleep, you'll leave me again."

The truth of the statement hit him hard. She was right: he would be leaving her. Not tonight, no . . . but as soon as they reached Pine Bend, she'd fork off toward her mountain and her cats and he'd head due south, toward Roland and his sister.

"Ah, damn it, Cait." He yanked her against him, crushed her to his chest, rubbed his face in her hair. He wished to God he never had to let her go; the time he spent with her was as close to heaven as he'd ever get.

But no matter how badly he wanted to make these days with Cait last a lifetime, he couldn't forget that she'd never be welcome in his world. And he couldn't go to hers.

He had a promise to keep to Josie.

Chapter 22

Four days later, Ethan sat bow-backed at the kitchen table in Josie's restaurant, the latest edition of the *Roland News* spread open in front of him. He stared unseeingly at the print and took a sip from the cup of coffee he'd been nursing. Too bad it wasn't something stronger. He'd welcome just about anything that would numb the pain in his chest.

He'd known it would be hard leaving Cait once they'd reached Pine Bend, but hellfire, he hadn't expected it to tear his heart in half.

With a heavy sigh, he raised the newspaper to an upright angle, vainly seeking some distraction. The headline COUGAR ESCAPES! did the trick.

Just as he finished reading an article about the cat's mysterious "escape," Josie entered the kitchen.

She came to a quick stop in the doorway. "Why, Ethan! When did you get back?"

"Late last night." He set down his cup. "How's Billy?"

Josie rubbed the small of her back with one

hand, her brow with the other. She looked so tired. "Resting. Doc isn't sure if he'll ever be able to use his left arm again."

"Time will tell." He pointed to the article. "I see the cougar's turned up missing."

"Since last week," Josie said, taking a chair beside him. "The lock was cut. No one knows who did it or why. Some are accusing you of letting it loose, since you left right before it happened, but others are defending you. They can't believe you'd do that after all the trouble you took catching it."

Ethan avoided looking at Josie by rising from his seat to pour her a cup of coffee. He doubted she would take well the fact that he'd helped free the beast that had attacked her husband. "Does Hullet know?"

"Ohhh, yes. I'm surprised you didn't hear him cussing all the way into Fort Benton."

Another damned lie. "Well, hopefully the cat moved on and we don't have to worry about anyone else getting hurt."

"That reminds me—I haven't thanked you yet for what you did for Billy."

"I didn't do anything."

"You saved my husband's life, Ethan. That is not nothing."

"Cait's the one you should thank."

"I would, if I knew where to find her." She shook her head, and a strand of blonde hair fell from the loose bun atop her head. "I still can't believe the legends are true. When Billy told me about her, I thought it was the fever talking."

Ethan dropped his gaze, unable to comment for the tightness of his throat.

"Is it true that she lives in the trees?"

The eagerness in her voice made him chuckle. "In a manner of speaking. She lives in a cabin made of trees, surrounded by trees."

"Can she really outrun a deer?"

The day he'd chased her through the forest and wound up kissing her for the first time came to mind. "She runs like the wind."

"Glory be, Ethan, I didn't realize you knew this woman so well."

"Our paths crossed a time or two." Blinking back the sudden spring of moisture in his eyes, Ethan found himself telling Josie about how Cait had caught him in the net, his later encounter with Sawtooth, then Ginger and Faw Paw. And he told her about the bear, and the cubs, and Cait's unending well of compassion. . . .

Having listened avidly to his tales, Josie finally exclaimed, "No wonder there are so many yarns spun about her!"

"Yeah, she really is an amazing woman," Ethan said with a sad smile. "But none of the stories have been proved, and I'd like to keep it that way. So that means you can never tell anyone what I've told you. If word gets out that she or her animals really exist, they won't stop hunting for her until they kill her—or worse."

Josie's brows rose, then a grin tugged at her lips, "Why, Ethan Sawyer, you're *sweet* on her."

There was no denying it, not to Josie. "Yeah,

I am," he whispered. Not only was he sweet on her, he'd gone and fallen in love with her. In fact, the depth and power of the love he felt for Caitlin Perry had his head reeling and his heart hurting all over again. "She makes it hard to remember what life was like before I met her."

"Well, I remember. It was filled with pain and anger and guilt. Go on back to her."

"I can't, Josie. I won't break my promise to you."

She slapped her hands on the table. "Ethan, I don't want you to *keep* your promise—why can't you get that through your thick head? I have a husband who is perfectly capable of taking care of his family; that isn't your role in my life anymore."

"So you don't need me anymore?"

"I'll always need you, brother. But out there somewhere is someone who needs you more, someone who needs you the way I need Billy. Maybe that someone is Cait."

"She's part Indian, Josie. Are you forgetting what happened the last time I brought an Indian woman home? These people all but ground you up and served you for supper!"

"Well, that won't be a problem this time, since I won't be around. Billy and I decided that as soon as he's recovered, we're going to open a restaurant in Pine Bend. Or maybe Helena. Anywhere away from here."

"Josephine," Ethan sighed her name, "it won't matter where you go. You've heard Billy talk about the natives—"

"He's softening, Ethan," she interrupted. "Give him time."

"I'm glad to hear that. But even if by some miracle he changes his views, you and I both know that his voice is only one of thousands chanting the same thing. Opinions like that exist everywhere."

"Except in the mountains."

Startled, Ethan realized she was right. In the mountains, he'd found relief from the constant strain of hostility. Up there, he'd discovered a place where the wind sang and the trees whispered and the mountains repeated a welcome. Wildcat Peak.

And Cait.

"Go to her, Ethan."

He lifted his gaze to his sister. She'd relieved him of his promise, had even given him her blessing to be with the one person who filled him with true happiness. And if Josie and Billy patched up their differences and left, he had no important reason to stay in Roland. Being one of the town founders no longer mattered, either. Hope burst in Ethan's chest, made his heart pound. Would Cait take him back? Would she forgive him for all that he'd said and all that he'd done to hurt her?

A sudden disturbance outside prevented Ethan from considering the possibility further. Together he and Josie hurried to the large window overlooking Main Street.

"Oh, shit...." The blood drained from his face as he spotted the source of the commotion.

Wasting not a second, he barreled out the door.

*   *   *

The fringe of her buckskins swayed in time with each deliberate step she took down the main street of Roland. Cait kept her gaze fixed straight ahead, her posture proud, her grip tight on the butt of the rifle resting against her shoulder.

And hoped none of the people lining both sides of the road smelled her fear.

Not of them, but of what she'd come here to do.

She thought she'd been prepared for the day Ethan would leave her. She'd told herself the morning she'd woken up in Mary's back room to find him gone that their parting was for the best. She'd found a measure of peace and contentment in the past six years, and the last thing she needed was some tenderfooted hunter disrupting her life and her emotions. Ethan Sawyer had a way of making her question everything she'd come to believe in, and damned if she had to put up with that.

But one night spent alone in her cabin made her realize that without him the simplest pleasures in life seemed insignificant. The aloneness she'd always found a sanctuary had become a suffocating loneliness that nearly crushed her under its weight. Without his laughter, his curiosity, his magical touch, her life had been reduced to a vast nothingness that even the company of her cats couldn't fill.

She didn't know precisely when he'd become the center of her existence, but she knew if she wanted him back, she had to be willing to fight for him.

Even if that meant taking on a whole town.

The whispers that followed her progress grew louder, the words more distinct.

"What is she?"

"It's a damn savage!"

"No, I think it's a white woman. . . ."

". . . Trousers! Can you imagine?"

"Disgraceful. Utterly disgraceful."

Head high, shoulders pulled back, mouth flat, Cait ignored the curious and the critical. Steady strides carried her past the livery and the saloon, toward a small shop in the center of town that smelled of saddlesoap and oak tree brands.

"It's her!"

The sudden outburst had Cait searching for the owner of the voice. Her gaze locked on the lean dark figure of Gypsy-man. He stood off to the right side, his mouth slack, his black eyes bulging.

"It's her! It's Wild Cat Cait!" He jabbed his finger in her direction.

A gasp arose.

"The crazy cat woman?" someone asked.

Cait inwardly winced, but kept walking.

"It's her, I'm tellin' you!" Gypsy-man started running along the rear line of the crowd. "Tooley! Tooley! She's here! Wild Cat Cait is here!"

A skinny cowboy with gaunt cheeks and wiry hair burst from the saloon. As he slowly straightened and gave her a leisurely once-over, a chill spiraled down Cait's spine. The mood around her took a detectable turn for the worse.

"Well, well, Louis, you're right. I'd know

that face anywhere," came the man's arrogant claim.

Cait didn't know what the hell he was talking about. She'd never seen him before. Yet he spoke with an authority that had the crowd hushing instantly.

"Folks! It looks like the mystery of the missin' cougar's been solved."

"She's a changeling?" Gypsy-man cried, going stock still. "Jesus H. Christ. . . ."

Cait might have laughed at his awestruck face if the situaition wasn't so serious.

"Naw," someone protested. "She's just a woman."

"Ah, but she's not—she's a heathen!" Tooley stated. "Everyone knows that Wild Cat Cait uses her powers to bend animals to her will. In fact, she prob'ly had the cougar attack Billy!"

A dangerous rumble of agreement passed through the crowd like a heat-wave. The people began to close in on Cait. Her heart started pounding erratically. She scanned a sea of heads for a glimpse of Ethan, yet the gathering had grown as thick as flies on fresh meat.

"You broke open that cage and set that vicious killer loose, didn't you, heathen?" a raspy voice accused.

"What did you plan, to set it on us in our sleep? Have it steal away our children?"

"Admit it!" came another cry.

Cait stood her ground. Integrity forbade her from denying the charges, pride wouldn't let her cower before these people.

Yet she couldn't stop the perspiration from beading on her brow.

Ethan had warned her what would happen if people identified her. They'd allow rumor and gossip to cloud their thinking. Though he'd said that most folks seemed happy just listening to the tales told about her, there were also those who'd take her, no matter the cost.

And it seemed that she'd made a serious error in judgment, walking boldly into town so soon after the cougar they'd all spent weeks hunting had disappeared.

She'd only wanted to prove to Ethan that she could be a woman worthy of his respect.

"Admit it, Wild Cat—" the one called Tooley ordered. "You turned that cougar loose!"

"She didn't," came a stunningly familiar baritone from the back of the crowd. "I did."

Her heart wrenched. Since everyone's attention had been pulled off her, Cait stood on tiptoe and craned her neck, frantically seeking a glimpse of her hunter.

And then the people moved back, parting like the Red Sea, until Ethan stood at the mouth of one end, she at the other. He wore the buckskin shirt and bear claw necklace she'd given him, and somehow looked more impressive than ever. More powerful. Unflappable. The perfect image of his stately grizzly spirit.

Then their gazes locked. Everyone else seemed to disappear.

It took all the restraint Cait could muster not to run to him, except given what he'd endured once over a woman of Indian blood, she couldn't do that to him in front of his people. She had to leave the final choice up to him.

With slow, confident strides that reminded

her of a lion on the prowl, he began to approach her. Her heart began a quick thud of hope and possibility. Closer he drew. An unnatural calm settled over the people.

Then he stood before her, his eyes shining with a mix of warm welcome and surprise. "You wouldn't happen to need a little rescuing now, would you?"

The glint of humor in the autumn depths tugged at her heartstrings and instantly soothed her fear. "Maybe a little."

Quietly he said, "You shouldn't be here, wildcat."

She tipped her chin and flicked her head, sending her braid over her shoulder. "You once said that you wanted a woman who would fight with you and for you. I'd planned to do both." With a crooked grin, she added, "I just hadn't counted on fighting a whole town. I'm slightly outnumbered."

"You're also crazy for coming here."

Funny, Cait thought—he sounded almost proud of that.

Tooley's gravelly voice intruded on the moment. "What the hell do you think you're doin', Sawyer? She set that killer free."

Ethan twisted at the waist to face the gaunt cowboy. "Do you have proof?"

"We don't need proof—she's a savage!"

"Yeah," another piped up. "She probably came here today to scout the town for scalps."

"All of you who are looking for someone to blame for the missing cougar are looking at the wrong person. Cait didn't set that cat loose, I did. If you want to hold her responsible for anything, let it be for saving the life of one of your own. She's got more kindness and compassion in her little finger than all of you put together."

His lip curled in disdain as he scanned the crowd with accusing eyes. "And you know what disgusts me? That I ever thought your approval mattered. All of you are nothing but a bunch of narrow-minded, bigoted fools. In fact, I don't know why any of you were so worried about the cougar killing those cows; you're depleting your own herds one by one. If people don't follow the standards you set and believe the things you believe, you shun them, toss them out. Did you ever consider that you were wrong?"

The faces staring back at him—some blank, some appalled, some outright furious—gave the townspeoples' answers. And that was probably the saddest part, Cait thought. They had no idea what they were doing to themselves. Or each other.

Then the crowd no longer mattered as Ethan turned back to her and asked, "Does this mean you love me, wildcat?"

A stunned hush fell.

"What?" Cait gasped.

"It's a simple enough question. Does your coming here like this mean you love me?"

Love. What a perfect word. Yet it seemed too small to hold the huge emotion she felt for this man.

Her gaze probed his as she searched for the answer. "If you're asking do I feel this great emptiness in my heart when we're apart . . . if you're asking do I hear the wind whisper your name across the mountain tops . . . if you're asking do I dream of every moment we've shared since the beginning of time—then yes. If that's love, then that's what I feel for you."

Her vision shimmered, her throat had grown tight. "I only know that I want to be wherever you are. I want to breathe the same air you breathe, walk under the same clouds you walk under, climb the same mountains you climb. It doesn't matter where. Here. There. I just . . . I just don't think I could bear this *nothingness* I feel when we're apart."

"I can't either." He held his hand out to her. "Will you come with me?"

Cait stared at his hand, then at his face in wonder. Ethan, whose moments of reckless daring invariably followed with cautious regret, waited with his hand extended. No doubt, no hint of regret showed in his expression. Rather, he looked at her with a brash arrogance and steely determination that had a lump of emotion rising in her throat.

In her entire life no one had ever had the courage to stick up for her the way this man had. Everything he had done for the last three years had been to earn the respect of the people around him. And in one morning he'd sacrificed it all . . . for her.

Humbled beyond words, finding courage in his courage, she proudly stepped up and reached for him.

And the instant Cait laid her hand so trustingly in his, Ethan felt a wave of completeness wash over him. He gave her a smile. And as he scanned the crowd, he finally understood why Cait couldn't stay on the reservation: survival, pure and simple. Had she stayed, it would have killed her. Just as staying in Roland would one day drain the life right out of him if he didn't leave.

Ethan realized then that just as there were different deaths, there were different prisons. The cougar they'd freed had been caged behind bars against her will. He and Cait—hell, they'd been stuck in prisons of their own making: he by remaining in an environment where he fit in only if he followed the rules set by others, and Cait by isolating herself rather than risk subjection—and rejection.

But if she had enough courage to break free of her prison, then he could damn well do no less. "Let's go, wildcat. There's nothing here for us."

"What about your shop?"

"I'll send someone after my things. Right now, I just want to go home."

Ethan grasped Cait's hand firmly within his own. With smooth, sure strides, he led the most important part in his life away, just as his father had done three years earlier. And this time, Ethan found what he had lost that fateful day. It wasn't the community's respect.

It was his own pride.

Epilogue

Five years later

After adding a sprig of mint to the bowl of dried apple peels in the center of the table, Josie stood back and admired her handiwork with a smile. "Perfect."

A hollow clomping drew her gaze to the stairs. Her heart swelled with pride at the sight of her husband, dressed in his Sunday best.

"Josie, I can't get this damned tie straight."

She met Billy halfway across the spacious dining room, empty for the first time since they'd opened the doors nearly five years earlier. Pine Bend had proved itself a successful risk for a restaurant—and for a relationship.

Gazing at Billy's bearded face as she adjusted his tie, she couldn't help but marvel at the difference in him. It had been a long, rocky road, but the man she'd loved since she was six years old had finally come home.

"You look very dashing, Mr. Gray," she said, kissing his cheek.

"Yeah, well, you're lookin' mighty pretty

yourself, Mrs. Gray." He stepped back and glanced at the table, where eight place settings of bone china waited on a pristine white cloth. "You've outdone yourself, Josie. I told you to stop working so hard."

She patted her rounded belly. "We're fine. I just wanted everything to be perfect. It isn't everyday that I get to have three of my favorite men and their families sitting down together at my supper table."

Billy cleared his throat, then confessed. "I'm a little nervous, Jo."

"You have nothing to worry about, darling."

"What if your pa and Ethan gave up on me?"

Tenderness tugged at Josie's heart. She cupped her husband's cheek in her palm. "They didn't. They always believed in you—just like I did."

The kitchen door suddenly burst open and a five-year-old whirlwind blew into the room.

"Caleb!" Josie cried, grabbing for the tow-headed rascal before he barreled headlong into her pretty table. "I've asked you not to run in here, something will wind up broken."

"But I forgot my stick horse, and Ted wants to play cowboys and Indians!"

"In your new clothes?" Josie cast a silent plea to Billy.

"Boy, your mama don't want you messin' up your duds. Now, our guests will be here soon, so you go on over and have a seat till they get here."

"Will you show me your scar?"

"You've seen it a hunnert times!"

"I know, but I wanna see it again."

Josie rolled her eyes.

Billy sighed but nonetheless unbuttoned his shirt with one hand. Their son sat on the woodbox, watching his pa with quiet interest as he revealed the trio of deep gashes down the left side of his chest.

As always, the sight turned Josie's stomach, for it reminded her how close she'd come to losing Billy. She turned back to the table and fiddled with the silverware and napkins while Caleb "Oohed" and "Aahed" over his father's scarred flesh.

"Ted was pokin' fun at you cuz your arm don't work," she heard their son say. "But I tole him that's okay, cuz you're the bravest man ever borned."

"Oh, yeah? Who says?" Billy asked gruffly.

"Mama."

"She does, huh?"

Josie gave her husband a smile and a wink.

"Well, son, normally I wouldn't argue with anything your mama says, but in this case. . . ."

She watched him head toward the fireplace, lower into a large, cushioned rocking chair, and pat his leg. "Climb on up here, boy, and let me tell you a little story about true bravery."

Once Billy had the tow-headed boy settled into his lap, he curled his arm around the scrawny shoulders, set the rocker to rocking, and stared into the fire.

Josie felt a lump of emotion rise in her throat at the sight. She knew what was coming. She'd watched this miracle play itself out many times in the last year, and yet it never failed to move her. Unable to resist, she lowered her bulky figure into one of the chairs and listened. . . .

"It all started on a cold spring morning when an ordinary saddle maker went in search of a wildcat—and wound up getting caught by a legend. . . ."

Author's Note and Acknowledgments

Some books are a work of love, others a product of research, yet others destiny from the start. This book was all three. *Wild Cat Cait* came to me as a title and took off from there. And as Cait and Ethan told me their story, I often found myself surprised and humbled by the choices they made.

From the start, I knew that Cait was a special woman, but I didn't realize how special until I met her cats. Sawtooth, Ginger, and Faw Paw are fictional names for three of my new friends—Kitty, Nala, and Katrina, a Siberian tiger, a lioness, and a cougar that I had the distinctive opportunity of interacting with, thanks to their owners, Mike and Mary Irons. Mike and Mary were invaluable to me as I researched and created *Wild Cat Cait*. They opened their home, their hearts, their humor, and their cages and allowed me a glimpse of their cats that I might not have known otherwise. These very special people often rescue exotic cats from abusive situations or from being put to sleep for one reason or another and find healthy, loving homes for many of them. The animals are also used as educational tools in schools, and are sources of joy to children and adults all over the region. I applaud the Ironses for their efforts, as raising exotic cats is a gift that takes up an enormous amount of time, patience, compassion, and love. For more information about the cats, the Ironses can be contacted at RR3, Box 433, Gilmer, Texas 75644.

Wild Cat Cait is a fictional story inspired by true historical events. Although I cannot find specific documentation supporting the endangerment of mountain lions in the year 1887, documentation does state that by 1900 man had nearly wiped out the cats or driven them from the area into Canada. Subsequently, state parks and national wildlife reserves were founded to protect endangered animals such as the mountain lion, the buffalo, and the grizzly. Thanks to their efforts, these species are thriving under careful breeding and reduction. I hope you will understand the literary license I have taken for the sake of the story.

I'd also like to thank Carlene Bockman of the Ronan, Montana, Chamber of Commerce, who patiently answered my endless questions about the area and gave Cait a beautiful place to live.

And to my readers, I hope you've enjoyed Cait and Ethan's story. I'd love to hear from you. You may write me at: Rachelle Nelson, Box 1217, Hughes Springs, Texas 75656.

Dear Reader,

Next month, there are so many exciting books coming from Avon romance that I wish I had two or three pages to talk about them all! But I only get one page, so I'll get right to it.

October's Avon Romantic Treasure is *A Rake's Vow*, the next in Stephanie Laurens' scintillating series about the wickedly handsome Cynster family. Vane Cynster has vowed to never marry, no matter that his cousin Devil has just tied the knot. But once he meets the very tempting, delectable Patience Debbington he decides that some vows are meant to be broken.

Kathleen Harrington's *Enchanted by You* is for anyone—like me—who loves a sexy Scottish hero! When dashing Lyon MacLyon is saved by Julie Elkheart he can't help but tell her how much he wants her—in Gaelic. But pretty Julie understands every scandalous word of love that this sexy lord says...

What if you could shed your past and take another's identity? In Linda O'Brien's *Promised to a Stranger* Maddie Beecher does just that, and discovers she's "engaged" to a man she's never met. Trouble is, she falls hard...for her "fiancé's" brother—enigmatic Blaine Knight. And when Maddie's past catches up with her, she must decide if she should tell Blaine the whole truth.

And if you're looking for a sexy hero to sweep you off your feet—and fix your life—then don't miss Elizabeth Bevarly's delicious Contemporary romance *My Man Pendleton*. When a madcap heiress runs off to Florida, her rich father sends Pendleton after her...but he never thinks his wayward daughter will fall in love.

Until next month, enjoy!

Lucia Macro

Lucia Macro

Senior Editor

AEL 0998

*W*e've got love on our minds at

http://www.AvonBooks.com

*V*ote for your favorite hero in
"HE'S THE ONE."

*T*ake a romance trivia quiz, or just
"GET A LITTLE LOVE."

*L*ook up today's date in
romantic history in "DATEBOOK."

*S*ubscribe to our monthly e-mail
newsletter for all the buzz on
upcoming romances.

*B*rowse through our list of new
and upcoming titles and read
chapter excerpts.

*If you enjoyed this book,
take advantage
of this special offer.
Subscribe now and get a*

FREE
Historical
Romance

No Obligation (a $4.50 value)

Each month the editors of True Value select the four *very best* novels from America's leading publishers of romantic fiction. Preview them in your home *Free* for 10 days. With the first four books you receive, we'll send you a FREE book as our introductory gift. No Obligation!

If for any reason you decide not to keep them, just return them and owe nothing. If you like them as much as we think you will, you'll pay just $4.00 each and save at *least* $.50 each off the cover price. (Your savings are *guaranteed* to be at least $2.00 each month.) There is NO postage and handling – or other hidden charges. There are no minimum number of books to buy and you may cancel at any time.

*Send in
the Coupon
Below*

To get your FREE historical romance fill out the coupon below and mail it today. As soon as we receive it we'll send you your FREE Book along with your first month's selections.

- -